# A Pinch
of Salt

FLOWERS OF SCOTLAND

Eileen Ramsay

# A Pinch of Salt

FLOWERS OF SCOTLAND

# ZAFFRE

First published in Great Britain in 1994 by Warner Books as *The Broken Gate*

This edition published in Great Britain in 2017 by
ZAFFRE PUBLISHING
80–81 Wimpole St, London W1G 9RE
www.zaffrebooks.co.uk

A CIP catalogue record for this book is
available from the British Library.

ISBN: 978-1-785-76224-6

*also available as an ebook*

1 3 5 7 9 10 8 6 4 2

IDSUK (Data Connection) Ltd

*For Ian, of course.*
*My bridge over troubled water.*

# 1

It seemed as if she had been running for hours; there was a stitch in her side that was almost unbearable but she knew that if she stopped, if she fell to the ground and sobbed as every fibre of her small being implored her to do, she would never find the strength to get up and so she kept going. She had to keep going or Mam would die, it was as simple as that.

*You haven't run so far,* she told herself. *It's not even a mile to the doctor's and not a mile from his house to the pit.*

'Doctor's at the accident,' had said Dr Hyslop's very superior housekeeper, 'and certainly will have no time for the likes of you tonight, Kate.' Her sniff implied that he would never have time for the likes of Kate Kennedy, but Kate knew better. Doctor Hyslop always had a smile or a word even though she sometimes found it hard to understand what he was saying.

'Speaks wi' marbles in his mouth', was how the mining fraternity described the cultured tones of the village doctor, and then, of course, there was the terrible speech impediment that – so rumour had it – had prevented him from becoming a rich and famous surgeon in a place called Harley Street.

Kate ran on, her breath coming in laboured gasps. She could not go on but she did, proving, not for the first time in her short life, that the will is stronger than mere bone and muscle. One leg followed the other, her breath was ripped painfully from her throat and tears, of which she was completely unaware, ran down her cheeks. They were tears of frustration and impotence and naked fear. *Why was the doctor not at home when she got there? Why did there have to be an accident down the pit, that loathsome open jaw that gaped open farther and farther under the ground; for months it stayed quiet, almost acquiescing in the rape and plunder of its precious fruit and then, when they were lulled into a false sense of security – it roared, demanding sacrifice – but why tonight of all nights?*

At last she was at the pithead. There were makeshift lights swinging from hastily erected structures and men running around as if they had no idea at all about what they were supposed to be doing. Women were standing huddled together for warmth or comfort more likely, and she recognized one of them. 'Mrs Brown, it's me mam; she needs the doctor.'

The woman looked at the girl and the effort to wrench her mind away from the horror of the coalface to the exhausted child was clearly written on her face. For a moment she seemed not to know her; she had a man and two lads down there. 'Yer mam?' she managed at last. 'Och Kate, the bairn's no comin,' she said impatiently. 'Look round ye, lassie. We're dealin' in death here. Away home, yer father'll have to manage himself. He got her pregnant easy enough, let him be in at the end o' it.' She turned back to her vigil and then, conscious of the child still at her side, she relented. 'Away and chap up Mrs Breen. She'll not be here and she's birthed more bairns than our braw doctor.'

Kate stood for a moment looking at the woman's back. She felt tears welling up again and desired nothing more than to submit to the luxury of being thirteen years old and to cry for her mammy, to be held in soft, warm arms, certainly not to have to face that three miles of dark fields and woods between the pit and her tumbledown home. Mam, she sobbed quietly and started once more to run – to run like a frightened hare back across the ground she had just covered so painfully. Her mother was in labour for the sixth time in thirteen years – not counting the miscarriages – and something was wrong. Kate was used to childbirth, the newspapers collected furtively for weeks and then spread on the old stained mattress, the neighbour women crowding in, glad that they were not lying in agony in that uncomfortable bed, ready to do what little they could to bring this new life into the world as easily as possible. They never sent for the doctor. His fee was minimal; but there was usually no way that Liam Kennedy could pay it – and why should he pay for something so natural as a woman's Godgiven function; this act of giving birth. Kate remembered huddling in the big box bed with her brothers and sisters, trying to block out the sounds of her mother's screams, soothing the frightened babies, telling them stories, crooning little songs. Tonight they were alone, well, Da was there, but he would be of little use what with Mam so bad and all the little ones there. When Kate had left, Da had been walking the floor with little Colm sobbing himself to sleep in his arms.

Mrs Breen. Mrs Breen. Kate turned and ran, her pains and fatigue forgotten. Behind her the desperate rescue work went on but she was already divorced from that tragedy and would never in the years to come be able to remember clearly anything at all about it.

Kate stumbled down the hill that led from the mine, reached what passed for a main street and turned left towards the miners' rows. The road ran along the river and usually she stood stock still and let the sound of running water seduce her but tonight she hardly noticed it at all; past the doctor's fancy big house with its beautiful garden – so much time, I've wasted so much time – and on to the foot of the village. Number six, that was Mrs Breen's house and it looked deserted, drawn in on itself like a tortoise. Everywhere else there were open doors and light spilling out. Of course, Mrs Breen had lost all her family long ago, no need to alert her to the trouble at the pit. Kate leaned on the door for a moment to get her breath; she had been running for ever and only the door stopped her legs from going on and on. Don't sleep, she admonished herself and battered on the door as hard as she was able. What a puny battering the door received; there was no strength left in the tired little body.

I can't wake her. Mammy will die for I'm useless. She picked up a stone that lay on the path and thumped it – with the strength of a dying moth – against the door, screaming and crying '*Mrs Breen, Mrs Breen,*' and not hearing a sound except the silence from inside the house. And then the door opened and the old woman stood there like a witch, her black shawl pulled round her voluminous flannel nightgown.

'Lassie, lassie, ye'll have the house down about ma ears. What's wrang?'

She bustled the slight, undernourished little girl into the kitchen assuring her that she could easily listen while she pulled on her drawers and her shoes. Kate poured out her story, grudging every second that the old woman took; it was years before she fully appreciated how fast Mrs Breen had actually been.

*

'Where is the doctor, lass? Did I not send you for the doctor?' Liam Kennedy's natural courtesy surfaced. 'Sorry, Mrs Breen, but I've had to send for the doctor, Mary Kate's been took terrible bad.'

Mary Kate was in labour – this looked to be the hardest yet – and he was almost out of his mind with worry but he would struggle to be polite to this neighbour, but Mrs Breen seemed not to hear him. Already she was over at the box bed where the slight figure with its huge distended stomach was struggling desperately to bring her child into the world.

Mary Kate gripped the old woman's hand with desperate strength. 'My Katie, Mrs Breen,' she whispered through cracked, bleeding lips, 'send her to bed; 'tis not a place for a wee lass.'

Mrs Breen smiled at her reassuringly but said nothing. She threw her shawls over the dilapidated old armchair and began issuing orders. 'Liam, boil water' – useless occupation but would keep him busy – 'Kate, hen, ye'll need to help me wi' Mammy. Where have you put the cloths, Mary Kate?' For weeks, Mary Kate would have been boiling and cutting up old sheets. 'Kate, get the cloths from the wardrobe, that's a good lass.'

The labour went on for hours. The echoes of her mother's screams never left Kate although on that awful night she was so numbed by fear and fatigue that she paid little attention to them. After a while she was completely anaesthetized, and although, for most of the night, her body did as it was bid, when her mother died she had dropped asleep by the bed. They left her there while Liam ran, at the old woman's bidding, for the priest. Mary Kate would have wanted a priest.

Liam didn't. All his life he had lived by the dictates of the Roman Catholic Church; he ate fish on a Friday when he could afford fish, he fasted before receiving Holy Communion on Sundays and holy days, he gave up everything he could think of – including the comforts of a sexual relationship – during Lent; in every way possible he tried to be a good Catholic. He had accepted every misfortune fate handed him, believing that his 'reward would be great in heaven', but this . . . this . . . Mary Kate lying there dead at the age of thirty-three . . .

'Get away from her,' he yelled at the boy, for that was really all the young priest was; 'don't prate about eternal life with me Mary Kate lying there in her own blood and me left with these babbies and Kate only thirteen . . .' he choked on his tears and visibly tried to control himself, his hands clenched and shaking.

'Now, now, my son,' began the young priest, desperately trying to say and do the right thing; he could not allow this child of the church to lose his immortal soul, 'you should have fetched me earlier but I have given her the last sacrament, Extreme Unction; Mary Kate is sleeping with the Lord.'

Liam, distraught, turned on him in a rage. 'Get out of my house and take your extremes and your unctions with you. Eternal life; damn you and your kind for ever – it's now she wants life. Now.' His voice broke and he turned away from the priest, brushing aside the younger man's arm as if he scarcely noticed it.

The old woman soothed the priest. 'Away home with you, Father, and say your prayers. He'll get over it, sure he will and be back to beg your pardon in a day or two.' Gently but relentlessly she pushed the young man, who spent what was left of the night prostrate on the concrete floor of his little chapel begging for help, out of the door. Then she returned to work that she had had to do far too often in her life. Forgetting her seventy-five years, she issued orders and instructions to the young man who stood bowed and help-lessly weeping beside the bed and when he was incapable of responding she carried them out herself.

'Ye'll need to shift the bairn, Liam. I cannae manage her.' For a moment she could not interpret the loathing on his face and then she understood. 'Naw, it's wee Kate. The undertaker'll need tae get in, that's if he finds time with an accident at the pit. Ye'll have to get him and the doctor; ye cannot bury her without ye've seen the doctor.'

Liam eventually got the doctor and the equally over-worked village undertaker. One hundred and nine men and boys had died in the pit, many others had been hideously injured and so, on the day that Mary Kate Kennedy was buried, mourners got mixed up and merely went from one grave to the next. What did it matter whether it was a boy born and bred in Dumfriesshire and his father and his father before him – fodder for the mines – or the wife of one of those Irish Catholics. Her man was a miner and miners all gave their wives far too many bairns, especially the Catholic ones. With any luck there would be some sister or auntie or grannie to come and help with the bairns for the women of the village who would normally have pitched in were all too busy mourning or nursing boys who would never walk again or husbands who would lie in the big box beds coughing their lives away.

Most of the vilage changed in the next few months for the miners' rows needed working miners and if the workers were dead, well then their widows would have to throw themselves on the mercy of relatives for the but n' bens were needed for able-bodied men. More Irish flooded in but Liam did not hold out the hand of fellow-ship. His spirit had died with Mary Kate and he rose and went to work and he returned and sat in his chair staring into the fire until he fell asleep.

There were no relatives and so at thirteen Kate became the mother of the family. On the day her mother died she had been at school and the teacher had mentioned a writer called Charles Dickens and a book called *A Tale of Two Cities*. Oh, how Kate hungered to read that book. Reading was for school children or the leisured classes and Kate belonged to neither. She could have asked Pat to borrow the book for her but when could she have read it? Without a qualm she forgot all about Sydney Carton, until years later she was introduced to the wonders of motion pictures and fell in love with a young actor called Dirk Bogarde.

For now, Kate set herself to rising every morning at half past three. She would rinse the sleep from her eyes with the ice-cold water she had left out the night before, pull on some clothes and then, while everyone was still asleep, she would rake the coals in the grate and throw on some kindling, hoping desperately that the fire would catch and that she would not have to start it all over again. Next the kettle would be set on the hotplate, and the pan of porridge that she had also prepared before going to bed. Only then would she wake Da from the exhausted sleep that never seemed to refresh him. Almost as soon as he pulled on his moleskin trousers she would hand a mug of hot sweet tea into his hand which was still grimy from yesterday's coal dust, and then set before him a heaping bowl of porridge. Liam would wolf it down without a word while she spread dripping over four thick slices of her own crusty bread and put them into the tin box carried down the pit every day. Falls of coal and rock were quite common, if not always dangerous, and it was the miners' tins that bore the brunt of them. Liam Kennedy's tin was bashed, as were his fingers, fingers that had once, long ago, teased such sweet music from his granda's fiddle. It was doubtful that he had any idea of that same fiddle's whereabouts and even more doubtful that he would have cared. Music belonged to his childhood in Limerick.

Did he ever look at Kate's childhood? Could he have borne it if he had? He would smile when he took his dented tin from her small hands – the smile for which a stronger woman than Mary Kate Kennedy would have left her home in Limerick.

'Thank you, Allanah,' he would whisper softly and she would watch him on his long walk to the pithead until his thin figure disappeared from view. Then, at the beginning of the day, she would have her moment of peace and quiet. She would set water on to boil for the washing – Mary Kate had been fanatical about cleanliness, mouthing all the old platitudes as if she had invented them; 'Sure isn't cleanliness nearest to Godliness' – and while Kate waited she would pour herself a mug of the thick, black tea, add three lumps of sugar, and sit down in Da's chair to enjoy both the tea and the solitude. If she was very lucky she might sit long enough to enjoy the morning song of the birds, but she would never ever waste time. There were always the baby's nappies to wash, and the other bairns' clothes, once a week the pit clothes that never got clean no matter how hard she scrubbed them on the scrubbing board. Then there were her own underclothes. She had made herself two pairs of knickers, one to wear and one to wash. As soon as she could manage, she would make a third pair for emergencies. She remembered her mother talking about a young woman who had died suddenly in the Main Street. 'Her underclothes was as clean as if she had just come out of a shop; you be sure, Kate Kennedy, that if you're ever hit by a cart, God forbid, you need never be ashamed of your knickers.'

As well as keeping her underwear clean, Kate had a hip-bath every Saturday night and it was then that she washed her long, blue-black hair with carbolic soap. Her hair was truly a crowning glory but no one ever said so, and Kate had neither the time nor the inclination to admire it herself. Perhaps if she had, she would have stolen a few more moments for herself, to brush and curl it. As it was, she washed it every Saturday and, for the rest of the week, was content to drag a comb through it every morning.

Kate sat with her feet on the fender and enjoyed her tea. As soon as her cup was empty she straightened her back in a gesture she had learned from Liam – like many miners of the time he spent his working day doubled over and so constantly had trouble straightening his aching spine – then Kate put all thoughts of leisure out of her mind until the next morning. By the time her brothers and sisters were awake she had the kitchen and tiny back kitchen as clean as scrubbing could make them. She had 'redded up' the back bedroom where her father now slept alone in the sagging double bed – no one thinking it at all peculiar that Liam should have so much space while Kate and all her brothers and sisters slept huddled together in the box bed in the kitchen – and she had butties ready for Patrick, Kevin, Deirdre and Colm. Little Bridie was usually the first to wake. She would crawl over to the edge of the bed and call, 'Katie, Bridie's up, come get Bridie, Katie.'

For a long time Bridie was to be Kate's most beloved child and only one person supplanted her in Kate's heart.

Kate liked it when little Bridie woke early, for then she had time to wash and dress her before tying her into a chair to eat her morning porridge. Bridie was a good child and seemed to know instinctively just how much of her surrogate mother's time she could claim. Not like Colm, almost five years old and about to start in Miss Timpson's infant class.

'And she'll soon sort you, you great big baby,' Kate would tell him as she administered a hearty smack to his wet behind. No one in 1910 was interested in the psychological reasons for constant bed wetting in a five year old. No one theorized that since Colm had been deposed as the baby of the house before his first birthday and had been bereft of his mother just after his third, he might just be in need of a little attention and reassurance. Colm's response was to rail heartily against overburdened Kate as she spanked him in the morning and to fight just as hard against his exhausted father who whacked him again when he found urine-soaked sheets drying on the clothes horse when he returned from work. It never occurred to Kate to wash the sheets every day. She made time for washing them once a week, merely drying them out in between, and in this she was a great deal cleaner than many of her neighbours. Who, after all, had time to draw water, boil it over a fire that one had to keep stoked, and then rub with raw knuckles on a washboard until the paper-thin dirty sheets were clean? Washing day was Monday; everyone knew that.

When the older children had gone running off to school, Kate untied Bridie and put her down on the floor with her 'toys' – a handleless cup and a tin spoon. Later on, if she had time to sit down, Kate would make the little girl a baby doll out of an old piece of clean cloth, but for now she was much too busy. She sent Colm out to play, with a warning not to wander. They both knew he would disobey but the mining village was small and Kate knew his favourite places. Like his big brothers and his sister, he carried his 'piece' and would be gone until either hunger or a skinned knee would bring him crying home.

'Ach, sure, won't it be grand to get him into school,' said Kate to solemn little Bridie, sounding for all the world like her own mother. Before her death Mary Kate had often teased her oldest child about her Scottish accent, but lately Kate had begun to sound more and more like Liam. Perhaps it was because his was the voice she heard most. Kate did not gossip on the back green as she hung out her washing and her neighbours no longer came to the door as they had done in the first weeks after Mary Kate's death. If they spoke of the Kennedys at all it was to say, 'Grand job wee Kate's doing wi' all the weans,' for all the world as if she was no longer a wean herself.

Physically she stopped being a 'wean' two months after the death of her mother. It was a terrific shock to her and also to her father who had no idea at all of how to cope with the onset of menstruation. One afternoon when Bridie was down for a nap and Colm was God knows where, Kate suddenly doubled up with the most appalling pain in her stomach. It was excruciating, low down on her right side, and so intense that she felt cold sweat break out all over her body. She doubled over, moaning until the pain receded a few minutes later.

*Sure, I must have ate something bad*, she decided to herself as she straightened up, and then the pain hit her again so that she cried out again and fell to the floor. Her mother's prayers came back to her. Oh God, am I dying? Here on the floor with the child alone in the house? Mercifully the pain receded and after a few days of waiting for it to strike like a cobra, Kate forgot about it. Then she found blood in her knickers. She sat in the smelly outside privy and wondered what to do. It wasn't a scraped knee that she could show Da. The blood had obviously come out of the unmentionable place between her legs for she had looked everywhere for a cut or boil and had found nothing. How was she to tell someone else that the blood had come from *there*? Did Kate really believe that she was dying or did some instinct tell her that what was happening to her was a natural part of her development? She was thirteen years old; her father was due in from the pit and his tea had better be ready whether she was dying or not. She struggled up from the cold, wet floor and went into the kitchen to cut bread and make tea.

She was still alive at bedtime and Da had noticed nothing wrong. Perhaps she had merely strained something hauling the tub of boiling water from the fire to the back kitchen. She fell asleep and woke up feeling warm liquid on the insides of her thighs. Her first hope that it was wee Colm come in for warmth disappeared; only Deirdre and wee Bridie were in the bed with her. Jesus, Mary and Joseph, she prayed in anguish. *I don't want to die. Oh, Mam, why did you ever leave me?* Even in the midst of her distress, Kate was aware of the other children; she did not want to wake them with her sobbing, nor did she want them to wake and find her dead in the bed. Her innate modesty made her shrink from approaching her father but it had to be done.

'Da,' she pulled at the blankets round him. 'Da, it's me, Kate.'

He did not wake immediately and from the smell of him she could tell the reason. It would not be the first time since his wife's death that Liam Kennedy had had to drink himself to sleep. 'Da, you have to wake up. I'm terrible ill, Da.'

That roused him – either the words themselves or the childish despair with which they were uttered. Blushingly, hesitantly, with downcast eyes Kate told him her problem. In dawning realization Liam listened to his daughter. What in God's name was he to do, to say? In the long, lonely nights since the death of his wife, he thought that he had visualized every problem the years ahead were to bring – but not this. Like his child in her despair, he too returned to the prayers of his childhood. 'Holy Mother of God,' he whispered and at the sound of his voice the child looked up. What did she see in his face? Was it horror, disgust? It was, in fact, embarrassment not unmixed with fear but Kate misread it and what she saw as his reaction coloured her own perception of a perfectly normal physical function for the rest of her life. Liam found his voice but the quandary in which he found himself made him gruffer than he meant to be.

'Ach, away with you, you silly wee bitch. It happens to every girl. 'Tis normal, sure. Away with you and put a clean cloth atween your legs till it stops. 'Twill be a day or two, no more.'

So ended Kate Kennedy's one and only lesson on the facts of life. Menstruation and everything connected with it disgusted her. She felt unclean, she hated the blood-soaked cloths that she secretly and furtively washed and dried. She hated having her body do this obscene thing for not one or two days but for four or five every single month, and perhaps because of her resentment her body inflicted her with cramps and nausea, two burdens that she bore in stoic silence. Who could she tell? Bridie, Deirdre? They were too wee. Liam had already shown his disgust with the whole business. Kate longed for someone, anyone who would listen to her questions, who would explain and put everything into perspective. There was no one. Mam would have told her, would have cuddled her and laughed and everything would have been all right. I'll pretend I'm talking to you, Mam. Maybe you can hear me up in Heaven.

If her neighbours were too burdened themselves to really consider Kate's plight, two people in the village did manage to spare more than a passing thought for her. One was the local doctor, a brilliant man, prevented from becoming the surgeon he had dreamed of being by a terrible speech impediment. Being a man of courage himself, he recognized the courage in the young girl and racked his brains to find a way to help her. Kate's brothers and sisters were as well cared for after the death of their mother as they had ever been. As he made his rounds in the miners' rows, Dr Hyslop saw the lines of washing bravely blowing, he saw the strips of carpet being thrown across the ropes to be beaten, and quite often he saw Kate herself tending the vegetable garden and he would stop to chat to her.

'Superb cabbages you have there, Kate,' he said with his usual difficulty and Kate, knowing how torturous speech was for him and what terrors casual conversation held for him, smiled warmly.

'Wee Pat does the digging, doctor. Will you have one? Sure, there's plenty.'

'Indeed I will. If you will have some flowers in return.'

They smiled at one another, their bargain agreed upon. Like most of the men in the mining community, the doctor spent most of his time in his garden, but while the miners grew vegetables to eke out their income, Dr Hyslop indulged in his passion for flowers. At all seasons of the year his garden was a delight to himself and all who passed. Kate stopped at the gate each time she was in the village and she and the elderly man had become good friends. He saw a wealth of potential in the girl; he saw the intelligence in her eyes and the beauty and strength of character in her face and he mourned at the waste. Unless some miracle happened, Kate Kennedy was already doing the work that she would do for the rest of her life. There was nothing else for her. Unless her father married again, Kate was doomed to spend her days washing, cleaning and cooking. She might marry, but if she did wed, her life would not change, except that she would be looking after her own husband and the children she would no doubt bear, year after year. That life script was all well and good, but only after she had been given a chance.

'This garden is quite an amateur affair, Kate,' he told her one evening as she stopped to admire his roses. 'Just fifteen miles away there's a castle with magnificent gardens. Once . . .' He stopped for 'once' belonged to the past, to the days of dreaming of worldly success. 'Kate, have you thought of going into service, of leaving the village?'

'No,' she said simply, 'who would look after me da and wee Bridie and the others?'

Who indeed? She left him then and he watched her straight narrow back as she walked towards the miners' rows. He wondered why her fate affected him. Service or matrimony or motherhood without 'benefit of clergy' was the lot of most of the village girls. One or two left every year to go into service; no girl to his knowledge had ever left to pursue further education. Kate Kennedy surely should have been the first.

The teacher of the village school knew that as well as the doctor. Miss Timpson was not particularly well qualified but she was conscientious and aware of her own limitations. In her classes Kate had learned to read, write and do basic arithmetic. She had absorbed a colourful, if not strictly accurate, history of her native land and had committed to memory most of the rivers and all the capital cities of western Europe. More importantly, Miss Timpson had passed on to Kate a love of poetry and for this the girl would be eternally grateful.

Once Colm had been enrolled in the infant class, Miss Timpson saw Kate as she fetched her small brother from school. Sometimes she had Bridie by the hand and at other times, usually when the weather was bad, Kate had the child swaddled tightly against her with an old shawl wound tightly around her own body.

'I thought you could trust Patrick to bring the wee one home, Kate,' she said.

Kate flew to her brother's defence. 'Pat's grand, miss. I was enjoying a wee walk.'

How anyone could enjoy a walk carrying a young child was more than Miss Timpson could understand. She guessed rightly that Kate was being brave and she shuddered for the girl. 'Can I do anything, Kate? Do you need anything?'

Here Kate lost the first of many opportunities. She wanted to ask for the loan of books, any kind of book, even *A Tale of Two Cities*, but false pride got in her way. She drew herself up haughtily to her almost five feet, hitched Bridie up on her hip, and said politely, 'No thank you, Miss Timpson. Our da provides everything we need.'

She was angry with herself as she half dragged, half herded the three younger ones home. Like all the *big* boys, Patrick would never walk home with his little brothers and his sister.

You have a big mouth on you, Kathleen Kennedy. You could have asked her for the loan of a collection of poems and copied some of them out, or even a story book, Walter Scott or Charles Dickens. You never got halfway through her shelf. Never mind, she brightened up, our Pat can bring them home when he's in the top class and no one the wiser.

Kate was preoccupied that night as she went about her never-ending chores but, as usual, no one noticed. Would they have noticed if she had neglected to do them? Probably. When there was no clean underwear or no porridge on the fire. Kate did not often feel sorry for herself; this was the way things were. She would have liked some time to herself, but she had a strong streak of practicality. Reading a book would be wonderful tonight but in the morning she could never catch up, and life was easier if chores were done regularly. When the others are older, she would tell herself, they'll give me a hand. For now Liam sat in the big chair before the fire dreamily watching the wee ones as they played about his feet. Eventually he sent them to bed and soon took himself off. In truth Kate hardly noticed him go for her mind was full of the doctor and the school teacher. What made them different from herself? The doctor spoke 'funny', not just because of his impediment but because his was a 'toff's' voice. He did not belong to the mining community. Vague rumours about his background circulated in the village from time to time, especially when some of his relatives visited him in their grand carriages. Dr Hyslop was a *gentleman*. But what about Miss Timpson or Mrs Campbell, the minister's wife or the minister himself? He didn't have 'marbles in his mouth' as the village said when describing the doctor's cultured tones.

Why hadn't she accepted Miss Timpson's offer of help? *I'll ask her for books the next time I see her,* she decided. *For it's education as makes them different from the likes of us,* declared thirteen-year-old Kate and, *one way or another, I've lost my chance of getting educated.*

# 2

Two events occurred in 1911 which were to have a far-reaching effect on Kate's life. One was the refining of a small pie that she had been making for the family since before her mother's death. The pie enabled her to put a tasty and nutritious meal before her large family for very little more than the meals of bread and dripping she had given them in the year immediately following her mother's death. Liam now gave his daughter every penny he earned as he had given it before to his wife; he had struggled with his grief and loneliness as he had struggled against so much adversity in his life and he had mastered it and the need for alcohol. He saw nothing odd in his sixteen-year-old daughter handing him back a few pence on a Friday night. Sometimes he joined his mates at the pub but more often he sat before the fire and listened with pride to his children as they practised their multiplication tables or read their lessons.

The other event which rocked Kate's small world took place in June. Patrick had his fourteenth birthday and was able to leave school and go down the pit with his father. Of school and the coalmines he found the mines the lesser of two evils. Liam had had the moleskin trousers bought and laid aside for weeks before his son's birthday and Pat could hardly wait to get into them.

'Putting on a pair of moleskin breeks and going down a pit is not going to make a man of you,' Kate told her young brother angrily.

'What do you want me to do, Kate? It's the pits or swilling out muck on some farm. The pit's better paid.'

'Can you not bide at the school another year and maybe get a nice clean job in a shop. You like horses, Pat. Can you not get taken on at the Co-op?'

'I cannot see myself delivering messages.'

'I wanted something better than the pits.'

'Kevin's got brains, Kate. Wait for him.'

'You're the eldest, Pat,' said Kate. 'It's you should have the chance.'

'You're daft, Kate Kennedy. It's time you joined the real world. There is nothing better than the pits for the likes of us.'

Kate looked at him and saw only a child, a half grown man-child with skin as soft and smooth as Bridie's. In a few months his thin white fingers would be gnarled and broken; the nails would be split and they would never be white and clean again. Dear God, he can draw flowers so nice you can almost smell them. How do miners' sons get away from the pits?

'It's not fair, Pat,' was all she said.

He smiled. 'I'll be earning near the same wage as Da once I've learned the job.'

He was so young, Kate thought, and so eager. He could not possibly understand what working for hours underground for the rest of his working life would mean; doubled over and crawling along the clammy wet ground like a rat. In a few years he would find it hard even to stand upright.

He would have to be well-fed and she could do that for him. All the weans liked to take her pies to school and Colm, the wee rascal, had been known to swap them or even sell them.

What a whack Kate had given him when she found him with a penny and a jammy piece.

'You wee toe-rag,' she had said. 'Selling my good, tasty food tae that dirty wee tinker. Don't you dare put that bread near your mouth; you dinnae ken where it's been.'

Liam was proud of his daughter's baking but when it had been suggested to him by Mrs Murphy, their next-door neighbour, that Kate should sell pies at the local pub he had been furious. Mrs Murphy had never set foot in a public house in her life but Tam Murphy, the publican, was a cousin of her late husband, and he wanted to add food to his menu of beer, beer and beer. A pub could be quite a genteel place, thought Mrs Murphy, if there was perhaps another room where food could be served.

'No daughter of mine will ever set foot in a pub,' Liam said.

'Kate wouldnae have to go into the pub, Liam,' Mrs Murphy explained, 'and it would bring a bit extra.'

'Kate has more than enough to do looking after the bairns and, forbye, I earn the money to look after my family.'

Mrs Murphy said no more. She was convinced that he was making a mistake but she would never argue with him. She had been amazed when Kate had mentioned her regret that Pat was going to become a miner.

'Kate, you would think the boy was your son and not your brother the way you fuss over him and, forbye, why should he not go down the pit with the rest of the laddies. Good enough for the likes of Mrs Breen's folk but not for your precious wee brother.'

Kate wanted to shout, *No, it's not good enough for us,* but said only, 'He's nobut a wean but he thinks he's grown-up; he's all bones, he's not even full grown.'

'He'll have his dad there to wipe his bum for him. You can't live their lives for them, Katie. Have you ever thought what it's going to be like for them when you have your own house and your own bairns?'

What an expressive face Kate had. Marriage for herself had obviously never occurred to her.

'I'd better away home, Mrs Murphy. A miner needs more nourishment than a school wean.' On the way home she wished she hadn't said that. How superior she sounded to herself sometimes, so how she must sound to other people she dreaded to think. *I just don't know what to say sometimes*, thought Kate sadly, *all the wrong words come out.*

No more was said about the rights and wrongs of fourteen-year-old boys going into mines and Pat himself was thrilled when the great day dawned. For the first time in his life he was awake before Kate and she came downstairs to find him, proud as punch, admiring himself in the first new clothes he had owned since his first Holy Communion suit four years before.

'You'd best sit down and have your porridge,' she said gruffly to hide the fear and dismay that the sight of her little brother pretending to be a grown man instilled in her.

Liam wondered why his eldest daughter, with a furious face, was savagely beating the already well-stirred porridge.

Patrick had to be forced to finish his breakfast so anxious was he to throw off his childhood and go down into the bowels of the earth. Today he would become a man; what did he want with porridge – but his father agreed with his sister and he was forced to swallow every tasteless morsel. At last, however, it was time to go, and he picked up his tin with his butty and, shoulders straight, accompanied his father up the road to the mine trying to look nonchalant. Kate watched them leave and another part of her youth went with them; Patrick would never be the same again. There were the others though.

'Our Deirdre, Kevin, Colm, get up all of you and get to school.'

School. School was the last thing any of them wanted to think about. Kevin, eleven months younger than Patrick, resented the months that kept him out of the pit, and his twin, Deirdre, spent all her time admiring her very pretty face in the tiny shaving mirror in the kitchen. She hated school but liked to go to see the effect that sidelong glances out of her large green eyes had on the boys.

'Lucky bugger, our Pat,' said Kevin through his porridge and got a clout on the head for his language.

'What's lucky about spending a day like this grovelling like a mole? Now hurry up and do your work so's I can get some blankets washed and hung out.'

Kate stretched luxuriously and smiled at her clothes line with satisfaction. If there were cleaner blankets in

Dumfriesshire, she would cat these. It had been a glorious June morning and so she had rushed to the palliative of hard physical work to forget Patrick and what she saw as her first failure in the promises she had made on her mother's grave.

'I'll take care of them for you, Mammy.'

She lost herself in washing their thin, worn blankets in the old tin bath. Getting the sodden blankets through the wringer had been a real challenge. They had soaked her skirt, her shoes, the ground – and she had congratulated herself on her forethought in hauling the old tub outside – but at last there they were, washed, rinsed and wrung, and now flapping in the pure, clear spring breeze. With luck, the weather would hold and she would get them back on the beds tonight. Again she stretched, feeling the tension leave her shoulders and the base of her spine where there always seemed to be a dull ache. It was good to stand straight and tall and feel the warm kiss of the sun.

Four-year-old Bridie, recuperating from measles, was also enjoying the sun. She had been in bed for over a week and Kate was delighted to take advantage of the healing properties of the sun. Suddenly Kate had a wild idea; she ran into the kitchen and to her relief the old wag-at-the-wall assured her that it was not even eleven o'clock. She would have a holiday. She would have to take little Bridie of course, but she would forget Patrick and the housework and escape to the woods. There would be primroses up the Baker's Burn; soft, clean pale lemon primroses and, if they were very lucky, some pink and even red ones. She would pick some and bring them back. Unfortunately there were no vases in the house that would show them off to their best advantage; they would be too small for Mam's blue bowl. A jam-jar would have to do; whatever they were in they would still be spring's loveliest gift. She would bring some for Mrs Murphy as well, as she hadn't really talked to her since the row over Patrick

'Bridie, love, we're away to see Mrs Murphy,' she called to the little girl who was solemnly digging in a tiny patch of dirt.

Without thinking, Kate hauled up her still-damp skirt and jumped, as she had done a thousand times before, over the fence between the gardens.

'And very nice too.' The voice was so unexpected that Kate stood stockstill for a moment, her skirts still kirtled up around her legs. Then, flustered, she dropped them in confusion and desperately tried to find something to say. A young man was standing laughing at her, a young man with black, curly hair and eyes so blue that they were almost purple.

'Mrs Murphy,' she stammered.

'My Auntie Molly, I'm Charlie Inglis. She must have told you I was coming for she has certainly told me all about you.'

Kate had decided that this cocksure young man reminded her of a proud little bantam rooster. He was rocking back on his heels looking at her and he was still laughing and she meant to be angry but there was something in his eyes; no one had ever looked at her like that before and she found herself blushing again even though her limbs were now decently covered. She felt breathless, there was a tightness in her chest and a funny feeling 'there' – a pleasant feeling – she had never felt one like it before. Heavens, she was still standing like a daft gowk looking into his eyes. That he was smiling into hers was neither here nor there.

'Well, she has never mentioned you, Mr Inglis. If you'll just tell her, och, never mind.'

'Did I embarrass you then, telling you that your legs were presentable. Gracious, there you go blushing like a beet again. What a sheltered life you must have lived. My auntie was telling me . . .'

'Kate, was you wanting to see me?' Mrs Murphy came hurrying out of the back door. 'I see you've met my nephew, Charlie. He's come down from Glasgow to give me a hand.'

'That's nice, Mrs Murphy,' smiled Kate as she backed away towards the fence. 'I'm away with Bridie for a wee while. I was going to bring you some primroses.'

'Lovely, can you get me a root, Kate? They're grand for spreading. Will Charlie not come with you to dig?' she added, almost coyly. Kate was over the fence again, more modestly this time. 'No thanks, the bairn's so weak we'll need to go awfie slow. He'd be bored to tears.'

Kate grabbed wee Bridie by the hand and bore the unprotesting child into the house.

'Well, what do you think of Mr Charles Inglis, Bridie? Fancies himself. The lassies in Glasgow must have spoiled him, wee bantam that he is. We like our men big, don't we, love – and modest.'

Despite her brave words, Kate was a trifle disappointed not to find Charlie waiting for her in the street. She had changed out of her wet frock and had put on her summer Sunday one, 'Just because it's such a nice day, Bridie' but there was no one on the road to appreciate it. Kate soon forgot Charlie and the odd effect he had had on her in the sheer joy of being away from the miners' row. It was wonderful to play truant, to feel the sun on her face and the little girl's hand in hers. A train was approaching the bridge on the road that led to the Baker's Burn and she hauled up her skirts like a child and ran to reach the tunnel to feel the roar and the power of the train above her.

'What do you like better, Bridie love; to be under the bridge when the train goes over so you get all scared and excited, or to stay on the road and wave to all the people on the train?'

'Both,' said Bridie.

'Aye, me too. Once a lady waved back at me, Bridie, a rich lady with gloves and a hat. When you grow up, Miss Bridget, you shall always have gloves and a hat.'

'You too, Katie.'

'Aye, me too.' They walked on, hand in hand, and Kate felt immeasurably rich. Her hands were rough and she had never owned a pair of gloves but the same sun shone on her and the gloved woman on the train and the woods and the primroses were hers alone.

There were thousands of them, soft and so sweet, and their perfume was the essence of spring. Kate buried her face in a bunch she found hidden among the roots of a massive beech tree. There was nothing in the world but the sweet, damp smell of the woods and the pale lemon and pink primroses. She would take the pink back for Mrs Murphy, but for herself, she would take yellow.

'Bridie, let's take some for Mam's grave. Mrs Murphy says they spread and so every year, even if you and me leave Auchenbeath she'll have flowers. She liked daffodils best, did you know that?'

But, of course, Bridie knew nothing of her mother's likes and dislikes. Kate was the only mother she knew; Kate was wonderful and, for Bridie, she always would be. The earth gave up the clumps of primroses without too much of a struggle. In 1911, in the woods around Auchenbeath, or any other little village, there were thousands of the sweet little flowers spreading their fragrant carpets, often unseen or unappreciated. Kate could not conceive of a world where primroses were an endangered species or where it was an offence to pick them.

How long had their truancy lasted? Kate had no way of knowing. She stood up and brushed the earth from her skirts, her Sunday frock, and that made her think of Mister Charlie Inglis again. Cheeky wee blighter. It was all his fault that she was up the Baker's Burn getting her Sunday-best frock dirty.

'Come on, Bridie, the hooter for lousing time will probably go any minute and what will we tell our dad and our Pat when they arrive hame and see no tea on the table?'

Kate gave her free hand to her wee sister and hurried back to the village. From the rise above the Kirkland wood they stopped for a moment on their helter-skelter flight and surveyed the ugly little village. Kate had never considered its beauty or ugliness before but today all her senses were finely honed and she saw Auchenbeath for what it was – an accident that had happened on an old post road. The former toll house was the only claim to beauty it possessed, unless one counted the two rather fine kirks that glared balefully at each other from opposing sides of the road. At one end of the village stood two quite grand houses although both hid themselves away behind age-old trees. One, for some obscure reason, was the headmaster's house and the other belonged to Dr Hyslop. The village proper consisted of some shops and a few rows of ugly little grey houses. As the Victorian mansions dominated one end of the village, the other end was subdued by the slag heap, that ugly evidence of the men toiling like moles beneath the surface of the earth.

I wonder if primroses could be made to grow over that ugly old bugger, Kate thought aloud, but Bridie could see neither beauty nor ugliness in a mountainous pyramid of slag. It was just there.

'Come on, Bridie,' Kate shrieked in alarm as the three o'clock hooter sounded, announcing to the world that was Auchenbeath that the men of the village would soon be on their way home, needing hot food and hot water in which-ever order they chose. The girls hurried along, back under the railway bridge – no time to think of waving to passing trains – and reached the main street just in time to join the exhausted crocodile of miners who spilled out of the pit.

Liam saw them, their black hair bedraggled, their eyes shining and their usually pale cheeks sunkissed, and his heart turned over. Dear God, what a beauty that child is, and then, as he noticed the bosom straining at the seams of the best Sunday dress, he realized with a shock that Kate was child no longer but woman – and the spittin' image of her mammy when he wed her.

'Hello, lassies, been after primroses?' was all he said.

'For Mam's grave, Da, and for Mrs Murphy.'

'That's nice. Better take them now sin' you're so near the kirkyard and I'll take the bairn hame. Our Pat is walking with some of his pals. He'll be a while.'

Kate looked after him for a full minute as he walked on down the road, wee Bridie skipping and jumping beside him. She was alone, completely and utterly alone for the first time since the death of her mother. She had an impulse to run, to shout, to do. . . . what, she had no idea. She was filled with exhilaration. Oh, she loved Da and all the bairns, especially wee Bridie, but just for once, for a wee while, no sticky little hand was clutching her, no fretful voice was calling, Kate, Kate, do this for me, Katie, do that for me, Katie. She turned and hurried out of the village, past the schoolmaster's house, past the manse and up the Great North Road to the churchyard where Auchenbeath laid its dead regardless of religious persuasion.

There was still time before the school bell tolled at four o'clock. Da would wash the coal dust off – or at least as much of it as would come – and that would take some time and then he'd be needing his tea. He would maybe put the soup on the fire. At the sheer imbecility of this revolutionary idea, Kate laughed aloud. No man would be cooking his own dinner. She had better hurry – Bridie would be hungry – would he give her a piece to keep going on? And the others would be tumbling in from school. Kate was unafraid in the Kirkyard. Even on the day of the funeral, distraught with grief, she had felt its peace. Now, with its beloved tenant, it was even more of a haven. She hurried to her mother's grave, aware of many – too many – new graves in five years. 'Beloved Infant Son', 'Dearly Loved Wife, in her Nineteenth Year'. Sad, sad. That was Gracie Flett, Mam, she was at school when I was there. She had to get married, and then she and the bairn died. Was she ever happy, Mam? Look at these primroses. If I can get you some daffodils, later on, I will but these are bonnie. Me and wee Bridie got them for you up the Baker's Burn. From down the hill came the sound of the school bell. I'll need tae go, Mam. I don't know when I'll get back up but I do think about you. Cheerio. Swift as a deer Kate whirled and ran until she reached the village and then she decorously tidied her hair and walked as in the year of Our Lord 1911, the eldest daughter of a respectable family should.

Charlie Inglis saw her as she sailed down the main street, glancing neither to right nor left. Looking as if she owns the place, he laughed to himself. Charlie was not inexperienced. Auchenbeath was a far cry from Glasgow and Kate Kennedy very different from any girl he had dallied with before. There would be no dallying here. For one thing, it was impossible to blow your nose in Auchenbeath without the entire community commenting on the event and he sensed that Kate was not the playing with fire type. A man would have to be very sure of what he wanted and what he was prepared to both sacrifice and accept before he paid court here. He knew Kate's history – his mother and his aunt had corresponded regularly over the years – and he knew Mrs Murphy admired and pitied Kate for the lot life had awarded her. But did Kate pity Kate? He could see no sign of self-pity, no sign that Kate resented the fate that had robbed her of her childhood and her mother in the self-same moment. Sure, life is harder in Glasgow for lassies like her, he thought. At least her da has a job and a bit room and kitchen and the air she breathes is clean and fresh. The skin on her, I've not seen skin like it and those eyes . . .

Charlie forgot all his doubts and hurried to catch up with her.

'Well, Miss Kate,' he began since he knew full well that he had come on far too strong at their first meeting, 'have you enjoyed your outing on this beautiful day?'

Kate had forgotten that he had embarrassed her and was able to greet Charlie quite naturally. 'It was lovely up there, up the Baker's Burn. You won't know it if you've just arrived.'

'Then since you wouldn't let me come with you, Miss Kate, you must tell me all about it and I shall think about it in the dark hours down the pit.'

Kate looked sideways at him from out of her clear, candid eyes. 'You'd be better off thinking about what you're supposed to be doing, Mr Charlie Inglis.' And then she laughed and described it to him anyway.

# 3

In 1914 a wireless set was a luxury that Liam Kennedy could not afford; neither did his wages from the pit run to the purchase of a daily newspaper. He and his family, however, always seemed to know all that was happening, not only in Auchenbeath but all over the world. There were newspapers in the miners' club and Liam went there regularly. As events in Europe became more interesting and more frightening, Kate began to call into the club on the way back from delivering Bridie to the school. This was a good time as the men were either asleep or down the pits and she had peace and privacy to read them from cover to cover. Coverage of the royal family fascinated her; they were real but unreal, gilded beings who lived cocooned in a world where there was no pain. No pain, that is, until a beautiful hot day in June.

'Some duke's been killed in a place called Sarajevo,' she told Charlie, who was on backshift and therefore at home. Together they looked for Sarajevo and Bosnia on Charlie's old school atlas, unaware of how their lives and the lives of countless others were to be changed by that assassination.

War was declared on August 4th, 1914. Kate read the official announcement again and again to unlettered boys and women who crowded into the miners' club.

'I'll need to away and tell my da,' she said and pushed her way out of the shabby room.

Liam was in the kitchen eating his breakfast and Kate was too upset by her news to really notice that their neighbour, Mrs Murphy, was sitting having a cup of tea with him.

Within a few days, Charlie was calling in on the way from the pit with news. 'They've made auld Kitchener Secretary of State for War.'

'Is that not great news, Kate?' said Mrs Murphy who was once more in the kitchen, having dropped in just as Liam was leaving for the backshift. 'He'll soon fix them like he did in South Africa.'

But he didn't and within a few days many men and boys had left the village to join up. Patrick ached to join them. He brought it up one morning when they were all at breakfast.

'What a grand life to be a soldier,' he said. 'What do you think, Da? Can I no leave the pit?'

'I see nothing grand in killing, lad. Putting on the king's uniform and rushing off to shoot German laddies like they was rabbits . . . you have a secure job, Pat, even more secure now.'

'Sure he's far too young and all, Da,' said Kate who always found herself more Irish than Scottish in moments of crisis.

Her mind went back to a similar breakfast just a few years ago, shortly after Patrick had gone down the pit. She always had trouble getting Deirdre and Kevin up in the mornings and it seemed that she was always yelling at them, for she was determined that they were going to get as much education as they could get, not Deirdre so much as Kevin. She had failed for Patrick but there was still Kevin.

'Get up, Kevin, and get to school. You're not going down the pit so you can get that idea out of your head right now. You are going to stay at the school and learn something decent like how to be a real artist. You're good at drawing, you are.'

The boy looked at her in amazement. 'Something's gone to your brain, our Kate. You dinnae get learned to be a painter, at least I dinnae think you do, and drawing pretty pictures of flowers and Christmas puddings is not art. Our Pat's right. There's nothing here but pits and farms and the pit pays better.'

'There's more to life than money. Eat your porridge, Deirdre,' she snapped as she became aware that the younger girl was only playing with her food.

'I don't like porridge, stodgy stuff. When I leave school, I'll never eat porridge again.'

'And what are you planning to eat for your breakfast, tell me that?'

'Kippers.'

Kate looked at her sister in amazement. 'Fish. Fish for your breakfast. Fish is for your dinner.'

'You're wrong. Janet Bell's sister's in service and she says the gentry has fish, so there, and they have mushrooms and eggs and real fancy things for their breakfast as well.'

'We're no gentry. Folk like us has porridge and we thank God for it.'

'I'll no thank God. I'll eat it because we don't have kippers . . .'

'What's a kipper?' broke in Colm. 'I never heard of such a food.'

'Don't you know anything?' Miss Deirdre was becoming quite haughty as befitted a young lady whose best friend had a sister in service to a titled gentleman. 'It's a fish.'

'It's no a fish, Colm; it's what a fish gets called when it's been prepared a special way,' Kate explained.

She never did get around to asking Deirdre if she ate kippers; she always meant to, for as soon as they left school, just a year after Patrick, Kevin had gone into the pits and Dr Hyslop had got Deirdre a lovely place in service. And now Patrick was talking about joining the army.

'I don't know where I've gone wrong, Mam,' she sighed to herself. 'I want to look after them all so well and to keep your laddies out of that hungry mouth in the earth but they go anyway, and now here's our Pat getting all excited about being a hero and maybe winning a medal but I think my da's stopped him. He'll listen to Da.'

Indeed the boy said no more and perhaps Liam believed that he had settled down. His sister did not. She shared her worries with Mrs Murphy.

'Our Patrick was talking about going off since so many of his pals have gone.'

'And here's you didn't want him in the pits. Tell him he's safer there than in the trenches.'

'What about Charlie?'

Mrs Murphy smiled at the girl coyly. Kate's question suggested to her an even greater interest in Charlie than Kate had formerly shown and she was delighted.

'Don't worry, lass. Charlie has more sense than to listen to daft talk. He's good at taking care of his skin is our Charlie. Mind you, he doesn't like the mines; he'd still be out in the fresh air in Glasgow if he hadn't thought so much of me when my man went. But here, have a cup of tea with me afore wee Bridie comes home. What a lovely child she is, Kate. Fair makes a body want to mother her.'

Kate bridled. 'I'm sorry, Mrs Murphy. I have some baking to do,' she said almost coldly. She was Bridie's mother; the child needed no one else. It wasn't the first time her neighbour had made remarks like that. They had started about the time Kate had begun walking out with Charlie. Not that she was walking out with him exactly. It was amazing how quickly a walk with Charles and at least one of her brothers and sisters had become part of her Sundays.

The family had their midday dinner together and then, once the dishes were washed and put away – a walk with Charlie. He had even asked her to take a walk with him on evenings after work and once he had asked her to a miners' dance at the club. She hadn't gone, of course, and he had taken Deirdre who was at home on her weekend off.

'How could you go, Deirdre?' Kate had railed at her sister who had slipped into bed beside her after midnight and with her breath smelling ever so slightly of beer.

'Just because you don't want to have any fun, you think no one else should have any.'

I don't want to have fun? thought Kate. Is that what they think of me? An old stick-in-the-mud who made them do their homework and keep their underwear clean? Dear God, I'd love to have some fun.

'That's not true,' she said, 'but Charlie is . . .' and here she had to come to a stop because she didn't know what her relationship with Charlie was or what she wanted it to be. All she knew was that when she did have some free time it was pleasant to spend it walking with Charlie and the bairns.

She tried to explain her feelings to Deirdre whose reply was to turn over in the bed and stick her rump over to Kate's side.

'And how long do you think a man's going to enjoy walking up the Baker's Burn with you and your bairns? The whole place is laughing at you. Now, if you dinnae mind, some of us workd for a living and need our sleep.'

The war went on. Mons, Marne, Aisne, La Bassée, Messines, Ypres. A few months before no one whom Kate knew had ever heard of any of these places. Now they knew exactly where they were and, more horribly, how many men had died trying to win them.

The world was insane.

'They do say laddies are lying about their age to get into the army,' said Charlie one afternoon. 'It was in the paper about a laddie from one of them fancy schools for rich bairns writing sixteen on the souls of his shoes so's he wouldnae be telling a lie when he said, "I'm over sixteen, Sir." '

'How wonderful,' breathed Deirdre. 'Did ye ever hear anything so noble and brave and . . . noble?'

'I never heard anything so stupid,' said Kate angrily. 'I hope he got a good leathering and sent back to the school.'

'He got killed,' said Charlie dryly.

If the sad little story had been written to frighten the youth of Britain, it had, if anything, a seemingly opposite effect. Hundreds of thousands of them rushed to join up.

It was not over by Christmas. Kate looked with pleasure at her brothers as they cheerfully devoured the succulent meat pie she had made for their Christmas dinner. 'They're here, Mam, alive and well.'

Patrick met her eyes and smiled his slow, shy smile. 'Grand pie, Kate; the best yet.'

The house was strangely quiet. Kate had made the pieces and her pot of tea and even started the water boiling for the wash and still the men had not appeared for their porridge.

How could they all sleep in? she thought angrily. Liam was usually in right behind her as if he waked with the shout she gave the boys as she passed their bed on her way to the privy. He came out after her and gave her some privacy to dress before coming into the warmth of the kitchen.

Sometimes the boys had to be roused twice – they slept the deep sleep of healthy young males and were always torn protesting from their beds – then they scurried around dressing and making enough noise to wake the dead. It was unlike Patrick, though, not to acknowledge that he had heard her shout.

Kate went first to wake Liam. Sudden deviation from the norm unnerved her; surely something had to be wrong for him not to be awake. Be calm, Kate; it's the lads who wake him. Sure enough, Liam was lying sound asleep curled up like a baby.

'Da, you've slept in. I'm away to get Patrick; hurry, you'll miss the cages.'

He was up before she had left the room and had pulled on his moleskins and his shirt before she had reached the big box bed where the three boys slept. Only Kevin and Colm lay like puppies in a tangle of blankets.

The bottom dropped out of Kate's stomach. She had no need to run outside to the privy; she knew she would not find her brother there.

'Oh, Patrick, dear wee laddie; why did you do it?'

The note was propped up on the wally dug on the mantlepiece – she had been too busy to see it. It was addressed to Liam.

Dear Da,

I have gone to join the army. Please don't try to stop me. Give my love to Kate and the bairns and make Kevin stay at the pit.

Patrick x x

She could hardly bear it. It was a bairn's letter with its wee x for kiss.

'You'll go after him, Da. He's too young for the army.'

'He's seventeen, Kate, been doing a man's job for years. I've been waiting for this.'

That was all Liam ever said about it. He left the house without his piece tin, a sure sign of his troubled mind, and Kate had to run almost to the pithead before she caught up with him.

Kevin was still in his bed when she returned to the house; she had forgotten all about him.

'Kevin, you lazy lump. Get up out of there. You've missed your shift.'

She hauled eleven-year-old Colm out too. It was much too early for school but Kate was too distraught to care. Only Bridie should be spared her grief and wrath and feeling of abject helplessness.

'Why didn't our Pat get me up, Kate? It's not my fault if he just left me there.'

And then she told the boys what their older brother had done and she railed at them for not hearing him move in the night. Somehow she would have stopped him, somehow. She thumped the unsuspecting Kevin on the side of the head.

'Were you at the pub last night with all the other louts? Is that why you couldn't hear your brother?'

Kevin stood up and looked down on her. 'Don't you ever hit me again, Kate, or I'll hit you back even if me dad's here. I wasn't at the pub. I was playing football with your precious Patrick . . .'

Kate paid no attention to his threat. Did she even hear it? Patrick had gone to the war and that had to be her fault, hadn't it?

'And he said nothing?' she said.

'No, but he's like Da; he's no a talker. Our whole shift's near away. There's been recruiters in the pub and posters everywhere. The government says if enough of us go it'll all be over soon.'

'Are you going, Kevin?' broke in Colm who had been speechless with excitement. He didn't mind being yanked out of his warm bed. He could hardly wait to rush up to the school and tell all his friends that his big brother had gone to be a soldier. If both of them went he'd be hero of the playground for weeks. If he played his cards right he could get sweeties, money, and he wouldn't even have to barter the piece Kate gave him.

'You wicked bairn,' scolded his sister as if she read his thoughts and she cuffed him.

Colm cowered. Oh, to be a man like Kevin and threaten to hit her back.

'I'll maybe go to the recruiting office to hear what they have to say. There's tae be medals and other "rewards of a grateful nation".'

'You'll do no such thing.' As usual when Kate was in a panic she took refuge in being tough. 'Since you were too lazy to get up for your work you can help me wring the sheets and you can dig the tatties for your dinner.'

Kevin said no more but fell in with her plans. Kate watched him intently while he went about his chores, her own day busy with calming Bridie and sending her off to school with Colm, and then the daily household tasks. All this while her mind churned.

Where was Patrick? What regiment? Most men from the village were either the Royal Scots Fusiliers or the King's Own Scottish Borderers. Could he possibly have been rejected and be even now on his way home? Was Kevin right? Would it soon be over? It would, of course it would. She would like to have run over to Mrs Murphy to talk, even though she did not really like their neighbour, but she was afraid to leave Kevin. As soon as Da was in she would go over; she needed to talk to another adult.

Charlie was there.

'Charlie, I need to walk; can you come with me so I can tell you?'

Usually she would have been conscious that Charlie, still damp from his scrubbing at the kitchen sink, could not have had his tea yet, but her mind was taken up wholly with her worry over her brother. She unburdened herself of her concerns to Charlie, Charlie who was always there, Charlie who would listen and commiserate with her.

'Good for him,' was Charlie's unexpected response. 'What did ye expect the laddie to do when all his friends are away to be heroes, Kate?'

They were walking up the road towards the Baker's Burn and for once Kate was unappreciative of the soft Scottish spring; she was also unaware that, for once, she and Charlie were completely alone. They walked slowly and he reached for her hand. Her mind was so full of her brother that she barely noticed but let him hold her hand, grateful for the human contact.

Charlie smiled ruefully and they walked on and climbed the dyke into the fields.

She became aware of his gaze and turned shyly to meet his eyes. She blushed hotly and he smiled and bent towards her. His lips touched hers; they were soft and warm and yielding. Heartened by her response Charlie put his arms round her and kissed her again more deeply. Immediately she stiffened and pushed him away.

'Damn it, Kate; I thought ye wanted that. You're that bonny and I havenae looked near another lassie since ye were fifteen; ye have to know how I feel. For once ye didn't bring the bairns and I thought that meant ye wanted to be with me.'

He sounded like Colm when he was feeling hard done by and she softened as she usually did for the children. 'Sure, I wanted to be with you, Charlie. You're my friend . . '

He turned away angrily. 'I don't want to be your friend, Kate, dammit. I want to be your . . .'

And this time he stopped himself for he was unsure what he wanted from Kate. Oh, his body knew well enough. He desperately wanted to throw her down on the grass and take her there and then. He ached to lose himself in her, in her glorious blue-black hair, between her thighs but . . . reason prevailed. In any other family a nineteen-year-old girl would have been married or would be, at the very least, wordly wise, but Kate . . . he looked at her troubled face. How lovely she was and how unaware of it.

'Ach, Kate, you have tae stop being so wrapped up in the bairns. They're yer brothers and sisters, no yer weans.'

'But I'm responsible for them, Charlie.' It was so clear to her. Why could he not see?

'Liam is responsible for them; they're his bairns.'

'You don't understand. It's like you coming here to look after yer auntie when her man got killed in the pit.'

'It's no the same. I pay the rent and she cooks and cleans. I come and go when I please. You never leave the house without Bridie or Colm. You should be at the dances with the other lassies – like Deirdre. Why cannot that wee besom take a turn in the house?'

Kate looked shocked. 'Heavens, Charlie, she works six days a week. When she's home she needs a bit o' relaxation.'

'And when do you get your bit o' relaxation? If you don't stand up for yourself a bit more you'll be cooking and cleaning for them a' when Bridie's grown up and married. You should encourage Liam to marry again and go and find a man for yoursel'.'

She stared at him in horror, her usually pale skin even paler. For a moment he thought she might faint and he put out his hands to steady her. She pushed him away.

'I've finally got through to you, Katie. You see what a miserable life you're going to have cooking and cleaning, everybody's favourite auntie.'

Her words proved him wrong. She wasn't thinking of a sacrificial existence as spinster sister and aunt.

'My father would never look at another woman. He was married to my mother.'

She was trembling with rage and turned away from him. In complete silence they returned to the village.

# 4

PATRICK WAS A Borderer and very proud of himself. He wrote to Liam within a week.

'Does he wear a kilt, Dad?' asked Kevin after they had pored over the rather short and uncommunicative little document until their hungry eyes had almost drawn the ink from the very paper. 'Our Pat'd be right embarrassed to wear a skirt, I would have thought.'

''Tis not a kilted regiment, the King's Own. I would like fine to have a picture of him,' sighed Liam.

'I'll draw him for you, Da,' offered Kevin, 'the first time he's home. I'll do a grand job, I promise.'

But Kevin did not wait to see his brother in his smart Leslie trews. Every day he went down the pit and his shift mates only wanted to hear the news, if any, of his brother. The football team, sadly depleted, sat around on the waste ground they called their pitch and talked of the war. Everyone had a brother or a father in the trenches. Everyone would go to fix the Huns if only 'Mam' or our Jeanie' would just let them. Everyone knew that the war effort needed only their presence for a successful conclusion. Kevin sat and drew little pictures of soldiers in what he imagined were Leslie tartan trews and eventually could bear the talk no longer.

Before the next letter came he too had joined the army; his farewell note to his father was scribbled on the back of a piece of drawing paper. On the front were two heartbreakingly young boys in uniform carrying rifles. They were smiling at one another and were easily recognizable.

'It won't matter that the uniform isn't right,' said Liam.

'He'll mend it when he gets his leave,' said Kate and hours after Liam had gone to bed she sat and looked at the little drawing. His scornful words came back, 'Drawing Christmas puddings isn't art.' But this was, the simple sketch on a torn piece of inexpensive drawing paper. Please God, let him live to get a chance. Then her mind seemed to fill with hundreds and thousands of boys who would never get a chance. I cannae help you, laddies, it's important men wi' power that's tae blame for the mess you're in. And another brick was built into the wall of determination Kate was building. Hers would get a chance. Anything she could do to make life better for those she loved she would do.

*Are they no grand words, Mum?* she asked. *What can a bit lassie like me ever do but feed them and keep their clothes clean? And there's Colm and Bridie to stay at the school, and so they will if I have to tie them to the desk.*

Then one day Charlie went, just like that. He got up in the morning, packed his sole change of clothes into a battered suitcase and took a train back to Glasgow where he joined up.

'He aye said he couldn't go because of me, Kate,' Mrs Murphy wept. 'He never told you but he wanted to go right at the beginning – he was that excited but he's all I've got now, you see, and I talked him out of it. Here, he left this letter, you read it so's you'll understand.'

Charlie was nothing of a writer.

Dear Auntie Mollie,

I have to join up; there were men in the mine said I was feart but you know I was never a coward. If I get killed you're down as my next of kin so you'll be alright. Tell Kate to wait.

Love from Charlie

Kate read the letter in growing anger. Wait, tell Kate to wait, wait for what? She was furious with Charlie for putting her into this position for there could be no doubt of what Mrs Murphy was thinking as she clasped Kate's unresisting hands and smiled at her through her tears.

'I knew right from the first day he saw you, Kate love, and I'm that pleased. You will wait, won't you? It'll be over soon and he's a good man, my Charlie.'

Kate pulled her hands away; somewhere in the very back of her mind, in a place she never wanted to visit, she could hear her mother screaming. She began to panic. 'I have to get home, there's the tea to see to. Da's fretting about the boys.'

'You're a good girl, Kate. I'll come over later and show Liam the letter. What a lot of grief we have suffered together.'

Kate could bear no more. What grief had old Mrs Murphy shared with Liam? She stopped halfway across the fence. Dear God and his blessed mother – she wasn't an old woman at all. Kate did a speedy reckoning in her head. Mrs Murphy was the same age as Liam and Liam, Liam was forty-five. That was old, old, old. Oh, face it, Kate, be honest. For the first time in her life she thought of her father as a man. This past few months he had been drawn and haggard because of his unvoiced grief and worry over his sons but usually he was tall and straight and strong, a man any woman would be happy to love. That was it. Mrs Murphy had been a widow since ever Kate could remember; naturally she was drawn to a man like Liam but that

Liam could ever think of anyone but his beloved Mary Kate . . . no, it was unthinkable. Liam could not possibly love Mrs Murphy. Why, she was nothing like Mary Kate. Kate felt almost lightheaded with relief. How stupid she had been to worry so. She skipped over the fence and went into her kitchen.

Her pies always gave her such a feeling of accomplishment. The thought of actually selling her pies for money surfaced again. Two less wages now. The Kennedys had been living the life of Riley these last few years with all that money coming in. The bairns had got used to a Saturday penny and even half a bar of chocolate some Saturdays when the grocer's laddie came round on his bicycle to tempt pit wives whose men hadn't drunk their pitiful wages away on Friday night. Well, belts had been tight before and could be again, but if she was to sell a pie or two at the weekends to the pubs she would be helping her less-fortunate neighbours in more ways than one. She would be supplementing Liam's wage and she would be helping those poor women out there who had to face drunken husbands as they staggered home from the public house. Was it not drinking on an empty stomach that caused the worst drunkenness?

For a few minutes Kate allowed herself to bask in the glow of seeing herself as a modern-day Florence Nightingale and then she laughed at her fancies and got on with her baking. Liam would never countenance it. So sure of this was she that she never even mentioned it to him when he came in dirty and exhausted. Coal dust. It got everywhere; under your fingernails, up your nose, in your hair, in your mouth, in your eyes and ears and every other opening in the body. Liam stood – in his drawers – and allowed Kate to pour bucket after bucket of cold water over him and then she filled the hip bath with the water she had been boiling and soon the smell of carbolic soap fought with the delicious smell of her baking pies and won – only to lose in its turn to the smell of coal that always hung in the air.

Mrs Murphy timed her arrival perfectly. Liam was clean, dry, dressed, and sitting at the table when she knocked tentatively at the door and came in.

'Oh, you're at your tea, Liam. I'll come back; a man needs his meal after his shift.'

Liam had jumped up as soon as she had entered the room. 'No, no, Mrs Murphy, you'll have a cup of tea with me, with us. Me and Kate fair enjoy our fly cup together afore the wee ones come in.'

'Just like you and the poor dear departed Mary Kate used to, I've no doubt, Liam. Wasn't it the same with me and my Frank.'

Liam could hardly remember his wife ever having time to sit and have tea with him. She always seemed to be running after one or other of the babies but he smiled at Mrs Murphy and held a chair for her, Kate's chair.

'Kate, love, there's enough for Mrs Murphy to join us, is there not? Set another place like a good lassie.'

And like a good lassie Kate did but her mouth was set with rigidly controlled anger. In one sentence he had relegated her from woman of the house to wee lassie. Sure, if Charlie Inglis had walked in the door she would have married him at once. Mrs Murphy was crying over the letter from Charlie.

Liam let her speak and spoke only when her emotional outburst had washed itself away.

'He's left you all right like a good son. Aye, I know he's your nephew but that's not the way you see him. To tell you the truth he's a better man than I thought he was. He couldn't let the bairns like my Kevin fight for him, now could he?'

He was holding her trembling hands tightly in his.

'Da?' said Kate before she could stop herself and he flushed a little and sat back in his chair.

'I'll take more tea, Katie love, and you, Mrs Murphy, you'll take a little of this pie. Charlie would want us to help you now and we'll not let him down.'

He smiled at Kate but she did not melt and kept her mouth set in disapproval.

'Is it worse for us old folks, worrying for our sons, Liam,' said Mrs Murphy with a return of her coyness, 'or is it them that's missing their lovers that's most in need of loving care and attention?'

'Neither. It's the laddies over there, on both sides, God help them, that's in need of our prayers.'

Chastened, Kate and Mrs Murphy smiled tentatively at one another and tried to enjoy their tea.

Later, when Mrs Murphy was leaving, having insisted on helping Kate with the washing up, she pressed Charlie's letter into the girl's hand.

'You keep this, lass; you'll want the address although I'm sure he'll be writing to you soon.'

Kate folded the letter up and put it away in a kitchen drawer. 'Charlie Inglis, you cheekie wee bantam, don't you dare propose to me through yer auntie – if that is what ye've done.' She would never write to him, well, not unless he wrote first. It would be rude not to answer a soldier's letter and him away fighting for home and hearth.

It was weeks before a letter did arrive, weeks in which Kate had almost forgotten the pathetic little letter to his aunt. There might be a war on but here in Auchenbeath one had to go on with the daily round of chores, chores that the war did not ease. At least there was no fear of Liam joining up. Every day he went to the pit where the talk was always of what was happening in France or Belgium and sadly of the losses of the men who had once worked beside them at the coalface. What had this glorious war brought them? They had exchanged the dark, frightening world of underground for the darker, even more frightening pits called trenches that ran with mud and dirt, death and disease.

Better to have stayed down the pit.

In his letter Charlie said nothing of his feelings of fear or horror; he never admitted that he would have been better to have stayed safe at home but Kate knew. Charlie, the brave wee bantam from Glasgow who had always had the answers at his fingertips, was adrift in a world he could not handle. His letters clutched desperately at normality and the normality was Kate. Suddenly she found that her friend who had joined the army had been replaced by a lover, the ardent lover of the Baker's Burn. He spoke of his delight in their simple picnics, of the beauty of the Baker's Burn and the joy he had found there – what joy? She had run away from him. He wanted to get this over with so that they could return to their idyllic pre-war existence, only now it would be more wonderful for he and Kate would be man and wife. He confessed himself surprised that he had never realized just how deep were his feelings but she was a woman and she must have known. She was to wait for him, she had to; he could bear anything here if she did. Other men were cracking under the strain but he had his dreams of Kate and the bairns and lovely, peaceful Auchenbeath and so he would survive.

How to answer such an epistle? Kate went to the miners club every day and read the newspapers from cover to cover. Often she had to share with other women and was still often asked to read the news for those who could not. Could the reporters really convey the hell of Charlie's existence? Enough; enough that Kate found it impossible to write to tell Charlie to slow down, she did not love him, she hardly knew him. She liked him fine; he made her laugh; but her life was Liam and the bairns, especially Bridie. How could she even consider marriage when Bridie and Colm had years at the school ahead of them and she would keep them at their lessons? She would not fail with these two as she had so abysmally failed with the others. Maybe one of them would – well Bridie anyway, for even the most devoted of sisters could tell that Colm wasn't all that bright – maybe Bridie would do something with her life . . . a teacher maybe . . . she had a nice voice . . . opera. Kate laughed . . . a miner's daughter from Auchenbeath an opera singer. I haven't the slightest notion how you get to be a singer, but I'll find out, you bet I will. That vow, like too many others, was buried under the massive slag heap of effort that went into survival.

Daydreams were not helping her write to Charlie. She stared at the blank piece of paper and gnawed on the end of her pen. No little voice whispered in her ear, 'Watch, Kate, handle the next few minutes with great care.'

I can't hurt him just yet. I'll tell him when this is all over but I can't tell a lie so I'll say nothing about marriage at all.

And for the next two years Kate wrote weekly letters to Patrick and Kevin and Charlie, letters full of homely family news, of how well wee Bridie could read, that Colm had finally stopped wetting his bed, that Deirdre seemed very happy in service to the Duke of Buccleuch. She hadn't liked the butler at first but she was used to him now and she really liked the duke who spoke to her as if she were a real person and not just a kitchen maid. She even had a dress for dances that one of the young ladies had given her; quite fancied herself in that dress did Deirdre.

By 1916 conscription had to be brought in since the first hysterical flush of enthusiasm for killing and being killed had long since palled and – Patrick was killed in a place called the Somme. The War Office regretted . . .

Kate didn't tell Charlie or Kevin. She had to write the first letter three times because tears kept spilling over and there was a pain just under her breast bone that made it very difficult for her to breathe. Words formed under her hand but all she could see was Patrick's sweet smile and all she could hear was his voice denying his talents or thanking her for services it had been her pleasure as well as her duty to carry out.

'Grand pies, our Kate.'

She put her head down on the table and wept again. Would these tears ever dry up? Patrick, what did you get to eat these past months? Did death hurt? You were always such a brave wee laddie. Please God, don't let it have hurt him . . . the way it hurt Mam. The memories came flooding back. Mary Kate on the blood-stained bed screaming and trying to be quiet because of her frightened children. Did you scream, Patrick? I wish I'd been there to help . . . Don't be stupid, Kate Kennedy, you're wallowing in your misery. There's Bridie and Colm and Da, my poor da, and Kevin, that must be told, and Charlie . . .

She reached for the paper.

We're managing fine here though things are quite dear. Da is doing the baith gardens and Mrs Murphy and me always has good soup on the fire though bread is not always available. It's little enough of a sacrifice . . .

Then one Saturday Deirdre did not come home for her day off. The woodcutter who usually delivered her at the foot of the brae had no idea why she had not turned up.

'I couldnae wait for her, Kate, wi' all this to deliver.'

'Well, maybe the duchess is entertaining and needed her. It's happened before. She'll get next Saturday.'

He looked troubled. 'The family's in Selkirk this time o' the year, but I'll be up next week and if she's coming I'll bring her.'

Kate watched him as he went off on his rounds. Something had happened; she knew it but just hoped that it was something that Liam could handle. The woodcutter brought the letter the following Saturday.

'She's fine, more than fine, but she'll have told you in her letter.'

He laughed and drove off and Kate looked at the letter. She hadn't liked that laugh. It was the way Charlie laughed sometimes, and even Kevin, at things she didn't understand.

'Oh God, not that.' The words of guilt and explanation and self-pity poured off the page.

We never meant to but it was the day we heard Davey would get called up and then when I missed he said we should get married fore he went and his grace didn't want to lose Davey and I've got the cottage you'll tell Da I'm no a bad girl and he'll love the baby and Davey's a fine man and a good worker he wanted to meet you and Da but the papers came the young ladies gave me a real silk dress for the wedding and the duke gave Davey real silver knives and forks the woodcutter will bring

you please come tae see me for Davey's away
I can work for a few months yet and I'm fine but I'm
frightened tae come hame till you tell me what Da
says

your loving sister Mrs Davey Spence

Inconsequential things forced themselves on Kate's attention. Deirdre's punctuation or lack of it. 'The wee besum
didn't pay over much attention at the school. How will
I tell Da? She's scared and she's lonely . . . and she's pregnant.
I wonder what that feels like. It should have been me first.'

By the time she got home Kate had recovered from her
slight fit of sullens that her young sister had experienced so
much that she had not and inexplicably she had been jealous. Right now, however, she had to find a way to explain to
Liam. In the end, stammering over the words, she handed
him the letter. He read it and turned without a word and
went out. Later she saw him digging like a madman in the
potato patch and she cautioned Colm and even his favourite, wee Bridie, to stay out of reach of his hard right hand.

'Mistress Spence will be frightened in her condition
without her mammy, Kate. Make sure you are with her
when the time comes.'

That was all he said for several months. Kate went to
see Deirdre several times. Sometimes she took Bridie with

her and they stayed in the tiny but comfortable cottage that was Deirdre's new home but Liam never asked about her and after her first hopeful questioning look at her sister, Deirdre stopped asking about him.

'I'm not a bad girl, Kate. You did tell him I'm not bad,' was all she had said and Kate felt guilty for she had actually never discussed Deirdre with their father. Liam had become so remote since Patrick's death, so tense as if he were waiting for even more bad news.

'He'll come round when the baby comes. He wants me to be with you. It's just the shock and Patrick . . . he's not over Patrick.'

Liam got drunk the night they heard that Kevin had died. 'What more do you want from me, God,' he yelled into the sky. 'Babbies, they were just babbies, them and the others, poor wee babbies greeting for their mammies and you let it happen. *Sweet merciful God.* Sure if you exist at all you disgust me.'

Kate dealt with him and then she stripped and scrubbed herself with cold water to rid herself of the smell of vomit. Exhausted, she crept into bed beside Bridie who pushed Kate's chilled body away in her sleep. All night she lay and listened to Liam crying in the next room and when dawn came she got up and dressed and made the porridge and Liam's piece. He would go down the pit again. His sons were dead but there were other children to feed and anyway there was no body to lay out and so one did what one had to do. He looked shamefacedly at his oldest daughter for a moment as she stood in the doorway with his tin.

'I'll not make an excuse, but it'll never happen again,' and through their pain their eyes met and consoled each other.

The morning went on. Kate fed Bridie and Colm. Got them brushed and off to school. Now she had time to think. Where to go to get rid of this unbearable pain? Who was there to talk to, to scream with, to cry with?

She was outside on the road to Sanquhar. She kept going – and then she had arrived. She sighed a deep sigh as she stood outside the door and the sigh seemed to loosen parts that had been frozen since her mother's death. She pushed the old door and it opened as stiffly as it had always opened. Nothing had changed. It was just as it had been the last time she had been there, the morning of Mary Kate's funeral.

The chapel was long and narrow, and as dark and quiet as she remembered. The little red light still flickered to show believers that Christ was present and Kate walked slowly towards it as if drawn by a force too strong for her weary soul to resist. She went down on her knees at the altar but stared straight ahead, not bowing her head subjectly and reverently as Mary Kate had taught her.

*Why, God, why?* she cried inside and then the tears came and she wept silently. She had not wept when Mary Kate had died, for after she had wakened from her exhausted sleep she had been too busy and confused to cry. Now she wept for her brothers and her mother and for her father's pain. How long she stayed she did not know, for she knelt quietly there for some time after the tears had stopped while the little light twinkled in the semidarkness, and a feeling of the most indescribable peace cradled her like a mother. At last she rose, and genuflected, and as she left, blessed herself with holy water from the little bowl at the door.

Painfully the old priest pulled himself up from behind the altar. The time was not yet. He had known who she was of course and his first impulse had been to go and comfort her and welcome her home. But not yet. For now the dialogues had to be between Kate and her maker.

Totally unaware of the presence of the old man, Kate left the chapel and walked on, in a daze almost, until a voice hailed her. 'Kate, I don't often see you out this way?'

She had reached Dr Hyslop's house without noticing. She looked at him. Here was someone she could talk to, someone who would take some of her pain and make it for a moment less severe.

'Kevin too,' was all she could say.

'My poor child,' he said and held her against him quite naturally for a moment while his eyes stared away into the distance looking for the face of another of the babies he had brought into the world and would never see again.

She moved away from him, gently warmed by the contact.

'I must away home. I've no idea of the time.'

'Just noon. Come,' he said and was surprised at what he heard himself say, 'take some lunch with us. Doctor's orders.'

Kate was shocked. Miners' bairns didn't take lunch with doctors.

'It wouldn't be fitting,' she said, deliberately becoming broader to show him the social gulf he had forgotten.

'Miss Hyslop is at home, Kate,' he explained, thinking that she was afraid. 'Lunch won't be so delicious as one of your pies, I'm told, but you need to rest.'

She smiled at him. 'You are a good man, sir, and I will never forget your kindness.' And she turned and ran like a tinker's lassie down the road to the miners' row at Auchenbeath.

# 5

THE DEATHS OF his sons caused Liam to withdraw farther and farther from his surviving children. Never a talker, he now spoke less and less, and Kate voiced her worries to Dr Hyslop. She did not consult him in his surgery on the Main Street, of course, for that would have been a professional consultation. Perhaps he watched for her; she never knew, but it seemed that more and more as she walked up to meet Bridie at the primary school, Dr Hyslop was in his garden. His garden grew more beautiful as the war grew more ugly.

'I seem to feel the need to be close to the earth, to create with God's help, perhaps just to take my mind off the war,' he told Kate one afternoon as she stopped, ostensibly to admire his roses.

'But you're a doctor, you create all the time.'

'God creates, Kate. Sometimes I wonder if I'm half as clever as these new mechanics for those motor cars.'

Privately Kate thought that was the daftest thing she'd heard him say yet they were not near so intimate that she could say he was daft to his face.

'You don't agree, Kate, but you see it seems to me that mechanics are between man and machine and I'd bet heavily on man every time but with medicine ... well, there's the doctor's knowledge and skill and experience but God has to have a hand in somewhere and the patient has to want to get well.'

Again he was talking nonsense. Surely everyone who was sick wanted to get well; no one wanted to die.

'And how is everyone at home? I see the wee ones ... getting bigger and bonnier every day ... but what about Deirdre and your father? He's a man with the world on his shoulders these days.'

And then she was able to spill it all out. How Liam was eating less and less each day and still working down the pit every hour God gave him, and not speaking much, even to Bridie whom he'd always adored, and never mentioning Deirdre who was so close to her time and scared and wanting her Da and her Davey who was in France too.

He sighed and straightened his back. 'Maybe the baby will be the best medicine, Kate. Somehow we have to get them together. Has he seen her since the wedding?'

'No, and he never asks how she is, but he leaves money for me to buy her extra things.'

'Then I would say that she should come home for her confinement. He'd not throw her out.'

She shook her head. 'I don't know. Last year I would have said "no", but since the boys, I just don't know.'

They stopped talking to admire a Red Admiral on a rose petal. The sun shone on the butterfly's wings and on the doctor's bald head and burnished the girl's blue-black hair, and all three were filled with a momentary sense of peace. There were other flowers to invade and the man and the girl followed the butterfly's flight until it disappeared into a sunbeam.

'Talk to Deirdre and let me know, Kate. I'll be there if she needs me.'

She almost forgot that she had promised to meet Bridie and Colm so full was her mind with the possibilities raised by her chat with Dr Hyslop. It was the first time that she had actually faced the physical facts of Deirdre's situation. She, Kate, was her sister, and since there was no mother to help, it would only be seen as natural that she help Deirdre. Deirdre would come home or she would go to Deirdre. Either way she was going to become intimately involved in the birth process and Kate, always honest, had to admit that the idea filled her with dread. What if Deirdre should . . . no, she refused to think of that. How many mothers had survived the birth process since Mary Kate's death? Dr Hyslop could have told her and told her too how many mothers had had babies over and over again since. It was a perfectly natural function. Deirdre would be fine and she, her big sister, would help her.

In the end it was not a grandchild who forced Liam from his depression, but Charlie.

Each week Kate sat down and wrote a letter and each week she found the letter harder and harder to write. Sometimes she found herself wondering who this Charlie was who took up so much of her precious time. She tried to see his face or hear his voice but the real Charlie was growing farther and farther away from her. The Charlie she wrote to was someone she had to protect from her sadness because he had too much of his own to tolerate. She had to pretend that everything was going well although it seemed as if every day yet another commodity was rationed, sugar, butter, bread, eggs. Where would it end? As wages became inadequate to sustain even the low pre-war standard of living of the working class, there were unofficial strikes all over Britain. Not much cheer to give a man who only wanted 'to get away from this hell and home to ma dearest Kate'.

She was not his dearest Kate. She was Kate who had promised her dead mother that she would nurture all her brothers and sisters; she was Kate who sometimes woke up in the night in a sweat of fear and dread because she had failed to keep that promise – two boys dead and Deirdre marrying because she was – but, dear God, how could she tell him this while he was in the trenches? He wrote to her of men who were shot as deserters because they desperately tried to get home to wives who no longer wrote loving letters. What a juggling act life was. And now here was Liam unable to eat enough to keep a wee lassie like Bridie alive never mind a miner.

And then came the day when Mrs Murphy cast herself into Liam's arms, hysterical with fear and dread because Charlie was 'Missing presumed dead'.

Immediately Kate forgot her own worries and set herself, with her father, to calming Mrs Murphy's fears.

'I'll make a cup of tea, Da. She'll be the better for that. Sit her down there at the fire,' for Mrs Murphy was making no effort to pull herself out of Liam's arms and he was holding her and saying 'there, there', as if she was a bairn needing comfort.

'He'll all I have left, Liam, and he's dead, the poor laddie.'

'Drink this nice strong cup of tea, Mrs Murphy.' Kate forced the cup into her hands. 'He's not dead, Charlie's not dead; sure it says only that he's missing.'

'Kate's right. Isn't it such a mess out there with smoke and rain and all, that you could be beside your brother and not know him. Didn't both my boys, God rest their souls, complain about the dark?'

It was a long speech for Liam and it had the right effect on Mrs Murphy. She calmed down and drank her tea and even played with a scone although her heart wasn't in it and Kate was startled to realize that Charlie's nice, fat wee auntie had lost a great deal of weight in the past months.

I've not been looking after her for Charlie, she thought guiltily. I've been so anxious to keep her away from Da.

'Mrs Murphy, stay and take your tea with us. The bairns'll be in from the school in a minute and Bridie always cheers you up with her prattle. I'll away to the back kitchen and get the soup on and a few more tatties and we'll have a grand shepherd's pie.'

She refused to look at the neighbour to see the effect of her invitation but punished herself for what she saw as her thoughtlessness by leaving Mrs Murphy and Liam alone together by the fire. She even refused to pray that the bairns would run straight down from the school instead of dawdling as they usually did. God must have decided that she was punished enough, if punishment were needed, for Bridie and Colm tumbled into the house a few minutes later, hungry as hunters and more than ready to distract Mrs Murphy's attention.

Kate dried her hands on her apron and bustled back into the kitchen.

'I'll make the bairns a sandwich to tide them over . . .' she began and then stopped for Liam was putting his coat on.

'I think Mrs Murphy needs something stronger than tea with the shock, Kate. I'm taking her up to the pub for some brandy. Sure her cousin will give us a glass in his front room; a public house is no place for a woman.'

Kate stared at them. What could she say? What could she do?

'The soup's on and the pie's ready for heating up.'

'We'll be back within the hour, Kate. I wouldn't want a decent woman in a pub for longer than it needs.'

'We'll be in my cousin's house, Liam,' smiled Mrs Murphy, 'but just you feed the bairns, Kate, and yourself too if you don't want to wait. We won't be long though; I'm that pleased to be asked for my tea.'

Kate could say nothing.

How dare she? How dare she? Feed the bairns, indeed. Who was she to tell Kate Kennedy what to do?

Liam, the least demonstrative of men, seemed to sense his daughter's distress. He put his hand on her shoulder.

'Would I let one of your pies get cold, my Katie? We'll be back afore you know,' and he smiled that special smile, the one that must have torn the very heart of Mary Kate Moore out by the roots all those years ago in Limerick.

'We have to help our neighbours, Da,' she tried to smile. 'It's just the. . . .'

'If I didn't take to the drink when my laddies went, Katie. . . .'

How could he be so blind? She wasn't worried about drink. That she could handle. It was his being with another woman. She could not explain.

'I'm sorry, Da. Away you go and have a nice time. Sure the pie will be the better for keeping a little.'

She tried to smile but as she stood at the window and watched them walk up the road towards the miners' club she knew that nothing would ever be the same.

And so it was. Mrs Murphy haunted the house or Liam was with Mrs Murphy; working in her garden, helping her write letters she wanted to write to nameless officials at the War Office, shovelling her coal into the cellar.

'Kate, when are we going to see Deirdre?' Bridie asked one Saturday morning a few weeks after the news had come of Charlie's disappearance.

Kate looked down at her little sister. Yet another worry. How much had the death of her brothers affected her? How concerned was she about her sister's condition or, perhaps, was the little girl merely excited about the arrival of a baby, something she perhaps saw as a little doll?

'We'll go to see her on Saturday, Bridie love. Would it not be fun if she was to come up here to have the baby. Doctor Hyslop thinks you'd be the world's best nurse.'

Bridie smiled and Kate looked down at her with love. She was not, even in the eyes of the most devoted mother, a pretty child, but something shone out of her grey-green eyes. What was it if not pure goodness?

She told Liam of the projected visit and it seemed for a second that he looked slightly embarrassed.

'I meant to tell you, Kate, and I should have afore this,' he tailed off.

'What is it, Da? Have you had news? There's nothing wrong, is there?'

'No, there's nothing wrong but Molly . . . Mrs Murphy thought, you're too young, Kate . . .'

(Dear God in Heaven, too young. Hadn't she been there, a mere babby when Mary Kate died?)

'Go down and take the wean, but Mrs Murphy suggested, asked if she might help at the lying in, and she'll stay till Deirdre's on her feet. Sure it will be good for her to have something to do besides grieve for Charlie.'

'*Molly* is taking a lot on herself, isn't she? Deirdre should be here in her own home with Dr Hyslop and me, her sister, and you her da, although you seemed to forget who you are . . .'

Never in her life had Kate Kennedy been insolent to her father and it was difficult to tell who was the more surprised at her outburst. Liam recovered first.

'You've not been yourself lately, Katie. Mrs Murphy was noticing as well. Weren't we talking about you last night. Sure, don't I know your heartbreak over

Charlie and the lads. A birthing would be too much for you.'

'I'm no grievin' for Charlie. Why can't you understand that? Oh, I don't mean I'm not sorry, of course I am, but . . .'

He wasn't listening to her. At least he was listening but not hearing. It was better to say nothing, to keep it all inside, to be controlled.

'And what about Deirdre . . . maybe she doesn't want a stranger with her at a time like this?'

Again Liam looked abashed.

'I heard from the carrier. She has nice friends in the staff at the castle. Even her ladyship is taking an interest. Deirdre wants to be there, Kate –' he tried to make her smile – 'with her kipper for her breakfast.'

'You'll need to away or you'll miss your shift. I have a wash to do.' And she turned and left him. She knew where she wanted to go but she couldn't, not yet, with the wee ones still to get up. She would hang out her washing, get the bairns ready for the school, and then walk them up the road. It was looking to be a grand day; a day for drying sheets and maybe even curtains.

Three hours later she was on her knees in the dark little chapel. The old priest had made one overture of friendship to her on one of her visits but when she rebuffed him had said merely that she was always welcome in God's house and that he was there should she wish to speak to him. She did not. Not yet. She was too confused. She knew only that here in the dimly lit little room with its spluttering candles she found something – peace, tranquility, reassurance, call it what you will. She was able to argue with herself, to see her unreasonableness over Liam's friendship with Mrs Murphy. Deep down she had been afraid that she might have been called upon to help Deirdre and yet she was angry that Mrs Murphy had taken it upon herself to do what Kate felt was her duty. Now she could breathe deeply and resolve to be grateful. Mrs Murphy had had a child; there were no mysteries to frighten her and helping Deirdre would, as Da said, help her come to grips with her grief over the loss of Charlie. It did not mean that she was going to marry Liam. There, she had said it. Marry Liam. And why shouldn't she marry Liam, a little voice whispered in her head. Would that be so awful? Grow up, Kate Kennedy. Men seem to need women more than women need men and it's not just because they can't cook and wash and sew. It's that other thing. If it wasn't for that, I would be enough for him. How will I face it if he brings her into our home? And Bridie? What about Bridie? She'll try to be her mother and I've been her mother all these years. No, Kate, you're her sister. Dear God, help me to bear it if Da marries her. I suppose I could go and live with Deirdre till this war is over if it is ever over.

The chapel or the one-sided conversation with God – was it one-sided; she was never aware that He answered, but somehow she always felt better about what she knew she had to do – worked its usual magic and she was able to face Mrs Murphy, if not with enthusiasm, at least with tolerance.

'It's good of you to help out with Deirdre.'

Mrs Murphy looked at her and smiled tentatively. She's afraid of me, thought Kate. Why on earth should she be afraid of me? Isn't it me that's afraid she's after me da?

'Good God-fearing men like your father, men that have lived their religion very seriously, take it awfully hard when one of their own breaks the rules, Kate. He was maybe frightened he hadn't brought her up right, no lettin' you go tae the chapel where your mammy would have wanted you to go.'

'You don't have to go to church to be a good person; there's no a finer man in Auchenbeath than my da and God knows it too.' Maybe she could get him to go back as she was going back. On her visits to the chapel Kate had thought only of herself. Now she would pray for Liam, for them all, for Deirdre.

It had been the wrong thing to say to Mrs Murphy, who assured Kate that she was the last person to need reminding of Liam's goodness.

'Hasn't he been so grand with me worrying about Charlie? Helping the both of you out with Deirdre will be my way of paying back. Or when the time comes I could help out here wi' feeding your father and the weans, Kate, if you'd sooner be wi' Deirdre?'

Wouldn't she love that chance? Oh, to be able to be in two places at once.

'I'll try to get Deirdre to come home when her time comes, but if she wants to stay in her own place, I'll be obliged if you'll help out.' There, she had said it. Not wholeheartedly, but she had said it.

Mrs Murphy smiled. 'The war'll soon be over and it'll be your turn.'

'I assure you that I will never have to get married,' said Kate stiffly.

'Goodness, Kate, what a thing to say? But you'll want to, when this bloody war is over, and the sooner the better.'

The war showed no signs of being over but on the very day that Deirdre gave birth to her first son, Charlie came home. Not to Auchenbeath. He had been injured at a place called Passchendaele and was to be in a hospital in England for several months.

Kate was relieved to know that he was alive. Perhaps now Mrs Murphy would transfer her interest to her nephew. She wrote to Charlie telling him how delighted they all were that he was safe. Perhaps she should not have said that they were all very anxious to see him home safely.

There was a revolution in Russia. Kate liked the aristocracy – they seemed to her to give stability to a wobbly world, even Russian ones who, after all, were related to the king – and was horrified that they had been murdered. King George decided to call himself Windsor and America entered the war. Colm was fascinated and learned more geography and history in a few weeks than Kate had learned in all her time at the village school.

'You wait and see, our Kate. The war'll be over in no time with the Yanks in. They're all millionaires and drive cars and they all own their hooses, even miners like Daddy.'

'And where did you hear this?'

'At the school and the miners' library. Did you ken that you could drop Scotland in one lake in America, it's that big, and if you had a motor car it would take weeks to drive from one side to the other. I'm going when I leave the school.'

'Good for you, Colm,' said Liam, 'and when you're a millionaire send for your daddy. I'd like fine to pick an orange right off a tree and eat it.'

'You shouldnae encourage him in his nonsense, Da,' said Kate but secretly she was delighted to have the loving Liam back, 'visiting America and picking oranges off trees, indeed.'

He was still not loving enough to invite Deirdre home and had not even seen his grandson, David Liam Spence.

Kate found this very difficult to understand. After all, had he not actively encouraged Mrs Murphy to stay with Deirdre? Deirdre herself was amazingly philosophical about the situation.

'He's still that Catholic and old fashioned, Kate. We'll have a christening when my Davey comes home and Da'll come round then, you'll see.'

Kate and Bridie were doting aunties and could only agree. How could anyone reject this most beautiful and intelligent of babies. Mrs Murphy agreed too but she had more on her mind than David or his grandfather for she was going down to visit Charlie. She was going to travel by train, in itself a terrifying new ordeal and she was to stay in a boarding house.

'Imagine me in a hotel. I'll be frightened I eat with the wrong knife.'

'Who is going to notice, Mrs Murphy, or care? You go and enjoy yourself. Pity it took poor Charlie near getting himself killed for you to have a holiday but pretend that's all it is, a nice wee holiday at the seaside.'

'At the seaside,' echoed Colm in a voice full of awe. 'Be sure and have a kipper then, Mrs Murphy, and tell us what they taste like.'

She did better than that. She brought kippers back with her and told Kate how to heat them up. It was not a success.

'Well, I'm sure they're very nice for the gentry, Da,' said Kate, 'but I'd rather have a nice bit of fish.'

'Do we have to eat them, Da?' asked Colm. 'I'm chok-ing on all the wee bones. Our Deirdre cannae really like them, can she?'

Kate put their supper on the back of the fire and cut bread for them instead. 'Dinnae tell Mrs Murphy if she asks you. Just say, very nice.'

'That's telling lies, our Kate,' said Colm grandly.

'Better a wee fib than getting your backside walloped for hurting somebody's feelings,' answered his father and the kippers were never mentioned or joked about again.

There were more important things to think about. Charlie was well enough to travel and was coming home. Liam went with Mrs Murphy to the station while Kate cooked a meal for him. The fatted calf, Liam had called it, although there was nothing of the prodigal about Charlie, unless the prodigal son had been emaciated and grey after his experiences. Kate could have wept when she saw Charlie. Nothing had prepared her. He was another man. Nothing of the cocky wee bantam was left. He was but skin and bones. Time, she knew, would help that, but his black curly hair was straight and quite grey and his once-sparkling eyes had lost their glitter. There was no bounce in his step; in fact he dragged himself around on crutches. His strength was all in his hands, or so it seemed to Kate as she examined the bruises left by his iron grip on her.

'I won't leave you, Charlie love. Sure, I'm only away into the back kitchen to get your tea.'

'There, pet,' said Mrs Murphy, 'didn't I tell you Kate waited for you. She's a good girl, our Kate, isn't she, Liam?'

Kate saw the smile of understanding that passed between them. 'I'm not your Kate,' she wanted to scream but there was Charlie, what was left of him, gazing at her.

'Don't worry, Charlie,' she said. 'We're going to get you well, you'll see.'

# 6

IT COULD NOT be happening; it had happened. My God, she was Mrs Charles Inglis. There was no way out. For a second a wave of panic swept over her and she fought down the impulse to run screaming from the little church.

*I never wanted this; how did it happen? Dear God, what will I do?*

For months Mrs Murphy had devotedly nursed Charlie back to all the health he was going to regain. Then she and Liam had taken to spending the occasional evening together at the miners' club and so Kate had begun to sit with Charlie, to read to him. She enjoyed that, time to sit and read without feeling guilty that there was perhaps something else she should be doing.

The dismantling of the machinery of war began on 11th November 1918 and the signing of an official peace took place seven months later. Deirdre's Davey returned and Deirdre made her peace with Liam who enjoyed the luxury of spoiling his first grandchild. And on the Sunday afternoon that Kate heard Mrs Murphy say to wee David, 'Come tae yer grannie, sweetheart,' she realized that her days as the mother of her father's family were numbered.

'We want to spend the last days of our lives together, Kate,' said Mrs Murphy when Liam officially broke the news to his children, 'but we will have to sacrifice our happiness for my Charlie. How can I leave him on his own the way he is after all he's suffered? He'll not live with me and Liam but he cannae live on his own.'

Liam explained his actions to Kate late that night as she sat darning socks by the fire.

'I'm not being disloyal to your mam. Can you understand that? This between me and Mollie isn't the same but I've been alone a long time.'

'You had us, Da. How can you say you were alone? Haven't I taken care of everything? I love looking after you and Bridie and Colm . . . and the others, God rest them.'

'It's not right, Katie. Molly and me need each other and you need a life of your own, a home of your own . . .'

She had not been able to find the words to make him understand, and so here she was surrounded by people, kissing her, hugging her. How dare they, how dare they?

At last a voice she recognized, a beloved voice. Bridie, my wee Bridie, my baby sister. The little sister whom she had promised to care for and whom she was now abandoning. How had it happened? When had she allowed herself to say I'll marry you, Charlie? Had she ever – or had it all been taken for granted and she had never had the courage or strength to say 'no'.

Dear God, I'm married because I didn't want tae hurt his feelings and him injured.

'Kate, there's a man tae take yer photo. Can I be in it?'

'Photographs!' Make the best of it, Kate, make the best of it; you're married, so get on with it. 'Charlie, we cannae afford such new-fangled ideas.'

He hugged her to him in full view of everyone, sending a flush of embarrassment over her. 'On yer wedding day, Kate Kennedy – naw,' he laughed proudly, 'Kate Inglis, ye can afford anything. Come on, darlin', and you too Bridie, Auntie Molly, Liam, we're getting our photo took for posterity.'

He bundled them out of the church and the photographer did his best to marshal them into line at the front door.

'Smile, please,' and Kate tried to smile. She smiled so grimly that the photographer tried to jolly her along.

'It won't hurt a bit, my dear,' he said and of course Charlie and his friends read a double meaning into the remark that set them off laughing uproariously, and so Kate's smile became even more wooden and, as such, was frozen for ever.

Mrs Murphy had hurried off as soon as Kate and Charlie had signed the register and the delicious smell of Kate's own pies greeted them as they returned to the miners' row. For once, Kate was not allowed to serve but sat in the big chair in the kitchen and tried to enjoy the party. Would it never end? Whisky was flowing freely and when Kate cut the wedding cake that she herself had baked, Charlie produced a bottle of champagne.

'Only the best on your wedding day, my darlin'. Come on now, drink up. Isn't that delicious?'

'Yes,' agreed Kate although the warm liquid tasted nothing like she had expected it to taste. Was it not supposed to be ambrosia, whatever that was? Deirdre took a glass and downed it at one gulp.

'Was there ever anything so delicious,' she cried in a voice that sounded quite intoxicated already. 'That's the drink for me. Champagne, Kate. We had bottles of it at our wedding, really good stuff from the duke.'

'Deirdre,' said David quietly.

What a difference he would make to her sister, thought Kate as Deirdre calmed down immediately she heard his quiet voice.

'Sure, you and the gentry are welcome to it,' said Kate and could not quite manage to take the sting from her voice. She wanted to quarrel with Deirdre, with anyone, just so that somehow, perhaps, this awful thing would go away.

She looked around the laughing red-faced group and prayed that the day would soon be over and then, as she realized that it was almost time for her to leave her father's house she prayed that it would never end. But of course it did, and Kate and Charlie, followed by shouts of drunken revelry – for those at the wedding party had almost one and all forgotten about the reason for the free drinks – set off to walk to their new house. Charlie, in common with almost every other man – and more than a few of the female guests – had had far too much to drink, but the chill evening air soon sobered him up.

'A grand wedding, Kate,' he said in tones chosen to mollify his bride. He knew well how much she abhorred over-indulgence.

Kate looked at him and remembered the photographer and the ghastly champagne and a wave of tenderness swept over her. He had a good heart, her Charlie, and although deep down inside she was sure that in marrying him she had made a grievous mistake, arm-in-arm with him on their wedding day she vowed that he would never know and that he would never have cause to regret it. Charlie misread the message, put his arm around her waist and almost carried her the rest of the way to the cottage.

Whatever Kate had expected, it was not this, and to give him credit, it was not what Charlie had intended either. He swept her up into his arms at the door, kicked it shut, and stumbled with her into the bedroom. No time even to take off the cover Kate had so patiently embroidered; no time either to undress and put on the new nightgown with the delicate lace around the neck. He pulled up her skirts and pulled down her drawers and then he was on top of her and her back was breaking and, dear God, what was he doing?

It was over; he was lying quiet on top of her. Strange how heavy he was and him still a slip of a man after the war.

'My hat,' she whimpered, 'you're crushing my hat.'

Hats, what did he care for hats? Was he asleep, collapsed on top of her; she lay, terrified to move.

'Jesus, that was rare,' at last he mumbled into her neck and then, oh dear God no, he was moving again, his breath sounding harsh in her ears, his spittle drooling down the side of her face.

'My hat,' she cried, but he was oblivious of everything but his need. Faster and faster he moved, deeper and deeper into her until she was sure that she must suffer some terrible harm, and then, with a cry of achievement, he collapsed once more upon her and then rolled off and lay there. She stumbled to her feet averting her eyes but not before she had seen IT lying there so limp, and wet, and . . . the smell! She was going to be sick. She stumbled outside and vomited into the weedy patch that was her front garden. Even in her misery she was alert enough to decide that there would be flowers, not vomit, there in the spring.

She returned to the front room of the cottage and filled the hip bath with water; then she pulled off her clothes and, clenching her teeth, lowered herself into the cold water. With a nail brush she began to scrub and scrub until her skin was raw and sore. Would she ever be clean; she could still smell *IT*. At last, too tired to scrub any more, she climbed stiffly from the bath and dried herself with a rough but spotlessly clean towel. Her new nightgown was in the bedroom but nothing would make her go back in there. She slipped her wedding dress back on and, after emptying the bath and drying it out, she curled up in the chair by the range and fell into an exhausted sleep.

She woke early and was making porridge when Charlie woke and somewhat shamefacedly crept into the room.

'I didnae mean it to be like that,' he muttered. 'It was just the waiting, all the weeks. It'll be different from now on.'

She said nothing. How stupid; she had actually thought that that was it. It was over; she was married and she had done it – or at least it had been done to her, but it was not finished. It was going to happen again and again. Oh, God, she would die. She shrank away as he tried to put his arms around her but then, with a tremendous effort of will, she pulled herself together and managed a wavery smile.

'It's fine, Charlie. I didnae know what to expect, that's all . . . and you ruined my hat.'

Relieved, he grabbed her and twirled her around in a hug. 'Your hat. I'll buy you a dozen hats.' He sat down at the scrubbed wooden table. 'Come on, Katie lass. Have some porridge. It's braw porridge. Then I'll have a look at that garden and see if I can dig a bit for a cabbage. Auntie Molly says we should get some more sprouts and all afore the year's out.'

Kate sat down and forced down some of the porridge. A dozen hats and him with no job and precious little chance of one. Well, she had coped with little money during the miners' strike of 1912, she could cope now with the pittance that was his disability benefit. Thoughts like that made her sorry for him again. Poor Charlie; sure, it wasn't his fault. Hadn't he ruined his health in the service of his country. So marriage was going to be far from perfect, but surely *that* would be a small part; she could handle it and, as for money, somehow they would manage. Charlie would never work but at the back of her mind there was that half-formed idea about the pies but for now . . . one day – and one night – at a time.

For several days they were left quite alone but then Kate had to walk into the village for some supplies, and if she was to be in the village, it would be silly not to stop in and see the family. Wee Bridie ran to meet her, closely followed by Colm who remembered too late that he was thirteen years old and too old to be running to meet a lassie even if she was his big sister.

'You're no to worry, Kate,' said Bridie earnestly as she proudly poured her sister a mug of tea. 'We're managing fine. Mrs Murphy's here that often they might as well be wed already and tae give her her due, Kate, she makes grand soup, and our Colm's a great help to me, he really is, much more than the laddies were to you.'

Colm blushed with pleasure and embarrassment but, as usual, said nothing. Kate looked at them, so young, so earnest, so self-important. It was almost as if it was happening all over again, as if Bridie was to become the mother of the family. What have I done? Left Bridie alone and for *that*. No, there was going to be the wedding, wasn't there?

'And me dad, Bridie. How's he gettin' on with no hot breakfast?'

'Colm gets it, don't you, Colm? He says you were his age when you were doing it all.'

'Aye, maybe, but I'm a woman; it's no job for a laddie,' said Kate and was annoyed when both Bridie and Colm laughed at her. *Poor wee lad*, she thought. *What kind of life is he having; cooking and cleaning and, next year, down the pit. Oh, Mam, haven't I made a terrible job of minding yer weans?*

She stood up and looked around the tiny room that already looked so unfamiliar. The damp little farm cottage on the road to the Kirkland Wood was now home.

'I'll no wait for me dad, Bridie. Come away up to the shop with me. I need a wee pat of butter.'

'This is great,' Bridie chortled with glee as she skipped up the road, her hand tight in Kate's. 'Imagine you a married woman. Is it nice, Kate, being married? Only two people to cook for and to wash for. What do ye find to do?'

Kate smiled at her innocence. 'Aye, well, there hasnae been much to cook and clean since the war. Dad's all right, is he, Bridie?'

Bridie was quiet for too long. 'He misses you but he's the same as he always was, since the boys I mean. It'll be grand when they get married.'

Kate was forced to agree. It would be better if Mrs Murphy were to take over the running of the house.

'I don't want Colm cleaning and cooking. When I make soup, I'll make a big pot and bring it down and the cottage takes no time to tidy up; I'll be down twice a week to clean so Colm's no to miss the school or you either.'

Bridie's murmured, 'What about, Charlie?' was dismissed. If Charlie didn't like it, he could lump it. After all, Kate had decided to lump one or two things herself.

Wisely, Charlie did not interfere. Like the rest of the village, he waited for Kate to fall pregnant; that would keep her in her own house where she belonged.

Mrs Murphy waited with the others but here was their three-month anniversary and no sign. She had a special gift for them to mark the occasion and toiled with it up the road, past the Presbyterian kirk, past the dark, forbidding wood to where the cottage stood, bathed for once in sunshine. Charlie was in the little garden, his plans for fresh vegetables not too far forward.

'Auntie Molly,' called Charlie in delight, and his voice brought Kate out of the kitchen.

'Come in, come in and I'll put on the kettle. What are you doing climbing all the way out here?' Kate scolded. 'Jings,' she exclaimed as the box she took from the old lady emitted an angry squawk.

Mrs Murphy laughed. 'I'll no open it till we've had our tea for it's a hen and you'll no want that in your nice clean kitchen, Kate.'

Charlie rubbed his hands in anticipation. 'Boy, never mind the tea. A hen? I'll hae its neck wrung in two shakes,' he finished, picking up the box and making for the door. 'Ye'll stay for a meal, Auntie.'

'You will not.' Kate spoke calmly and Charlie knew the tone well enough to know that her mind was set. 'Oh not you, Mrs Murphy, you're more than welcome' – what else could she say to someone who was her husband's aunt and would, one day very soon, be her step-mother? 'But it's soup we'll be having and not chicken soup either.' She smiled cajolingly at her husband. 'Charlie, think; a hen means eggs, fresh eggs near every day and then when it's past laying, it's soup and a bit stew too. It's a wonderful present. Thank you very much.'

'Well, I suppose it's me that'll have to be making a pen for it.' Charlie accepted the loss of his dinner philosophically. 'That being the case, I'll have some of that tea.'

The pen was never made for Jessy – as Kate named her hen – but for a while, until the winter, she remained near the cottage and laid a large brown egg in a nest of dead leaves in a tumbledown outhouse three or four times a week. Shortly after the first frost Jessy disappeared.

'It'll be one of the foxes,' sniffed Kate, half in anger, half in sorrow, for she had come to rely, not only on the lovely eggs, but on the cheery chirping with which the brown hen had invariably greeted her. She pulled some Brussels sprouts – not Charlie – he got too tired for much heavy digging. 'Just when I really needed you, Jessy,' she muttered as she looked at the dark earth and saw not it but the bright brown eye of the hen as she had pecked in the dirt beside her. For Kate had 'fallen' at last and fresh eggs were supposed to be really good for someone in her condition. How she had dreaded her weekly visits to the village shop where it seemed the only subject worth discussing was her fertility. She had actively discouraged such prying into her private life and to her chagrin, had earned an undeserved reputation.

'Here comes Madame Hoighty-Toighty,' had whispered Violet Fenton from behind her counter. 'Always was above herself with the books she wanted tae read at the school and her always chattin' up the doctor. Wonder if he'll rush up the hill to deliver her weans, if such a skinny body could ever get one in the first place.'

At last, however, Kate had discovered that she was pregnant. During the few short months of her marriage she had welcomed her monthly period for, although the word menstruation was never mentioned, Charlie never sought his connubial rights during these times. She never counted the days but would find herself thinking as she lay waiting for Charlie to be deeply asleep so that she could get up to clean herself, *another few days and I'll get a wee rest*. This month there was no respite and it was in fact Charlie who had noticed. He had climbed into the bed beside her as she lay with the covers tucked up under her chin and pulled up her nightgown before rolling himself on top of her. 'Can I have a wee go, Kate? Has the curse of Eve no struck yet?'

He did not wait for an answer but began his violent bucking while she lay totally unresponsive beneath him. The curse of Eve, her detached mind thought. 'That's right; I'm late. What's wrong with me? Oh dear God, don't say

I have to put up with this every night, for Charlie now had his hands tightly clamped to her buttocks as he tried to fuse their bodies together until he exploded into her with a confused babbling and that slobber down her neck that she hated almost as much as she hated the sticky, smelly fluid now pouring down her thighs.

'Jesus, Jesus, Jesus, Kate, that was the best ever and do you know why? I've given you a bairn, Kate, that's why there's no curse. Damn, if you'd listen to the men wondering if I was man enough to fix you, but I have, haven't I? My lungs are buggered but there's nowt wrong wi' this.' Proudly, and almost fondly, he patted his limp penis and hurriedly Kate averted her eyes. 'Bloody hell, Kate, could you no even pretend you like it? Do you think for one moment that don't know ye jump up as fast as ye can tae clean me off; that's probably why you took so long to fall.'

Still she said nothing.

'At least put some water on the fire with the winter coming. If you have tae wash yourself', I'd as soon you washed in warm water.'

She climbed out of bed and went into the front room. Differing emotions were warring in her troubled mind. Anger with herself that she had not realized that her haste to wash herself after Charlie's lovemaking had hurt him; a very real distaste for all aspects of the physical part of marriage; and now a swiftly growing euphoria that she might indeed be expecting a child. This last feeling would, in the months to come, be in danger of being swamped by terror of the actual process of giving birth, but for tonight there was only joy.

A baby, a baby of my very own.

Tonight the memories of her mother's confinements remained hidden in the recesses of her mind; they would rise soon enough to taunt her. Tonight, as she scrubbed, she did not feel the bristles; she thought only of a small, defenceless Bridie, but this Bridie would be her very own to love and to keep for ever and ever. 'My baby,' she thought and her ecstasy was the nearest she came to orgasm in those early days. 'My very own baby.'

# 7

KATE WAITED SEVERAL weeks to tell Pa and Bridie. Firstly, she was not sure that she could bring herself to see her dear Dr Hyslop as a patient and for such an intimate condition. Secondly, her realization that she was about to bring new life into the world had forced the terrible dilemma she was in over religion to surface again. She had married in the Kirk because nothing had seemed to matter too much after the deaths of her brothers, but she had still been drawn to the dim peace of the Roman Catholic chapel. She had gone there several times but never with any real purpose in front of her. Life and its partner, death, were more bearable if one believed in God, and, as she knelt on the hard wooden kneeler, she thought about her life and about Liam and her brothers and sisters, yes, and Charlie. She never consciously prayed and never used the prayers she had learned as a child but when she left the quietness she felt at peace.

Now, with the knowledge of the baby, all the half-remembered lessons came back. She had been baptized a

Roman Catholic, she was still a Catholic and here she was expecting a baby and her marriage had taken place in the Kirk. In the eyes of God was she married at all?

As usual she communed in her heart to the ghost of Mary Kate and one day she had a visitor to whom she told everything. One cold morning she had gone out into the garden and there, looking like a king, dressed in his magnificent autumnal finery, had strutted a cock pheasant. He did not fly off with the usual violent whirring of wings but, after sizing up the danger to be expected from the small figure in the doorway, went on about his business.

'Well, that's me well and truly in my place,' laughed Kate, 'not even a bird's frightened of me.'

'Have you a family, my fine sir?' she asked the pheasant. 'Sure, you have the look of a family man about you, or is it the founder of one of them grand dynasties, more like?'

She rested her hands lightly on her flat stomach and moved out into the thin sunshine; still he stayed, pecking the earth.

'I, sir,' she said slowly to savour the pleasure of telling, 'I, sir, am going to be a mammy. What do you think of that then?'

He looked at her out of his hard little eye but made no move and Kate went on. 'Right now, it's the embarrassment, you see. I have to go to the doctor, but he'll know what Charlie's been doing. Sure, I know he knows, they all know, but now they'll really know, and I hate all the little eyes on me. I wish my mam was here.'

*Oh, Mam, how can I be so happy and so scared at the same time? Sometimes I think of having my own wee baby and there's joy in me like I've never felt before and then, sometimes, at night when Charlie's asleep, I get frightened for I remember your screams. But on a morning like this...* forgetting the bird, she took a further step into the garden and, with an angry whirr of wings, he rose straight up into the air.

Kate watched him fly. *Is he not bonny, Mam? I'd like to fly from my worries. Must be grand. Another thing's bothering me lately, Mam. Will I go to hell if I die because I married in the Kirk? I'll need to talk to a priest; a pheasant cannae help or you either, Mam, unless it's you that's leading me.*

She smiled. Of course, that was it. The spirit of Mary Kate was telling her what to do.

'I'm away in to the surgery,' she told Charlie who was cleaning the grate. 'And I'll maybe see Bridie and me dad if he's no at the pit.'

Charlie straightened up and smiled at her. 'Great. To tell you the truth, Katie love, I was a wee bit worried that you wouldn't see the doctor. Away ye go and I'll have this old range fair gleaming when ye get back and a nice pot of tea waiting.'

'That'll be grand.' She put on her hat and, pulling on her gloves, went to the door. 'If I see your auntie?'

'She'd be that pleased if you was tae tell her. She'd throw away yer father and come up tae take care of you.'

Kate was not amused. 'I can take care of myself,' she said sharply before she could stop the angry words and then felt ashamed of herself. Why she was antagonistic to poor Mrs Murphy she did not know. Everything was so jumbled in her mind. Had Mrs Murphy pushed her into marriage with Charlie and, if she had, was that too bad? Apart from *that* aspect of marriage, she liked being married to him; he was really a very nice man. Was it that Liam needed someone else? Was she jealous or did she feel a failure, that she wasn't enough for him. She looked at Charlie and softened. 'Ach, Charlie,' she added, 'if the doctor says everything's fine and I see my da, then I'll tell her next.'

Since Mrs Murphy, who had known for herself without being told, had been knitting small garments for the past month, Charlie found himself praying that his aunt would do nothing to set up Kate's bristles.

Liam was down the pit when his eldest daughter visited the village and Bridie and Colm were at school. The visit to the doctor's office had not been so fraught with difficulty as Kate had feared. Even the examination, with her eyes and teeth tightly clenched, had been over quickly.

'And now, what about the garden, Kate?' he had asked as she dressed herself again and she had relaxed and told him of her vegetables and her poor hen and the pheasant and her plans for the spring.

'You must let me give you some cuttings and some dahlia tubers. A garden can only support so many plants and you, as a gardener yourself, must know that we gardeners cannot bear to see any of our children die.'

Gladly she had agreed to call, with Charlie, at the doctor's house, the following weekend. And no matter what he said about saving cuttings which would otherwise be sent to the compost heap, she would pay for the plants with one of her pies.

She did not know then how this proud gesture would change her life. In the meantime, however, there was another visit to be made.

'Father O'Malley, my name is Kate Inglis and I'm a lapsed Catholic.'

The old priest smiled. 'Come in, Mrs Inglis, you'll have a cup of tea. With a charming young visitor I can allow myself a biscuit and so you will be doing an old man a favour by permitting him to indulge himself.'

She followed him into the cold, dark, chapel house and soon found herself pouring out her entire history while he poured tea. He listened quietly, saying nothing, but occasionally nodding as if he understood, or, yes, that was perfectly understandable. They drank the pot of tea; just the way Kate liked it, strong and hot.

He made no judgements.

'According to the law of the land, Mrs Inglis, you are, of course, legally married. The Church does not recognize your marriage and you can be married in the Catholic Church. If you do not, or if you cannot marry in the Church, you may have your child baptized; for that you do not need the permission of the father. Have you spoken to him, discussed this with him?'

She shook her head.

'Then talk to him, my dear. I think that's the first thing to do. I am always here and you can talk to me at any time. If I can help you I will. It will take a little time – a marriage that is – you have neglected the Sacraments, but, while you were a child, that was not your fault. You must decide what you want and you can and will be welcomed back.'

She thanked him and left. He had not asked her to pray with him and for that she was grateful; she was not yet ready, but she felt better. It would take time to work things out but she had made up her mind. Her child would be baptized in the Roman Catholic Church. What would Charlie say? She would have to talk to him. Baptism . . . getting married again, getting married for the first time is how it would be – according to the Church. Charlie wouldn't like that idea. They were married, well and truly; that's what Charlie would say.

'Is this one of them queer like notions women in your condition get, Kate?' is what Charlie said. 'We're married and I have a wee paper to prove it so no more of your havering.'

'According to the law of the land we're married.'

'That's good enough for me.'

How could she reach him? What could she say?

'It's not good enough for me, Charlie. It's the laws of God I'm worried about.'

He wasn't often angry but he was angry now. 'What papist mumbo-jumbo is this? I won't have ony of that nonsense in my home. We were married in the Kirk afore a minister. Are you trying to tell me that that's no good enough?'

'But I'm a Catholic, Charlie.'

'Since when?'

'I've always been.'

'Never in all the years I've known you, or Liam or the others.'

She told him about the night her mother died. 'She was buried by a priest, Charlie, but Da wouldnae let us go to Mass after.'

'Good for him; he saw the light. It's nonsense, Katie, all that stuff, incense and chanting and a man dressed up like an old doll, nonsense, and I won't have it in my house.'

She turned to face him. She was frightened now, but surely Liam would protect her. 'Then maybe you won't have me in your house either, Charlie,' she said defiantly. 'My da will take me in.'

They stared at one another, both young, both frightened. Charlie capitulated first. 'You couldn't bring such shame to me, Kate. Think on my side. You went out to see the doctor and me near sick with the worry because you wouldn't go afore, like you were ashamed you were having my bairn, and you come back and tell me, not that you've seen him and all's well with you but that you want to become a Roman Catholic.'

He began to cough as he always did in moments of stress and he tried to push her away as she went to assist him. Kate helped him into the chair by the fire and held a towel to his lips until the spasm passed.

'I'm no ashamed, Charlie. I'm that happy about the baby but I want everything to be right for him. I've been to the chapel a few times since my mam died just to sit or to kneel and I feel right there. You haven't been to the kirk since the day we were wed. One of us should go to church to show the bairn the right way.'

'What will folk say, you going to the chapel?'

'We'll no hear them, Charlie, and that's all I want, just to go now and again and think. The priest's nice; he's no pushy . . .'

'That'll make a nice change. Ach, maybe it's right a mother should go to church. Ministers have aye christened, married and buried us, and that's aye been enough; that's what they get paid for.'

'They'd all starve to death, Charlie, if everybody thought like you. Now, have we sorted this or do I go to my da?'

'You're no still talking about walking out? And let me tell you, Kate Inglis, Liam's more like to belt ye and send you home where you belong.'

They both knew that was untrue. Kate sighed and kissed Charlie lightly on the forehead and he sat and waited for her to make their meal.

'That cough's tired me,' he said after a while. 'I think I'll hae a wee lie down. You wouldnae like tae join me; a rest in the afternoon would be good for you, Kate.' His eyes told her that she would not be resting.

She shouldn't have kissed him. What was it about Charlie? The slightest sign of weakness or affection and he thought she was ready for whatever it was he did in the bed. No, by God, she was not going to put up with it in the afternoon too.

'I've this tattie soup tae finish, Charlie. I'll shout you when it's ready.'

'I'll bide here then, Kate, and watch you. I had planned to walk up the road after dinner and see the farmer;

there's maybe something I could do. I was aye good with horses.'

'The morn'll do, Charlie.'

'Aye. I'll feel better the morn.'

On the Sunday following her initial visit to the doctor, Kate rose early to make her pies. They had to be ready to carry into the village in time for Mass, which Kate had decided to attend, and there would be no time to return to the cottage before visiting Dr Hyslop. It was a beautiful morning; by seven o'clock a weak but valiant sun was trying to melt the frost that had crept over the garden and the surrounding fields. The trees in the garden, a magnificent chestnut and an equally imposing beech, were beginning to change into their autumn finery, the chestnut already almost a pillar of fire. Kate stood for a moment in the doorway throwing dough to the visiting pheasant. Was it the autumn air, that incredible crispness and clearness, or was it her condition that made her feel so happy and fulfilled? She took great gulps of the cold fresh air and, filled with oxygen and euphoria, returned to the kitchen. The three pies were wonders of the baker's art; she had never been so pleased.

'Will I come with you, Kate, no to the chapel, but I could maybe help you with the pies; precious use any other way.' Charlie was awake and Kate was touched by his concern. For a moment he was like Liam, the Liam who would push a pram in an age when such an action was deemed unmanly; here was Charlie offering to help carry pie dishes.

'That'd be grand, Charlie,' was all she said but it was enough for they walked happily to the village, stopping every so often because Charlie was sure that there were still brambles on the bushes that clambered over the dry stone dykes. He did find a few and they shared them like greedy children, but there was that look in his eye that made Kate glad that they were on their way to church.

He did not go into the little chapel with her. 'I'll have a walk by the river and fetch you later,' and Kate was more than content.

Dr Hyslop was in his garden when they walked past later on their way to see Liam.

'Going to your father's, Kate? Sunday luncheon? Come in. I have several cuttings for you.'

He showed them into his greenhouse. 'Have a seat; you take the comfortable one, Kate. I'll be back in a second.'

Obediently Kate and Charlie sat down, and, too nervous even to talk to one another, they looked shyly at the beautiful plants.

The doctor returned with, not cuttings but a tray of coffee, and he kept up a flow of small talk while Kate, both embarrassed and honoured at being treated like a guest, sipped her coffee – the first cup she had ever had.

'What a gentleman, Charlie! Is he not? And his thanks for my pie; did you hear him say he has friends coming, golfing friends, and he'll serve it to them? Just think, Charlie, real gentlemen eating my pies,' babbled Kate as, her arms full of cuttings and her heart full of joy, they walked to the miners' row.

'And why not, Kate Inglis? Why did you think I married you? Was it not all over Dumfriesshire that Kate Kennedy was the queen of the bakers?'

Liam Kennedy was not a demonstrative man. Kate waited until they had finished their dinner, not their luncheon, before she told him that he would be a grandfather again in the spring. 'That's nice,' was all he said, but he rose to put on the kettle for the tea thereby conveying some new status on his eldest daughter. It was as if he was recognizing that she had waited hand and foot on him and the others for years, even before the death of her mother, and was no doubt doing the same for Charlie. To put on the kettle would be a small thing to do for her but Kate read all the unspoken messages and her heart warmed afresh.

Bridie was thrilled at the prospect of a new baby but Colm appeared sheepish as if here was proof positive that his sister really participated in the unmentionable but secretly exciting things the boys discussed at school.

'What do you want? A wee girl would be nice. What about names?' asked Bridie all in one breath. 'You'll need to write to Deirdre. A wee cousin for wee Davey, and let's away in to tell Mrs Murphy, she's got news hersel' ... I shouldnae have told ye.'

'News?' asked Kate. 'Have you set the date?'

Liam stood up and stretched. His back was always stiff and sore from the constant doubling up in the pit. 'Away and fetch your auntie, Charlie. I cannae think why she wouldn't come for her dinner. Did I not tell her Kate always makes enough?'

Mrs Murphy, of course, had shown great understanding by refusing her intended's invitation. She had rightly supposed that Kate was going to make her announcement and felt sure that the girl would prefer her not to be part of the family gathering. Now she pretended great excitement and surprise.

'And you'll give me the right to help a little, Kate, now me and ye da's finally getting married. Hogmanay's a lovely time for a wedding and Liam has a day off the pit.'

The wedding was very different from Kate's and no doubt the wedding night was too, if the besotted looks the new Mrs Kennedy gave her husband were anything to go by.

She's not frightened, thought Kate, and she's been through it all before.

What was wrong with her that she could barely tolerate, never mind enjoy, that part of marriage? Even Deirdre was gazing into her Dave's eyes and sending messages that anyone could read.

The wedding had taken place in the register office in Dumfries and all the surviving family were there, looking stiff and uncomfortable in the clothes that had not been worn since Kate's wedding. Mrs Murphy had refused Kate's offer of help – 'too much work in your condition' – and Liam took them all for fish suppers which they ate on the bus back to Auchenbeath.

'That pair'll be under a tree long before they get home,' laughed Charlie as the bus deposited Deirdre and Dave at the end of the road leading to their cottage.

Kate kept silent, hoping that Liam had not heard his son-in-law's remark. Charlie was not a coarse man in spite of what he did to her almost every night in their bed. What made him say these vulgar things? Even if his own daughter were not involved, Liam would not appreciate Charlie's levity.

'Maybe we'll find a tree ourselves, Katie,' whispered Charlie. 'Is that what ye need, lass, a wee bit of romance?'

'Don't be silly, Charlie. It's Hogmanay; it's freezing cold.'

'My practical wee wife,' said Charlie, and to Kate's surprise, when they did eventually reach home, she did not have to endure the nightly fumbling, for Charlie had fallen asleep before she joined him. A stronger man than Charlie might well have fallen asleep too, for after the bus had finally deposited them in the village, there had been that long cold walk through driving sleet to their cottage.

'You'll need a hot drink, Charlie, or you'll catch your death,' had been Kate's New Year greeting to her husband, but he had dropped his outer clothes onto the floor and climbed, in his combinations, into the bed. She put his mug of soup on the table beside him and gratefully and quietly so as not to disturb him, had eased herself into the bed, already warmed by his body.

*I'll be grateful if he doesn't get the cold*, Kate thought but she was more grateful to start the new year without *that 'nonsense'*.

On her first visit of the new year to Dr Hyslop's surgery he had some news for her.

'Not the best time for you to be thinking about something like this, Kate, but it could solve a lot of problems.'

'I'll think about it. I'm real grateful and I'm flattered, I don't deny. If I wasn't . . . having a baby, I'd jump at the chance, once I'd talked to Charlie, of course. Can I tell you, next time I'm in to see my da?'

She went out into the driving wind and sleet and, wrapping her thin shawl about her, set off up the hill to the cottage.

I could have a decent coat for a start, she told herself, and a nice cot for the bairn, and a pram.

She struggled the mile to the cottage and arrived on the doorstep, soaked through and hungry, to find the fire out and the cottage cold and dark. Charlie was in bed, his face grey against the sheets.

'I'm sorry, lass,' he whispered, 'a wee attack. Take off yer clothes and get in here with me. I meant to bank up the fire for you.' He had said too much and collapsed coughing.

Alarmed, Kate forgot her cold and fatigue. 'I'll run back and get the doctor.'

'Get yourself dry, Kate, and mend the fire. A bowl of your soup later and I'll be fine again.'

That reminded her but it wasn't the time to tell him. She went into the kitchen with some dry clothes and, after pulling them on, she redded up the fire and heated the soup. When she was warmed up and she had managed to spoonfeed Charlie, she sat sipping her own bowl and told him her news.

'Charlie, one of Doctor Hyslop's friends owns lots of grocery shops and he wants to sell my pies.'

Weak as he was, Charlie struggled up in the bed. 'No wife of mine is going to work,' he tried to shout but the effort was too much and he fell back, coughing.

Kate held him until the fit had subsided but she could almost feel the steel forming inside her. She looked around the damp little room with the fungus growing on the walls. *This is what I'm to be content to bring my son to,* she thought – for he would be a son. *Well, Charlie Inglis, I'll lump a lot. God knows, I'm not used to much, but this is for my child. There's a chance for us, him and me, and you too, and I'll fight for it with every weapon I've got.*

'You're a good man, Charlie Inglis, but you'll never work again so we'll stop pretending. I *am* going to sell my pies. This is a once-in-a-lifetime chance, Charlie, and you'll be in it same as me. This Mr McDonald knows about the baby and he's prepared to wait for a wee while to go into . . . well, to order a lot, but in the meantime he wants pies in the local pubs, seemingly he has *interests* in them as well. I've thought it out. I'll get your Auntie Molly to help and Deirdre, she could use a bit extra. My recipes, two other good bakers. You'll deliver them to the pubs, once you're over this attack. Now, rest a bit, while I'm away to write to Deirdre. She'll have to talk to Dave who'll be as daft as you but she's near Thornhill and that's a grand market.'

Trembling at her temerity, Kate hurried off before he could say anything and left Charlie fuming at his infirmities and wondering at Kate's almost uppity talk when her dander was up. 'I'll talk to Liam,' he croaked eventually. 'He'll sort you. His wife and his daughter working for a living; he'll never lump the idea for a minute.'

Liam, no doubt persuaded by his new wife, whose relations, after all, ran one of the local pubs, came to see his son-in-law.

'In a perfect world, Charlie, a man would be able to provide a decent home for his wife and bairns, but it's not perfect. You shouldn't have been gassed; my boys shouldn't be dead. That bloody war changed a lot, and not always for the better.'

'There's talk of pensions, Liam. I'll get a pension. You can't want Kate working?'

'Think on it this way, Charlie, they're not really working, not like going down the pit. It's baking wee pies, man, women's work. So they're going to make a few extra and sell them, let them. In the summer maybe you'll be better able for a bit farm work and Kate'll have her hands full with her babby.'

They smiled; nature would take its course. It did and almost four months after Liam's wedding, Kate went into labour. The child was late, almost as if he knew that he was hardly arriving at an opportune time and had kept out of his mother's way as long as possible. Kate had refused to move back to Liam's home to await the baby. She was standing up in the kitchen of the cottage when labour started and her last words through clenched teeth to a distraught Charlie were, 'Mind and take they pies out of the oven in ten minutes and then you can go for your auntie.' It was Dr Hyslop however, who, returning from a sick call, found the exhausted Charlie stumbling along the road and took him up in the pony and trap.

'Can you help, man, or should I fetch her step-mother?'

'I'll manage, doctor.'

Charlie meant well, but he was not intended to pursue a career in midwifery. Each and every one of Kate's fears, both rational and irrational, returned to plague her and she was sure that she was going to die. Charlie almost swooned at the sight and sound of his wife in agony.

'Go and boil water, man,' said Dr Hyslop, taking the old way out of getting rid of useless help without offending it.

'Mam,' screamed Kate, 'my mam's there, doctor. She's taking me. It hurts; no more, please, no more.'

'She's here to help, Kate. Push, lass, push; it'll soon be over and you'll have your baby.'

Kate moaned and shook her head. 'I want to go with her. Mam.'

She opened her eyes, stared wide-eyed beyond the doctor's back, and rallied, and finally the exhausted doctor dragged the unwilling infant from his mother's torn body.

'You have a fine boy, Kate,' Dr Hyslop whispered and he returned the cleaned and warmly wrapped infant to her. Did she feel a kiss dropped on her brow? She could not be sure, but she felt surrounded by love. With all her determination and strength she grabbed the feeling and held on to it and then focused on the warm baby nuzzling at her breast. How strong his little mouth was; strange that so small a child should have so much power. She felt the milk, the nourishment, passing from her breast into the greedy little mouth and with it went her heart, whole and entire, for ever and ever. She was his from that moment on, and she would never love anyone or anything with half the passion she felt for this son.

'Hello, my wee lamb.' Her whole being exulted.

She did not hear the doctor leave. Charlie's incoherent outpourings of love and sorrow affected her not at all; indeed she barely heard them. Patrick Hyslop Inglis attached to her breast. She was asleep.

# 8

KATE'S EUPHORIA AFTER childbirth lasted for but a few days, the love for the rest of her life. Dr Hyslop had gone out of his way to inform her father of the birth of his second grandchild and later on the day of Patrick's birth, Liam and his new wife arrived to look after Kate. They stayed to care for Charlie who had had another recurrence of his lung problems brought on by strain and over exertion.

Kate was up and at her baking three days after Patrick's birth and when he was a week old, she loaded up the old pram – bought at a jumble sale at the Kirk – with the baby, and her delivery of pies, and set off for the village.

The walk exhausted her and she was glad to reach her father's house and to sit down by the fire while Bridie fussed over her and Colm fussed over his nephew.

'He's bonnier than wee Davey,' was his verdict.

'Boys are handsome, not bonny,' said the doting mother, 'but I quite agree with you.'

She went off into the bedroom to suckle her son. Never had she imagined herself doing such a thing there in the room where Liam had slept with Mary Kate and where he now slept with Molly Murphy.

*She's a nice enough woman, Mam,* said Kate to the ghost who was never far from her, *but how Da could marry her after you? Well, that's no my business, is it? What about my bairn? Is he no the most beautiful creature ye've ever seen?* And then, while she watched the child pull hungrily at her breast, she began to formulate the actual plan which had been lying at the back of her mind for years and which Doctor Hyslop had given her the courage to accept. *I'm going into business, Mam. Charlie's no pleased. He's that silly. He's got this idea that he has to provide.* Unaware that she was repeating her father's argument almost word for word she went on; *Well, in an ideal world, maybe . . . but the world's no ideal. If it was you'd be here, wouldn't you? I'm a wee thing tired after the walk down the brae with the pies but I'm leaving a note at the doctor's . . . I'd walk through fire for that man, Mam, pure goodness, but anyway, I'm going to start the business proper. I've asked at the pubs for good bakers to give me a hand . . . for a decent wage. I'm not getting above myself, Mam, but I want a chance for my bairn; I'm not after wealth and kippers for my breakfast. I'll work all the hours God gives and one day your grandson will go to the university and* – she could say it in her head but not yet aloud – *he'll be a good Catholic, Mam.*

The baby thus discussed with the dead told his mother in no uncertain terms what he thought of her conversation by burping loudly and regurgitating most of the milk he had hungrily swallowed across her bosom and down the front of her dress, for, modest as ever, Kate had unbuttoned only enough to allow access to her nipple.

Lamb, lamb, was Mammy no paying attention to you? It's for you, Patrick, all my working, for you and for your uncles, God rest them. Maybe they hadn't it in them to be great artists but they never had the chance, lambkin, but you'll have all the chances you want, if your mammy has to prop herself up at the oven to bake her pies to give you that chance.

Patrick yawned heartily and fell asleep.

For the next few months, while Charlie chafed irritably in the bed which Kate never slept in, she baked single-handedly in the little kitchen. Every day she would load up her pies and her baby and walk to the village. First stop was the pub which she never entered and next she went to the miners' club and then to the village shop. Molly and the two miners' wives she had accepted from among the many applicants for jobs baked for the shop in the next village and Deirdre supplied the shop in her somewhat larger village. Almost from the start it was obvious that it was not enough. Mr McDonald, her employer, owned shops all over Galloway and he wanted mass-production of the pies even in the face of the poverty brought on by strikes among the miners, railway workers and even the police. Kate was stopped several times a day by women anxious to work for almost anything and even Liam had to be glad that his wife was earning something. Charlie, of course, her proud wee bantam, would never admit that he was grateful for his wife's earnings. He wasn't. It was all wrong and despite the rallying words from Liam he wondered what he had fought and almost died for. Was it so that his wife could work so hard that he very rarely even saw her, and that his newborn son should be carried around the village in a pram full of pies?

Liam put a stop to that. He arrived at the cottage one morning just after Kate, who had been up for hours, had given Charlie his breakfast.

'Da,' Kate was surprised and then worried. 'Is it Bridie? Is something wrong?'

Liam looked around the tiny kitchen which was already full of the mouthwatering smell of baking and his eyes stopped at the blankets in the big chair by the fire. 'Not in my house,' he said.

Kate blushed. She had meant to sleep in the chair for a few days only, to let Charlie rest and gain his strength. She folded the blankets and put them away in the wee press beside the fire.

'Some tea and a bap, Da? Are you here to sit with Charlie a wee while?'

Liam accepted the freshly baked morning roll and a mug of hot sweet tea. 'I'm away to hire myself out as delivery boy for Kate Inglis Bakeries.'

Kate was overwhelmed. Her proud father – a delivery boy. Then she remembered that Liam Kennedy had pushed prams and rocked babies when most of his peers thought such tasks were unmanly.

Kate Inglis Bakeries. It had a grand ring to it.

'Do you mean it, Da? You'll deliver my pies?'

'With pride. ''Tis better too for you to be at home with your baby. I'll work for you till this strike is settled and then Charlie'll take over. He'd best see the doctor about all the walking but, sure, I can't see that being in the fresh air ever hurt a body. Pushing a pram at the same time will be Charlie's worry, added to any other ills the poor man might have.'

He got up and went off into the bedroom to see his son-in-law and came back less than fifteen minutes later with Charlie leaning on his strong arm.

Kate rushed to her husband's side. 'Da, what are you daing? You're no fit, Charlie. You should be in your bed.'

Exhausted by the short walk from the bed, Charlie could say nothing but Liam answered for him.

'A wee sit by the fire will do him the world of good, Kate. Sure he can even rock that precious wee boy of his while he watches the mammy working. When I get back from the village I'll help him outside for a sit in the sun. Better medicine than lying in his bed.'

'Your daddy's right, Kate. I'm letting myself be an invalid. A proper man would get himself a job to look after you and the wean but this I can do; I can mind him while he's awake and I can take him for a wee bit of fresh air.'

Kate was not so sure that she would allow an invalid, for that was how she had become used to thinking of her husband, to hold *her* baby outside. What if he should drop him on the stony path? But she smiled and fetched her husband another cup of tea and then prepared a delivery for her new delivery man. Liam covered the distance to the village in no time at all but when he came back he found that Kate had taken the opportunity to air the cottage. The windows and doors were wide open and the coverings on the bed had been pulled back to let fresh air into the mattress.

'Is it one of these compulsive workers you are, Katie?' asked Liam gently. 'Are you forgetting how to sit down and let God's sunshine warm you?'

Sit in the sun. Was it mad he was? Kate ignored the question. 'I thought about washing the sheets but I'm frightened they wouldn't be dry by the time Charlie would need to get back to bed. The first day you're able to sit up all morning, Charlie . . . What in the name of heaven is that, Da?' for Liam had certainly delivered his pies in the bairn's pram but he had returned with a large empty grocery box.

'This is going to be an outside cot for Patrick.'

'A box for my bairn?'

'Won't I have the pram at the village? Fill up the bottom with papers so it's not damp and the laddie can lie in the sun with his daddy and kick his wee legs.'

Kate hated the idea but Patrick loved it. With less and less swaddling on as the summer progressed, his little limbs grew stronger and would have got browner if his mother had not interfered.

'My son is not a tinker, Charlie Inglis. It's indecent the way you have him lying there.'

The baby had progressed with the summer from his box to an old rug and he now delighted his parents by suddenly turning from his back to his front, a feat which excited him so much that he proceeded to repeat the performance till he had mastered the technique.

'Isn't he the cleverest baby you've ever seen, Charlie?' Kate said to her husband who was standing beside her in the garden. She turned to look at him and found Charlie looking at her and not, as she had thought, at his son.

He put his arms around her.

'Charlie, it's no right. In the middle of the day and the bairn seeing us . . .'

'Aye, he'll die of shock seeing his parents kissing. It's all he'd see, isn't it, Kate? I've forgotten how to do anything else.'

'I never meant . . .' began Kate but, luckily for her, for she had no idea how to explain what she had never meant, Liam called to them from the road.

'Is this not the best day and you two out in the garden. I've got the post. Did Jock Thomson not say he loved coming up here for his tea with you? But there's nothing for the farms and so he's off home to get his garden in.'

'He's over late,' said Kate with relief as she took the letters. 'There's one from Mr McDonald,' she said in some puzzlement. 'It's a wee thing early but it'll be a grand cheque this month. Da, can you bank it for me when you're back in the village. Bring the bairn, Charlie. I'll get you two your dinners and feed him in the back room.'

They heard no more of the daily post till they were well in to their mince and tatties. Kate came through from the bedroom looking dishevelled and to her father utterly charming; to her husband completely desirable, and totally oblivious of the effect she created.

'Da, Charlie, you'll never guess. Mr McDonald wants to see me . . . in Glasgow.' She said Glasgow as if it was as far as the moon instead of a bus journey, albeit a long one, away. 'Our business plans,' he says. 'I didn't know we had any business plans. Well, I'm no going to Glasgow. Gracious, I have a baby to feed, and a bakery to run.'

'And a husband forbye,' added Charlie sotto voce.

Kate heard but paid no attention to Charlie's wee joke. It *was* a joke, wasn't it? Of course she knew she had a husband and didn't she show he was important by working hard to feed him? She was rereading her letter. 'He says it's time we was on a more businesslike footing. Oh, Daddy, what if he'll no sell my pies?'

If Liam did not think it strange that Kate should voice her fears to her father, Charlie certainly did.

'Glasgow is the business capital of Scotland, Kate,' he said, 'not Siberia. We'll all go. You come too, Liam, and me Aunty Molly. It'll be a grand day out.'

'It'll be like a tinker's flitting,' laughed Liam. 'No, you two go. You know Glasgow, Charlie, and you can mind wee Patrick when his mammy's at her meeting. You can afford a new frock. Molly says the Co-operative has nice ones.'

Kate listened to them planning her life and wondered at them. If she had come into the room demanding new clothes for a business meeting in Glasgow they would have thrown up their hands in horror and found a million reasons why she should not go. Now they were discussing the probabilities of trains running, the times of buses, and the logistics of breast feeding (although the word breast was never mentioned) on the said buses, as if they had been wholeheartedly behind her business ventures in the first place. Contrarily, for the first time, she would have welcomed their interference. The thought of a long bus journey to someone who had only once been as far as Dumfries, with a business meeting at the end of it (whether or not she was bolstered up by the wearing of a brand-new, shop-bought dress) was making her feel more than slightly sick. If only Charlie would rage and storm, 'No wife of mine is having a *business meeting* in Glasgow or anywhere else.' It would then be easier to acquiesce quietly and go on as she was. Here she was at the turning point, wife and mother or businesswoman. The thought was terrifying but strangely exciting.

'You'll need to get a writing tablet at the post office, Kate,' Liam went on as if he had been arranging meetings every day of his life. 'They'll have what's suitable for business letters and then,' almost as an afterthought he turned to Charlie, 'she should go and buy a frock . . . maybe a coat too, and a hat.'

He smiled at them both, well pleased with his organizational skills and Kate and Charlie looked at one another in the confusion engendered by the word hat. To Kate, and she felt sure to Charlie too, it brought back memories of their appalling wedding night. She remembered her beautiful wedding hat, shop bought too, and the only one she had ever owned.

'A hat would be too much. Wouldn't they think it was the queen herself coming, Charlie, but I'll get gloves,' – a smile lit up her face – 'and some for Bridie.'

She would not listen to their surprised reaction to the thought of Bridie with gloves. It was a promise, a promise from long ago and for the first time ever Kate felt as if she was beginning to make good her promises. She had money in the bank, for none of the profits from the pies had been spent, and they owed money to no man.

'I'll see what the Co-op's prices are,' said Kate bringing herself back to reality. Meeting or no meeting she was not about to put her hard-earned money on her back. Was it not for Patrick? But she and Bridie could have gloves surely and she could wear her wedding dress and her shabby old coat. Mr McDonald need not see the coat for she could take it off and have Charlie mind it for her while she was talking to Mr McDonald.

'Talk to your daughter, Liam. Every penny profit goes into that bank to make more.'

Charlie was the man for the grand gesture, champagne and photographers at his wedding when he had not a shilling to fall back on. Kate, more practical, smiled at him. A new frock, just this once. She was sorely tempted.

'Kate's a grown woman. It's for you to tell her what to do,' said Liam.

This was dangerous ground. Kate knew fine what Charlie wanted her to do and what that moment in the garden had made her realize that she would have to do.

'Aren't we wasting time here?' she said. 'If I'm coming into the village, Da, we'll need to get the pram ready.'

'Stop fussing over that bairn. He'll no die with me here to mind him and he'll probably sleep till yer back,' Charlie said angrily some time later as Kate tried to get herself ready.

'You'll no let him lie wet and these are all aired nice. Charlie, I've not left him afore.'

'I'm his father, Kate. Look for a blue frock . . . to match yer eyes.' He smiled at her; it was almost the brilliant-blue smile of the cocky wee bantam she had known before the war.

*Oh, God, what's wrong with me that I can't respond to him?* thought Kate almost wistfully, aware deep down that something was missing, something that could make life so much fuller. *But I can't, I can't; if he touches me I'll scream. Breathe deep, Kate; it's Charlie and it's not that awful.*

Kate and Liam walked off down the road, Liam wheeling the pram and Kate looking back to wave again to Charlie still standing in the doorway.

'Will I not wheel the pram, Da?'

'It's heavier with pies than with the bairn, lassie. My goodness, Kate Kennedy. What would yer mam say if she could see us walking together to the bank and maybe a blue frock. Changed days. Don't let Mr McDonald talk you into working harder. Have you not a nice little business and all your own work? Maybe it's time I retired and let your man have my job. A man needs to feel he's doing his share.'

'That's daft, Da. Charlie will never work again. What's wrong with me working for the both of us and the bairn? Look, is that not the doctor's sister in her pony and trap. What's she doing out this way?'

The little blue cart drew up to them and Miss Hyslop looked down at Kate and her father. Her eyes, so like her brother's, had none of the friendliness that always lighted up the doctor's homely face.

'Good afternoon, Kennedy,' she nodded to Liam. 'Dr Hyslop asked me to give you this, Kate,' she almost sniffed with the appalling realization that she was playing messenger to the ragged miner's child who had once knocked fiercely at her door demanding the doctor. She handed down a letter and Kate had to stop herself bobbing a curtsey. Instead, Kate Kennedy Inglis, businesswoman, smiled her dazzling smile and thanked Miss Hyslop for her kindness.

'I'll get blue, Da,' said Kate watching the retreating trap, 'and maybe even a blue coat.'

'Her brother would have taken us and the pies up beside him,' said Liam. 'Open your letter. Two letters in one day. Don't I think I'm in the presence of somebody special.'

Kate did as asked and read the letter from Dr Hyslop in quietly growing pleasure. 'Oh, read this, Da. He'll send me in his trap to Ayr and then I can get a direct bus to

Glasgow. That'll save hours and he'll pick us up – he says he knows fine I won't leave wee Patrick for the day – if we get the last bus home. Why is he so kind to me?'

'Isn't he kindness itself to everyone, Kate? I think he sees something he can do to help you get on. You know when your mammy died he was dead against you leaving the school. "She's bright, Kennedy," was what he said, "and deserves her chance." He was silent for a long moment. 'Wasn't he right but there was nothing else I could do.'

Kate said nothing for her heart was too full. To walk beside Liam like this, on her way to that grand building on the main street that she never entered without a thrill of pride, and to have him talk to her not as a father but as an equal was absolute joy.

'I won't be frightened to get lost in Glasgow with Charlie with me. A big place like you could confuse a body, do you no think, Da?'

'Aye, especially if her mind's taken up with a new dress,' Liam interrupted and they laughed. They had reached the village and while Liam strode off with his pramful of pies, and surely with even more pride in those strong shoulders, Kate went to the bank. She was always amazed to see the totals growing larger and larger every week but, as Charlie had pointed out, nothing had ever been taken out and she almost hated to do it now. She made a quick calculation, added two whole pounds in case of emergency, and the money was counted out to her.

'Always a pleasure to serve you, Mrs Inglis,' said the bank clerk and she nodded to him politely as if bank staff were always saying such things to her. And one day they will be, she determined, when I'm Kate Inglis Bakeries.

According to Mr McDonald, sole proprietor of McDonald the Grocer, that day was on the very horizon.

'I've ordered lunch, Mrs Inglis,' he said after she had been shown into his beautifully appointed office. 'You must be starved after that journey. You're staying overnight in Glasgow, I take it?'

Kate shook her head and heard the words, 'I have a bakery to run, Mr McDonald.' She must have said them for he was laughing.

'A holiday never hurt anyone and if your bakery was on the right footing you could have had a few days; nice shops, restaurants, art galleries, a wonderful city, Glasgow.'

They talked, at least he talked and she murmured something now and then, of Glasgow and Charlie and wee Patrick as they walked along thickly carpeted corridors to a private dining room. Kate had never imagined that he would invite her to lunch and at the bottom of her stomach was lying a bacon sandwich that Charlie had insisted she eat at the bus station. Even without it she doubted if she could have eaten in this lovely place. All she wanted to do was look around and dare to touch the fine linen on the table when her host turned his head to address the hovering waiter. Behind his head on the wall was a painting and Kate admired it with rising excitement. It was of little boys and boats and the sea looked as if any minute it might splash out of the canvas and soak the floor.

'It's a McTaggart, Mrs Inglis. Incredible, isn't it? Do you know, I used to wrap that picture in brown paper and carry it home with me at night so that I could look at it there too. I ordered a meal to save time so I hope you like what I've chosen . . .' Kate nodded dumbly while part of her mind wondered why he no longer carried the glorious painting home to admire at night – was he so rich that there was another one just like it in his house? 'We need to talk, Mrs Inglis.'

And for the next hour, while fish followed soup and beef followed fish and the lightest most delicious pudding followed the beef, he talked and Kate listened and tried to remember what he said and what the food looked like. She could not eat a bite. She did try but the bacon butty seemed to have moved and to have become lodged somewhere between her throat and her stomach.

'You don't care for white wine, Mrs Inglis. Try this claret,' and she sipped from a glass that she would have thought too fine even to sustain the weight of the liquid and wondered that he could pick them up so nonchalantly in his great hands.

The bacon sandwich slipped down and the second gulp spread a warm glow across Kate's stomach and down her legs to her toes and she wiggled them inside her brand-new shoes. The only alcohol she had ever tasted had been the champagne at her wedding.

She gulped again. 'This is very nice,' she heard a voice say and it must have been hers. 'Much, much nicer than champagne.'

He refilled the glass. 'I knew you were a woman of impeccable taste, Mrs Inglis. All the ladies of my acquaintance swear by champagne, a highly overrated beverage in my opinion and obviously in yours too. It's almost time for your bus though.' He signalled the waiter who poured coffee. 'I'm not asking for your decision today. It's a lot to take in and quite an undertaking with a new baby, but the business plan is carefully set out for you here.' He patted the fat folder beside him. 'You should have brought Mr Inglis and the baby with you. It was remiss of me not to think of them, but next time. If you'll excuse me a moment . . .' and while he was gone a neatly dressed maid showed her into a bathroom and asked if there was anything at all madame needed.

Madame looked at herself in the grand mirror. I was so scared but now I'm not. She felt distinctly unlike herself and experienced a rush of nausea that made her hold onto the marble basin for support. What am I doing here, and then her heavy breasts reminded her of her son and she came back to reality in terror that she might be leaking over her new dress.

She splashed cold water over her face and looked at it in the glorious mirror. It was Kate Inglis, wife of the war-wounded Charlie and mother of wee Patrick who looked back at her and not 'Kate Inglis Bakeries'. Kate was delighted to see her. 'You were almost daft for a minute there, Kate,' she told her reflection.

'My car will take you to the bus station,' said Mr McDonald as he handed her the business plan. 'I'll be down for your answer in two weeks, Mrs Inglis. It's been a pleasure.'

She must have thanked him as she must have added something to the conversation at lunch but she could never remember having said a word. And now here she was sitting in a motor car and what Charlie would say when she arrived at the bus station she could not imagine.

Charlie said nothing but handed her a sobbing, soaked baby. 'I'll get myself a piece and a cup of tea if your lady-ship has enough time to attend to yer wean.'

It wasn't fair, of course it wasn't fair. She looked at the public clock. How could she have spent so long with Mr McDonald? There was barely enough time to attend to the baby before the last bus. She sat in the lavatory and pushed her aching breast into Patrick's hungry little face and as usual his eagerness to suckle made her laugh. Poor wee lambie. Was it a bad mammy to leave you alone while she had her fancy luncheon with a city gentleman . . . and your poor daddy. But he knew it would take a while, Patrick, and he said it would be all right. Ach, but who would like to sit in a place like this for three hours with a crying baby – she bent to kiss his downy little head – except your mammy, lambie. I'll make it up to yer daddy. Wait till he hears about yon grand office. Office; a palace more like and now Mammy's got to think about the business plan and talk about it with Daddy.

But Charlie had no interest in the business plan. 'I'm exhausted, Kate. Let me sleep,' he complained as the bus drew out of the city and sought the road to Ayr.

Kate saw the greyness in his face and felt guilty again. Business plan, she thought to herself. We're living nicely on the earnings now and Charlie's getting better. What if he should have a relapse because of me? She remembered the words beautifully printed out on the crisp sheets of white paper . . . new premises, more bakers, weekly deliveries to Ayr, Thornhill, Dumfries, building up to deliveries to Glasgow and eventually into England itself. For a moment she saw herself sitting at a desk like Mr McDonald's, with the glorious painting hanging behind her. Then she looked at what she saw as reality. She was an uneducated girl from the mining village of Auchenbeath. She had been terrified in that office and wouldn't she always feel out of place in such an office. 'I could hardly feed you in a grand place like yon, lambie,' she addressed the sleeping baby and briskly dismissed the thought that Mr McDonald would not have minded at all.

# 9

Did dr hyslop sense that all was not well after the trip to Glasgow? He chatted inconsequentially all the way to the cottage and refused Kate's offer of some tea.

'You must all be exhausted,' he excused himself. 'A good night's sleep, or what's left of the night. You'll be up at the crack of dawn baking, Kate.'

It was Charlie who answered, bitterly spitting the words out. 'Afore dawn. Never gets to her bed at all these days, would you believe. Thank you for your kindness, doctor.' And he went in, leaving Kate to bid the doctor goodnight. The baby lay heavily in her arms so that she felt that any second she would drop him on his little head on the pathway.

'Was it not a success, Kate?' Dr Hyslop asked gently. 'McDonald seemed to have so many plans for you. I hoped for really great things.'

'Too great maybe. A lot of thinking has to be done, doctor.'

'Well, don't think when you're tired from such a long journey. You should have stayed at a hotel. Get some sleep, Kate.'

She watched him until he had turned the trap and, with a cheery wave of his hand, was headed back down the road.

Charlie was standing in front of the fire which Liam had tended during the day. The bakery fire could not go out or the oven would not be hot enough for the pies in the morning.

Gratefully Kate put the baby in his cot and reached for his clean nightdress.

'Leave him alone, MRS INGLIS, and attend to me.'

She looked at him in surprise.

'Get your clothes off, Kate, everything.'

She had never seen Charlie like this before; he had gone mad. There could be no other reason. She was terrified.

'Damn it, woman, do as you're told. For once I'll see what's hidden under those prim and pretty corsets.' He looked at her standing there, trembling, half-crying. 'All right, I'll do it for you.'

He was not gentle; perhaps he did not know how to be; perhaps if Kate had helped, had tried, but she was physically and mentally exhausted from the events of the day. He pulled her clothes from her shivering body and then he was pushing and pulling her down onto the rug where the firelight cast shadows over her secret, hidden treasures. He drank it all in while she turned her head away, sobbing. His hands, oh, God, it was indecent; would he never stop? There was a moment – his mouth tightly encircled her heavy breast – a spark of pleasure flared at the base of her stomach and, if he had but known, he could have blown up a flame that would have consumed them both, but he did not know the moment existed, and he ground the spark into oblivion as, with a hoarse cry of mingled pain and pleasure, he pushed himself between her shaking thighs and possessed her. When it was over he was aware only of how chilly the room seemed and of how silly he must look collapsed on top of his naked wife with his trousers and drawers around his ankles.

'Fucking in firelight's supposed to really turn a woman on,' he said in an attempt to recapture the bravado he had had a few minutes ago. 'Get up for God's sake afore ye catch your death.' She stood up trying ineffectually to hide herself from him. 'Make one move for that kettle and, so help me, I'll belt ye one. I should have done it long ago.'

He pushed her before him into the bedroom and pulled back the blankets. 'Get yer bloody nightgown on. I'm not away to sully yer body again the night, Madame Business Woman, but you'll sleep in this bed from now on and you'll act like a proper wife and mother and no like you were making some great sacrifice for the nation.'

She pulled on her nightgown and stood for a moment by the side of the bed. In the front room the baby began to wail. He was wet and he was hungry. She had to attend to him, no matter what Charlie said.

'Charlie?'

'Attend to your precious son,' sighed Charlie bitterly.

When she was gone he wearily undressed and slipped into the bed. His thoughts went to his wife and child in the next room. Her beautiful breast would be offered to that greedy little mouth and he, he, her lawfully wedded husband was not even allowed to see. He groaned in remembered pleasure and then pain. *Why, Kate, why did you make me act like that? I raped my own wife, damn it. Was I punishing her and for what, trying to make our lives better? Or was it because I'm no man; I cannae even provide a decent dry home. She's taken my right place as breadwinner. Does she think she's head o' the house too? Well, I'm still a man. I proved that the night.* He turned over and pressed his head into the pillow. *Oh, Katie, Katie, I want you to love me, to let me kiss you.* He thought of her white trembling body in the firelight and desire rose, swift and hot, in his groin. God, it's no wrong to want your wife. What did she marry me for? And then he remembered how frightened she had been and all desire for anything but oblivion left him. He felt Kate slip into bed beside him. *No need to lie on the edge, Katie darling,* he thought, *is that not where I am already?*

Kate did some hard thinking too. She tried to avoid remembering the experience in the front room; Charlie had been angry because he had been alone with the child so long while she had been sitting, with no thought for husband or even child, being feted by Mr McDonald. She determined to show Charlie that she still thought of him as an important part of the family, even if it meant being more . . . welcoming. His quick fumbles at least left most of her body inviolate. Perhaps if she held him while he moved?

When they woke that first morning Charlie had been shamefaced. 'Forgive me, Kate.' Echoes of their wedding night.

'It's all right, Charlie.' She looked at him sitting like a bairn that had been belted, head down, afraid to look at the wielder of the strap. 'I wish I could be more like what you want. I'll try to . . . to . . . no be so frightened.'

She hurried out into the garden, afraid to say too much too soon. A few minutes later he heard her voice, raised in excitement, calling him.

'It's Jessie, Charlie, look she's come back.'

The brown hen was busily pecking away in her vegetable garden.

'Would you look there, Kate.'

Under the cabbages, in and out among the Brussels sprouts ran . . . seven, eight, nine little chickens, not yellow chicks, but browns and golds and blacks.

'Noo, what in the world fathered them?' asked an incredulous Charlie.

Kate knew. It had to have been her winter visitor, the beautiful pheasant. Everything was going to be fine; she knew it.

'Do you think you could maybe build a pen, Charlie?' The day before she would have said, 'you'll need to build a pen,' but things had to change.

Nine months later, Kate had been welcomed back into the Catholic Church and Patrick had been, with the permission of his father, duly baptized. Jessie and four of her children were happily laying eggs in their pen at the bottom of the garden and the other five, all little cockerels, had made fine soup.

Unfortunately, by Kate's way of thinking, she was also in labour with the child conceived on *that* night, or was it the next night, or the next? No matter. The pregnancy had been nothing but a nuisance although, thankfully, she had felt well all the way through and had been able to continue with the growing business, for it was growing and Kate was well on the way to becoming a rich woman.

As a peace offering, Charlie had asked to read the business plan. 'The man's mad,' he had said as he finished it. 'This "high finance" stuff is no for the likes of you, Kate. You're a wee lassie that left the school afore ye were fourteen. He's maybe wanting more than your pies.' He looked at his wife questioningly but it was obvious that she had no idea of what he was thinking. Maybe it had been just excitement that had made her look so, so . . . different that day; her eyes, her skin glowing as they never did for him, sitting in a motor car like a princess of the realm. 'Delivery vans.' He started to laugh. 'Does he know his pies are delivered in a pram? We can paint Kate Inglis Bakeries on the sides to give it a bit class.'

'Inglis Bakeries, Charlie. We're partners.'

'Take it slow, lassie. What about yer bairn? Aye, I thought that would get through.'

'I would never hurt Patrick. The work's for him, Charlie.' She looked at him still unsure, afraid to wound, . . . 'And for you and me too and, look, I've even given my own father work.'

'Aye, he must be a proud man walking up and down the streets wi' a pram selling pies.'

'He's proud to be earning a wage and paying his own way.'

'Well, for God's sake, buy a wee pony and cart, and I'll take the pram for a wee while till ye can afford a second one, but none o' this "Elegant, distinctive delivery vans". What would the village say?'

The thoughts of what the village might say bothered Charlie more than they bothered his wife. At first it had seemed a bit strange when girls she had gone to school with had called her Mrs Inglis when they had come looking for jobs but she had become used to it and accepted it. Then, one or two, assuming a friendship that was not there, just because they had sat side by side in the same classroom, had attempted breezy familiarity.

'Well, Kate, ye've done right well for yersel'. It'll be grand us working together.'

So easy to smile and respond in kind. Harder to rub her sweating palms against her skirt and straighten her back.

'Mrs Inglis in the bakery, if you don't mind.' And they had flushed and accepted the rebuff for jobs were not going abegging in the 1920s. It was correct, for if she was going to be an employer there had to be a barrier over which no one could tread. It would make working relationships easier. None of them had been friends after all. When she thought back to the long-ago days of her schooling she realized that, even then, she had been too busy with her brothers and sisters to make friends.

'If we're taking on more bakers, you'd best get on with your two carts, Charlie.' Remember, remember, he is a partner and must always be consulted.

They said nothing of the new premises idea that had been in the business plan and since the thought of a 'real' bakery terrified Kate herself, she decided not to voice the question; not yet. She knew every word of that business plan and one day, some day, there might be a bigger kitchen. But there would be no bank loan. She preferred to overwork herself, her step-mother, Deirdre, three mining wives and even wee Bridie, rather than expand too quickly. The more popular the pies became, the more frightened became the baker trying to keep up with the demand, and then she had realized that she was pregnant. It could hardly have happened at a worse time. Please God, don't let it have been *that* night.

'I'll need to get another baker. I think we'll afford another trap before Christmas and I'll need to get everybody into my ways afore this bairn comes.'

Luckily, because the doctor could never have got to her in time, the birth was completely straightforward. Auntie Molly delivered Katherine Margaret Inglis at four o'clock on a cold, frosty morning in March 1921. Twenty-four hours later her mother was again in her kitchen and business was more or less as usual.

'Kate, do you no think you should hae stayed in yer bed a wee while longer?' asked Charlie. 'Auntie Molly's managing fine. Come on, sit down and I'll fetch you a cup of tea.'

He put his arms around her to lead her to a chair and, despite herself, she jerked away from him. Was their relationship always to be one step forward, two steps backward? If she could just explain that when *it* was happening she began to hear the screams and she couldn't bear them, couldn't bear . . . she wanted to be soft but she was abrupt. 'I have to get back to the business. If there was one thing I didnae need at this time it was another bairn.' There, she had said it. She hated herself for feeling it, let alone saying it, and she was angry with herself for being glad that there was no milk for this baby and that baby Margaret had to be bottle-fed. It had meant that wee Patrick had had to be weaned and Kate sorely missed those precious moments of closeness with him. Charlie spent more time with him now than his mammy did but that was a sacrifice she was prepared to pay. *He'll thank me for it one day*, thought Kate, and as she made pastry she went over and over her conversations with Mr McDonald; the pictures of a different life that he painted. 'Grab this chance with both hands, Mrs Inglis. I'm on my way to being the biggest wholesale grocer in Scotland and you could come with me, but you need a bakery, not five wee kitchens all over Auchenbeath.'

What was holding Kate back? Was it that already there was more money in the bank than she had ever dreamed of? She had two carts and two drivers and paid the wages of seven people. What did she need with an assembly line and motorized transportation? In the dark of the night she would lie beside a gently snoring Charlie and compare herself with Dr Hyslop or Mr McDonald or even her own old schoolteacher. *The only difference between me and her is education, no breeding. I'm frightened to talk to people I don't know and tied down with two bairns . . . and as for Charlie, he hasn't a shred of ambition. He's more than content with what we have now and maybe I should be too.*

Six months before baby Margaret's arrival, Charlie had received a pension from the War Office; five shillings and sixpence a week. He thought he was a millionaire.

'At last I'm paying the rent on this place,' he had said and Kate could only be grateful that his euphoria satisfied him and he did not feel the need to prove himself in bed quite so often.

She had been determined to carry on working, working, before and after the baby. But two pregnancies in less than two years took their toll and finally she had to sit down; her overtaxed body could take no more – and there at the door was wee Bridie all set to take over. She did not get the reception that she expected.

'Bridie, it's lovely to see you and you can bide for yer dinner since you've walked all this way but I want you back home and at the school in the morning. Me and Charlie and yer Auntie Mollie can manage fine and you need to look after Da and Colm.' Kate sighed in exasperation. Would anyone in this family ever get an education? Aye, her wee Patrick would; he would stay at the school and he would even go on to the university. There was a glimmer of a dream of what he would be but she would not tempt fate with that yet.

She was distressed to see Bridie so mutinous; she could understand that the little girl had been thrilled at the idea of staying with her big sister and looking after the babies. Playing with real babies was a lot more fun than playing with one with a china head.

'Da said I could come up to yer lovely wee cottage and help you; please Kate, I fair get bossed around at home by Da and Auntie Molly and even Colm. I'm just waiting to be old enough to leave school and get a job in the bakery.'

Not a wise remark to make to her sister who was worrying, worrying, not only about her own lack of education but of her failure to ensure an education for her brothers and sisters. For her pains Miss Bridie received another lecture about, to her, boring books.

'Come on, Bridie,' said Charlie. 'You'll no shift her once her mind's made up. Give Kate the babby and you and me will take Patrick with us in the cart. I'll let you drive.'

'Da said I could stay a week. He said I could sleep in the big chair and do the first baking. I've grand light hands.'

But Kate was adamant. She refused to listen but after their midday dinner sent Bridie off with a well-wrapped-up-baby Patrick while she sat down with her new little daughter in her arms. 'Let's enjoy this, my wee Margaret, because there won't be many days like it, but just think, when you're a big lassie like Auntie Bridie you can help your mammy after school, and when you're really big we can stay together every day. I bet you'll be a better baker than anyone.'

She was, but baking pies was the last thing young Margaret would want to do with her life.

# 10

IT WAS CHARLIE who decided to move. A one-bed-roomed cottage that was cold and damp in the summer and freezing cold and even damper in the winter was hardly the ideal place to bring up two children.

'Forbye, Kate, I cannot move for cots in the room and I dinnae like the bairns there when we're, well you know what we do.' She knew what he did; she merely lay there and prayed; one, that just once she would be able to relax and enjoy it; two, that it would be over even faster than the night before, and three, that she would not get pregnant again. 'And I cannae move in the front room for pies,' Charlie continued, 'could we not put our name down for a council house?'

Kate looked at him and then at her reflection in the spotted mirror above the fireplace. Their wedding photograph was on the mantel just below the mirror and it was strange to look at how they used to be and at their real selves at the same time.

'We must get a likeness of the bairns, Charlie, to put beside our wedding picture. Do you not think we're better-looking now? You've filled out a bit and it suits you.'

He blushed with pleasure. Kate never gave compliments and, indeed, as if regretting that she had let her guard down she moved away from him and from the two views of herself. I look older though, she thought to herself and – surely not – do I look hard? I never meant to get hard.

'We don't want a council house, Charlie. I have enough trouble running a business from here. You know how much Thompson has raised the rent on this ruin since we started to make a go – can you imagine what rent a council would ask from us, even if they would let us run the bakery in the first place?'

Charlie reached down and retrieved his daughter from her investigation of the coal scuttle. 'Ach, lambie, your face is near as black as yer beautiful hair.'

'Tie her in her chair, Charlie, and give her a good hard slap. Wee midden. Patrick never ate coal.'

'Aye and the sun rose and set on his head, we all know that.' Four-year-old Patrick, who was sitting at one end of the table drawing on a slate, looked at his father in surprise. He had no idea what Daddy meant but he knew it wasn't nice and he had no way of knowing how he had displeased him. Patrick spend his entire day trying to please.

First Kate who was so busy that she hardly saw him, then Charlie who sometimes patted him on the head and took him in the cart with him, and even Margaret who either pulled his black curly hair or bit him.

'Don't be silly.' It wasn't fair, thought Kate, if he's angry wi' me he shouldnae take it out on Patrick, good wee laddie that he is. 'Patrick, go and get your sister a clean frock. She's such a pretty bairn you'd think she'd like to be clean.' Kate opened the oven door and drew out the baked pies. 'This is the new one,' she said, holding it up in the air to be admired, 'we'll have one for our dinner, then you can take one to Doctor Hyslop on your way in, Charlie, and maybe you could ask him about a house, and give this third one to Molly.'

Charlie stopped in the act of undressing the squirming Margaret and looked at his wife. 'Ask the doctor about a house? Is he on the council?'

'We'll need to buy something,' said Kate firmly, 'Not too big, mind. A house with enough rooms and maybe a great big kitchen or one or two rooms that could be made into a bakery. The doctor'll maybe know if there's anything near the village. We cannae be too far away because of the school for Patrick next year, and I doubt there's anything in the village.'

'Buy a house?' To Kate it was obvious that Charlie had never contemplated such a step, and why should he?

In the village of Auchenbeath very few people owned their homes. Even the Manse, the Chapel house and the Dominie's house were not really owned by their inhabitants.

'You'll need to do the looking, Kate. Buy a house. You said that like you say, get me some more milk.'

Kate was already putting the next lot of pies in the oven while Charlie still had a half-naked child squealing in his arms. 'When am I supposed to have time to look for a house? You're not after Buckingham Palace, love. Just a house with a bit garden for the bairns and my hens and a big kitchen.' She turned and smiled at him, the dazzling smile that he very rarely saw these days. 'And do ye know what I'd really like, Charlie, an inside lavvie and maybe even a bath.'

Charlie knew his limitations. 'You'll have to do this yourself, Kate. I'll mind the bairns and we can get Bridie tae help.'

Kate went on taking pies out to cool and putting others in, moving back and forward between the table and the ovens and still fully aware of Charlie and her children.

'Don't bother, I've just minded on yon Mr McAndliss. According to Mr McDonald I already pay him to do my legal business. Well, this is legal so he can start earning his, what was it cried . . . retainer.' Kate smiled in satisfaction and reached for her daughter. 'Patrick, put your coat on and take Margaret out to play and keep her away from the hens, lambie.'

Quietly Patrick did as he was told while Kate efficiently dealt with little Margaret who had been fighting Charlie's administrations with all her considerable energy. Kate smacked her daughter's behind, so encased in cloths that she felt nothing, and pulled the sparkling white frock over the angry little head.

'Daft colour for playing,' said Charlie as he helped with the coat.

'I suppose you're right but I love tae see her bonnie. Would I no have killed for a frock like yon and this wee tink has too many.' She put the child down on the floor, 'Away out with yer big brother, pet, and don't chase Mammy's hens.'

Charlie left with the children to see to the ponies and Kate sat down for her first quiet time of the day. She relaxed in the big chair by the fire and sipped her hot, sweet tea while her mind went over the problems of house-hunting. She had discovered that when she was really afraid of something, it was much better to confront it head-on. *I'm away to buy a house, Mam, me, your Kate*. It was a big step from farm cottage to owner occupancy. She retraced the route into the village. Nothing there but the Toll House and the Manse. In the village there were no properties big enough. *I'd need to circle the village* with the pony and trap, she told herself, there has to be something but first I'll write to Mr McAndliss. Charlie can hand it in to his office.

Kate took down the big dictionary from the shelf beside the fireplace and got a jotter, her pen and her writing-paper. She would make a rough copy and check the spelling and then she would write the letter. Another new experience, writing to a solicitor. When would she ever take such things for granted? If all gentlemen were like Dr Hyslop how easy it would be. When Charlie returned, she had the letter ready.

'What do you think, Charlie?'

Charlie read the letter. 'You could have been a solicitor yourself, Kate Inglis.'

'Away and don't be daft.' But Kate smiled at his obvious pride in her. A solicitor. She doubted if she had ever heard the word while she was at the school. How could anyone from Auchenbeath become anything? Surely some children left the village school for places of higher education. It was scandalous if they did not. The steel inside her hardened even more. Patrick, she vowed, Patrick.

When they had gone she cleaned the tiny cottage and did her washing. What satisfaction a line of washing blowing in the good fresh air gave her. Even more than a tray of pies wrapped in paper with your name on it? Yes. No. Just the same. They're both for Patrick, she told the dancing sheets . . . and wee Margaret and Charlie too, she added guiltily. Everything she did was for her family. That each and every one of them would have preferred five minutes of her time never even occurred to her. She stood for a moment straightening her back in the old gesture she had learned from Liam. A bird flew over her head so close that she could hear the loud slap of his wings against the air. The hills had never looked more beautiful.

I hope Mr McAndliss finds me somewhere where I can still see the hills, she told the hens. That was one joy of the damp little house where she had lived for almost six years. From windows and doors one could see the hills. I'd hate to give that up. She toyed with the idea of buying the cottage from her landlord, renovating and extending it. She looked back at the open door and she saw herself being pushed through it on her wedding night. She could see the rug where . . . no. Some memories she would be happy to leave here. As for the hills – she could always take a day off now and again – take the bairns for a picnic. Goodness, how Bridie had loved a picnic in the hills. She would find time to take Patrick. A day off with a book and the bairns playing among the primroses.

It was a strange year. The Earl of Carnarvon entered the tomb of a pharaoh in Egypt and died two months later. Kate knew that it was as the result of a curse. The King's second son, the Duke of York, had, according to Kate and Auntie Mollie, the great good sense to marry a Scot, Lady Elizabeth Bowes-Lyon. Kate enjoyed the luxury of poring over the newspapers at the miners' club; she just happened to be passing by on her house-hunting expeditions. There too she read of the appalling earthquake which almost razed the cities of Yokohama and Tokyo to the ground and for the first time in her life Kate sent money to an international appeal.

'There was hundreds of thousands of people dead, Charlie,' she told him when she returned from the bank. 'I cannot imagine all those people living in the one place or even two cities. Seven thousand factories was destroyed.'

'Is Japan a big place then? Sure that's more factories than in the whole of Britain.'

Kate could not assimilate the newspaper report. 'It looked like two wee dots in the ocean in the newspaper drawing, Charlie. Where did the people all live?'

To Kate, Charlie was an experienced traveller. He had seen Glasgow, London, Liverpool and even Paris. 'Ach, ten in the one room is nothing, Kate, and here's me complaining about having to step over my own babies.'

'That's something we'll have to talk about when we get them to their beds. You'll never guess what house in Auchenbeath Mr McAndliss says is for sale and absolutely perfect for converting? The Toll House.'

Kate had seen the Toll House almost every day of her life. It stood just outside the village and had been a toll house in the days of horse-drawn carriages. The house itself faced the road, and was small and white with beautiful windows, into which had been blown lovely glass bubbles. The front door opened directly on to the main road and that would be both an advantage and a disadvantage. Great for business, dangerous for small children, even though a motor car passing through once a day was still a novelty. Kate and Charlie both knew that the motor car would soon take over from the horse and cart but they determined to fight it off as long as possible. On the north side of the house was a huge and beautiful garden, a perfect place for growing children, and what made the property perfect for Kate's purposes were several solid outbuildings and a wide, cobbled courtyard. The original house was seventeenth-century but the outbuildings had been built later, probably replacing earlier stables.

'There's an old man lives in it, Charlie. He'd wanted to start a horse-drawn bus company after the Boer War but somebody else got in afore him. He's been wanting to sell since about 1905, poor man, and we can have the lot for less than five hundred pounds.'

Charlie nearly choked on his tea. 'Five hundred pounds. My God, Kate, you say that so casual. Where would the likes of us get a hundred pounds, let alone five?'

'It's in the bank, Charlie, well almost, and Mr McAndliss says the bank would be honoured to lend us the rest for the repairs that's needed.'

'You're out of your mind, lassie. Borrow money from a bank? Never in my born days have I owed a man a penny and I'm no about to start now.'

'Charlie, it's for our bairns. At least let us go to see it. We'll do it up bit by bit; this year the kitchen. There's a barn kind of building right up against the side of the hoose and we could make it the bakery with big ovens and have all the women that bakes for us in the village come there of a morning.'

'They'll no like that. How can they mind their bairns and hang out the washing . . .'

Kate interrupted him. 'If they want to work for me, Charlie, for Inglis Bakeries,' she added quickly, 'they'll have to make arrangements. I have a list of names as long as my arm of lassies wanting work and at a proper bakery I could make sure everything was done my way. We could put off having a bathroom till the ovens was paid for . . . Oh, Charlie, it's not near so much as Mr McDonald wants; he'd have us with vans and preservatives, whatever that is. It was you said we needed more room, Charlie, and we have to get nearer the village afore Patrick starts the school. He couldnae walk through the snow and rain and the school's near next door to the Toll House.'

'And why could he not? It's hardly more than a mile and he has stout shoes and a coat.'

Eventually Charlie agreed at least to see the house. The rooms were even smaller than those of the cottage and the ceiling was very low but they had a charm that the damp little cottage had never possessed. And although from the windows one could see only the Great North Road, beyond the garden and the courtyard there stretched fields and woods which reached up to the hills. Kate could not foresee the day when the fields would be ploughed up to become housing estates or that the corner on which the house stood would one day become one of the most dangerous blind spots in the whole of Britain. She saw generations of Kennedy and Inglis families who had never dreamed of owning their own homes; she saw an indoor lavatory and a gleaming white bathroom with hot and cold running water where her babies would be safe and comfortable; she saw separate bedrooms for her children. Perhaps it was her whispered 'I'm afraid Patrick can hear' – a remark she later regretted – that swayed him, but Charlie submitted. They bought the Toll House.

Mr McDonald was delighted and so too was Dr Hyslop. Liam was not so sure. He could not bring himself to say, 'How will you manage if you have another child?' So far, Kate was following almost in her mother's footsteps. Another child was overdue. She should be like Deirdre who, since the war, had produced a living child on the average of every eighteen months and weren't she and Dave as happy as the day was long? Kate's poor showing in the maternity stakes was due more to prayer and good luck than anything scientific.

To Charlie, a pregnant woman meant only that she was married to a *real* man. He did not want his wife to die in childbed, and indeed, the fact that Kate was so seldom pregnant meant that he could enjoy her body more often. But he would not tolerate any artificial means of contraception. He wanted more children – that was only natural – and, although he was sure that Kate did not artificially prevent impregnation, her jumping up and scrubbing herself with hot water immediately he had withdrawn from her did not help; he would not fight her. She allowed him access to her body every time he wanted. No doubt most normal marriages were like that.

Kate's recurring nightmare was that there would be another child. Not that she did not dearly love Patrick and Margaret. Sometimes she felt wicked; that the feelings she had for them bordered on idolatry, and she sternly forbade herself to pet and play with the children. At other times she would succumb to her emotions and sweep them up in her arms hugging and kissing them, dancing madly round the kitchen with them, revelling in the firmness of their small bodies. 'You'll want for nothing, my lambies,' she would tell them, 'nothing, not while there's breath in Mammy's body.'

Patrick would hug and kiss her in return; Margaret would soon squirm and fight to be put down and the game would be over, but even Margaret would stay for a while on the floor beside her, playing with her doll while her mother worked.

And Kate would look at them and at the long table of numbers on the positive side of her bankbook and pray to her mother, not to God – that would be wicked. *Don't let me fall yet, Mam. How did you manage so many bairns? Two's such a handful. I sometimes feel I'm just getting into my bed when I have to get out of it. Mr McDonald's coming down to go over the Toll House with me. He's always asking me up there but I'm no going to Glasgow again until the bairns are older. I've told him that.* 'Get a sleeper on the train, Mrs Inglis,' he says to me. 'Let me put you up in a hotel,' he says. Charlie near had a fit when he read that letter. 'My wife's no staying at any hotel,' says he, 'and if she ever does I'll pay for it.' I'd quite like to stay at a hotel, Mam. Your breakfast cooked for you . . . can you imagine?

Mr McDonald drove down in his chauffeur-driven car and Kate showed him round the new premises while the chauffeur terrified Patrick and delighted Margaret with a drive around the village.

'You should have done this years ago, Mrs Inglis,' said McDonald as they sat at the kitchen table. That was one of the things Kate liked about him; he could be at his ease in his private dining room or drinking tea at her kitchen table. 'Mrs Inglis, do you know how many shops I have now? Two hundred. I had one wee shop in Glasgow in 1909 and if it hadn't been for the war I'd have an outlet in every village in Scotland and maybe England too. You should take a trip to London, go to Selfridges, or Fortnum and Mason. Lipton is my hero; good groceries to the working classes; that's what we want, Mrs Inglis. Good quality at reasonable prices and everything produced as cleanly as possible, like the pictures of Bournville or Sunlight Dairies. We could do an advertising campaign round you and your pies, Mrs Inglis. Once this place is knocked into shape. Gleaming marble baking tables, sparkling ovens, tiled floor you could eat the pies off and a beautiful young woman in a pretty apron, not that sensible one you're wearing now, Mrs Inglis, but a bit of lace.'

Kate laughed in delight.

'You think I'm joking, Mrs Inglis, well I'm not. And you, Inglis, how would you like to see a huge picture of your wife staring down at you from a billboard?'

'I would not, sir. Kate's not that sort of woman.'

'More tea, gentlemen,' said Kate ironing over the difficult moment as women had done for centuries. 'Can you stay to see the architect, Mr McDonald?'

Kate sighed with relief when he agreed but added that he was dining with Doctor Hyslop and so could only spare a few hours.

Late that night, as Kate lay unresponsive under her husband's bucking, sweating body, she went over and over the plans drawn up by the architect. The bathroom was going in at the same time as the kitchen, much against Charlie's will, which, no doubt was why he was exercising it at the moment. 'Makes more sense,' had said McDonald, 'too much upheaval, one improvement after the other and really, Inglis, in this day and age, a bathroom is basic, wouldn't you agree?' And Charlie had agreed. Now, at last, he lay still across Kate and then rolled off. She did not move. Sometimes when the business was going particularly well or, like today, there was some interaction with a man like Mr McDonald, Charlie would try to do 'it' twice. She never used the euphemism 'making love', there was nothing, she felt, about love in this almost violent use of her body. Thanks be to God, he had stopped the passionate kissing which she sometimes thought she hated more than the intercourse. At least down there she wouldn't choke. Poor Charlie. The words came into her head often at times like this though why she should be sorry for him she did not know. He was getting what he wanted, wasn't he? No, he wants more, and so do I, but how. Stop thinking and pay attention to him . . . it was too late.

He was asleep. She slipped out of bed and past her sleeping children. Soon they would have their own wee rooms. They were sound, wee lambies; nothing had disturbed their rest. The kettle was gently steaming on the stove; she had known hot water would be needed. She filled the basin, pulled off her nightgown and began to scrub herself clean. There was a poet died in the war who'd talked about the benison of hot water. When there was money to spare for such nonsense, she would buy his book. Brooke, that was it, Rupert Brooke.

You knew what you were talking about, Mr Brooke.

# 11

HOW QUICKLY THE world moved in the days when her children were growing up. It seemed to Kate that every tooth, every new word, every inch of growth was marked by some equally momentous – but perhaps retrograde – step in the world. Outside the Toll House life was becoming noisy, dirty and very, very fast. Kate tried hard to tolerate developments that made her life easier. She applied for an automatic telephone in November 1927 when she heard that just such an exchange had been established in Holborn. How much more convenient and private than waiting for connections to be made. Besides, she was quite sure that Masie Ward at the Post Office listened in to every conversation, and surely she couldn't if the line was automatic. Kate had great faith in science. Sometimes Maisie mentioned village matters in the bakery that she could only have heard by eavesdropping. Not that Kate's telephone conversations were exciting or scandalous. She ordered flour or butter or assured the waiting grocers that Inglis Pies would certainly be delivered. Had she ever let them down?

They had moved into the Toll House six months after having signed the contracts, six months that Kate felt went so slowly as to make her almost scream with vexation. What took workmen so long? She wanted to visit them every day but restrained herself urging Charlie instead, or Liam, who would have made a much better employer, to check as they were passing, that everything was being done as the architect had planned. She did supervise the connecting of the ovens and the installation of her bathroom. It seemed to her that every child, every man who was out of work, and every woman in the village (all of whom should have been at home looking after their families) also supervised the unloading of the bath.

'Have you nothing better to do with your time?' she asked a group of women tartly as she tried to manoeuvre past them to see that the delivery was in pristine condition. She was nervous and embarrassed and a little guilty that she could afford such luxuries and so spoke more sharply than she had intended.

'Stuck-up Mick,' said one of the women, 'I mind when she was at the school and no a pair o' shoes to her name and look at her so la-di-da now.'

Kate heard and lifted her head proudly. She was now stuck-up and she had earned that bath by the sweat of her brow, and if these workmen would do their jobs quickly she could enjoy bathing her children in it.

What is there in the human condition that made some of the villagers resent her and her family once they had moved into the Toll House? To almost everyone, even people she had known all her life she became Mrs Inglis while Charlie remained Charlie. Kate was so busy that it was actually several years before she even noticed that hardly anyone addressed her as Kate and by then she was too busy with her growing children and her business to admit that she cared.

Patrick and Margaret were at the village school and every July Kate took an afternoon off to watch them climb up onto the platform of the Kirk Hall to collect their prizes. She and Charlie, together with Liam and Mollie, sat in their best clothes and tried not to let their pleasure and pride show. That could come later, when they were safely inside the gates of the Toll House.

Kate shook hands with the headmaster, an old man now, nearing retirement. He had been headmaster when she had attended; she, with every other child in the school, had been terrified of him and the tawse he carried everywhere, and here he was shaking her hand.

'Well, Margaret is certainly your daughter, Mrs Inglis. Everything comes so easily to her. If she is a worker like her brother as well, she will go far.'

Kate heard only that Patrick was a worker. 'Oh, he does work hard, doesn't he? I sit with him every night after school while he reads his book and learns his lessons. He likes to get everything off by heart.'

'Children like Margaret have to, Mrs Inglis. Margaret now. I'm quite sure you don't have to go over everything with her a dozen times.'

Kate laughed, the pride in her children's prizes still bubbling inside her. 'Margaret's daddy does her work with her. I can hardly get the pair of them to sit down for fifteen minutes to be quiet for Patrick, before they're away playing somewhere.'

'I should have thought five minutes would be enough for Margaret,' said Mr Cairns drily, and so bound up was Kate in her plans for her son that she did not understand and promised to make Margaret work harder.

At the Toll House the family gathered for tea to celebrate the prizes. Charlie had wanted to buy the children presents but Kate had over-ruled him.

'You would spoil the bairns, given half a chance, Charlie Inglis. Presents are for birthday and Christmas, not for doing their lessons well,' but Charlie had slipped them each a half crown and felt better for it for he had a feeling that their grandfather had been handing out sixpences.

'Was there ever a family more blessed?' said Kate later. The meal had been cleared away. Patrick was sitting in the window seat reading his new book and Kate could hear Margaret screaming with pleasure as Charlie and Liam pushed her higher and higher in the garden swing.

'That one should hae been the laddie,' said Mollie as she poured herself one last cup of tea. 'She won't read her new book till she's made to.'

Kate sprang to her daughter's defence. 'She'll read it in her bed, the wee besom. She knows fine I think books are unhealthy in the bedroom but I'm always finding them under her pillow.' She looked again at the early evening sun distorting itself as it pushed past the bubbles in the windows. It lay across Patrick as he sat engrossed in his book and moved on to her comfortable upholstered furniture and gleaming fireplace. On a small table there was a blue Wedgwood bowl full of roses whose scent filled the room. How different it was from the room in which she had grown up. And down the hall there was a bathroom with a bath, a handbasin and a lavatory, and everything with running water. Bridie and Colm came for their Saturday baths but not Liam or Molly.

'Liam's frightened he'll drown in all that water, and it hot into the bargain,' laughed Charlie.

'The Council will need to put indoor plumbing in the village. In a year or two everybody will have a hot bath on a Saturday night just by turning on a spicket.'

'Aye and we'll all have these cursed telephones and motor cars and fly away to the sunshine for our holidays.'

Kate was not ready to agree with Charlie's ridiculous ideas. He was only joking anyway, wasn't he? But Charlie refused to be drawn.

It was time for Liam and Molly to go home. They had promised to watch Bridie and Colm play tennis at the local court. Kate wasn't so sure that mad dashing around on a tennis court was a suitable sport for a young girl but there was one redeeming factor. Knees had become the most prominent feature of all young women of the late 1920s but at least the tennis skirts of Auchenbeath had not yet caught up with prevailing fashion and for a few hours every evening the knees of the athletic girls, and especially of young Bridie Kennedy, were decently covered.

Margaret, as usual, caused the delay by demanding to go with her grandparents.

'It's already past your bedtime, Margaret,' scolded Kate. 'You can watch Auntie Bridie at the weekend.'

Margaret was well aware that she would never change her mother's mind once it was made up. She could not, however, acquiesce quietly in any decision that concerned herself and usually argued till her overburdened mother slapped her. Kate hated slapping the child, a fact of which Margaret was also well aware but she still felt compelled to put up a fight.

Margaret argued and Kate threatened all the way to the front door while Liam muttered 'maybe just this once' under his breath.

It happened so quickly. Kate opened the door on to the main road for her father and then turned to Margaret who was still muttering under her breath.

She said 'Enough, lassie,' and slapped Margaret hard. Liam, already on the road, turned as if to protest. Neither he nor the driver of the lorry that had just hurtled round the corner even saw one another. There was a thump, a horrible noise of metal on bone, and then an appalling screech of brakes and of people screaming.

Kate could remember very little of the hours that followed. Everyone was screaming except herself and Liam, who lay on the road in his best suit like a tailor's dummy that had been tossed aside because it is out of fashion. She thought she slapped Margaret again, on the face this time, to stop the hysteria. Always she could see the imprint of her hand on the child's cheek. The lorry driver vomited on to the road, or was that Charlie?, and it had to be the driver who kept sobbing, 'I didn't see him, I couldn't see him.' Molly said nothing, not for months.

'He died instantly, Kate,' said Dr Hyslop as he once more bound up the wounds of the Kennedy and Inglis families.

'There was no time . . . I always hoped he would see a priest,' Kate whispered.

'I said "Into thy hands, oh Lord," ' said Patrick. 'I don't know why, Mammy, but Grampa went flying and I said it. It didnae hurt him, did it, Doctor Hyslop? It was a horrible noise,' and then he began to cry.

'Shock,' said the doctor, 'just like his sister and his granny.'

'She's not his granny,' snapped Kate and instantly hated herself for saying it.

'Oh yes she is, Kate,' said the doctor mildly, 'and she'll need them even more now.'

That was when Kate realized how much she had always needed her father. For a few months after Mary Kate's death, Kate had been more mother than daughter to Liam but as he had learned to cope with his grief, his steady, quiet love had surrounded her. She remembered his smile as he had taken his piece tin from her, 'Thank you, Allanah.' He called no one else that, not even Margaret whom he almost worshipped. She remembered the early days of the bakery when he had tramped the village proudly pushing a pram full of pies and even a baby as well. It was shame that had made Charlie follow his father-in-law. If the job didn't demean Liam Kennedy, it certainly couldn't demean Charlie Inglis. One or two had laughed at Charlie; no one had ever laughed at Liam.

She did not ask Father O'Malley to bury her father but she did ask him to pray. The wee kirk was full of mourners;

miners Liam had worked with over the years, boys now men, who had survived the war and been friends of his sons; women to whom he had delivered pies, and to Kate's joy, Dr Hyslop.

'Wouldn't he have prayed for me, Kate?' said the doctor when she thanked him for coming. 'I won't come back for the wake, I'll look in on Mrs. Kennedy.'

Molly was unable to attend her husband's funeral. She lay in bed and silent tears coursed down her cheeks. If Bridie lifted a cup of tea to her lips she drank it but otherwise made no move.

'I'll need to stay with her, Kate,' Bridie had explained. 'Doctor Hyslop says it'll take time. I can bake from the house if you want me to, but I can't leave her.'

'I interviewed two lassies this morning, Bridie. I'll take them both on. They can at least learn how to keep the place clean if they cannae bake. Tell Colm to take his dinner with us; that'll save you to nurse Molly.'

But Colm preferred to keep to his own routine and to take turns sitting with his step-mother.

'There's neither of them bairns, Kate,' Charlie consoled her. 'You're like one of yer own hens; you want Bridie and Colm roosting round you. You'd be really happy if all three of them would move in here for you to look after. Poor Auntie Molly; she was right fond of yer father, Kate. She'll take a while to get over it.'

Kate turned away. How long would *she* take to get over it? She could hardly bear to look at Margaret for every time she did she heard that dreadful sound of the lorry hitting Liam's body. She's only a wee lassie and it was your own fault for hitting her. That's what made him turn round. She deserved the slap. No, she didn't. She's only a bairn; her fault, your fault. The words went around in her head until she thought she would scream.

Charlie had no idea how to comfort Kate; he could not hold her in his arms as easily as he could hold and soothe Margaret. Kate had never been one for physical contact, for the easy embrace. She had never had them as a child, of course, since Liam was not demonstrative and all Mary Kate's outward pourings of physical affection had flowed over whichever of her children was baby at the time. That her mother loved her, Kate had known. It had not needed to be said to be real. But now, when she really needed tenderness and love, she had no idea how to seek them and poor Charlie had no idea how to give them. He tried to show her his sympathy and love in the only way he knew how and for the first time in their married lives he was pleased to feel Kate cling to him. She forced herself to look into his face while he moved on her and tried to see only his face and not Margaret's and certainly not Liam's. But she could not block it out and at last she cried and the tears washed away Liam's face and she fell asleep for the first time in her husband's arms. She woke stiff and sore from lying on his bony arms and remembered that she had not washed herself. Charlie heard the bath water running, shrugged his shoulders in exasperation, and went back to sleep.

If Kate had not become pregnant that night she might have become a very wealthy woman. Mr McDonald was, as he said, doing very well.

'People will always have to eat, Mrs Inglis. Come on, we survived the strikes and it's time to grow. I know we have always advertised your pies as "home-baked" but I think you must face the fact that you must automate. People in the Borders want Kate Inglis pies; in the Shetlands they want them and I want them to have them. Faster transportation is the answer and preservatives. Be realistic. You can't bake a pie in Auchenbeath at four o'clock in the morning and sell it in Edinburgh at nine.'

'I never thought of selling them anywhere but Auchenbeath,' Kate almost whispered, 'or Thornhill with Deirdre near there. I can't take all this in, Mr McDonald. I work so hard now and I have so much, more than I ever dreamed of . . . my own home, my own business, money in the bank for my children's future.'

The grocer looked around the spotless kitchen. 'How many times have I sat in a kitchen with you over the years?' he asked Kate. 'You don't mind my saying you look older? How you manage to remain so pretty though, I'll never understand.'

Kate raised her hand as if to stop him but he went on.

'An old man can say that, can he not, without causing offence. The business, two lovely children, your husband to nurse every so often ... you're a remarkable woman. Why don't you consider some domestic help?'

'People like us don't get people in to do our work for us, Mr McDonald.'

'Why ever not? You work too hard, Mrs Inglis. Time to work with your head and not your hands. Get a house-keeper to look after the house. Another bank loan to extend the bakery or—'

The door had opened and Charlie and the children came in. Patrick stood quietly by the door and smiled shyly but Margaret rushed to Mr McDonald. 'You've got a new car; it's beautiful and a new driver. He wouldn't let me get in ...'

McDonald rose, lifting the girl up in his arms. 'Hello, Charlie. I'm glad you're back; want to have a word but first we'll see about giving Madame here a wee hurl, and you too, Patrick. Do you want to see my new car?'

'Yes please, sir,' said Patrick although he was not too interested in cars – they reminded him of Liam – but felt it would be impolite to tell the complete truth. 'Is it all right, Mammy?'

'Of course,' said Mr McDonald. 'Do we have your permission, Mrs Inglis? Burns can take them round the village while we fill Charlie in on our plans.'

'Be careful going out,' Kate called to the children as, permission received, they rushed to the door.

'I'm parked well away from the corner,' Mr McDonald said quietly. It was three months since Liam's death but it was still very much in everyone's mind. He looked up the road as he instructed his chauffeur. Not a car in sight and he doubted that anything had passed while he had been in the bakery. What a tragic fluke the accident had been. Mind you, not everyone in the south of Scotland was so resistant to progress as Kate Inglis. The motor car was on its way. Even Edgar Hyslop was talking about having one. What a boon it would be to a busy doctor and to an expanding businesswoman. He returned to the kitchen determined to argue with her.

'You'll spoil those bairns,' Kate smiled at him. 'I've been telling Charlie that you want us to expand again.'

Charlie stirred his tea thoughtfully before he spoke and the others waited, McDonald quietly, Kate busy with the children's tea. 'I'm not an educated man, Mr McDonald, and I'll be honest and tell ye that all this talk of, what is you call it, expansion – scares me. There's never been one o' my family with his own house and here we have this big place and the bakery and enough work for the two of us so that I can hold up my head afore my bairns. But Kate works too hard now. She cannae work harder; it's no fair to her or tae her bairns.'

Kate looked at him in a mixture of surprise and pride. Never had he said so much at one time. Patrick was quiet like his father, she realized. She had always compared her son to Liam who had been a quiet man, but Charlie was too.

'Where's your ambition, man?' asked the grocer. 'The years of really hard, sweating labour are over for the two of you. It's time to work with your head, not your hands. Sit back, relax. Hire more people, a housekeeper and a nanny for a start. Move your family out of the bakery, out of Auchenbeath even. Better schools in the city, theatres, restaurants, art galleries.'

It was the mention of a nanny that ruined it. If Kate had known the word ostentatious she would have said it. Nannies were for the rich, for royalty, not for the children of a delivery man from Auchenbeath.

'Ambition is a funny thing, Mr McDonald,' she said, 'and maybe I don't have the right kind of ambition. I don't want to be rich. I wouldn't know what to do with any more money. I want, *we* want, our children to grow up to be good people, to have the chances in life that we didn't have. Patrick will be old enough at the end of this school year for the big school,' she looked at Charlie hesitantly.

'We want him to go to the university, to get an education, to be . . . a teacher even. That's our ambition.'

The street door had opened and they had barely noticed the children return from their drive in the big new car. 'A teacher, Mammy,' said Patrick, who had obviously overheard the end of the conversation. He took a deep breath and looked at his father who never went to the wee chapel with them even at Christmas or Easter. 'I think I want to be a priest.'

'A very laudable ambition, Patrick,' said Mr McDonald since Kate and Charlie seemed to have lost their voices. 'You won't make any money at it.'

'I want to have a brand-new yellow car every single year,' said Margaret and that roused her mother from her adoring contemplation of her son.

'Get to your homework, miss.'

'I haven't had my tea yet, Mammy. Neither has Father Patrick.'

Had Mr McDonald not been in the room Kate would have slapped her saucy daughter. As it was, her look boded ill for Margaret's future.

'The child's right, Mrs Inglis. I've outstayed my welcome and you and Charlie have a lot to think about. There is another solution and I'll have my solicitors write and explain it all to you, a compromise, as it were. You don't expand but I sell Kate Inglis pies in every shop the length and breadth of Scotland. Don't worry about it tonight.'

The compromise was that Kate agree to sell her recipes and all rights to the McDonald grocery chain. By the time the solicitor's letters arrived she would have sold him anything. She had realized that she was pregnant and, unlike her other two pregnancies, this one was accompanied by all the symptoms that Kate had hardly believed existed. She sold over her rights to her recipes and even to her own name. But a huge cheque went into the bank; no thoughts here about investments or stocks and shares.

'That money is going to sit there in the bank getting bigger and bigger,' said Charlie to the children. 'Can you imagine that. Now Mammy's not very well so you two be good and quiet and maybe she'll let me take you to the pictures.'

Kate tried to joke. 'I'd let Amy Johnson fly the both of them to Australia with her.'

'This is no like you, Kate. Will I phone the doctor?'

She smiled at him. Charlie had always had an incredible knack for doing or saying something to cheer her up. He hated the telephone and never used the machine unless there was absolutely no alternative. 'I feel better already,' she said with some truth. She certainly felt better mentally if not physically.

When they had gone Kate sat down by the fire and sipped hot, sweet tea hoping against hope that it would stay down, then she re-read the letters from the solicitor and tried to assimilate what selling her recipes and all rights to her own name really meant. Heretofores and whereuntos and the party of the first part. I wish I really understood all this. Again they were back to the question of education, that magic word. With an education, a proper one, Kate felt sure that she could understand the terms in which the formal contracts were couched. She had sold her name. How could she sell her name? She was quite sure that she had never agreed to do any such daft thing. But there were all those pounds lying there in nice rows in the bank, growing and growing all the time.

Would you like to be an executive, Mrs Inglis of Kate Inglis Bakeries? Should you get a nanny for the bairns and a housekeeper and a fancy car with a man to drive it? Would you enjoy being driven up to Glasgow and God knows where else for executive meetings? Mr McDonald says it's not too late; if I want I can go in with him and become one of the country's leading businesswomen. Do I want that or do I have enough already? She stood up. No, it's done. I've told them I'm staying small. That's what I want, isn't it, just a nice wee business here to provide work for Charlie and a home for the bairns? She looked around. 'I'll walk down and tell Bridie about the bairn. Maybe that'll cheer Molly up.

She looked in the mirror as she adjusted her hat, one of the dashing new Robin Hood hats. You look like an executive, Kate Inglis Bakeries, and it was with more than a hint of regret that Kate went out closing the door behind her.

# 12

Charlie learned to drive.

'What's the point in trotting around behind a wee pony, Kate? We have to move with the times.'

'It's madame has put you up to this, Charlie Inglis. You would never have thought of it yourself. You don't even like cars.'

Charlie refused to be drawn. He and Kate would never agree about Margaret, who wanted to follow her big brother to the secondary school in Dumfries.

'A van will make deliveries faster and it'll get Patrick home faster.' The second argument won his case. A van was bought but to Margaret's fury it was black, not yellow, and had The Toll House Bakery painted on the sides.

'Teach me to drive it, Daddy,' Margaret begged. 'It's perfectly safe around Auchenbeath.'

'Away ye go, you wee monkey, and you not even fifteen yet; you'll get me hung with your wheedling. Aren't the cars crawling along the roads like beetles these days?'

Margaret learned to drive. She kept her newfound skill from Kate as she kept many things from her mother. It seemed to Margaret that the older her mother got, the harder and harder she worked and it was all so useless. Kate Inglis pies were being sold all over the country and yet Kate received not one penny from them.

'I'd never have sold the recipes and the name, Patrick,' Margaret confessed to her brother. 'We could be millionaires now.'

'A slight exaggeration, Margaret,' said Patrick who as usual was sitting at the scrubbed surface of the bakery tables trying to study.

'We could too. Look how hard Mammy works trying to keep a share of the market in this area. Mr McDonald cheated her. Well, he wouldn't cheat me.'

'Mr McDonald is a good man. He didn't cheat Mam; he gave her a very good price for her recipes and the right to her name.' He put his pencil down and turned to look at his sister. 'I think Mam could probably afford to stop working, Margaret. I just don't think she knows how to stop.'

'She doesn't want to stop more like. She loves getting up in the freezing cold when she could be lying in her nice warm bed. Well, you won't catch me working when I don't have to work.'

Patrick sighed. That was patently obvious. Margaret had already finished her homework and he had only done

one assignment. No point in suggesting that she read over what she had written. They both knew there was no need. Margaret's would be correct and she would remember everything she had written.

'God wants me to work harder,' he said to himself. 'It's his plan for me to test me, to see if I'm worthy. If I get my Highers it'll be a sign that he really wants me and then I'll tell Mam.'

Since the day Patrick had told his mother of his intention to become a priest the entire household had revolved around him and that troubled him but he was as inarticulate as Charlie and could not explain his feelings to his mother. He really wanted to be a priest. Since the day of Liam's death in front of him he had thought of nothing else, even when Mam talked about lawyers and teachers and doctors. It was a priest like old Father O'Malley, a gentle, quiet man who offered Mass every morning and to whom Patrick confessed his sins every Saturday but not his doubts. For Kate wanted him to be a Jesuit which meant going to the university first.

'If I get my highers it'll be a sign that that's what God wants too.' Patrick knew that it wasn't what he wanted but he had always done as he was told. He wanted to please his mother. She worked so hard for him and she wanted him to go to university. Not much to ask for, Patrick, three or four more years, after you've finished school, of swotting desperately to understand or even remember enough to pass the examinations. Margaret never had to swot; mind you, she hadn't got to the really hard stuff yet.

'Don't think, Father Pat,' his sister would tease since she knew he hated it. 'Just learn it all off and spew it out at exams. That's exactly what teachers want; remember everything they say, and write it down to show them how clever they are.'

'Don't be so cynical, Margaret. Facts are important and have to be learned.'

'Then learn them, Patrick, but I would have thought that why they are important is more important than just reciting them, if you know what I mean. 1066. Norman Invasion. Who cares that it was 1066? Why is the Norman Invasion important?'

Patrick looked at her in exasperation. 'The date's important too. It's . . . tidier. Go away. You're giving me a headache and I have loads to do.'

She looked over his shoulder. 'The subjunctive. We haven't got to that yet but I could do your geometry for you. I can easily work the proof out.'

'That would be cheating. Go away and play with Liam.'

Margaret jumped off the table, her skirts knocking several of her brother's books and his inkpot onto the floor. Unperturbed she picked them up and dumped them all unceremoniously back on the table. 'I think I'll teach him to read. That'll really upset Miss Timpson. Another Inglis she won't know what to do with.'

'What's that, Margaret?' Kate had come in. 'I hope you're not annoying your brother.' Her eyes softened as she looked at her son. 'What a lot you have to do tonight, Son. I'll away and bring you a wee cup of tea and keep you company for a while. If you're finished, Margaret, there's ironing to do.'

Quietly Margaret left the bakery and went through to the kitchen. If she did the ironing quickly and put everything away tidily there was just a chance that she could talk Kate into giving her money for the pictures. She put the kettle on first. That little gesture would soften her mother too.

'Where's Daddy?' she asked as her mother reappeared.

'Oh, you've put the kettle on, lass,' Kate smiled at her daughter, standing so patiently ironing one of Patrick's shirts. 'Make sure the iron's nice and hot now and get a good crease in the sleeves. Your Da's taken the bairn over to your gran's for a wee while.'

Margaret looked in amazement at the clock on the mantelpiece. 'At this time of night? It's way past his bedtime. I was going to give him his bath and read him a story for you, Mammy.'

Kate smiled at her daughter and stretched her back in the old familiar gesture. How nice it was to be chatting to Margaret who for once seemed as soft as when she was talking to Charlie. Usually Kate felt that, for some unknown reason, Margaret was on the defensive with her. The thought came – Am I too hard on the lassie? And the answer – No, isn't everything I do for her own good. Please God she'll realize it one day.

'You're a good girl,' she said. 'Your Auntie Bridie came for a wee while and said your gran was a wee bit upset that Liam hasn't been to see her this week; it's been the rain.'

'Granny Molly could easily come to see him,' said Margaret with an almost vicious swipe at the body of her brother's shirt.

Kate agreed with her, but not even to her daughter would she criticize Molly. She changed the subject.

'There's a letter from Uncle Colm on the mantel there. He's coming for the weekend; says he wants to take his girlfriend to the pictures. Now, who could that be?' Kate spoke teasingly, enjoying herself.

Without thought to the shirt Margaret left the iron and went to find the letter. Colm had joined the army two years before. He had said he wanted to see the world. Margaret felt sure it was to get away from Molly who had not allowed herself to recover after Liam's death.

'He says he wants to borrow the van, Mam, to take me to Dumfries. Does Patrick want to come too – there's talkies at Dumfries – and we can have our tea at a cafe. You'll let me go . . .'

Kate almost dropped the tray she was carrying to rush to the ironing board. Margaret watched her mother fearfully as she lifted up Patrick's best shirt which now had a large scorch mark in the middle of the back. Kate stared angrily back at her daughter. 'And here's that teacher trying to tell me that you're the clever one and you can't even iron a shirt without ruining it. You're just like your Auntie Deirdre – nothing in your head but the pictures and film stars and that lipstick you think you've been hiding.'

'I'm sorry, Mammy. I'll get it out. The iron was cooling.' Margaret desperately wanted to get her mother's mind away from the beautiful lipstick, the envy of every other girl in 2A. 'Take Patrick's tea, Mam, and I'll have the mark out before you get back.'

To her relief, her mother picked up the tray she had been preparing. 'Is it a good hard slap you need, Margaret Inglis?' Margaret knew that was a rhetorical question and needed no answer. A smart reply would certainly lead to a slap since Daddy wasn't here to protect her. Not that Kate slapped her often. Margaret tended to goad her mother but wisely chose times when Charlie was there to quietly diffuse Kate's wrath.

'It's a good talking to this lassie needs, Kate, and I'll see to her while you get on,' he would say, and Kate would 'get on' with one of the million tasks she found to overfill her day.

'Get that mark out, madame, and everything ironed and put away afore I get back or it's you will be ironing all weekend while Uncle Colm sees this talkie on his own.'

She didn't mean that. She knew it and Margaret knew it, but it was a game they played. Margaret set herself to removing the scorch mark, and was re-ironing the shirt when Charlie and four-year-old Liam returned. Liam was a very important young man. His father doted on him as did his older brother and sister, his aunts and uncles, his grandmother and, when she had a moment to spare, his mother. Dr Hyslop, who had retired to a cottage in the Lake District two years after Liam was born, believed that it was the child's existence which had prevented Molly from dying of grief, if not from spending most of her day lying on the settee being waited on hand and foot by her devoted step-daughter.

Margaret scooped up the child who had run to her but carefully stood the flat iron on its end first.

'Hello, my wee lambie. Did you see your grannie then?'

'Put him down, Margaret. He's away too heavy for a wee lassie like you. He's near too heavy for me an all. Aren't you, ye rascal?' Charlie looked around. 'Patrick still at the books?'

'Aye, Mammy's taken him a cup of tea.' Margaret, still carrying her young brother whose arms were tightly around her neck, carefully lifted the cooling iron and set it down on the fireplace before dislodging the child.

'Now, I'll get your cocoa, Liam the lamb, so away and see Mammy. I've to put you to your bed.'

Liam obediently trotted off to the bakery and Margaret started to prepare his supper, but Charlie stopped her. 'He's that full he'll burst if you put anything else in him, lassie. Sit doon and let's have a wee crack afore the others come back.'

Willingly Margaret sat down. She loved these times alone with her father when they talked non-stop, or at least Margaret did, about anything and everything that mattered. Charlie would have surprised his wife with his comprehensive knowledge of the latest in fashions, in hairstyles, in filmstars and even lip colourings.

Unlike Kate, Charlie thought their daughter suited the bright-red lipstick. Against her white skin, and framed by the cloud of dark hair she had inherited from her parents it looked, he thought, very nice. He loved watching her chatter with animation, a look that sadly her mother saw very seldom for the girl tended to be quite wooden around Kate, unless they were fighting when she was too animated for her own good.

'Did you see my Uncle Colm's letter, Daddy?' she asked now. 'He says there's going to be another war.'

'Nonsense, lassie, and for heaven's sake, don't let your mother hear you talk about war. Didn't she lose enough in the last one?'

'But it's Germany. Do you remember Hitler in the twenties? He tried to take over then and he's at it again now.'

'I've no heard that name afore, lass. Tell me about the school; that's away more interesting than some wee German laddie.'

And obligingly Margaret talked about school and about how she loved mathematics and science and languages.

'Changed days from when I was at the school, Margaret. Imagine a wee bit lassie like you learning Latin. Your brother doesn't like the Latin and I cannot say I blame him.'

'Och, it's easy, Daddy. It's just learning words and things like tenses. Poor Pat has an awful job with his tenses.'

Charlie got up from his seat by the fire and began to fill his pipe. 'You're not to tease him. I cannot understand it. You're that quick at the learning but he works away and gets there in the end but, my, if he does go away to the university, what a dull time the poor laddie's going to have.'

'Aye, he'll be at the lectures all day and then he'll be stuck in his room all night trying to remember what he heard.'

'Sure, that's what university's for.'

'Away, Daddy. I'd have a grand time in the city; you wouldnae get me stuck at the books all day. I'd try everything.'

'And what would you learn, miss?'

'Everything. That's what university's for.'

'It's not for lassies, Margaret. You don't need to fill yer head up with facts, a bonnie wee thing like you. Some handsome prince . . .'

'Some handsome prince will do what, Charlie?'

They had not heard Kate return. She looked at them and, not for the first time, envied the warmth and ease of the relationship between father and daughter. How she would love to sit at the fireside of an evening and giggle with Margaret, but she was always too busy. Even her attempt at playfulness with the girl this evening had been spoiled because of Margaret's thoughtlessness and selfishness. So anxious had she been to see Colm's letter with its promise of pleasure for her that she had carelessly burned her brother's shirt. Kate took refuge in anger. 'He'll not marry a lassie that cannae iron a shirt or who promises to tell her wee brother a story and doesn't.'

Margaret had jumped up. 'I'll do it now, Mammy. I'll away and run his bath.'

'He's in his bed and that's where you should be. By the way, do you mind a George Bell at the primary school with you and Patrick? He's coming up the night to apply for the relief vanman job and I want to know if he's the type that was in trouble at the school. No use asking Patrick. He cannae see badness in anyone.'

Margaret stopped on her way to the door. 'There was a lot of Bells at Auchenbeath, Mammy. I cannae mind that I ever heard anything about a George.'

'Well, he's a year older than Patrick so maybe he was too big for you. Put the pipe out, Charlie, or smoke outside where you can breathe at the same time. Your lungs are bad enough without that.'

Margaret had reached the door when the bell rang. 'I'll get it,' she called and opened the door. For a full minute she was bereft of the power of speech and, to her intense mortification, felt that horrible red blush coursing across her cheeks.

'Mrs Inglis is expecting me,' the young Greek god at the door said to break the silence.

'She's in there,' said Margaret and fled to her room where she rushed to the window and pressed her hot face against the glass. Where had her sophistication gone when she needed it? Where had the bright-red lipstick, that would have devastated the most beautiful boy, no, man – he was a year older than Patrick, that made him seventeen – been when she had had a chance to really test its seductive powers? What an idiot she had been. She threw herself on her bed in an agony of embarrassment. She could just hear him with his pals. 'I met Pat Inglis's wee sister. What a gawk; stood there looking at me with her tongue hanging out and ran away when I spoke to her.' Oh, God, she could kill herself. George Bell, George Bell. Beautiful George Bell. How could I have forgotten you? There had, not that she thought about it, been a George Bell at the school, tall and skinny with blond hair that was always far too long, haystack, they'd called him, and his bum halfway out of his breeks. She laughed at the memory and that made her feel better. Well, the next time he saw Margaret Inglis, he would see a changed woman. She pulled her frock tight across her front and looked at her reflection in the mirror. Was there any chest there at all? None worth mentioning. It would have to be the lipstick and silk stockings. How could she get the silk stockings on when George Bell was at the bakery and her mother, who would definitely kill her if she discovered the silk stockings, was not? She had an utterly, terrifying, devastating thought. What if he didn't get the job? She fell on her knees beside the bed. Dear Blessed Virgin, please let him get the job, and let him see me when I look nice and I'll never tease Patrick again about being a priest and I'll iron everything perfectly for the rest of my life.

George got the job and Margaret planned her campaign very carefully. It had to be a Saturday; Kate spent most of the morning in her office doing accounts and Charlie, who would be in and out filling his van, wouldn't notice anyway and Patrick, who would say nothing, although he would look at her mournfully as if she were in danger of losing her immortal soul for the heinous crime of wearing silk stockings, would be up at the primary school playing football for the Auchenbeath Eleven. For several Saturdays

George was not at the bakery. His employer did not need his services but then, at last, either she felt more secure with him or the pace of deliveries hotted up, for nearly two months after he started work for The Toll House Bakery, George arrived on his old bike just as the family were finishing breakfast.

'Come away in, George,' Charlie welcomed him. 'There's time for a fly cup.' He sat the boy down at the table and George, who was the only member of his large family out of bed at seven o'clock on a Saturday morning, was only too pleased to sit down and demolish the rolls and tea Kate put in front of him.

'We should do him eggs, Mammy,' whispered Margaret when she followed her mother into the kitchen. 'He looks starved. I bet you he's no had his breakfast.'

'You can do some bacon for him when he gets back from Sanquhar, Margaret. Now, I want this place cleaned up when I come through. Keep wee Liam happy; he can play outside if it stays nice but wrap him up, and help your daddy with the orders.'

'Can't I go in the van with Daddy?' asked Margaret whom wild horses would not have dragged from the premises. She always argued with Kate about Saturday chores and certainly did not want to rouse her suspicions.

'They should be back about ten. Have the bacon ready and I'll have some tea in the office. Now I want

the place spotless.' She whisked off to the glorified cup-
board she called her office and Margaret hurried back
to the bakery.

Unfortunately she would have to keep the awful white
apron on until Charlie left because he would wonder
what on earth she was doing wearing her second-best
Sunday dress. She could pull the ghastly cap off though,
because the baking was all done. Better not change the
stockings or apply the lipstick just yet. There was a limit
to even Charlie's indulgence. She brushed her hair furiously and bit her lips to make them red.

'You'd best put your cap on, lassie,' said Charlie. 'Mrs
Inglis is very fussy about hygiene in the bakery, George.
Check off the order book, will you, Margaret, while I go
over the Thornhill route with George.'

Thornhill. If George were sent all the way to Thornhill
he would hardly be back before dinner time and that was
when Kate closed on a Saturday.

'Would you not be better to go to Thornhill, Daddy?
You could take Liam; he'd love to see his Auntie Deirdre,
wouldn't you, lambie?'

'George is doing the Thornhill run. He's got the best van.'

'Do you know the way, George?' asked Margaret and
knew immediately that she had made a fatal mistake.

'Aye, lassie,' said George smiling at her in a way that
made her blush like a silly loon. 'If I point the van down

the hill and keep on for fifteen mile I'll hit the Burns statue in the middle o' the town.' He laughed and picked up a tray of pies to put in the back of the van.

Margaret wanted to burst out crying. She could hear herself. 'Do you know the way, George?', like a right idiot, and Charlie was looking at her in a fair puzzled way. What was even worse was that George had called her a lassie. He didn't know, how could he? and her in this ghastly apron that hid the little she had, that she was a woman of the world with a treasured pair of silk stockings and a red lipstick.

'I'll take the bairn,' said George to Charlie, 'if he wants to see his auntie.'

'No, lad, thanks, his mammy's frightened of cars with him. He's got to be sitting on her lap for her to be easy.'

With a general wave George drove out of the yard. He hadn't even looked at her, not as if she were a person, and Charlie was staring at her.

'You're not yourself this morning, lass. Are you feeling all right? Should you maybe get back to your bed? Tell your mammy . . .'

'Oh, Daddy, away you go on your run. I've this bakery to scrub. You'd think Mammy would get some of the women in to do it but, no, Margaret can do it. That's what lassies are fit for, scrubbing floors and washing dishes, nothing atween their ears but air.'

Charlie looked after her. Sometimes she worried him with her antagonistic attitude to Kate. 'You're no fair to yer mammy, Margaret,' he wanted to say, and maybe he should have. Instead he shook his head and climbed into his van while in the kitchen Margaret almost threw the breakfast dishes into the sink. A cup broke when it hit a plate and that calmed her down. If Kate came in to see what all the noise was about, there really would be trouble.

# 13

PATRICK PASSED HIS Higher examinations by the skin of his teeth and to Kate's almost unbearable joy was offered a place at Edinburgh University.

They sat around the kitchen table and read and re-read the beautiful piece of paper.

'Look at it, Charlie.' Kate could hardly speak for pleasure. 'Our bairn at the university.' She passed the official letter to Charlie who looked at it for a while and then passed it to Margaret.

'I never thought you'd make it, Father Pat,' she teased and hurriedly passed the paper back as an angry move from Kate made her realize that even at the advanced age of sixteen her ears were not completely safe from her mother's hard right hand.

'Can you not share your brother's joy, miss?' asked Kate. 'Do you have to spoil everything with that smart tongue of yours?' Where had she gone wrong with Margaret, thought Kate. It seemed that the girl antagonized her with every word that came out of her mouth. This past year she had been almost impossible and just when her mother had begun to think that perhaps the girl should go on to higher education, her examination results had been poor. Well, I was right all along, thought Kate, Patrick's the one to do great things.

'I was only joking, Mammy. Patrick knows I'm pleased for him.'

Look at the face on her, thought Kate, acting as if she was misunderstood. I understand you only too well, madame. She lost herself again in the study of the paper. Eighteen years, eighteen years of hard work, of sweat, of fear, of disappointment and of great joy. Maybe every mother felt the same, experienced the same.

'I'm glad you're pleased, Mam, and you too, Dad, but I'm not sure about the university.' Patrick's doubts disturbed her euphoria. 'Should I not go straight to the seminary? I want to be a simple parish priest, not a Jesuit or a doctor or a lawyer or a teacher. What good is a university education going to be to me?'

'It's not just the chance of being a Jesuit, love, but I promised your dad, love,' said Kate, 'and you still feel that way don't you, Charlie? You want him to go to the university first.'

Charlie stood up and reached for his pipe, a sure sign of stress. 'You know where I stand, Patrick. I don't want you to be a priest, I never have, but I'll not stand in your way, if that's what you really want. Just go to the university first; who knows what you'll learn there? Ach, give yerself a chance, laddie. You're not even eighteen yet.'

'It's just because you never had the chance of university; you want it for me, but it's not what I want. I'm not clever enough. I might not be clever enough to be a priest either but I want to try.'

Charlie looked at Kate but she sat quietly, refusing to interfere. For years they had argued; night after angry night in the big bed almost from the night of Liam's death. 'Our boy wants to be a priest, Charlie. I never hoped or even prayed for such a blessing and I never said a word to him. He decided himself, from seeing his Grampa die, I think.'

'It's no natural, being a priest. I want him to be a real man, no half a man.'

'Oh, Charlie. Men like you think *that's* what makes a man, groping away at some poor woman night after night. Well, there's more to being a man than that.' She hadn't meant to say it; she would have cut her tongue out rather than ever utter such hurtful words but they were flying there in the air around them and nothing could ever bring the words back. She had to do something to make it up to Charlie. Although she hated doing it, she had found herself suggesting that Patrick test his vocation by doing a degree course at the university first. If he still wanted to be a priest after he had achieved his degree, then his father would say no more. Charlie had agreed but it was over a year before he ever touched her again. At first Kate had enjoyed the abstinence, had even begun to go to bed without that feeling of trepidation but then she had begun to worry. Had she wounded her husband so deeply that he no longer loved or wanted her? She doubled her efforts to make his home life as pleasant as possible. After all, perhaps it was just age, perhaps it had nothing to do with what she had said. The house shone with polish and the bakery gleamed in its hygienic whiteness. Margaret could have testified to that because it became one of her jobs after school to scrub the tables.

If the house and bakery were not spared Kate's zeal, neither were her children. They did not gleam with polish but as she sent them off to school each morning, with their nourishing pieces, their homework all done and as far as she could gather, correct, she would thrill with pride. Were there any smarter, better turned out children in the whole of the south of Scotland?

'Take Liam with you on your rounds this morning, Charlie,' she began to say. 'He's aye under my feet, but I've told him he's to behave and not touch the wheel. I have a lot to do this morning.'

'You have a lot to do every morning, Kate.' Charlie enjoyed the company of his youngest child but, despite his mother's dire warnings, Liam was becoming a handful, always trying to figure out how the van worked. He couldn't be left alone for a second or he'd be driving away.

'The sooner you're at the school and all, ye rascal,' Charlie laughed.

But now, not only was Liam at the primary school at Auchenbeath, his brother was finishing his sixth year at the academy in the big town and would soon be off, somewhat reluctantly, to university.

'You're really something, Patrick Inglis,' Margaret berated him on the bus home. 'You've got the chance to get away from home, out from under Mammy's thumb, and you're moaning and groaning. Boy, if she'd let me go to the university I would be gone without looking back.'

'And what about George? When would you see your darling George?'

Margaret blushed furiously and rounded on her brother. 'What are you talking about? Have you been spying on me, you nasty sneak? If you've said anything to Mammy, I'll kill you.'

'Calm down, Margaret. Which heroine of the pictures are you playing now?' Patrick laughed at her terror. 'Of course I haven't said anything to Mam for I think you should tell her yourself. You're sixteen, hardly a wee lassie, and George is a nice enough fellow.'

Tell Mam? The enormity of the suggestion. Margaret could hardly assimilate it. When had she ever been able to tell Kate anything? Even if she had wanted to have long cosy chats with her mother about boys and clothes or the pictures, Kate was always busy or, what was worse, totally condemning of her interests.

'Is Hollywood all you have in that head of yours, madame?' Kate would say with her bitter, hurtful sarcasm. Tell her about George? Never.

'Why don't you go on to the university?' Patrick went on. 'You'll get your Highers if you stop mooning over big, blond George and make a little effort. You're brainy, Margaret, far brainier than me.'

'You know fine Mam wants me to work in the bakery to take over from her eventually.'

'She let you stay on at the school. Would all that education no be a waste and she hates waste?'

Margaret leaned back in the seat. Go to university. What would she do there? She hadn't too much idea of what a big city was like but it had to be full of more challenges than Auchenbeath, and the people! There would be people from foreign countries at the university. Maybe somebody French on whom she could practise this daft language she'd been learning for so long. Her Latin was even better but nobody spoke Latin now except priests and she certainly could not become a priest. Who would want to anyway? She looked across at her brother. Poor Father Pat. Latin was his worst subject. Just as well he only had to read it.

'Patrick, you don't think Mammy knows that I'm going out with George? We only meet at the pictures or sometimes for a walk up the Baker's Burn.'

'Mam's not devious, Margaret. She would say something – at least I suppose she would if she disapproved.'

'How did you find out?'

'Och, Daddy and I used to have a good laugh at you trying to attract George's attention. You'd have done better tae hit him over the head like the caveman. He thought you were just my wee sister till last summer and then he saw you when you didnae see him and you weren't acting the femme fatale. You're a bonny enough lassie without your lipstick and that stuff you put on your eyes. Just as well Mam's over busy all day; she'd kill you for that.'

'You can imagine what she would say if she knew I was seeing George.' She stayed quiet for a while as the bus groaned its way along the winding road to Auchenbeath. She looked out of the window but she was not seeing the trees, the hillsides that in spring were covered in primroses; she was seeing George, George whose hot mouth and seeking hands both excited and frightened her so that she would do almost anything to be with him, to sit with him in the darkness of the picture house, sweating hands tightly clasped, or more daringly to walk with him on the hillside beyond the bakery.

'The world's full of Georges,' Patrick disturbed her thoughts, 'and an awful lot of them are at Edinburgh University.'

'You're daft, Father Patrick. There's only one George, but I'll see about the university. Maybe I'll come in your last year and we could get a room together and I would look after you because you'll starve to death on your own.'

But Kate had taken steps to ensure that her son did not waste away from hunger at the university. Margaret and Patrick could sense her excitement as they walked in from school. Kate waited until the whole family were seated around the table at their tea.

'And guess where we are going on Saturday?' she asked the expectant faces. 'Edinburgh. We're away to look at rooms for Patrick. There's an area called Morningside, Patrick love. It's a very nice part of the city with good clean homes and this lady offers her rooms to students. She takes three students and she does a full breakfast and an evening meal. I spoke to her on the telephone today. Your daddy will drive us up in the van, she'll see you come from a good family and that you can pay her charges. Aren't you excited, lamb?'

'He's terrified,' said Margaret before she could stop herself.

'Go to your room and stay there, miss. You have a genius for spoiling everything with that tongue of yours. Well, maybe we won't take it with us on our trip.' Kate was furious.

'Mammy, she just meant I was nervous about all the changes,' said Patrick, as usual trying to be the peacemaker between these two women whom he loved and whom he knew, loved each other. Why couldn't they show one another? Was it because they were women? Mysterious beings. His mother and his sister were the only two he knew really well and half the time he couldn't figure them out. 'And I am,' he went on. 'University'll be a right change and then there's living with folk I don't know and all.'

'You'll get used to it in no time at all, will he not, Charlie? Here's your Daddy has been in foreign lands, Patrick. That'll be the next thing for you. You'll be phoning us up and saying, I'm away to France or Italy or some such place for a grand holiday with my pals, for I want you to have friends, lambie. Don't we, Charlie, no sitting night after night studying. You're to join clubs and do exciting things in your free time.'

'Can I not go?' demanded Liam, and got a hug from his mother for making his big brother laugh.

The day's outing was a great success. The drive itself, through the magnificent Dalveen Pass, was an excitement in itself. Charlie, his heart in his mouth, as he crept slowly along the road with its perilous drop on his left side, almost spoiled the day before it started. 'Next time, if there is a next time, you can drive, Margaret.' He looked at the horrified realization that her daughter could actually drive a motor car dawning on his wife's face and hurriedly added, 'or you, our Liam, for Daddy's frightened we fall off the edge.'

Liam hooted with laughter for he loved cars and would want nothing better, and Margaret breathed slowly again and deliberately kept her face to the window so that her mother had no chance of seeing her eyes until any suspicion roused by Charlie's ill-judged remark had faded. Mam would undoubtedly want Patrick to learn to drive first. The knowledge that her daughter had been driving for years would not please her one bit.

Yet again Margaret misread her mother. Driving was yet another twentieth-century step with which Kate was having to come to terms. She would be excited and pleased when her children learned to drive but because she basically distrusted the motor car, she would always be afraid when they were driving.

In Edinburgh itself there was panic again, for although Charlie had no fear of a big city, when he had lived in

Glasgow he had walked the streets pushing a barrow, driving in unfamiliar towns was a different matter. It was the castle that saved the day, for everywhere they went they were conscious of it towering above them and the excitement of actually seeing it took away the terror over being lost.

'Can we not go up and see it better?' asked Liam peevishly.

Kate smiled at her youngest. This was going to be a day to remember. 'We'll do better, lambie. We'll find the direction to Patrick's house, if he likes it that is, and then we'll find a nice place to eat our picnic, and after your daddy and me has talked to the landlady, we'll take the tour of the castle, and you'll see swords and crowns and all kinds of things.'

Eventually, with Patrick almost beside himself with suspense, they found the neat little row of terraced houses, and surveyed them from afar. Auchenbeath was nothing like this.

'Very posh,' said Margaret enviously.

'Don't talk slang,' said Kate automatically but not angrily for she felt the same herself. If the house were as nice inside Patrick would be bound to be happy there. They went back to the car to eat their sandwiches.

'Save the apple for cleaning your teeth, Patrick. We want to make a nice impression. Liam, you'll have to stay in the van with Margaret; it'll look like a tinker's flittin' if we all go in,' ordered Kate, ignoring the look of disappointment on the girl's face. She knew Margaret would love to see inside the house where her brother might stay for the next three years but she would have plenty of opportunities later. 'We'll go and see one of the nice big shops on Princes Street, lamb, maybe find something special for a good lassie,' she finished to ease the disappointment.

The house was well furnished and comfortable. Mrs McGregor was as neat as her house, and as well upholstered. The bedroom Patrick would have had a single bed, a wardrobe, an easy chair, and a little table and chair by the window which looked out over the garden.

'That's an apple tree, Patrick,' said Mrs McGregor. 'But a country boy like you would know that. It's particularly beautiful in the spring and, of course, Mrs Inglis, my students are always more than welcome to the apples.'

The kitchen and the bathroom were inspected and approved, and the ladies discussed suitable meals for growing young men with all the enthusiasm of good cooks. 'He'll not starve in this house, Mrs Inglis, and I can easily make him a piece to take. That would be extra, of course, or he could buy his own things and keep them on a separate shelf. Most of my young men prefer to do that. It is a little cheaper, I suppose, and allows for differences in taste.'

A price was agreed and Patrick was registered to come up in September so that he could get used to Edinburgh before the start of term.

'You're not the Kate Inglis of Kate Inglis Bakeries by any chance, are you?' asked Mrs McGregor at the door and when Kate modestly said that she was, Mrs McGregor shook her firmly by the hand. 'I have admired your products for years, Mrs Inglis, and your courage in running a business. Had I been allowed to work as I wished to do when a young girl, I would not now have to supplement my income by letting my rooms. Not that I am not delighted to welcome healthy young men into my home. Mr McGregor and I were not blessed with children,' she finished sadly.

Kate and Charlie said all the right things and returned to the van. 'Well, he'll be all right if she doesn't talk his head off,' said Charlie in answer to Margaret's questions. 'She sounds like an old primer I had at the school, the day or two I was there, that is.'

'Nonsense,' said Kate. 'Mrs McGregor is a most superior person and her home is lovely, as clean as our own. You will be quite at home.'

'As bad as that,' Margaret whispered to her brother.

'I won't see much of her, Mammy,' said Patrick somewhat loudly, 'but it's a nice room with a big tree just outside the window, Liam. I'll sit there and study and pretend I'm at home.'

Could he have said anything better calculated to please his mother? The rest of the day was just as perfect. They spent hours in the castle where Kate cried when she found her brothers' names in the War Memorial. 'I never knew, I never knew,' she sobbed. 'All these years. I wish my da had seen this.'

'Come on then, lass, let's take Margaret to the shops,' said Charlie who had seen some names that had brought back unpleasant memories for him too.

Kate agreed and they walked down Princes Street where Kate thrilled her daughter by buying her a dress in Jenner's, the most wonderful shop Margaret had ever seen in her life. Just wait till George saw her in this.

'Are you not having something for yourself, Kate,' teased Charlie, 'something blue to match your beautiful blue eyes?'

'Away you go with your nonsense, Charlie Inglis,' said Kate although she was pleased at his silliness, 'have we not a son to outfit for the university and fees to pay and lodgings? I'll tell you what we will do for a treat. We'll have a meal in a restaurant, not fish and chips but a proper meal, soup and meat and pudding, and even coffee after. What about that, Miss Inglis?'

'Can I wear my new dress?' breathed Margaret and a side street was found and eyes modestly turned away while she got herself into the dress in the back of the van.

'We'll all have to stay a step behind Miss Jenners here,' said Charlie and Kate looked at their daughter and agreed that, yes Margaret was quite a pretty young woman but there was much more to life than beauty and forbye was it not only skin deep.

'Mammy's just frightened you'll be swept up by yon fellow on the white horse afore you're twenty,' whispered Patrick to his crestfallen sister. 'She thinks you're a right smasher as well.'

Kate heard and was moved by her son's maturity. How she wished she could explain to her daughter all the fears that lurked in her mother's mind. The girl thought marriage was undying passion. There was no such thing; that was only on the celluloid screen the lassie devoured with such enthusiasm. She glanced across at Charlie, nervously trying to find the wee restaurant a guide at the War Museum had recommended. I think I've grown to love him in a sort of way. We're used to one another. Even *that* had settled down to a few mintues once in a while. He's a good man, doesnae drink, or beat up the bairns or me for that matter. Maybe that's all there is if you're lucky. I don't want my wee lassie tied down with weans and a man and work, work, work. Not for a while yet. Maybe she should go to the university. My God, what would Auchenbeath say if Kate Kennedy sent two bairns to the university?

# 14

THE SUMMER PASSED too quickly for everyone, especially Patrick. The news from Europe was bad, for the wee German laddie, whom Margaret had talked about a few years ago, was causing more and more trouble. He had annexed Austria, and then, despite all promises and declarations, had marched into Czechoslovakia. A bloodless annexation of Poland was finally what he wanted and Britain issued an ultimatum. Colm, whose unit had calmly been preparing for a war seen by most as inevitable, had tried for years to prepare his sister for the fact that she had an eighteen-year-old son and that there was going to be a war, at least in Europe.

Kate refused to listen. She had great faith in Chamberlain whom she classed as a perfect English gentleman, someone like Dr Hyslop, well educated, calm in a crisis, reasonable; a man who would never let you down.

Adolf Hitler, unfortunately, was not a middle-class Englishman.

Kate and Charlie left Auchenbeath with Patrick and Liam and everything Kate could find to make her son's life comfortable in Edinburgh after the bakery officially closed at noon on Saturday August 2nd, 1939. Margaret was left with a list of chores to do.

'George'll be up to wash the big van; you could give him a cup of to in the bakery, lass,' suggested Kate, and Margaret did.

'There's a dance the night at the miners' club. Let's go to it, Margaret,' suggested George.

Lovingly Margaret poured him some tea, deliberately pressing close to him as she passed.

'My mam thinks only painted women go to dances.'

'She's away. She'll never know. Come on, for once I can come up here and take you out without having to slink along to the pictures like a criminal.'

The wireless was on, as it always was in the bakery. Margaret and the girls knew all the latest songs by heart. Now some dance music was playing and George got up and pulled Margaret away from the table. They danced frenetically for some minutes and then, exhausted, rested against one another. George pressed Margaret close against him and began to move slowly around the room with her to the beat of the love song now being crooned across the sound waves. She felt him stirring and instinctively pushed herself closer against him. They stopped dancing and stood kissing and stroking until George almost threw her away from him.

'God, you'll get more than you bargained for if we go on like this. I'll away and finish the van.'

Trembling, Margaret sat down on the hard wooden bench. It was wonderful. Love was wonderful. She wanted George to come back, to dance with her again, to kiss her the way he had just done. Clark Gable couldn't kiss like that, nor Ronald Coleman. I'm going to the dance with him, she decided. It would be so nice to go to the miners' club with George, to walk boldly down the main street of Auchenbeath, not to sneak around like a criminal. It was highly unlikely that anyone would tell Kate; she had no casual acquaintances and the women who worked in the bakery were too much in awe of their employer to indulge in gossip in her hearing and if Charlie was told, well, she would handle that problem when it confronted her. She had always been able to deal with him.

George arrived for her at the appointed time. He was quiet on the way into the village.

'It's no right, Margaret,' he finally said, in answer to her questions. 'It's no right we should be seeing each other without your mam knowing.'

'Wait till our Patrick's well settled; she's that nervous the now. She'd take it hard.'

'Take what hard, that you're going out with a common vanman?'

The question was so unexpected that Margaret laughed. 'Don't be daft. My mam has a million faults but being a snob's no one of them. It's just, oh, I don't know, George; it's just not the right time.'

'You know her best, I suppose, but Margaret, would it not be better to tell her afore we . . .'

He stopped and Margaret turned to him breathlessly, 'Afore we what, George?'

'We'd sure enough have to tell her if we want . . . to get married.'

Margaret squeezed his hand tightly. Was that a proposal? Her ideas of love and romance were all culled from Saturday matinées. She should now hear bells and birds and perhaps even glorious music. Better still, George should go down on his knees, singing. Romance had nothing to do with parents and certainly not with a marriage like theirs. What did they know of love, of the passion that had overpowered Rhett Butler when he had carried Scarlett O'Hara up those stairs, the feeling that was surging up inside her now, that made her want to . . . to . . . melt?

'Margaret?' George's voice was funny, as if he was choking somehow. 'Here's the village,' he said, almost as if he were a tour guide. 'I'm looking forward to the dance.

Now, not too many dances with other laddies, you're my girl, Margaret Inglis.'

Heady stuff. She was George's girl, she would not want to dance with anyone else. But she did dance with others. Almost every man in the hall wanted to dance with her. George refused to ask anyone else and, over the shoulders of her partners, she would see him glowering at her from the side and she revelled in the power she had over him and that she seemed to assert over these others. Yet when she danced with George there was such a feeling of rightness that when she was gyrating savagely around with someone else, she ached to be with George instead.

Margaret rejected the sturdy young miner who asked for the next dance.

'I'm with someone,' she said demurely and turned into George's arms.

George was jealous. 'Nice of you to remember. Come on, it's hotter than hell in here. I want a drink.'

Margaret was even thirstier than George. The first two alcoholic drinks she had ever had slid down as easily as the nice cup of tea her mother recommended in hot weather.

'Come on, it's the last dance and I'm dancing it with my girl.'

It could hardly be called dancing. Margaret was un-aware of her feet and could not have given them coherent instructions if she could have found them. She moulded herself to George and he pivoted her around the crowded room, intoxicated not only by too much alcohol but by the smell and feel of her in his arms.

The night air sobered them up a bit and, arms around one another, they stumbled along the road towards the bakery.

'It's bloody cold all of a sudden,' said George.

'If my mam's not back, you can come in for a minute to warm up.'

Margaret had the key to the bakehouse. Even if Kate were back she would be nowhere near the bakery. Only the big van was there. Margaret and George slipped into the nice warm, welcoming bakery. They did not risk a light but stood in the moonlight and one kiss led to another; kisses to which Margaret abandoned herself as she had never been able to do in the back seat of the one-and-three seats at the local picture house. She took off her coat only because it was so hot, and a moment later they were lying on it and George's hands were reaching places he had never hoped to touch. He slipped his hands up inside her blouse and undid her bra and perhaps there was one moment when she could have said no, but she wanted his hands, his mouth. When she felt his hungry mouth closing over her hard little nipple, wetness flowed from that awful place *down there* and she pushed herself against his hardness. She helped him tear off her clothes and she lay stretched out wantonly in the moonlight watching him pull off his own clothes. She could think of nothing but how wonderful he was, and that these feelings which were over-whelming her, had to be appeased. He entered her, pulling her hips up closer and with primal instincts, virgins both, they struggled to satisfy themselves and each other. Even the sudden pain when he thrust more deeply was soothed by the mutual climax that left them lying together, soaked with sweat and overwhelmed by it all. It was better than anything George had ever heard of; no one had ever achieved such a climax, and Margaret lay, her whole body pounding with the fever of lust fulfilled, and glorified in her power.

It was Margaret who returned to reality first. Her temperature cooled and so did her thoughts. She pushed him off and, too late, tried to cover the nakedness she had glorified in a moment before.

'I'm going to Hell,' she wailed and burst into tears, and it was years before she could laugh at the unbelievable astonishment on George's face.

'Quiet,' he managed eventually. 'If your mam's back she'll hear you.'

Mam. Hear her. She would kill her.

'Quick, get dressed, get out.'

'Oh God, oh God,' she muttered as shamefacedly they hurried to dress, turned away from one another, embarrassed by the glimpses of what had appeared so beautiful only a few minutes before.

'Will I see you the morn?' whispered George as she pushed him from the bakery. 'Up the Baker's Burn?'

'I don't know, I don't know, please go.'

She locked the door behind him, picked up her coat and switched on the light to see that no evidence remained. Then she crept up to her room and fell on her knees beside the bed and begged the Virgin Mary not to let her go to Hell. Had it not been dinned into her and every other Catholic child in the village that sex without the sacrament of matrimony was a mortal sin and punishable by banishment from God's presence? She could not go to confession to the new parish priest either. He would recognize her voice and know her for a wicked harlot and he would condemn her, she knew it. Dear Blessed Virgin, why could something so wonderful one minute be dust and ashes the next? I never meant to be bad; how did it happen? Oh, Mam will kill me and I'll go to Hell.

She heard her parents return in the early hours with a tired and tearful Liam and was surprised and frightened when Kate cautiously opened her door. Could it be that her mother cared for her as she cared for Patrick and was peeping in to see that she was safe in her own bed? Perhaps it was because she lay so quiet and still pretending to be asleep that sleep finally came but it did not revive her.

*

Kate roused her early the next morning to go to Mass but was too full of her own awareness that Patrick was no longer there to notice her daughter's unusual quietness and sudden devotion. If she had thought about the girl's bent head and closed eyes at all, she would probably have said high time too.

Margaret was still heavy-eyed when they sat down to breakfast later.

Charlie knew she was not herself. 'What's wrang, lassie? Did you no sleep well? Did we disturb you when we came in this morning?'

It was a yawning and irritable Liam who answered for her. 'I bet she was out canoodling with her click.' Did anything get past the eyes of an observant little boy?

'Shut up, you little squirt.'

Kate was not thinking of her precious Patrick now. 'I've told you about your language before, madame.'

'And what about his language and his spying and creeping . . .?'

'Enough, Margaret, don't talk back to yer mam.' It was Charlie who spoke. 'Sup up your porridge, Liam.' He leaned over to his daughter and touched her hand. 'Have ye got a laddie, Margaret? Somebody at the academy or, wait a minute, who in this wee place could possibly take the place of Clark Gable?' To his amazement, Margaret burst into tears and rushed from the room.

'Girls.' Liam almost spat out the word. 'I'll tell ye, Daddy. Mammy, do you not want to know about our Margaret?'

Charlie grabbed him and something in his face made Liam quiet. 'Away and feed the hens afore I leather your backside.'

Bursting with the awareness of the unfairness of adults, Liam stomped from the room and Charlie turned to his wife who was standing looking out of the window.

'Could our lassie have a boyfriend, Kate?'

'A boyfriend?' The thought had never occurred to Kate. 'She's at the school, far too young to be interested in any of that nonsense.'

'I don't know; she's near seventeen. What are you watching for the postie for? The laddie's hadnae had his breakfast yet, never mind wrote ye a letter. Forbye, it's Sunday.'

Shamefaced, Kate laughed and sat down. 'Daft, isn't it? It's just that . . . he's gone, Charlie. It'll never be the same again. When he comes back for the half term he'll be different, no our laddie at all.'

'Well, that's what ye want, woman. He'll not become a priest if he stays your bairn. Now, let's have a cup of tea and some toast in peace. I'm glad it's Sunday and we can have a rest after that drive.'

# 15

MARGARET SAT UP in her room looking up at the hills. Usually on Sundays she would gaze out of the window thinking that soon she could go up and up that little road to be with George and she would tremble with anticipated delight. But not today. She had had little sleep and her outpouring of repentance and beseeching at Mass had not brought the balm she wanted. She had woken up praying that it had been a bad dream but it had been real. It had happened and she was doomed to everlasting fire. What could she do? She threw herself on the bed. Was it her own fault or was it George's fault, the lustfulness of men? She coloured again at the memory of her wantonness. She had disported herself naked in front of him. It was the beer; it had to have been the beer. She would never have done such a thing in her right mind. And then the memory of how sweet it had been, of the closeness she had achieved, of the rightness of being with George surfaced and she moaned again with remembered ecstasy. It could not be wrong.

She was fast asleep when Liam came rushing up to tell her that 'if you're no down in two minutes to help with the dinner, Mammy's going to skin you alive.'

She felt better after her sleep. How silly she had been. It wasn't too terrible or serious. She loved George and he loved her and everything would be fine. It would never happen again, well – and she giggled to herself – not until they were married. That would be glorious.

George was waiting at the railway bridge on the way to the Baker's Burn. The September sun was shining on his fair head; he looked so beautiful and so dejected that Margaret ached with love for him. They did not touch but turned together and walked up into the country. When they came to the fairy ring where Kate and Charlie had stood not so many years before, they stopped and turned to one another.

'No, no kissing, George, we have to talk first. I mean I don't want any kissing . . .' She stopped and looked at him, his lock of hair falling over his eyes, such sad eyes, like Liam when Charlie could bring himself to punish him.

'I never meant to hurt you, Margaret. I couldn't control myself.'

Margaret smiled. So it had been his fault. Relieved of part of her burden, she took his hand. 'You didn't hurt me, only just at first a wee bit. It was wonderful.' She looked up into his eyes, 'It's just that it's against my religion and you can't do it again.'

He reached for her and she allowed him to pull her into his arms. Very gently and sweetly he kissed her. 'We'll get married as soon as we can.' He kissed her again, more deeply this time and at once she pulled away.

'I meant it, George. No nonsense. Do you realize that if I die right this minute I'll go to Hell for all eternity?'

'What a load of rubbish. We love each other. That's just a way of showing love, real love. Would you do it with anyone else?'

'No, of course not. What do you think I am?'

'Well then, don't be daft. It's only wrong if you do it with different people. We're in love and we're getting married but we'll not do it again in case . . . well, you know.' He looked at her in confusion.

Again the burning pit opened before Margaret's feet. She had never thought of that. 'Oh God, my mother'll kill me.' She threw herself into his arms. 'What am I going to do, George?'

'We'll get married as soon as we can. We'll need to save. I haven't a penny to my name – what with the money I give my mam and the pictures and the dance – but if we just see one another up here I can put by a bit. I'll take care of you, I'll always take care of you.'

She leaned against him. 'But what if . . . you know?'

'We'll away to Gretna Green. Don't worry, I'll not let nothing hurt you, Margaret, ever. I'm no planning to be a

vanman all my life or even to stay in Auchenbeath. I want
a nice house and a decent life for my wife.'

'Your wife, George.' Margaret kissed him tenderly and
did not demur when the kissing grew more and more passionate. His wife, his wife, those beautiful words.

Regretfully she pulled away from him while she
could. 'We'll have to stop, George darling. I'll need to tell
Daddy . . . that we're going out together, and he'll help
me tell my mam, and then, if, well if everything's fine,
we could maybe tell them at Christmas that we want to
get married. Don't you think Christmas would be a nice
time to get engaged, and then we could get married after
my birthday?'

But they did not tell Charlie or Kate that Sunday for
when Margaret got back to the bakery that evening she
found out what most of Britain already knew. At six
o'clock, while many of his subjects were enjoying their tea,
the king had broadcast to the Empire. Britain was once
more at war.

Kate's sole concern was for her son. She remembered
1914 and her brothers and Charlie and how they could
hardly wait to throw themselves into the hands of the rav-
enous war machine. Charlie was too old and too frail, but
Patrick? He must not be infected by the patriotism that
would no doubt be fuelled by skilful politicians who did
not have to fight themselves. She telephoned and then sat

down to write Patrick her first letter in which she reinforced everything she had said on the telephone. He would be more useful to the world as a priest, a man of God, and so he must, absolutely must, resist all desires to fight for king and country. He was to stay at the university.

'I pray to God he gets the chance to stay at the university, Kate. If there's a war like the last one, he'll have no option,' said Charlie.

'He's a baby.'

'He's older than Kevin was when he was killed.'

Kate stared at her husband, aghast at his brutality, and to their mutual surprise, like their daughter a few hours before, Kate burst into tears.

It was her daughter who comforted her. 'Don't cry, Mammy. Here, sit down and I'll get you another cup of tea. They'll no call up university laddies; it'll be the working men that goes first, the ones without privileges.'

Kate looked up at her daughter. There was something in the girl's voice, some bitterness. 'I believed Mr Chamberlain. Did he not tell us he'd sat down with Hitler and they said no war? Peace in our time, he said, and I believed him.'

'He believed it himself, Mam. But it'll no last long this time, no with all the airplanes and things. It cannae last long.'

# 16

EDINBURGH AND THE university completely overwhelmed Patrick for his first few weeks. He was constantly exhausted, by work, by the long walks back and forward from his digs in Morningside and from the heady excitement of being away from home and actually at the university. He panicked at lectures because he could not write quickly enough to put down, word for word, everything the professors said. Eventually he worked out a shorthand that he could understand, and spent his evenings rewriting his notes so that they became more comprehensible. At last he was able to hold his head above the water and look around. The first thing he saw was a girl, Fiona Rutherford.

'Do you mind if I sit down?'

He looked up from the book he was reading and there she stood, as small and dainty as his sister Margaret, but not nearly so pretty. She had shocking red hair, freckles, and the merriest green eyes. He couldn't help smiling back.

'Please,' he stammered, getting to his feet.

'I'm Fiona Rutherford,' she said as she put down her tray. 'I'm in one of your classes.'

How easy she was to talk to. Patrick was basically very shy and, because of his shyness, had grown up knowing only two women really well. Fiona was not like either Kate or Margaret. She bubbled over with life and interest. By the time they had finished their lunch, not their dinner, Patrick knew that her father had been a Church of Scotland Minister in Perthshire and that he had died of tuberculosis when Fiona was a baby. She had wanted to be a painter but since her mother had pointed out that art did not pay she had decided to teach English instead. Fiona knew everything about Patrick except that he wanted to be a priest.

I wasn't being dishonest, he told himself later as he went over his self examination of the day's events. It's too precious and too doubtful yet; I don't want anything to intrude on it in case it gets spoiled.

He had also promised to join a Great Books Club. Fiona had joined almost every society she could find time for.

'You owe it to yourself and your parents to get as much out of university as possible, Patrick,' Fiona said. 'Join everything and drop the ones you don't like.'

'I couldn't spare the time for more than one, Fiona; I'm not really very clever. But my mam wants me to join things; I may even be able to go on hill walks some Saturdays.'

'Good,' smiled Fiona. 'I'll see you on the Pentlands then.'

Patrick blossomed. Where before he had lived for Sundays when he could go to Mass and pour out his love and fears and doubts, he now found that Wednesdays became more important because Wednesday was Great Books day and it was the day that he could sit in class and watch Fiona Rutherford's animated little face as she listened to the lecturer. She never made notes.

'He's so wonderful, Patrick; it's easy to remember. I write it up in the dorm.'

And so she did, for when Patrick found that he'd missed something important because of watching her, Fiona was able to tell him what Dr Fenn-Smith had said.

He looked out for her during the rest of the week and sometimes saw her and the day brightened. She drew people to her like moths to a light and was always surrounded by other students, laughing, talking, even – to his horror – smoking. If she saw him she smiled and waved and gestured to him to join them but he was always too shy. It was enough to see her. In another age he would have practised self-flagellation and often, on his knees at night, wondered whether he should punish his body for the thoughts he could not banish from his mind. For a few days he would avoid the Students' Union altogether and then he would find himself turning up for a Pentland walk.

'I need fresh air; I need fresh air. It's got nothing to do with Fiona,' and he knew he lied. And so the first term ended.

Patrick went home for Christmas, his first term's exams successfully, if not triumphantly, completed. Kate decided to put all the worries about war, together with the niggling little doubts she had about Margaret's well-being, behind her for the holidays. The girl had been acting uncharacteristically, one moment singing the latest love song until Kate thought she would scream with the boredom of its repetitions, the next creeping around the house in the blackest of moods and refusing to answer any questions with anything but 'leave me alone, I'm fine.'

Patrick was himself; more than four months away from her and not a bit changed. She was overjoyed. The family sat eagerly around the fire and listened to him talk, for had he not seen and done so much that they had never experienced. To Kate's great joy he had taken her advice and had joined a literary society for recreation. He told Kate and Charlie all about the meetings and the group of enthusiastic young students who formed the group. Kate was so preoccupied remembering her own aborted schooldays that she failed to notice that one name came up more than any other and it was not that of a writer; unless, perhaps, there was a writer called 'Fiona Says'. As usual Kate heard only what she wanted to hear and she soaked up all Patrick could tell her about the world of books.

'I've a whole lot back with me, Mam. You should read them, Dickens and Dostoevesky, Jane Austen and F. Scott Fitzgerald but you probably wouldn't like him so much, and lots of others.'

His soft lowland speech had refined itself, the speech of an educated man.

'Does he not sound like a man of the world, Charlie?' Kate asked in the big bed on Patrick's first night home. 'Nothing put on, or trying to sound like Doctor Hyslop, but just nice grammar.'

'That's what you've always wanted, Katie,' agreed Charlie, 'just as long as he doesn't ever get above himself and look down on his illiterate old father. Mind you,' he added with a laugh, 'seems to me it would depend on what Fiona says.'

'What are you talking about, Charlie? To get too big for his boots is not in his nature,' protested Kate. 'That's more like our Margaret. I was glad she behaved herself the night and enjoyed being in listening to her brother. She's done some gallivanting this year; I don't know how she passed her exams.'

'She's clever, Katie, like her mammy.'

Modestly Kate denied this but she revelled in the unusual compliment and vowed to start reading Patrick's books. Hadn't she promised herself for years to read *A Tale of Two Cities*? Surely now she could find the time? She would even try the Irish fellow – he had to be Irish with a name like Fitzgerald. He wasn't, of course, and Patrick was right. She did not like him.

The family were all together for New Year's Day, except Colm who was with his regiment somewhere ... They had driven down in the big van to see Deirdre, whose two eldest sons had already joined the army.

'They didnae want to wait to be conscripted; this way they got to choose their own regiments, Borderers, just like their daddy and their uncles.' Deirdre seemed proud and not at all worried. 'And what about you, our Pat? Will they call up you clever laddies?'

'No they won't,' said Kate before Patrick could speak. 'Let's not talk about war the day. It doesnae seem like a real war anyway, not like the last one where we were in right from the start.'

'It's real enough, Mam,' said Patrick, 'and it's going to get a lot worse.'

He was right. By May of 1940 Norway had been overrun by Germany and many people blamed the hesitations and procrastinations of the Chamberlain Government. Sir Archibald Sinclair said that the trouble was that Britain was working a one-shift war while the Germans were working three shifts. Amery quoted Oliver Cromwell when he spoke in 1652 to the Long Parliament which he thought was no longer fit to run the affairs of the nation. 'You have sat here too long. . . . In the name of God go.' And, helped along by Winston Churchill's brilliance, the Government went. On 10th May 1940, Winston Churchill became prime minister.

Patrick telephoned. 'Did you hear his speech, Mam? Isn't he great? Fiona says with a leader like him, we'll easily beat the Germans, you'll see.'

For Kate it was merely echoes of 'over by Christmas'. 'You'll no do anything daft, Patrick; you'll not join up?'

Patrick hesitated. Fighting for justice wasn't daft. Watching Fiona Rutherford, listening to her speak, admiring the way her green eyes flashed with anger or amusement; that was daft. 'If I pass my exams, Mam, it'll mean God wants me to stay.'

'You'll pass, of course you'll pass. Study hard.'

'He was that excited, Charlie,' she told her husband. 'He's all fired up. And you were right about his having a new wee friend. Fiona something or other. Oh, what will I do if he joins up? And where's Margaret? If that girl's been in one night this week . . .'

'She's playing tennis, Kate. There's no harm in that. Even George belongs to the wee club they've got there. All the young folks are in it.'

'Aye, I suppose tennis is safe enough. Never did our Bridie any harm. Mind you, she never found a man there, if she was looking for one. I worry about her sometimes as if I let her down, never really looked after her the way I promised my mam. She waits hand and foot on your auntie . . .'

'Her step-mother,' broke in Charlie.

'Who's perfectly capable of running a duster round the place.'

'Colm,' Charlie won the argument. 'Till Colm marries, she'll stay wi' him.'

Kate was quiet. If she hadn't married Charlie she would be looking after Colm. Would Bridie have married? Had there been a nice fellow at the tennis club? Was there a nice fellow there who interested Margaret? In the privacy of darkness she could admit to herself that her daughter was a very pretty young woman, girl, she was still a girl. Maybe it was her fault that the girl was so reticent with her. They hadn't sat down to talk to one another in . . . Had she ever sat down to talk to her children? Patrick, perhaps. She had almost always found time for Patrick. And Liam? He needed discipline. Charlie spoiled him. Not even fifteen yet and he had been at that tennis club till nearly midnight. Was Margaret in yet? Pity tomorrow was Monday and the busiest working day of the week but she would make an effort, she would find time to discuss further education with the girl. Maybe girls *should* become doctors and lawyers and such. There were plenty of women in Patrick's classes and in his Literary Society, this Fiona – giving her opinion of Winston Churchill. *Am I doing right, Mam, sending her to the university? I failed Bridie. I think though, Bridie always seems to be happy, especially with my bairns to spoil.* She rolled over. 'Charlie, what do you think about sending our Margaret to the university with Patrick?' But Charlie was already asleep.

Long before Christmas Margaret had realized she was not pregnant. Her first period after her 'indiscretion' with George had been a few days late and she had gone almost mad with terror. One thing to tell Kate that she wanted to marry her vanman, another to tell her that she had anticipated matrimony and had been punished accordingly. Never had she been so relieved to see those stains in her knickers.

'We got away with it, George, this time, but until we're married it mustn't happen again.'

George held her gently. 'You had me near as scared as you, sweetheart. See, God wasn't angry for what we did. It was natural. You're my woman now and we'll tell your parents that we want to get married.'

'No!' Margaret almost shouted. 'Then she'll know I've been deceiving her and she'll be furious. We'll build up to it gradually. She's been at me to work harder, not in the bakery, at the school, and she's frightened Patrick fails and gets called up. What about you, George? Some lads have been conscripted since last May when they were still telling us there wasn't going to be a war. Will you get called up? You'll not volunteer?'

'I'm no daft, Margaret, but I'll have to go if I'm wanted, and I want everything right between us afore then.'

She interrupted by kissing him passionately but he did not respond.

'I meant all right with your parents. If you're not ashamed of me, tell your mam, or is it that you don't know whether you want to marry me or not?'

'Of course I want to marry you, especially after . . . but we're so young. I'm only sixteen, George. My mam wanted me to leave the school last year and work in the bakery. I like being at school learning things, I wanted to go to the university. I'm far brainier than poor Father Pat.'

'Too brainy to get stuck with a vanman, especially one that could get called up and killed.'

He turned away from her and began to stride towards the village.

'George, no, don't leave me. I'll do anything . . .' He turned towards her and in the moonlight his pale face and hair shone with an almost ethereal light. 'I'd die if anything happened to you.'

'I'll no get killed,' he muttered into her hair, 'and I'm no going to be a vanman for ever. There's money to be made out of this war, Margaret, and I'm going to make it.' He looked down at her lovely face, at the tears glistening on the ridiculously long lashes and then gently he kissed them away. 'My brother told me how to do it so you won't get caught,' he whispered and began to kiss her softly and then, as she relaxed against him, more urgently, parting her warm, moist lips with his tongue.

She struggled a little, protesting, 'It's wrong, George,' but the feelings she had been stifling since September awoke and began to scream for relief, and she responded with all her passionate young body. He grasped her hand and began to run, pulling her along with him, until they reached the shelter of the wood. The pine needles lay thick and dry under the trees and he pushed her down and they struggled to remove as much of their clothing as was necessary.

It wasn't right and wonderful as it had been the first time; in fact it was almost distasteful. Margaret was aware of her skirt round her waist and her knickers round her ankles and she wanted to protest, 'No, not like this.' Then he began to touch her and in spite of herself desire for him overpowered her. When he pushed himself into her she was almost as ready for him as she had been that night in the bakery. She climaxed quickly and lay there looking up through the branches to the starlit sky and waited while George moved violently on her soft belly. She felt the cold earth under her and held his head against her and tried to feel primitive and all-powerful but all she felt was the November cold seeping into her bones. Eventually he lay still.

'Jesus, it's cold,' he said. 'Come on, we'll get our death up here.'

On the way to the bakery he pressed her again to talk to her parents. 'We was supposed to announce our engagement at Christmas and here it is November and they don't even know we're walking out.'

Kate was sitting at the fire when Margaret breathlessly opened the door.

'Where have you been and don't tell me the pictures because the late show finishes at just after ten?'

Margaret was terrified. Was there dirt on her coat? Was her hair too untidy? 'I was at the pictures, Mam, and then we went for chips to the Tallies.'

'With the good food you get here you have to fill yourself with that greasy food. I'm all for helping poor refugees, Margaret, but I don't want you standing around that wee cafe with all the riffraff from the village.'

'There's nowhere else to go, Mam, just the miners' club and you don't like me going there either because of the drink.'

'You could bring the lassies here, miss. Haven't we provided a lovely home for you?'

'Yes, Mam, I'm sorry. I'll do that.' Margaret edged towards the door. If Kate shouted her back with, 'What's that mud on your skirt?' Please God, please, don't let her find out and I'll never do it again. But Kate was already turning down the gas mantles and, apart from the glow from the ashes in the grate, the room was dark.

'I know it's Saturday, Margaret, but I don't want you washing your hair for Mass tonight; it's far too late.'

Dutifully Margaret agreed and, closing the door, fled along the corridor to the haven of her room. Her knickers were full of pine needles. They were all over the place. My God, I've left a trail; she'll kill me. She put on her dressing gown and lay on the bed waiting for her mother to fall asleep so that she could go to see if any pine needles were on the carpets. Her stomach felt sticky. That wasn't romantic; nothing beautiful and right about skulking under a tree like an animal and after a few minutes of intense feeling there had been nothing but awareness of the damp and the cold. And it's wrong; whatever George says, it's wrong. I had a chance there to tell Mam. Why didn't I? Because I was too scared and if she finds any pine needles she'll know I was lying to her. Oh, God, Mam, go to sleep so's I can have a bath and wash this off. She got up and crept to the door. All was quiet. She would risk it. She crept back to the front room and turned up the gas. She was exhausted by the time she had crawled inch by inch over the floor picking up pine needles here and there, not many, but enough for Kate to wonder and, Margaret thought, her mother was far from stupid. She would know immediately that they didn't come from the chip shop.

The next day was wet and cold, the kind of November day that makes staying beside a roaring fire with a good book an ideal occupation, but Margaret couldn't settle. What was the point? Why study for Highers if Kate was going to insist that she leave school and work in the bakery? Why study if she was going to marry George? Marriage didn't take brains. Surreptitiously she looked at her parents. Kate was writing a long letter. What did she find to say to her precious Patrick every Sunday? Charlie was struggling with a jigsaw with Liam who was good-naturedly taking out most of the pieces Charlie was putting in. Her father was only pretending to be stupid, she knew. Mind you, he wasn't all that bright. Kate was the bright one. Why had she married Charlie? They could never have felt as she and George felt, could they? Her icy mother (whose eyes softened only when they looked at Patrick) and her poor father with his weak chest locked in a soul-stirring embrace was a ludicrous picture. She remembered yesterday afternoon in the bakery watching George loading the van. She loved looking at him, touching him, being kissed by him, making love. Had Kate ever felt like that with Charlie? She looked at the book in her lap. Was there anything wrong in wanting to have George and an education too? God, life was complicated, and there was her soul too. She had gone to communion that morning because if she had not Kate would have wanted to know why. Walking down the aisle to receive the wafer she had had a moment of terror that God would choose to punish her for her wickedness right there in front of the entire Catholic population of the village; she had expected a lightning bolt to strike her dead to her mother's everlasting shame in the village. It hadn't come. Was God too busy with the war? She had not been making a good confession in months either. She wanted to stop going. She wanted to go and say, I made love to my boyfriend, and thus get the whole sorry mess off her shoulders. But she could do neither. She was a wicked, proud girl. God would forgive her if she was truly sorry. Surely Father Brady would not judge her. He would not shake his head sorrowfully every time he saw her in the village. She knew that but still she could not tell him.

The winter passed. Margaret lost weight. She couldn't sleep, she couldn't eat. Patrick came for Christmas and still Margaret could never find words to explain her feelings to her mother; she could not talk about getting engaged when her parents didn't even know she was walking out and worse. And then there was Patrick.

He was talking about the air force and one's duty to humanity and Kate was distraught with fear that he would do something stupid. She took a day off, an unheard-of occurrence, and Charlie drove her to Edinburgh to confront their son. Margaret was left in charge of the bakery.

George came of course. They made love. She had not intended it to happen but one kiss led to another and somehow she or George had pushed them along the passage to her bedroom and they were naked in the bed and it was the most wonderful experience that anyone had ever had in the entire world, until Margaret came to her senses. He had not withdrawn.

'Jesus Christ,' George almost screamed at the girl sobbing into her pillow, 'God will not send you to Hell. Hitler'll go to Hell.'

'And so will I, George. You're not supposed to make love till you're married.'

'We make love and everything's wonderful and I feel I'm the luckiest man in the world. I've got it all. The next minute you make me feel like I should be flogged at the cart's tail, or whatever it is they do with, what is they cry them . . . seducers. I thought you wanted it too. I don't remember ever forcing you. You want it and then when you've had it you do this going to Hell bit. I'm getting bloody fed up. I don't know why you're so scared of your mam; she's aye been a good boss to me but if you can't talk to her . . . let's get married on our own for I'm fed up.

It's near a year, Margaret. Either it's all over, or I find out about Gretna Green and you come away with me.'

'We can't get married in the church?'

'Not unless you tell your mam.'

'My mam hardly knows I exist. The only person exists for her is her precious Father Pat. She'll not take a day off the day I run away.'

'Maybe it's for the best this way. I'll never make anything of myself working for your mam. I'll find out about marrying in Gretna and you have a few things in a bag and we'll leave from the tennis club one night.'

When he had gone, Margaret tidied up and packed her schoolbag with a few of her favourite clothes. The decision made, she was very calm. It was the right, the only thing to do. She returned to the bakery in case there were afternoon customers. *I wish I could get married in church, in a beautiful white dress. One day though.*

They met at the tennis club and George had Kate's small van. 'We cannae steal this. After we're married we'll leave it at the nearest station with a note.'

'Why, Charlie?' said Kate when she eventually read the note. 'She never even said she liked the laddie. Why should she do this? George always seemed such a nice lad despite the awful parents. What was the need for all this underhand business? Goodness, I only want the best for my children. I've tried to bring her up to know that and, all right, I did want better than a vanman for her; that's what I've worked for. Could she not see that?'

Charlie could only stare mutely at her. 'She should have told me,' he said. 'I would have protected her.'

Protected her, Kate thought. From whom? George . . . or me?

# 17

KATE AND CHARLIE received a letter from Margaret a month after the wedding. In it she told them that she was happy, that she knew she should have spoken to them about her love for George but she hoped that they would forgive her. She and George were legally married and she would try to make everything right with the Church as soon as possible. They already had good jobs, she in a factory and George at the shipyards – they were desperate for workers in Glasgow – and they had a little flat. As soon as it was really nice she would invite her parents to come to see her.

Kate read the letter which had come in the post together with a letter from Patrick in which he spoke about the obscenity of war. Was there, he asked, an even greater obscenity in young men who should be fighting to remove the blight from Europe, wasting their time in lecture halls, filling their heads with knowledge and principles which would do them no good in the world which Hitler and his ilk planned to create?

Margaret received a short answer to her plea for understanding. She was assured of her mother's love, but, that same mother asked, what had possessed her to carry on behind her back? She was also very hurt and disappointed by George. Why had he not straightforwardly asked for permission to marry her daughter, and did he realize what a predicament he had left the business in by going off like that? She also included an extremely generous cheque. She didn't say so but she hoped Margaret would use it to make the flat nicer more quickly so that she could then carry through her promise of inviting her parents to visit.

'What did I do wrong, Charlie? What possessed her? I've worked and worked so that she wouldn't have to, so that she'd have a better life than mine and what does she do? What made her run off with the vanman?'

Charlie looked at her sadly. 'She maybe had to.'

Kate stared at her husband. She was unaware of the talk in the village. To the villagers there was only one reason for a young girl to run away from home. A bun in the oven, they said. Serve hoighty-toighty Kate Kennedy right. That would teach her to think she was better than the rest of the village; her precious Margaret was not the first lassie to wed in a hurry.

Charlie had heard the talk and agreed with it, but had said nothing to Kate. She would learn of it soon enough.

'No,' she gasped, 'not my Margaret. She wouldn't do such a thing. It was George, wasn't it? You and your precious tennis club, running about half dressed. We'll be the laughing stock of the entire village. Wait till you see the custom that finds its way to the bakery.' In her distress she unconsciously wrapped her arms round her body as if to seek comfort from someone, even herself, and returned to her first problem. Why had Margaret not discussed George with her own mother? Where had she gone wrong that her only daughter could not confide in her?

'Charlie, was I too strict with her? Should I have told her we were thinking of letting her go to the university too? She's only seventeen, a bairn, Charlie, just a bairn.' She moved around the room, picking things up and putting them down, tears of which she was unaware streaming down her face, and took refuge in anger. 'I never want to see her again.'

'Oh, lassie, lassie,' cried Charlie. 'You cannot mean that. It's grief and hurt that's talking. The blame's no all yours, Kate. She could have told me and she didn't, and I'll carry that grief with me to the end of ma days but I'm no throwin' out my own wee bairn.'

She rounded on him, the need to hurt someone paramount. 'Aye, you spoiled her, Charlie Inglis. One smile from her and you did what she wanted. You would have let her marry her precious George.'

'Aye, I would, and why she didnae talk tae me, I'll never understand. I'll ask her just as soon as she walks in that door.'

Kate looked at him and knew that his mind was made up. He did not often force his opinions or wants on the family but when he did no argument could move him. She hadn't meant what she had said about not seeing Margaret either. That had been anger and unhappiness talking. 'George isn't welcome,' she said. 'Not a bit of character in that entire family.'

She tried to put Margaret's possible condition out of her mind and set herself to finding a second driver.

'As if rationing wasnae enough to contend with,' she complained. 'Now with the call-up I've had just two replies to my advert for Geo . . . that job.' Nothing would make her say George's name again. 'I wouldnae let either one of the dottery old souls near a bike let alone a van. It'll be a grand summer job for Patrick if you can manage for a few weeks, Charlie. Here's all this carry on over Margaret, and now Patrick's trying to talk himself into joining up. Best have him work here for the summer. You help me persuade him that feeding the nation's a war effort an all.'

'Why don't you learn to drive yersel', Kate? You don't need to be in the bakery every minute. Go out and meet your customers instead of stayin' cooped up here.'

The idea did not appeal, especially now that her customers, she felt, would be avid for further scandal about Margaret. Well, they would get nothing from her. In the bakery Kate became even more remote from her bakers, speaking to them politely, but only when absolutely necessary. Apart from attendance at daily Mass, her few excursions had been to see Bridie or to do such shopping as could be done in the village. She got into the habit now of telephoning her order and having Charlie fetch it in the van. They had no real friends of their own generation. In their early married life they had had no money for entertaining, then they were too busy with work and children, and Charlie had never really been well. He tired easily and after work he liked to sit in his chair by the fire as Liam had done, and to watch and listen to his children. Charlie had his wireless for companionship. Kate had her work and her letters to her son. She would try to have Charlie or even Liam communicate with Margaret. Her own letters were bound to be stilted. How could she pour out on paper what she had never been able to say face to face? For one thing, if she confessed to her daughter that she had never really been 'in love' with Charlie and that she had always wanted something better for her child she would be being disloyal to Charlie who must never ever know that she did not love him. Or did she? Charlie, dear, sweet Charlie who surely deserved so much more than she had given him. I love him now, she admitted to herself, but I could never tell him. Why not? He never, ever said he loved her. 'That was rare,' at the end of *that*. Was that the same as 'I love you, Kate'? Not for Margaret, not for her child; no fear or trembling or distaste. For Margaret it had to be special; that was why she had worked so hard.

She could speak to her priest.

'Is it yourself or Margaret you're thinking about, Kate?'

'I don't know, Father.' As always, Kate strove for total honesty with herself. 'I'm hurt and I'm angry and embarrassed to walk all the way down the Main Street to get here. I feel everyone's looking at me and laughing. You see, I wouldn't let her play with most of the village children, just one or two from better homes, clean homes. I'm not sorry for myself, Father, but I've worked so hard, every hour God gave man, and it was all so's my bairns could have a better life than mine. I was going to let her go to the university; I should have told her but I'd always thought of the bakery for her ... money for Patrick to get him through but the bakery for Margaret. A good job, independence. I had a chance, years ago, to get really big and I turned it down because I was scared, and I didn't have much schooling but Margaret could have done it. She's got the education. She'll not be pressured into marriage, I thought, not throw herself away. Marriage for me hasn't been easy, Father; my own fault probably, but I wanted better for my lassie.'

'What makes you think George isn't right for Margaret?'

She looked at him. What could he possibly know of the intimate and, to her, degrading side of marriage? 'She's just turned seventeen, Father. Marriage to her is what she sees on the Saturday pictures, lovely music, roses. It's not like that. It's being up night after night with fretting weans and walking the floor with them at all hours so your man can get some sleep, and working till your half dead on your feet to pay the rent and put food in their mouths.'

'Loving George and being loved by him will let her hear the music, Kate. At least enough of the time to make it worthwhile.'

Oh to have the courage to shout out, 'Sanctimonious twaddle.' Was that what he saw when he walked around the village, people with nothing who thought it all worthwhile because of love? If he wasn't a priest she would say he saw too many Saturday matinées himself.

'And there are the children,' he went on, 'they make it worthwhile.'

Her face softened. 'Enough of the time to make it worthwhile, Father.'

'You'll let Margaret know that she's welcome?'

'Aye, but how I wish I could understand where I went wrong.'

Briskly she walked back through the village. She felt a little better after her chat with Father Brady. At least he was more responsive than her mother or that pheasant she had talked to all those years ago in the cottage garden. I've failed with my daughter but there are my sons. Liam will have the bakery when he leaves the school, and there's Patrick. How many women would he comfort in the years ahead? It was a glorious vision. He must not leave the university.

He passed his examinations, not well but he passed, and he came home for the long summer holidays. Summer 1940.

Night after night they sat together with the blackout curtains stretched across the Toll House windows and prayed for the people in London and the south of England. One night a bomb fell on the Main Street, the only bomb ever to hit Auchenbeath.

They had heard the planes flying low overhead, that horrible, low humming noise. Were they friends, were they enemies?

'It's the Luftwaffe,' called Liam excitedly, 'I wish I could see them. Let me go out, Dad.'

Patrick grabbed his brother who was heading for the door. 'No, you fool, that one sounds too low.'

'They'll not bomb Auchenbeath,' said Liam struggling fiercely in his brother's surprisingly strong grip. 'They're away to bomb the bridges on the Forth and the Clyde.'

And then he stayed, paralysed in his brother's arms as there came that frightening whistle, heard too often over London that awful summer but never before over Auchenbeath. There was a loud dull thump and the house shook and ornaments, including Mary Kate's wally dug, Kate's greatest treasure, were thrown from the mantelpiece and shattered on the hearth below.

'Jesus Christ,' prayed Charlie, 'we've been hit. Put out that lamp, Patrick, I'm away to open the door.'

'I'll get our gas masks,' said Liam excitedly. 'Wait, Daddy.'

'No,' screamed Kate, 'Patrick, stay here. You too, Liam.'

She grabbed her younger son and held him back forcibly while Charlie and Patrick ran out onto the Main Street. The night was alight with the flames from a fire and there were already people running from all over the village towards it. Liam pulled himself from her arms and she hurried after him into the night. About halfway down the street flames were shooting into the sky which was now empty.

'It's the Co-op, Dad,' said Liam, who had caught up with his father and brother.

Patrick was laughing, half through hysteria and relief and half through genuine mirth. 'No, Liam, Jerry did us a favour. He dropped his bomb on the local eyesore.'

And so he had. A bomber limping home after one of the nightly raids on London had shed the remains of his cargo as he headed for the sea and Germany and it had hit the ghastly brick structure which some well-meaning town council had erected to fill what they saw as the pressing personal needs of the occasional lorry driver who visited Auchenbeath on his way up or down the Great North Road.

Kate stood silently and watched the flames destroy the little building but it was not the remains of the public lavatory she saw but the pit at Auchenbeath all those years ago when she had been looking for the doctor. The voices of the Civil Defence unit and the wardens as they scurried around were the voices of women waiting for their men, their husbands, their sons. She forced herself back to 1940.

'Come on, Liam,' she pulled at her younger son's resisting arm. 'We can do nothing here and no one has been hurt, thank God.'

'No, I want to watch. I've never seen a fire. We've been bombed, Patrick. Will we be on the wireless like London and all they places?'

'Sweet Jesus,' groaned Patrick. 'Auchenbeath and London. We shouldn't say them in the same breath.'

Auchenbeath got its mention, at least in the local press, but it was a very small item since that night had been one of the worst nights of the summer for Britain. The skies above the gallant little island nation had been crossed and recrossed by the enemy in their attempt to totally destroy the capital, and by those immortal little British Spitfires which had sent the survivors back across the sea dropping their unused bombs anywhere as they desperately sought their own safety.

For the rest of the long university break, Patrick spent many of his free hours in the little chapel. His mother was not so delighted as she thought she would have been.

'He wants to join up, Charlie. He's got chums in Clydebank and Edinburgh and some of the laddies have already left and joined the air force. Help me talk him into staying at the university,' begged Kate.

'We fought so that they wouldn't have to'. Charlie was staring at pictures only he could see in the fireplace where a small fire burned to combat the late evening chill, 'And, my God, what was it for? Never again, we said. Yer brothers, most of my friends. Our bairns'll be safe, we said; we've saved the world for them, we said.' He looked up at her. 'I dinnae want my laddie in the war, Kate, but he'll maybe have no choice if he waits.'

Kate was desperate. 'Patrick's precious air force has saved us. That's what the papers are saying. The German air force is gone, useless; the war'll end now and he should stay and finish his education so's he can help the way he's best fitted for when the laddies get back.'

Charlie looked at her for a full minute. 'It's not over, Kate. Face reality. It's just started.'

And so it seemed.

The Battle of Britain went on into September as Germany desperately tried to crush her cocky little enemy. Seven hundred British pilots and crews died, but in death they were victorious. Patrick, still torn by conflicting emotions, returned to Edinburgh and his studies.

'They're bound to call me up this term, Mam. Maybe I should enlist in the air force. I should have been up there this summer.'

'They were near all killed, Patrick. God has other plans for you. Accept his will,' Kate reasoned despairingly.

Patrick put his arms round her in an unfamiliar, consoling gesture. 'I won't die if I'm meant to be a priest, Mam.' With that Kate had to be content.

The war not only went on; it escalated. Kate hired a woman to drive the van. Bessie had driven a field ambulance in the First War and had never touched a vehicle since.

'I tried for this one, Mrs Inglis, and if it gets much worse, and it will, and they change their minds, I'll go. Too old, they said; why, I could drive this van right up the Miller's Burn and not spill a pie.'

'Cows don't buy pies,' said Kate drily. 'If you can keep the van on the main road between here and Thornhill I'll be pleased enough.'

With petrol rationing, Charlie, and Liam when he wasn't at school, found themselves two-wheeled transportation. Kate put the big van in storage and pies were delivered locally on bikes, but sales and profits fell drastically.

Molly died in the spring of 1941 and Bridie, who had found herself, through Colm's foresight, the legal tenant of their council house, decided to stay to make a home for her brother for when the war ended.

'I get money from the army as his dependent, Kate,' she said when Kate tried to persuade her to do something else with her life. 'I'll be here to help him when he gets back if he needs me. We'll grow old together.'

'Don't be daft, Bridie.' Kate was angry. 'You're not forty yet; you could marry, have children.'

'I'm going to sit out the war doing nothing. You should try it, Kate. Leisure's a grand thing.'

But Kate couldn't sit, especially after Deirdre's two boys were lost in the summer of 1941. She was often on the bus between Auchenbeath and Thornhill. Deirdre, who had seemed so jaunty just a year ago, had shrivelled up like an old plum in just a few days, and Kate sat and talked to her or cleaned her house around her, or stood in Deirdre's kitchen and cooked and talked and waited for Deirdre to answer her, to say anything.

'I don't need to go to school, Auntie Kate,' Alice, Deirdre's oldest girl, said resentfully, 'I can stay at home and look after Mam. The doctor says it'll just take time.'

'Your mother likes you to go to school, don't you, Deirdre love?' said Kate to the silent form in the chair, but Deirdre sat, rocking tirelessly, pressing invisible babies to her empty breasts.

'I'll need to go if I'm to catch the last bus, Alice. I'll be back on Saturday.' At the door she turned, 'Talk to your dad about that chair. He should maybe burn it or put it in an outhouse till your mam gets better.'

She walked the mile to the main road alone. Before, when Kate and Charlie and their children had visited, one or more of Deirdre's lively children had skipped along beside their auntie who always brought chocolate or new clothes, but now they would not leave Deirdre even to walk through the wood with her.

Who'd stay with me if my mind went? It was a tired and dispirited Kate who allowed herself a little self pity. Liam wouldn't notice I was ill unless I fell in the engine he was tinkering with. Margaret, dear God, Margaret. Margaret who had confounded the gossips of Auchenbeath by not producing a child in her first few months of marriage. Here she was now, months later, and still no word of a child. Not that Kate was in a hurry to become a grandmother. She was still not reconciled to her daughter although Charlie and Liam had both gone to see Margaret in war-torn Glasgow. Kate had been in a state all the time they were gone. What if a bomb should drop on them – but she had to have first-hand news of her daughter; she had to know that Margaret's letters were not a sham and that her child was indeed happy in her marriage.

George, it seemed, had something called asthma, and had failed his physical.

'God knows what they're paying in the shipyards, Kate, but they're living like kings,' was Charlie's awed announcement.

Where was George's money coming from? One more worry. And Patrick, never robust and lately more emaciated than ever. She had never thought of him as pretty but the thinness accentuated his dark eyes and his face was almost ethereal in its beauty.

'There's more eating that laddie than guilt about not being in the war,' Charlie had said once and Kate, whose innate honesty compelled her to agree with him, had taken refuge in anger again.

'All of a sudden you know everything about Patrick. You paid little heed to him for years and now you can see inside his head.'

'When did you ever let me pay attention to him? Once or twice on the cart with his daddy, but he was aye Mammy's precious bairn, wasn't he, Mammy's precious boy that she was going to make a priest.'

Kate reeled back from the unexpected attack. 'I never forced him. You can't say that. You cannae force a vocation, Charlie.'

'You damn well tried.'

'I never did. I wouldn't even let myself pray for such a blessing on this house.'

They stared at one another and then turned away, silent. Too much had been said already but more guilt had been added to Kate's burden. Something was bothering Patrick. Was he in doubt about his vocation? Was he unhappy at the university? Surely he had been glad to go, to be the first person ever in the Kennedy or Inglis households to remain in full-time education. She turned to her sure comfort. *I'm right, am I not, Mam? The laddie should have the benefit of a grand education and then, if he wants to be a priest at the end of it, after meeting all the folks from all parts, will he not be a better shepherd to his flock? They're no all unlettered folk like us in the Catholic Church.*

Liam got fed up with the strained atmosphere and took himself off, without a word, to Margaret in Glasgow.

They didn't even know he was gone until one night the telephone rang. Charlie answered it for he knew that at night the caller was usually Margaret. He listened for a while and then held the receiver out to Kate. 'Do ye no want to speak to her? Here's a grand chance. She's got our Liam with her. He says he's near old enough to leave the school so he's left. Speak to her.'

Kate sat clutching at the folds of her dress around her stomach. Her mouth was dry. At last she managed. 'Liam? Is he all right?'

'Yer mam's had a bit of a scare, Margaret. If you keep the laddie till I get over wanting to blister his backside for the shock he's given her . . .'

'Could you not have spoke to her, Kate?' he asked sadly when he replaced the receiver.

She looked at him with painfilled eyes. 'I wanted to, Charlie, as God's my witness, but the words wouldn't come. I couldnae lift myself from the chair.'

Kate the all-powerful, the invincible, admitting to weakness. Charlie was dismayed. 'Let's put you to yer bed and I'll get the doctor.'

At this sign of devotion Kate smiled. How afraid Charlie still was of the telephone. He could be persuaded to answer it and he had forced himself to chat on it so that he could have conversations with his absent son and especially his daughter, but the initial act, the actual ask-ing at the exchange for a number, that was still an almost insurmountable challenge.

'I'm fine now and the books have to be done. You listen to yer wireless and later we'll have a wee cup of tea. You can tell me what you think of this eggless sponge I'm trying.'

He sat down in his usual chair by the fire but made no move to turn on his wireless. He was staring into the fire. Was he trying to conjure up the faces of his absent children? Did the pictures refuse to come as they some-times denied themselves to her? Kate tried to shake off the mighty feeling of foreboding.

'It's you and me by ourselves again, Charlie, at least for a while. The house feels empty and quiet.'

He looked up at her and smiled a gentle smile; a smile without the growing warmth that she had used to fear. He was fond of her, she knew, but it was a long time since he had approached her in bed. She had failed there too. Was there to be no end to her failures? Her daughter had run away and although she wrote letters and occasionally telephoned when she knew her mother would be up to her elbows in flour and therefore unable to speak to her, she had never returned to Auchenbeath. No doubt she feared the reception from her mother. And Liam had run off to his sister without even a note or a word of explanation. Liam, her baby, her direct link with her dead father. She had made the wrong decisions there too. Could mothers ever get it right? Why was bringing up children so complicated? Surely the hardest part should have been over with the actual giving of birth?

Sighing, Kate went to the table and sat down at her books. The profits were minimal but still there was more money in the bank in the Main Street than she had ever dreamed of when she was Liam's age. She could close the bakery and never bake another pie and, oh, that sounded sweet – no baking, no deliveries, no tradesmen, no slow payments, no decisions – no challenge.

*Stop feeling so sorry for yourself, Kate Kennedy. You have a business to run, people to keep employed, that silly old ambulance driver for one. The army would be desperate afore they hired her. Liam can have a wee holiday in Clydebank; that'll cure him of thinking a bombing's a grand time, and Patrick. Dear Blessed Virgin, I never pressured the laddie into thinking he wanted to be a priest, did I? Did I ever once say the words, 'Patrick, how happy I would be if you were to be a priest?' Mam, have you ever heard me say that to him? I wanted it, dear God how I wanted it, but only if God chose him. Oh, Mam, I've made a right mess of everything and I cannae tell how. What did I do that was wrong?*

The question was still with her as she went to bed and as she lay sleepless beside Charlie, but the thin steel inside that had been steadily forming over the years refused to break, nor even to bend.

*I'll away up to see Patrick and we'll have a real talk, and Liam will come back and I'll find time for him too. After all, the bakery's not near so busy, and Margaret . . . I'll ask her and her . . . husband to bring him home and stop for a few days. It'll be good for them to get out of Glasgow, and I'll keep the business going for Liam even if I have to do both the baking and the delivering. I can only do my best and if that's not good enough I can't help it. And Charlie; I've failed with him too. Maybe there's a chance to do something about that. It cannot be that awful. Margaret likes it well enough. Maybe if I'd known what to expect when we were first wed and if Charlie had been, well, if he'd been patient and gentle. There's something missing in me that seems to be in every other woman including my own daughter. She turned to her sleeping husband, very gently, so as not to wake him. You're no Clark Gable, Charlie, but maybe, if I hadnae been so frightened of the whole thing, we'd have been happier. Could we talk, do you think, or would you brand me a wicked woman at my age to be thinkin' on such things?*

The next morning, Kate rose refreshed even after so few hours sleep. 'I've decided to go to Edinburgh, Charlie,' she said as she put his breakfast on the table in front of him. 'Eat up that nice fresh egg. I doubt the king and queen are getting eggs like that.'

'I doubt they're worried about eggs. Did our Deirdre not always say the nobs ate kippers?' Charlie neatly severed the top of his egg. 'You can still get a kipper. What about Deirdre if ye go tae Edinburgh?'

'Bridie can go. The bairns like their Auntie Bridie.' She sat down across from him and played with her toast. 'I'm going to spend a night in a hotel, Charlie, for I'll never get to Edinburgh and back the one day. Do you want to come?'

'Army barracks was hotel enough for me, Katie. I'd like fine to see the laddie but I'll bide here. Forbye, Liam might take it into his head to honour us with his presence.'

'And pigs might fly. I'd better find out about hotels. I'll ring Patrick to ask him.'

'Jesus Christ, did you hear that?' Charlie interrupted her.

'I hate the wireless these days, Charlie. You know I—'

'Shut up, for God's sake, woman. The Japs have destroyed the American fleet at some place in the Pacific – Hawaii – I think . . . some kind of precious stone, he said.'

Pearl Harbor, Kate heard, what a really pretty name.

# 18

SHE HAD BEEN expecting the telephone call but yet, when it came, she was shocked.

'I'm doing the right thing, Mam,' said Patrick. 'You must believe and have faith in me.'

'I'm trying, Patrick,' Kate wept into the receiver, 'I was coming up to tell you to follow your conscience, not to do things for me, but for yourself.'

'I hope I'm doing them for God, Mam. I've had a bad time this year, a lot of thinking to do.' He stopped and she waited for him to elucidate further but after a few minutes he went on. 'But I'm fine now and so at rest, you can't believe. I'll get over this, Mam; the Americans will come in after this terrible bombing and we'll crush Germany and the Japs. I've talked to the university authorities – there's no problem about continuing where I leave off – please God, I'll be a better man for having gone. I would probably have been called up anyway and, this way, enlisting off my own bat, I've got into the air force.' He tried to sound happy and excited but she could feel that he was saying what he hoped she would want him to say. 'You know I've always been fascinated by planes, and won't our Liam be pleased to have a big brother one of "the boys in blue"?'

When the connection was finally severed and she could hear what she assumed was the air of England humming along the wires she wearily lowered herself into a chair and leaned towards the fire for greater warmth. The bakery was always warm but somehow she felt chilled, so cold and so old. Already she felt as if he were a million miles from her. Well, no use sitting here all day moping and feeling sorry for yourself. That wouldn't change his decision; he was gone and she would have to make the best of it. It would make him a better man. Oh, Patrick, love, weren't you as good as they already come? No, those were the sentiments of a doting mother. Come on, Kate, you have bread and pies to bake.

'He's joined the air force, Charlie,' she said baldly as Charlie emerged from the bathroom and sat down at the table for his breakfast.

'I heard the phone.'

'We'll just think about having everything wonderful for him coming back. And Liam and Margaret too,' she added hastily. They were all her children and she loved them. Would she not be forgiven for thinking her firstborn a little special? Didn't every mother think the same? 'Liam's room could do with a bit of paint, a man's colour; high time we painted over the ducks and rabbits. We should have done it long since. You can see Sam the painter on your deliveries this morning and fix a time. Handy, with the laddie away for a few days.'

He said nothing for a while but stirred and stirred his porridge as if it was still cooking on the fire. 'I canna see his face,' he said and she knew he was thinking of Patrick, not Liam. 'Tell me why that is. I'm thinking and thinking and trying to see his face; he was only here a few weeks ago, and in my heart I can see a wee laddie, sitting up wi' me on the cart and laughing. I cannae see the man at all. He loved that old pony.'

'Aye, he did. There's folk waiting for pies, Charlie. I have great faith in America. It's a rich country and with them in now . . .'

'Not afore time,' said Charlie bitterly into his porridge.

'Well, they're in now and it'll soon be over. I've a slice left of that wheat bread you like. It's a bit stale but if I toast it, you'll never notice.'

The house seemed even quieter in the days that followed, the days of waiting for Patrick's first letter. Kate knew that was a silly fancy and dismissing it from her mind, made more of an effort to talk to Charlie, to fill the great gaps made by Liam's absence. That Charlie missed the boy more than she did was obvious. She had always been busy but when Charlie was home from his rounds there had been Liam with his football scores and his cars, cars, cars.

'Maybe Margaret will bring him home for Christmas, Charlie, and then we could discuss leaving school. There isn't a job for him here but we could let him have a bit of pocket money and old Tom might take him at the garage as an apprentice or something.'

The decision taken so easily, in the depths of the night, to try to salvage – no there was nothing to salvage – to create a relationship with her husband, was not quite so simple to handle in the light of day. Charlie was not the same man he had been in the early days of the marriage. It was not that he had callously dismissed her overtures, he simply did not recognize them. His mind was full of Liam who refused to return. George had got him a full-time job in a garage and he laughed at Kate's idea of a little pocket money for helping old Tom with his broken-down bus and his unreliable taxi.

'I'm making a fortune, Mam,' he confessed into the phone, 'and Margaret and George are great to me. You should come up and see their place. They've got a cocktail cabinet, but George won't let me have any so don't get your dander up, and there's gold taps in the bath that's shaped like fish, the taps I mean, and George is getting Margaret a fur coat for Christmas. I cannae come for Hogmanay; I'm working.'

'You're going to Mass, aren't you, Liam?'

'Och, Mam, I'm too old for that stuff; if Margaret goes to Midnight Mass I'll go with her. She went the Sunday after our Pat joined the air force and she says she means to get married again in the church one day, but my dad and George have never been to the kirk and they're fine.'

Kate swallowed hard. What to say? 'They weren't baptized in the Church, Liam.'

'I'll have to go, Mam. See you.'

The telephone was indeed a mixed blessing. It could bring a distant loved one right into the living room but if the conversation got too hot to handle it was only too easy to hang up.

'He'll come home when he misses his mammy waiting on him hand and foot,' said Charlie.

'I cannae compete with gold-plated fish.' She didn't tell him about the fur coat. That sounded too much like a fallen woman. 'How about everybody here for Hogmanay, Charlie? We'll put all our coupons together and have a right feast and we'll blow our petrol on bringing Deirdre and the family. She's about ready for a wee outing. I'll write to Dave and let him know when you can fetch them.'

The party was a grand success. Kate had provided more than enough food, allowing her conscience to slip a little because it was New Year's Eve and there was, after all, a war on. Offered extra eggs, bacon and butter, she happily paid out for these precious commodities. It would be a Hogmanay to remember. It was. For the first and last time in her life Kate Kennedy Inglis found herself entertaining well into the first hours of the New Year. A few hearty villagers stumbling around in the dark, enacting the age-old ritual of the First Foot that 'no bloody Jerry is going to stop, Mrs Inglis', arrived at her door and were welcomed in with 1943.

'Don't give them any more drink, Charlie,' she ordered at four o'clock in the morning.

'Lassie, lassie, there's a war on. Is it not the first party we've ever been to in the dark? We'll not know who they were the morn's morn and they'll never mind they were here.'

At last, at last, the merry revellers left and Kate began to tidy up.

'Leave that, Kate,' said Charlie. 'You've been grand, lassie. I know ye hate strangers in yer house.'

Kate looked at him, the dim warm glow from the coals in the hearth showing all the grey the years had painted in his dark curls. 'I didnae mind at all, Charlie Inglis. It took a war to bring my neighbours to my door for anything besides a loaf of bread.'

It was easy, after that, and completely unexpected. Kate had forgotten her 1942 resolution and had not yet made any for 1943. When Charlie turned to her she rested for a moment against him as if at last her tired spirit knew where it should lie and then she kissed him, the first time in her life that she had ever done so.

He held her for a second, without speaking, without breathing almost.

'Oh, Katie, lass, my wee Katie,' he whispered.

Was it better for having been denied so long? Kate did not think. All she could do was feel and react, and abandon herself to the feelings that surged up out of the depths of her very being. She was a quivering mass of sensations that had to be satisfied. As dawn broke she whispered her husband's name with tears streaming down her face and fell into an exhausted but satisfying sleep.

'And a Happy New Year to you too, Mrs Inglis,' was all Charlie said when at last they woke.

Everything was different but at the same time nothing was changed. They ate, they slept, they worked, but at last they did it together. It was not that every night was a glorious night of passion; usually they were too tired to do anything but hold each other tenderly for a few minutes before sleeping, but even those few moments were fulfilling. When they did make love Kate gave herself with desires only to please and to be pleased and without any thought of distaste. Who that other woman, the harder, frightened one, was, she could not remember. She waited for the mornings to bathe and wept over the benison of hot water and the younger Kate who had missed so much.

No point in trying to find out why, she told the ghost. Oh, Mam, you had this with my dad. I wish I'd had the joy and the . . . it's the closeness, Mam. . . when life was so hard. At four o'clock in the morning with fretting bairns and an oven that won't fire, you can feel so alone, Mam. But the hard parts are all over now.

Poor Kate.

Patrick was stationed in the south of England and he seemed to spend any free time he had in writing to his relatives. He said nothing at all about air force life, apart from telling them that he loved the work and was very happy. He had met the Catholic chaplain and had told him of his dreams and desires.

'He's wonderful,' he wrote, 'and was in the air force long before the war started. A grand life, he says, but I still think that if God wants me for one of his priests my destiny will be a small village not unlike Auchenbeath. I miss the country and you both.'

And so his letters continued throughout the war. Kate and Charlie heard second-hand about the courage and audacity of Britain's armed forces but neither Patrick, nor Colm when he surprised everyone with a letter, said anything at all about what their own units were doing. Kate wondered if their reticence was misplaced. Did one worry more, imagine worse, when one was kept so unconsciously in the dark, for she never imagined for a moment that either man was being deliberately secretive? That Colm was overseas was readily apparent and it seemed that Patrick was to remain in England. Kate was pleased.

Strangely, she worried more about Liam. Auchenbeath sometimes heard the planes of both sides flying over – it was a sound Kate was to hate for the rest of her life – but Glasgow was often a target and she waited for the news that she was almost sure had to come. She felt almost fatalistic about it; obviously she had been a bad mother to both Liam and Margaret, for they had both run away from her. Sitting night after night in a blacked-out room she felt that she wanted to change things, to go back and do things differently, to spend more time with her children, to love and be loved; at least to let them know that they were loved for they seemed to need to have what she felt was obvious put into words. Had she felt so unloved herself that she had been afraid or unable to love others openly?

The next morning, however, as she helped prepare the day's pies and worried about how she was possibly to keep these desperate women employed when she had fewer orders and more difficulty in getting ingredients, she remembered the early years in a cold, damp cottage, miles from anywhere, with a sick husband, a young baby, and less than ten shillings a week coming in to the house, and she straightened her aching back again. I did what had to be done, she told herself. I kept them from starving, and I kept a roof over their heads and clothes on their backs, and we all had to sacrifice a little to have that.

Charlie came into the bakery one morning with a smile on his face that made her remember the bold little Charlie with the tight dark curls and the naughty blue eyes; the dear, sweet, funny Charlie she was finding again after twenty years. But this was not what she had expected.

'Good morning, Grannie,' he said and, putting his arms around her, he whirled her into a mad dance until he started to cough and she had to help him into a chair.

'Grannie?' she asked, when the coughing had subsided.

He nodded. 'Aye. You'll go to Glasgow now, lassie? Did ye not hear the phone? George, from the hospital. A wee lassie, as bonnie as her grannie.'

Kate knelt on the floor beside his chair and first a wave of the purest joy swept every fibre of her being, to be followed by the utmost misery. Her new joy was too tenuous, too tender a flower to withstand this onslaught.

'A bairn, Charlie, and she didn't want her mammy.' And she burst into tears.

Charlie patted her heaving back. 'You're the first one to know, lassie. I'm to tell George's folks when I'm down the village. It's to be Elizabeth after the princess. Is that not a bonny name?'

'Elizabeth.' Kate pulled herself together and stood up. 'Aye, Charlie, a bonny name. We'll see if she's bonny too when her mammy brings her down to see us.'

'Och, lassie, lassie. A new baby cannae travel and there's a war on. It's plain she wants you, or George wouldnae have phoned. Like enough, she thought a baby would be a lovely surprise and you two could make up.'

It was as if she had not heard the end of his conversation. 'Auchenbeath is safer than Glasgow. She should have been here, or I should have been there, Charlie. Why didn't she tell me? Nine months, nine whole months; I could have got her room ready for a lying-in or she could hae had our room; it's bigger.' She was quiet for a time, her memory showing her the magical moments of long ago, that first cold, frosty morning when all the fears of childbirth had abated and she had for the first time exulted. 'Waiting for your first bairn is the most wonderful, precious time in your whole life, Charlie. I cannot describe it so's a man would understand, but the time I was expecting Patrick all I thought about was how I missed my mam more and more every day; how I wanted to share . . . the hopes, the fears, the countless wee joys. To the end of my life I'll know that my daughter didn't need me, didn't even want me.'

'It wasn't like that at all, Kate'. Charlie tried desperately to comfort her. 'Yer gettin' yersel' worked up for nothing.

You've no spoke in years. No doubt she's been thinkin', "Wait till Mammy hears about the baby; she'll be up like a shot, if she has to push the old bus." '

'And so I would, Charlie Inglis. I'd have been up like a shot, and I'd have pushed Tom's old bus through the hills if I'd had to.' She stood up and wiped away the tears and the momentary weakness. 'You'd better get yourself some tea if you're away on your run and I'll look at the pies. I cannae trust Mrs Thomson to get them baked just right.'

She returned to the bakery where the women were listening to the wireless. She would have to let two of them go, there just weren't the orders these days. It never occurred to her to tell them that she was a grandmother. 'If you have nothing to do,' she said, 'I suggest you find some machinery to clean and a good scrubbing would certainly improve your table, Mrs Flett.'

The workers had noticed the new tenderer Kate who had blown in with the New Year. 'She's blown out again,' said Mrs Thomson. Quietly, they invented work for themselves until the pies came from the ovens and were set out ready to be wrapped with the waxed paper imprinted with the design of a coach and horses and the words, 'Toll House Bakery'. Kate looked at the wrapping but saw the old paper that had said Kate Inglis Bakeries and wondered again if she had done the right thing by refusing to expand and, indeed, by selling her original recipe to Mr McDonald.

'He filled it full of preservatives, God rest his soul,' she said to herself. 'In the end, all he was selling was my name.'

She had seen the name in the shops in the village. Why they chose to buy synthetic bread when the real thing was baked half a mile up the road was more than Kate could understand.

'Nothin' so queer as folk,' Charlie had said when she had told him, and looking now at her pies cooling on the table she had to agree.

'The bike's getting a bit much for you,' she suggested to Charlie as he got ready to follow Miss Peden as she went off with the van. Nothing, nothing must harm him now. 'We'll maybe have to lay old Bessie off and let you have the van back.'

'Away, woman, I'm happier with the bike, especially in weather like this. We'll think again next winter. Forbye, if ye let Bessie go, she'll away and join up and then where would Britain be – more danger on our own side.'

Had he always been able to make her laugh? She needed to laugh in the days that followed, days of worrying and fretting over Liam and Patrick, but now, for the first time, mainly over her daughter. The bakery was so quiet that her absence would hardly have been missed had she gone to Glasgow as she desperately wanted to do. Several times she made up her mind to telephone Margaret but could not bring herself to pick up the receiver. *Mam, Mam, help me do the right thing. I can't condone that she did a wrong thing, running away with George and no getting married in the church, but I can understand now and forgive. I want to forgive and maybe even be forgiven. Oh, if there had just been a bit more time, more time for me to get used to this ... Oh, Mam, this quiet new joy and peace. Has my lassie always had it? The peace as well as the joy?* The longer Kate delayed, the more impossible it became. She should ring and ask me. She doesn't even need to say she's sorry she ran away. She should just say, Mammy, will you come up to see my wee girl?

Eventually, just before Christmas – did everything awful happen at Christmas time, the time of peace and joy? – Margaret phoned. Kate did not even recognize her voice, so changed was it by years of living among soft west coast accents.

'I'm sorry, Mam, there's been an accident.' Stunned, Kate listened but there was absolute silence on the line. She shook the receiver as if that would help. 'It's Liam,' began the voice again. 'Oh God, Mam, he's dead,' and then Margaret's control snapped and she broke down crying and George had to finish the phone call.

Liam, it seemed, had built himself a motorcycle and had ridden it everywhere and in all weathers. He had skidded in the slush and slid right under the wheels of an army transport lorry.

With her eyes on Charlie who was lying white and speechless in his chair, Kate managed to tell her son-in-law that she and Charlie would get the first available bus or train to Glasgow. Then she spoke to the operator again and asked to be connected to Dr Wyllie.

'Aye, I thought you would need him, Mrs Inglis,' said the girl on the exchange, thereby confirming Kate's suspicions that she listened to almost every conversation, but she was too shocked herself to complain. What did it matter? What did anything matter?

'I can't come up, Margaret.' She phoned again herself. 'I can't leave your father. No, the doctor says it's just a wee shock but I can't leave him even to bring . . . Liam back. Can you leave your work, you and George? I'll arrange everything here.'

They came by train, bringing the body of Kate's youngest child with them. Unable to stay in the damp, cold waiting room, Kate walked the length of the platform and waited. No matter how hard she tried, she could not picture the boy's face in her mind. *He's dead, Mam. She sought refuge* and comfort from the beloved ghost. *My baby's dead and I didnae know him. I cannae even mind what he looked like. I see a picture and I don't recognize it. And Charlie? My God, Mam. Charlie's in what they story writers cry flat despair. He's no eating, no sleeping, lying there like some zombie. Oh, Mam, what'll I do if he dies too? Never once in our life together have I said I love you, Charlie, and I do; even with this pleasure that's come to me so late, I've never actually said the words. He's beginnin' to look up and smile the way Dad did whenever you came in the room. So many years of eating and sleeping together and not being together, Mam. Oh, dear God, the awful waste there's been and now we've found something and I don't want to lose it afore I really have it. I'm that frightened for Charlie I cannot think on my bairn. Oh, don't let me make it all wrong again.*

The train was pulling in and just in time for Kate to regain the iron control of herself that she had almost lost. A young woman stepped down on to the platform. Surely Auchenbeath had never bred such a figure of elegance; black fur coat, neat little feathered hat, shoes that looked like they had been cast on the dainty feet that wore them, white, white face and a very red luscious mouth.

For a long moment the women looked at each other while the young man behind Margaret seemed to hang suspended from the train, almost afraid to step down, and then Margaret stepped forward and hugged her mother; the breach was healed. In a reversal of roles she tried to console her mother.

'I'm so sorry, Mother, so sorry,' she repeated as if she was sorry for not only the death of her brother. 'It was so fast he couldn't have felt a thing.'

With her arms still protectively around Kate, she looked along the platform for the undertaker's men and signalled to them. 'We phoned in case you'd not been able, Mam, but I'd forgotten how strong you are, how efficient,' she finished, almost bitterly.

The coffin was closed.

'I'd like to have seen him,' were the first words Kate spoke to her daughter. 'I hoped he was peaceful like his grandfather.'

'I've got the taxi for us, Mrs Inglis.'

Kate looked at her nervous son-in-law for a long moment. 'George,' was all she said, but it was enough.

She was disappointed later when she had time to wish they had brought baby Elizabeth with them. A bairn, especially Margaret's, might have been good for Charlie. As it was, he struggled up in the bed and tears of joy washed his face.

'And you a mammy,' he murmured as quite naturally they embraced. Charlie had not held his daughter in his arms since she was six years old.

'You're spoiling that little madam,' Kate had said and although it had not been said with any real malice he had set the little girl down from his knees.

'Is Patrick coming?' Margaret asked her mother as they sat around the table later.

'Compassionate leave,' said Kate calmly. Perhaps if she'd seen the boy's face this whole nightmare would be more real. It was as if it was happening to someone else and she was merely observing.

'I've closed the bakery the day of the funeral. I told the men, Wednesday; that should give Patrick time to get here,' continued Kate and did not realize how much she had shocked her daughter.

'You're never baking tomorrow?'

'There's a war on, Margaret. My bakers have men and boys at the front; they need the money . . . and the occupation. I'm sorry your room's as you left it. If I'd had time . . . I'll say goodnight to your father for you, will I?'

But Margaret had already spent a long time with Charlie. 'I'll stay a wee while and help you nurse him, Mam, if you'd like, and then I must get back to Elizabeth. George's sister is her nanny, works out grand. I've brought you some photographs. They're doing a sort of colour wash now; really lovely effect. You can see her big blue eyes, but she's fair like her daddy.' She put a restraining hand on Kate who was beginning to clear the table. 'We'll do that, if you want to get off to bed.'

And Kate, who suddenly found that she could not bear to see her daughter go to her old childhood bedroom with this nervous man who was her husband, was only too pleased to leave the dirty dishes on a table for her daughter to wash.

Margaret had set a coloured photograph of baby Elizabeth on the table beside Charlie's side of the bed. Kate lifted it up and looked at it. A bonny baby. Flesh of your flesh, she told herself, and tried to feel something.

Patrick was on the doorstep in the morning when she opened the bakery.

'I got in about three, Mam, and don't tell me I should have come straight home. I'll appreciate my lovely warm bed better tonight. How are you coping, Mam? Are you all right?'

Now I am, she thought exultantly. With my son beside me I can cope with anything.

'Aye, love,' she said softly. 'Go see your dad; he's brighter I think since Margaret came but he took it awfully hard.'

Margaret was already at Charlie's side and the brother and sister sat with him for hours. Kate insisted that she take in a breakfast tray.

'I could have got that, Mam,' said Patrick and Margaret together. They were united in their love for their father and their sorrow for their young brother and the blow his death had dealt Charlie and it seemed to Kate that they viewed her with something like suspicion. Did they think she felt no grief? Would they have loved her better if she had fallen apart so that someone else would, for once, have had to carry on the load of this family? My God, how could they not know that she wanted to pull her hair out and scream and scream and fight with this God she kept trying to find but who kept taking from her those whom she loved? And she did love Liam. Had loved him. Love was more than kissing and hugging and spending every minute listening to your children; it was toiling in the dark hours of the night when you were dead tired and hungry and everyone else was asleep, just so that they could indeed sleep soundly, accepting that there would be a hot meal on the table in the morning, clean clothes in the wardrobe and shoes that would happily keep out rain or snow on shoe trees in the hall.

Kate returned to the bakery.

'Can you not just tell us what to do the day, Mrs Inglis?' suggested Mrs Thomson. 'Folk'll not mind if it's not so perfect.'

'I'll mind, Mrs Thomson, but thank you. My family are all here to help. If you get the deliveries ready, I'll start the food for the wake. All Liam's friends from school are coming.'

'Always sad that it's a funeral that fills the house.' Mrs Thomson had the last word.

All day Kate stayed in the bakery and Margaret and Patrick between them prepared the meals and looked after Charlie. Patrick brought soup into his mother and insisted that she drink it.

'You do too much, Mam, you always have. Auchenbeath could have made its own bread tomorrow.'

'They'd have bought Kate Inglis Bakeries at the Co-op. I had to keep going, lad. Margaret can't see it, and God knows it isn't the money. Isn't the amount in the bank already indecent? I'm responsible for a lot of people. They'll have a paid holiday tomorrow, but the day after they'll have to run to catch up. I've never let a customer down yet, Patrick, not since afore you were born and that's something worth hanging on to.'

Patrick refilled the soup bowl and put it down before her with a slice of her own thick bread liberally spread with butter. She scarcely noticed the appalling waste. 'Come on, Mam, eat up, and then I think a wee rest would be a good idea.'

'Take to my bed afore bedtime?' Kate laughed with something approaching real laughter. 'Wouldn't your poor father get the shock of his life if I crept in aside him?'

They sat quietly for a moment while Kate finished the bread. 'That was delicious, Patrick Inglis, but I could have buttered a whole loaf with that amount of butter.'

'It was good for you.'

'And what about you? There's so much I feel I don't know about you, Patrick.' For a moment she thought she saw a dark shadow pass across the young face but dismissed it as a trick of the firelight on his stubble. He hadn't shaved. Dear God, her son was a man who needed to shave. 'Here's you all grown up and we never seem to have had time to sit down and talk, and you're here now but it's illness and death that's brought you. Did I neglect

Liam, Patrick? Was I a bad mother to the three of you? I was always here where you could find me if you needed me, wasn't I?' Desperately she sought assurance.

'I can't remember you ever sitting down, Mam. You must have, to nurse Margaret and Liam, but you seemed to be baking or washing or ironing. Weren't the sleeve creases on our shirts the envy of every other bairn in Auchenbeath?' He stood up and gently pulled her to her feet. 'Enough for now, you need to rest. I'll pray by Liam for a while and then we should have an early night.'

'Don't stay too long. You've spent over much time on your knees lately by the look of you.' She reached up and touched his face. He bore her no ill will; perhaps Liam had not either. She could find peace. 'God bless you, Patrick.'

When she had gone, he looked around the bakery at the carefully covered pies and tarts laid out on the tables, at the best cups and saucers and plates taken down from the big store press and washed again before being used.

'God have mercy on me, a sinner,' he said and went quietly to kneel by the coffin of his young brother.

This death was not a punishment; he believed that. If he thought God was a vengeful God who wanted to punish him for his human weakness he could not go on. As he knelt he allowed the memories to return. He gave himself up to them as part of his punishment. Had he not avoided them too long? Days when he should have been studying when he could not for thinking of Fiona – Fiona with her warm smile, her childish, pure laughter. Walks beside her on the Pentland Hills when it had been enough to listen to her attractive voice as she ventured opinions on everything under the sun. Evenings in the coffee bars, part of the group around her. What was it she had? Not beauty; there were many more attractive girls in his classes; not intelligence; even he could tell that sometimes her opinions were naïve. She was good to be with. Simple as that. She made people feel happy; with Fiona there was laughter. And that one night of madness, that one time only, dear God, there had been more. John Christie, one of their Great Books Society friends had joined up and been killed within weeks.

'The waste,' sobbed Fiona, 'the waste.' For John had been the clever one, the one who would change the world and, oh, his death had changed the world for Patrick.

They had stayed in the Students' Union, quiet, frightened. Some of them heartbroken at the loss of a friend. All of them sickened by the waste of just one more priceless and yet so easily disposable life. Were the boys thinking 'It could have been me – it might be me?' And the girls. They sat, some motionless with huge staring eyes that saw nothing and others sobbing, tears running down their cheeks and turning their faces into grotesque masks.

'We'd best get these girls home,' Patrick had mumbled and they had pulled themselves out of their misery or self-pity and arranged safe journeys through the blacked-out streets.

Fiona still sobbed. He remembered wondering if perhaps she had loved John.

At her door, she had fumbled for a key and he had taken her bag from her and found it.

'Will you be all right? Are the others here?'

'Oh, God knows where they are these days. I'll be fine, Patrick'. And then she should have gone in and closed the door behind her but she had turned almost into his arms as he stood holding the key. 'Cocoa,' she whispered. 'Would you like some cocoa? I have to make it with water but it still makes me think of home.'

Cocoa. Mam and Dad; Margaret and wee Liam; fire-light and gaslight and thick slices of good bread.

Fiona still sobbed and her hands shook. He held her hands to steady her and her tears came again.

'Why, Patrick? Why John? Why is it always the good who die so young?'

He had never held a woman in his arms before but he did it now naturally. They stood holding one another, giving and receiving comfort and then – who kissed first? It didn't matter. They were on the sofa, still kissing and still discovering. Had he undressed her? Had he undressed himself? Never ever had he felt like this. Feelings were bursting up within him and he could not think, only act with a primeval instinct. Had Fiona led him, or had she followed his lead? He did not know. He did not care. He woke hours later, Fiona snugly in his arms, like two forks fitted into a kitchen drawer. He was frozen and his arm, where her carroty head rested, was asleep. He welcomed the pain and the cold. He had, oh God, what had he done? He had stumbled to his feet and found his clothes and, not daring to look at Fiona who still slept, he had lurched from the flat and run through the darkened streets to his digs. He had spent the rest of the night on his knees, praying, beseeching. 'Oh, dear God, let it not have happened.' What a stupid prayer. He was unclean, unworthy. He had prayed for death, even for a bomb to fall out of the skies but then, awareness that such a bomb would kill not only the depraved Patrick Inglis but everyone else in the house, had sobered him. Show me what to do, he prayed. Tomorrow. I'll join up tomorrow. Mam, oh, dear God, what has my wickedness done to Mam? He had risen to his feet, again cold and cramped, as the dawn light had broken over the beauty of the city. How can such beauty hide such wickedness, he had thought, or am I alone the stinking evil? He had reached the cathedral but had been unable to find the courage to go to confession and the mass had not brought him comfort. There had been months of tortured misery before it had.

Now he knelt and scarcely noticed the cold as he allowed himself to remember. Moaning with anguish and grief, but for himself and not for his brother, he prostrated himself on the floor beside the coffin and, finally, began to pray.

# 19

CHARLIE WAS TOUGHER than he looked.

'I didn't have a heart attack,' he told Margaret when she continued to fuss over him after the funeral. 'Just a wee bit shock. I'd like for you to bide a wee while but there's a bairn waiting you in Glasgow. Away home and bring her down soon to see her grampa.'

Kate looked at her daughter. How out of place the girl looked in Auchenbeath. Such a short time had made so much difference. It was more than the cropped hair and the bright-red finger nails; how could they do any work? It was an attitude of mind perhaps.

*As she had grown older, Kate had believed that she had felt the friendly presence more and more; she had even confessed her wonderment and joy at the tenderness and pleasure experienced with Charlie. Maybe I could understand and get close to her if I'd had a chance to know you, Mam.*

Patrick was returning to his unit and had decided to spend one night with his sister on the way. 'I'll give you a first-hand account of wee Elizabeth, Mam, and next time they come down, they'll bring her with them.'

At the station, Margaret kissed her mother goodbye. It was not the genuine outpouring of emotion there had been just a few days before but an elegant gesture that meant nothing. She had learned it from Hollywood via Glasgow – powdered cheek to powdered cheek. Her mother's cheek smelled not of the latest in panstick but of Lifebuoy soap and hard work. For some obscure reason that made her angry again.

'Why mother never expanded, I simply cannot under-stand?' she told Patrick and George as the train pulled out of the station, leaving a small, frail-looking figure waving on the platform. 'And why she never even got herself some household help; she could have afforded it years ago. It was because she had me to do it.'

Patrick thought carefully before he spoke. 'I don't think it was that at all, Margaret. In her, our class, women did their own housework. Being a businesswoman has never altered Mam's attitude to life. Being as big as she is terri-fies her.'

'That's stupid. Every Friday, for as long as I can remem-ber, she walked into the bank on the Main Street and put money in; when did she ever take any out? George will soon be making more than Mum ever dreamed of and it won't sit in the bank because we're scared Auchenbeath will think we're too big for our boots. We'll travel when this bloody war is over; we're going to build the most marvellous house, we'll send our kids, girls as well as our precious little boys, to the best schools.'

'I'm away to the corridor for a cigarette,' said George, 'I'll bring the both of you a stiff drink. You sound like you need it and I certainly do efter a few days with your terrifying mother, if you'll pardon the expression.'

Margaret smiled at him, an intimate, understanding and yet promising smile that made Patrick vaguely uncomfortable.

'Thanks, George, a drink will be fine,' said Patrick and waited until his brother-in-law had left the carriage. 'Mum isn't you, Margaret, and she doesn't need the trappings of wealth to make her happy. She would feel uncomfortable with gold-plated spickets in her bath room.' He leaned back on the seat and looked out of the window, again seeing, not the Scottish countryside but Auchenbeath. 'You don't remember our first house, do you? It was tiny and damp and the only warm room was the kitchen because she baked there, morning, noon and night, just to pay the rent because Dad couldn't. The house she grew up in, in the miners' row, Auntie Bridie's, yes, it's quite swish now since Uncle Colm took it apart and rebuilt it, but it was worse, and Mam, our wee mam made enough money to buy the Toll House. You grew up used to a house that your family owned. You grew up accustomed to nice clothes and good food and a car, even if it was a delivery van, to travel in. Elizabeth will be used to even more, but never ever forget, Margaret, that you owe it all initially to the hard work of one small woman.'

He sat back, somewhat embarrassed by the vehemence of his long speech, and Margaret found that she could not answer immediately. She wanted to argue that their mother was as tough as old leather and that the lifestyle of her own children would owe nothing whatsoever to their grandmother, but she was honest enough to admit that there was some truth in what her brother had said.

'Perhaps if their grandmother had allowed their mother an education they would have owed her even more.'

Patrick turned from the window in surprise. 'Education? You're not telling me you wanted to go to the university.'

'Father Pat,' laughed the old Margaret, 'you sound as if I had said I wanted to run naked through the streets of Auchenbeath.'

'But why didn't you say something to her or to Dad? He thought, still does, that the sun rose and set on his wee lassie's head. Why didn't you tell him?'

'What was the use? All our lives we heard that you were going to the university; God had great plans for you. And as for me, me that could do your homework without even taking your classes, I was going to take over her bakery and be the best baker. God alone knows where wee Liam was supposed to fit in. God, where is George with that drink?'

'Margaret, why didn't you tell her?'

Margaret laughed. 'I thought I was, loud and clear, every time I came home top of the class while her blue-eyed boy struggled to even pass.'

Patrick clenched and unclenched his hands. 'Margaret, if you'd just—'

'For God's sake, Father Pat. When was I ever able to talk to her? When did she ever talk to me and not at me? Your frail, struggling little heroine is pretty formidable. Look at poor old dad. "Yes, Kate, no Kate." You don't think I would have married George when I did if I'd had your chances?' She stopped as if she regretted giving so much away and then laughed. 'Hearing my confession, Father, and you not even in the seminary?'

Patrick could hardly see her through the tears he was struggling to control. 'I can't handle this, Margaret, I can't. I thought you loved George. I was so happy thinking of you in love and with your own precious wee baby.'

'Of course I love George, but I married him to save my soul from eternal Hell and damnation; something your brother priests had been scaring me about all my sinful life. Things got out of hand and all I could think of was all the horror stories of what happened to women like me, women who . . . shall we say anticipated the joys of holy wedlock, the harlots and trollops. Not that I can expect an innocent like you to begin to understand.' She looked at her brother who was so green he must be about to be sick. 'Oh, don't get upset, Pat. George appreciates my brain; we're well matched in every way. He's another one that should have been at the university instead of being hauled away by that slut of a mother of his to work on a farm before he was fourteen years old. We're doing pretty well without all the so-called advantages, and we've hardly begun. She looked out of the window as if she was talking, not to her brother but to herself. 'I made my bed, Patrick, and believe me, it's an extremely comfortable one.'

To Patrick's relief, George returned with the drinks.

'That went down the hatch quick enough, Patrick. What's my Margaret been saying to upset you?'

'He didn't realize we had had to get married, love,' Margaret answered for her brother.

'Well we didn't as it happened.' George laughed. 'What a state our Margaret was in about Hellfire and brimstone. I hope they don't fill your head wi' nonsense like that at your priest college, Patrick.'

'God knows about all our weaknesses, George. He created us after all, and He forgives us if we are truly sorry that we have given in to them.'

'That's enough religion for now, Patrick. You're not a priest yet. Wait till you see your niece – and what about a meal, George? There's maybe nothing in the house.'

'We'll put the bairn to bed and take Pat to The Villa Sorrento. How about that, Patrick? A slap-up meal in one of Glasgow's finest restaurants afore ye go back to the war.'

Patrick wanted to say he would be happy with bread and cheese and some tea but he was over-ruled. He did not enjoy the meal. He was honest enough to admit that he could have enjoyed the delicious food and wine with other companions. What had happened to George? The George he had known at school had been quiet; the brother-in-law who had crept around his mother's house was quiet. This George was loud. He shouted at waiters; he talked boisterously about his acumen in business so that not only his own table but every table in the surprisingly crowded restaurant was privy to his conversation. If Margaret was right, George had an excellent brain, but his brother-in-law thought he showed too clearly the want of education. Margaret didn't seem to mind. In her own way, although she spoke quietly, she was as loud as her husband. It wasn't the colour of her dress; that seemed to be rather dull, but there was something about the cut that made Patrick avoid looking at her. Every other man in the room could hardly take his eyes off her. She was beautiful. Compared to all the girls he had known at the university, yes, Margaret was beautiful, although there had been a quality about – no, Patrick, don't think about that – Margaret's beauty that was disturbing and not at all restful.

And I always said she looked like Mum.

He was glad when the meal was over and he could get back to the flat to fall on his feet beside the bed with the Divine Office and pray for his dead brother and his parents and Margaret, George and wee Elizabeth, and God have mercy on me, a sinner.

Active combat took away the time for thinking. It was only in the space between sorties that dark thoughts came and hopeful ones too. 'When this is over,' was the beginning of many a conversation and many a letter.

Bridie, sitting happily knitting for soldiers, got such a letter and brought it to Kate.

'Bud, what a strange like name,' said Kate.

'Has Colm no mentioned him afore to you? He's aye talking about Bud this and Bud that,' explained Bridie. 'I thought you knew all about him. Bud's from Canada; some wee place in Alberta; he grows apples. Colm says they're bigger and redder and sweeter than anything we've ever tasted here.'

'And now our Colm wants to go to Canada after the war with Bud and grow red apples,' said Kate. 'Oh, Bridie love, and here's you sitting keeping his home safe and clean for him.'

'He . . . they want me to go with them, Kate, all the way to Alberta, Canada.'

Kate took the letter and read it through again. Automatically she made more tea from the kettle always steaming away on the stove.

'You won't go,' she said when she had refilled the cups and sat down to stir in her sugar.

'It sounds nice, Kate, and what is there for me here?'

Kate looked at her sister, her first baby, and saw a woman approaching middle age. 'I wanted so much for you, my wee Bridie,' she said softly.

'You were my mother, Kate, my sister, my friend. You gave me all that, and don't think I threw my life away looking after Molly and Colm. What else was there to do? That's been your attitude to the blows life hands out, right, Kate. Get on with what there is to do because nobody else is going to do it for you. If I do go, it leaves you alone with Deirdre . . . and Charlie. Will he ever get over it or is he going to be like his Auntie Molly? She never did get over Dad's death.'

Kate straightened her back as she always did when confronted by a problem. 'Charlie's much better since Margaret was here; he'll get up a bit this afternoon.' She smiled a soft secret smile that made her look like the young Kate, the Kate who had run through the meadows, looking for primroses, the Kate who had thought that owning a pair of gloves was the height of ambition.

'By the spring you'll see a difference in my Charlie. But right now we have to think about you. Maybe this Bud'll be rich and handsome and fall madly in love with you, like in our Margaret's films.'

'Sounds more like he's in love with our Colm, if such a daft thing was possible. They're wantin' a cheap housekeeper, the pair of them and our Colm has always liked his food.'

'You have lots of time to think it over. Get some books from the library about Canada and especially this Alberta place. Wonder who it's called after?' suggested Kate and when Bridie had gone she sat down and cried a little. She gave into such weakness more often these days and railed helplessly at herself.

I don't know what's the matter wi' you, these days, Kate Kennedy, but you're as ready to greet as a bairn. It's your age, your time of life, as Molly used to say. Goodness, the sins of omission that are committed by women havering about 'the time of life'. You don't have the time, woman; there's a business tae keep from disappearing out from under you and there's Charlie. Aw, Charlie love, get well soon for we've so much lost time to make up – and there's Deirdre and her crew needing every bit of work or money you can put her way. Her Dave'll never learn tae work they new machines the duke's buying for his farms and then what'll Deirdre do wi' a man that knows nothing but horses that naebody wants, and now Bridie, my ain wee Bridie. I never once thought she'd leave me. To get married, maybe; I can say that with feeling now, that's the right job for a woman, but Canada. She goes to Canada and I'll never see her again. But what's right for her? This war has to end soon and then what'll the country be like having to build itself up again. And if Colm goes, the Council'll maybe want her house for a miner, a family man, coming back from the war. She could come here; there's aye Margaret's room. Aye, face it, Kate. Margaret's left Auchenbeath; she'll come back now and again to see Charlie, maybe she'll even bring her bairn to see us, but that room'll lie empty, and Colm's still wi' its wee ducks.

The ducks gave her spirits a lift. That was what was needed, she would get Colm's wee room ready for Elizabeth. Rabbits would be nice for a wee lassie and Margaret's room should be readied for a married woman. She would make Margaret realize that she was welcome and George, of course. What had happened to George? He was nothing like Mr McDonald, the only Glasgow businessman she had ever known. How could a quiet wee man like George, who had crept around the house in Margaret's wake and almost run every time he had seen his mother-in-law possibly be the enterprising business man Charlie had assured her he was. Mind you, if Margaret's diamond rings were real, and they were so big as to be almost vulgarly fake, somebody was making some money.

'Bridie was here when you were having your wee sleep, Charlie,' she told her husband when she took him his midday dinner. 'She's maybe away to Canada after the war. What do ye think of that?'

'There's grand pictures of Canada in the *National Geographic*, Kate, a beautiful place. What's put Canada into her head? She's never been further than Edinburgh with our Colm.'

'It's Colm's taking her to Canada,' explained Kate and told him about the letter and Bud and beautiful red apples.

'I got a red apple all the way from Canada once,' said Charlie. 'It was a lucky day for me, one of the few I went to the school, and there was this fella had gone to Canada from Glasgow and made a packet, thousands of pounds a year the man was making and he never forgot his roots, the teacher said. You know I wondered for years what the hell roots had to do with people. Put a funny picture in my head; this wee Glasgow Keilie in Canada carrying around roots like a tattie. But roots or no, they didn't hold him back and when he made his millions he sent a crate of apples every year on a ship to Glasgow and every bairn in the school got one. Never tasted anything like it. Fair makes my mouth water to think on it. I've always liked apples.'

Kate looked at him and almost wept again. Never once in their married life could she remember Charlie expressing a like or dislike. Always he took what was put in front of him and said, 'That was nice, Kate. Aren't you the grand cook?' How little she had really known of him. They had been married for twenty-five years. They had been alone for a while, then the children had come, and now they were alone again. Thank God it was not too late or too foolish to think about getting to know him. She could now say easily that she loved him, that she had probably loved him all the time but had been too frightened, too emotionally immature to admit it. It had to be more than duty that had kept her by his side, more than the words of the marriage service – until death do you part.

'You're looking at me like I was something in a zoo, Katie love. Was you surprised to hear me talk about being a bairn? Were ye ever a bairn yersel', my wee Katie, or were ye always minding other folk?' He laughed at himself in embarrassment. 'Do ye know I mind the first time I ever set eyes on you, skipping o'er the fence wi' yer skirts up and the taps of yer stockings showing. Our Margaret's no half so bonnie as ye were, Kate, and as ye still are to me.'

'Charlie,' whispered Kate. 'I wish you'd just once told me . . . you like a red apple.'

'I like bananas, and cabbage with a bit butter, and I like you, Katie Kennedy Inglis.'

'I like you too, Charlie Inglis. In fact . . .' Kate sat on the edge of the bed and he shifted over to make room for her, 'In fact,' she blushed like a teenager and could say no more.

Charlie laughed and softly shook his head. 'Katie. Last Hogmanay was the grandest and happiest night of my life. Did I show you then that I loved you, Mrs Inglis? And if I had the strength I'd show you again right now.'

'I love you too, Charlie. There, I've said it.' She leaned over and kissed him full on the lips and somehow she was lying on top of him and instinct showed her how to do most of the work and when they climaxed together she screamed his name, 'Charlie, Charlie, oh, dear God, I love you.' She lay like a wanton, her blouse open and her skirts around her hips and then they slept. When she awoke she cried for her dead son and the waste of his young life and all the wasted years of theirs.

Charlie patted her back. 'Ye never cease to surprise me, Katie Inglis. I wonder what yon fine doctor fellow would think of the medicine you've just given me. It's too cold to get up yet, but the first day of spring, whatever he says, I'm getting out o' this bed and back on my bike.'

Charlie was never able to ride his bicycle again but as the years of the war went on with victory following defeat he was able to take a more active part in the business. Kate hired a convalescing soldier to deliver pies locally and Bessie went proudly on down the middle of all the country roads while Charlie stayed at home and became a wrapper. Kate soon realized that it was very important for her husband to feel useful and that he would rather sit at the scrubbed marble bakery tables and wrap baked goods than sit at his fire and listen to his precious wireless. He sorely missed Liam and never again took any interest in football but he hungered to see his granddaughter.

'She'll bring the bairn in the better weather,' Kate would assure him. Or: 'She's teething. Margaret won't want us to see her girny; mind how Margaret's teeth kept us up half the night. Tell her to give wee Elizabeth a chop bone to help bring them through.'

The only comfort to Kate was that George's family seemed to have been abandoned by the young family too. George's blowsy mother, who had never been a customer at the bakery, began to walk the mile from her crowded council house to the bakery to attempt to establish some kind of camaraderie between herself and her daughter-in-law's family. Kate hated these visits. She had never been good at making friends and she certainly could find nothing in common with Mrs Bell. As always, she tried to be courteous but, as Mrs Bell got more and more hurt by her son's neglect, it became more and more difficult.

'Our Annie says they treat her like a servant when their smart friends are in. She has to call your Margaret Mrs – can you imagine that? Her own sister-in-law and a wee lassie that was at the school wi' her. And she calls her own brother mister, in company like. Your Margaret always was stuck up but my George. And we're not welcome up there in their smart apartment; it's not a flat like everybody else has, it's an apartment and they've bought it outright, nae money going tae the bank every month like what you probably have to do wi' this place unless it's paid up wi' all the money you've made all these years.'

'I've labelled the pie without onions, Mrs Bell,' said Kate repressively.

'Well, I'm not wanting yer pie, *Kate*, with or without onions. I can see where your lassie gets her toffee nose. You're no better than the rest of us, Kate Inglis Bakeries. I mind on you, the ragged bairn of a ragged miner and an Irishman at that. I wouldnae have yer pie if ye gave it o us.'

Kate watched Margaret's mother-in-law stomp out of the bakery and sat down. She felt sick and dizzy.

'I can't gossip, Charlie,' she told her husband later. 'I never have been able to, and certainly not about my own daughter.'

'It's wrong if he's not speaking to his own mother.'

'I know it's wrong and that she was hurt and upset and wanted to find out how they treated us. I suppose if I had told her we haven't been up to Glasgow either, she would have left feeling better, but she stood there and her fat, beery face just got redder and redder and seemed to get bigger and I wanted to be sick.'

'You should have called me. I would have sorted her for you. You should know that without asking, Kate Inglis. There's never been much ye've asked me to do, Katie, or that I've been able to do, but I can certainly throw loud mouths out of yer kitchen for ye.'

'Oh, Charlie, my proud wee bantam,' Kate almost wept and, quite naturally, went into the haven of his arms.

He held her against his chest gently, almost she felt, as if she were Margaret. For a moment they stood while Kate drew strength from her husband and then, just as gently, he held her away from him.

'A bantam,' he laughed. 'And here's me spent my hale life thinking I was the cock o' the north.'

He sat down in his chair by the fire and leaned back against the old comfortable cushions.

He's an old man, thought Kate. I nearly left it too late. Please God, let me have made him happy. She put her hand on his shoulder gently. 'My dear wee bantam. Come on. Let's sit and listen to the Brains Trust. Julian Huxley is on the panel and ye always like him. I'll make a wee cup of tea . . .'

He covered her hand with his. 'I meant to tell ye the news, Kate; that's why I came into the bakery. Operation

Point Blank has started; that's a massive bombing pro-
gramme. The Huns'll be sorry they ever dropped their
wee buzz bombs on London; we're out to flatten Germany
and wi' Russia squeezing the wee bugger from the west the
war'll soon be over and Patrick will come marching home.'

Patrick's letters were also full of the sense of impend-
ing victory. I can't explain it, he wrote, but, in the middle
of all this madness I have the most overwhelming sense
of peace. I'm not going to be killed; don't ask me how
I know, but I just feel that Almighty God has other plans
for me. Would it hurt you too much, Mum, if I did not
return to the university to finish my degree but went
instead straight into the seminary? I think maybe Margaret was right when she said I didn't have enough brains to
be a university man. I think too it's got something to do
with being able to learn what one's heart is really interested
in. Studying at the university was torture but I can't wait
to study for the priesthood. Every page of every textbook
will be a joy because it will bring me closer and closer to
my Lord. All I ask is to be allowed now to serve Him but
I will finish my BA if that's what you want.

'Germany can't hold out much longer. For the sake of
the poor people of Germany, who are not to blame for
this insanity, Hitler must be stopped. I'm helping out here
with some adult literacy courses. You wouldn't believe the
number of men who can't read or write; they've never had

the chance but they feel the war is almost over and there's got to be a better world for all of us after this terrible struggle. There are thousands of courses being offered to help give these men a better life after the war. And Rab Butler is raising the school leaving age to fifteen and everybody is to get proper secondary education, not just extended primary lessons. Have you heard too that there is to be a family allowance, five shillings a week for each child after the first one? What a difference that is going to make to Britain. Keep your wireless on, Dad, and hear about the grand world and all the opportunities for poor people. A free National Health Service, can you imagine, and can you think what a difference that would have made to your lives, you and Mam?

'Well, it all sounds almost too good to be true, does it no, Katie love? Free everything for the people. Does the money grow on trees to pay for it?'

'All I can think of is that this war will soon be over and he'll be coming home. We'll write that we don't mind about the university, Charlie, if that's fine with you. I was wrong to push him into it, wasn't I? Seems I ruined all their lives and, God knows, I only wanted the best for them.'

She could say it to him now. She could sit companionably with him in the evenings and listen to his favourite programmes, *ITMA* or the *Brains Trust*, and they could talk as they had never done before. Their life together had reached a pleasant stage. In bed they lay happily talking, sometimes – but not often – touching and loving. Charlie seemed to have reached a stage where he no longer needed so much sex; perhaps it was age or frailty and although Kate harboured a little regret that her decision to be more of what she saw as a real wife to Charlie had come so late, she accepted the new stage in their relationship with gladness. Whenever they did make love she was fulfilled, even if she did not always reach that breathless stage of intensity, that pleasurable, almost painful, climax that left her quivering with ecstasy.

'If I'd really thought the laddie couldnae handle the lessons, Katie, I would have put my foot down. I always knew he wasn't as quick as Margaret and that's maybe where we made a mistake, the both of us, Katie love, not telling her earlier that she could go to Edinburgh as well. Ye were a grand mother, Kate Inglis, to the three of them. There's not many people that'll come to the end of their days and be able to look their maker in the face and say I never hurt anybody and I always did my best.'

'My best wasn't good enough, but I cannae see as how I could have done anything any different. I'll live what time's left to me hoping our Margaret will show me she doesn't hold it against me by bringing wee Elizabeth down to see us.'

'She's your lassie, Kate. Write and tell her she's welcome if you cannae speak to her on the phone.'

Kate did. She swallowed her pride and telephoned her daughter. She had written down everything she wanted to say on a piece of paper so that she could not forget in the excitement of the moment. Since Liam's death she had spoken several times to Margaret, but this time she was going to talk to her daughter, really talk, and please God, she would make her understand. She didn't get the chance. Margaret was too busy to have a long chat.

'I'll bring Elizabeth down as soon as we have a week-end free, Mam. You can't believe how busy we are. The business is expanding. George is going to be ready for the end of this war, but we will come down just as soon as I see my way clear to take some time off. You can't believe how big she's getting and I want to show her off to her grandparents.'

The war went on inexorably to its final moments and Kate stopped begging Margaret to visit them. It had to be enough that at least they could speak to one another occasionally on the telephone. Even Elizabeth began to chat to her grandparents on Sunday evenings and Charlie lived from Sunday night to Sunday night. Kate, however, lived only for the end of the war and Patrick's return.

# 20

As always, Kate woke early. She looked at the clock on the dresser as she dressed and, to her joy, realized that there was time to go out into the garden before she started baking. She filled the kettle and pulled it on to the always warm stove and then opened the door to the May morning.

The grass was wet under the trees and the blue wild hyacinths bowed their heads under the weight of the dew that had not yet burned off. Kate walked slowly, savouring the moments, occasionally bending to snap the deadhead of a daffodil off its stem. She smelled the lilacs, white and purple, and smiled at her memories.

'Mammy, Mammy, there's purple berry trees in this garden.' That was Patrick, the spring they moved in, and they'd always called lilacs purple berry trees after that.

Will you be here afore my purple berry trees bloom again, Patrick? Surely Germany can't hold out much longer.

*She went to her borders, filled with memories of Dr Hyslop. It was still too early in the year for flowers but the plants were beginning to grow green and sturdy and strong; she knelt down and pulled out a few weeds that had managed to germinate themselves in the few days since she had been in the garden, and then she straightened her back in the old way and looked up towards the hills.*

*The spring's glorious, Mam, and there's nowhere nicer than a garden on a morning like this. Do you see this place, Mam, your Kate's? A bit different from the garden in the miners' row, is it not? And look at my house, still sleeping there in the early morning mist. My Charlie's there, a good man, Mam. I wish you'd known him. I've stood here winter and summer and pictured my bairns asleep in their beds, warm and clean. They're gone, Mam. Maybe you and my dad have Liam with you. I like to think on that. And my lassie; she's away from me too and she never comes back, always talks and makes excuses, but never comes, and Charlie frets for her and my heart hardens but he says no. Give her time, he says, she's busy like you always were, Katie love, building up her business. What business it is, she never says, Mam, but they have a big house in Glasgow and a woman to cook and clean and one to look after wee Elizabeth. Best not to think on Elizabeth; she'll be at the school afore long and I've never seen her. What would you say to me, Mam, about your granddaughter? Go and see her yourself, Kate Kennedy. But I'm frightened; isn't that daft, a woman my age, but I want her to say, Can you and my dad not come up for a few days? She talks that posh now. Charlie says, that's what ye wanted, Katie, ye'd never think she grew up in a mining village. Be pleased for her. And I am, Mam, but it hurts sometimes not to see her, but more to think she doesn't really want us, or she'd make an effort, would she not?*

*Dear God, it's a glorious morning and it's going tae be a beautiful day. My heart's singing – is it just for the spring or is there something in the air? You'd never believe there was a war on, not with the May blossoms rioting in the hedgerow, that pleased wi' itself to be blooming again.*

Strangely at peace, Kate returned to the house to find her bakers already at work and the tea made.

'There's a tray all ready for Charlie, Mrs Inglis,' said Mrs Peden. 'We didnae want tae disturb you, having a wee while to yersel' in the garden. It's awfully bonnie this time of the year, is it not?'

Kate was touched by the unexpected kindness and smiled. 'It is bonnie, Mrs Peden. I think sometimes I'd like fine to retire and spend my days in the garden. I'll cut some lilac for each of you to take home later. I love the scent of it in a room.'

She picked up the tray and went out leaving the women staring after her in surprise. 'No often ye get a bit of chat from the missus. Mind you, since the bairn got killed, she seems a bit softer, would ye not say? Mind, we'd better get to work afore her mood wears off or she'll have us scrubbing from floor to ceiling.'

But Kate's good mood did not wear off.

Charlie heard it first on his wireless in the bedroom.

'Kate,' he called, 'Katie, come quick,' and, her heart in her mouth, she ran.

'It's over, Kate.' He was trembling and she pushed him back against his pillows. 'Naw, Katie love. Help me out o' the bed for I want to tell ye again standin' on my own two feet.'

'Charlie, what's wrong? You'll give yourself' a turn. Lie back and tell me. What's over?'

And then she realized what he was saying, what he had to be saying, and she put her arm around his waist and helped him out of the bed where he had spent most of the last few years.

They smiled at one another while he said solemnly, 'The war is over, Mrs Inglis. That wee German bugger has committed suicide, God rest his soul, and the Jerries have surrendered.'

Kate could say nothing but stood with her arm around her husband while she tried to take in what he had said. The war was over. Whether Hitler had committed suicide before or after the surrender was immaterial; the war was over and, oh dear God and His blessed mother, her son, her son would soon be coming home.

'Patrick's coming home, Charlie,' she said and burst into tears.

'Katie Inglis, that's about the third time in our married life ye've started to cry and ye always choose the daftest like times. Here, help me to the side o' the bed afore I fall on my face. My legs is that wobbly.'

'Charlie, you're no ill; don't be ill now with our laddie coming.' She looked at him almost in terror. It would be too cruel were he to have a relapse now.

'I'm fine, Kate, just fair excited. You'll see. I'll be up for him coming home. Right now, let's have some cocoa. I can hardly wait for this week's *ITMA*. Tommy Handley'll be right up on this one.'

Tommy Handley was not the only comedian to make political statements in the ensuing weeks. Another of Charlie's favourites, Tommy Trinder, began to campaign strongly for the Labour Party and its promise of a free National Health Service. The coalition government was dissolved on May 23rd 1945 and a caretaker government, under Kate's hero, Winston Churchill, took over until the general election. Kate and Charlie, while politically divided, had never been closer as they waited for the real end of the war.

They had no idea where Patrick was. He had not come straight home as Kate had innocently supposed he would on that wonderful day in early May. There was still a terrible war waging in the Far East and a worse ending was being planned for it. While Kate and Charlie and millions of others throughout Britain rocked with laughter at the antics of Colonel Chinstrap and Mona Lot of the *ITMA* show, or argued hotly about the relative merits of the Labour or Tory parties, a team of refugee scientists together with several American and British scientists exploded a bomb in the south-west of the United States of America. Three weeks later, duplicate bombs were dropped on Nagasaki and Hiroshima.

Charlie was stunned. 'I always thought an atom was a wee thing but here's these atom bombs killing hundreds and thousands o' wee Japs. Some o' them was maybe old folk like us, Katie, waitin' for their laddies to come home.'

'It had to be done,' said Kate grimly. 'It says in the paper it was the only way to end the war without killing millions by invading. It's over now, Charlie, for us all, Scots and Jerries and Japs and all, and that's all that matters. Our laddie's coming home.'

Most of the world went mad with joy and, in her own small way, Kate went mad too. She planned a party. It would be the most wonderful party that Auchenbeath had ever seen and everyone, her whole family, would be there. The war was over. Patrick and Colm were both alive; the party would say Welcome Home and, at the same time,

Goodbye to Colm and Bridie who were planning to leave for the apple farm in Canada as soon as the papers could be arranged.

Margaret would come. How could she not? Kate wrote to her and explained that the party would be held as soon as they knew for sure on what day both men would be demobbed. It seemed to take for ever but at last they heard from Patrick. He would be arriving in Glasgow and, since it would be late at night, he would stay with Margaret and travel south the next day.

'My spiritual adviser suggests that I have a few weeks' holiday to make quite sure that I know what I am doing but I feel I can't wait any longer. I'll stay with you and Dad for a few days, Mam, and then, with your blessing I will go straight to the seminary. What a roundabout route I have taken but at last I am on my way.'

'It's all meant, Charlie. Bridie's meeting Colm in Glasgow to go to the Canadian Consulate for their papers.'

'You'll miss Bridie. She was always more like yer own bairn than yer wee sister, Kate, and I suppose you'll feel the same about Colm but, you know, I hardly knew him. He was aye sae quiet, and then he's been gone since he joined the army, hardly home at all.'

'I think I'll miss them later,' said Kate. 'Right this minute I haven't room in my mind or heart for anything but our laddie. Will the seminary be a sparse-like place with poor food; seems a shame to live for years on army rations and then eat seminary food.'

'Likely he'll never notice what he has to eat, Katie, but feed him up when he comes if it gives you pleasure.'

He looked at the evidence of Kate's preparations around the kitchen. 'I never heard he was bringing the entire British air force wi' him.'

'Are folk no good, Charlie? I have Bessie's butter and sugar ration and Mrs Peden's. She says she cannae afford to buy it most weeks anyway, the way her man drinks. I felt a wee bit guilty taking her coupons but I gave her a bit extra, and then she'll have some of the food home with her after the party.' She lifted a tea towel to reveal a bowl full of large brown eggs.

'Kate Inglis, you're not keeping eggs back?' Charlie almost gasped at the sight.

'No, they're from Deirdre and no questions asked. Two of them you're going to have lightly boiled for your tea.'

'Here's me near forgot what a fresh egg tastes like, and us wi' hens in the gairden. You'll have one of them, Katie?'

'No. I'm having two of my own, so there.'

She laughed like a young girl and he sat in his chair by the fire and watched her swift, neat movements as she moved around the kitchen.

At last the letter came bringing the good news of the actual date of Patrick's arrival. Kate held it to her breast as if it were the beloved child himself. 'What he must feel like, Charlie, and all the other laddies, Colm and all, finally coming home.'

Patrick felt serene and at peace. This last year of the war he had felt no fear, just a sure certainty that finally everything was going to be all right. He went about his duties, not in a daze, no. He would have been no use to himself or the other men and boys in his squadron if he had not always been aware of what could happen if he was not totally alert. Almost every spare minute he spent in prayer or quiet meditation, but not on his knees when there were others around. He lay on his back on his bunk so as not to embarrass them, or even sat in a chair in their midst but his heart and mind were completely singing with quiet joy. The war would soon be over, the war was over, and soon he would be going home, home to study for the priesthood. At last he felt almost worthy. He had committed sin, the sin of a young, weak and frightened man but he had repented and he had been forgiven. Perhaps intimate knowledge of the frailty of human nature would make him a better priest. He prayed so.

He stayed the night in Glasgow in his sister's grand house and enjoyed it for her.

'Come home with me, Margaret,' he pleaded as he held his niece on his knee. 'Wouldn't Mam and Dad love to see this poppet. You're a wee treasure, aren't you, Elizabeth?' and Elizabeth, well aware of her worth in the scheme of things, solemnly agreed.

'I've left it too late, Patrick,' said Margaret, almost sadly. 'I always meant to go back and to take Elizabeth, but you've no idea how busy we've been. How Mother managed with three children and no help, I'll never understand. Mind you, she never had to do the entertaining I do. It's non-stop, but it will be worth it in the long run. Connections, the right connections, are vital. We're diversifying, putting profits into other things. There's going to be a boom in house building. And then some of our business will naturally disappear or change with the war over.' She hesitated. 'We were in war-based activities – I'll be honest with you, Father Pat, and call the Black Market the Black Market, but, as I told you years ago, George is bright and he saw ahead. Unfortunately to be on top of trends all the time doesn't leave much time for other things we would like to do.'

'Like keep in touch with your parents,' said Patrick quietly and saw Margaret colour.

'We're in touch,' argued Margaret defensively. 'Elizabeth rings them up every Sunday regularly and George sends money to that awful mother of his, but we can't have her up here, Patrick. We've got nothing against George's people but they're not right for here while we're making our lives. Mother ... and Dad are welcome, but she's as stubborn as I am. I'm always asking them to come. I do want them to see Elizabeth; she's their grand-daughter for God's sake. And I know it's childish, but I want Mam to see what I've got. There's nothing wrong with that, is there? We've worked hard. Maybe I'll have time to have another child. George wants a boy and Elizabeth needs to have her nose put out of joint a few times, don't you, Mummy's precious little lamb?' She took the child from Patrick. 'We can't help spoiling her, can you blame us? She's beautiful, isn't she?'

'She is lovely, she's like you.' He wanted to add, 'and like her grandmother,' but thought better of it.

The next morning he bid a loving farewell to his tearful sister.

'You'll be writing to me, Patrick, even from the seminary?'

'Of course I will, Margaret, and I'll keep you in my prayers if that helps you.'

'Yes, it does, and I'll come to your ordination and maybe you'll be the priest to marry me in the church. Wouldn't Mother be a happy woman then, her son ordained and the wicked daughter back in the fold?' She looked around the busy station. 'Uncle Colm can't have got demobbed yet; he and Auntie Bridie were going to meet us here if he got everything done. You'll have no one to talk to on the way.'

He smiled quietly. 'I'll write to you, Margaret,' he said and kissed her for the first time ever.

She stood and waved as the train pulled out of the station and Patrick sat down in a corner of the carriage and gave himself up to the joy of realizing that he was finally going home. He was sure that all his companions had to know what he was thinking. He was so unbearably happy; it was over, the war was over. He was going home and in four days' time he would be where his heart and soul had always wanted him to be. The train gathered speed as if it too wanted him to get on with his life, his vocation. As it flew along the lines he watched the countryside blurring past, closer and closer and closer to home, closer and closer and closer to God.

There was no one to meet him at the station, he was alone on the platform. He smiled away his disappointment for Kate had said in her letter that she would be there and maybe his dad too if she could stop him from getting too excited. Patrick picked up his small bag that contained everything he owned in the world and, heart still singing, walked almost at a run, up the road towards the Toll House. Smoke was coming from the chimney. They were inside. Mam would be killing the fatted calf. He threw open the door.

Charlie was sitting in his usual chair by the fire. In his arms was a rather dirty little girl with tangled red hair.

Where had he seen hair like that before? The child's streaked face showed that she had cried herself to sleep. Of Kate there was no sign.

Oh God, please no. You said it would be all right. I was sorry, sweet Jesus. You promised.

Charlie looked at his son. 'Welcome home, Father Pat. Meet Holly. She's your daughter, Patrick, and her mammy just doesn't want her any more.'

# 21

KATE STOOD IN the garden and gave herself up to the peace of it. Winter was coming, there were but a few days left to enjoy it. November. Soon it would be Christmas, another Christmas, and then the new year coming. No, she could not allow herself to think of other holidays; Da off the pit, or later the bakery closed for the day and the children, all three of them, cooped up against the cold, standing at the open door to shout 'Happy New Year.'

The hills were bare; too bare even for the sheep. It would be a hard winter; she could feel it in her bones. 1947 would come in on a blizzard.

1947. Elizabeth was at primary school and . . . despite her vows, her rigorous self-control, she thought of the other one. Holly, the Christmas child, the child born at the season of peace and goodwill and whose birth had brought nothing but trouble. 'Poor wee thing,' thought her grandmother, 'you didn't ask to be born.'

No, thinking was too painful.

Damn them, she shouted silently. Damn them both . . . and honest as ever, she added . . . and me too, for my reaction didn't help him cope.

She looked at the garden but it was Margaret she was seeing, Margaret, Charlie's best-beloved child who was always too busy to come down to see him.

'Oh, Margaret, why can't you come to see him? He won't be here much longer to plague you with his working-class voice and his working-class ways.'

'It's not me keeps her away. I've done everything but get down on my knees to that girl and I'd do that too if I could ever see her.'

'Next summer, Mother, next summer when we can take some time off. You were so right not to expand,' said Margaret, the businesswoman, just a hint patronizingly. 'You have no idea how time-consuming it is. I hardly ever see Elizabeth and there just isn't time to have another child.'

Oh, there was no limit to the amount of money Margaret spent on telephone calls – every Sunday evening – but she had not been near Auchenbeath since Liam's funeral. And Patrick? Her knees suddenly weak, Kate sat down on the rusted garden seat, her businesswoman's mind automatically registering that it needed attention. 'It's me that keeps him away.'

A groan escaped her and she hugged herself to keep the pain inside. 'Patrick, my bairn. Why, why, when you'd worked so hard, when you were so close, why did you do it?'

She remembered the night they had waited for Patrick's return from the war; the table heavy with food, the chairs ready for all the family.

Charlie in his suit, his hair brushed into order, walking up and down, up and down, hours before the train was expected.

'Kate, is it not a taxi at the door? He's come in a taxi.' And then the young woman and the wee lassie, another man's bairn that the new Yankee husband couldn't accept. Patrick's wee lassie. She couldn't believe she had heard the words.

'Don't think too badly of me, Mrs Inglis,' the woman had said handing over the sleeping child. 'Patrick and I . . . well, we were only friends . . . in the Great Books Society, and then one night . . .' She had stumbled and cried over her memories and the husband had muttered consolingly, 'There, there, honey.' That was all Kate heard him say and part of her registered – Honey – Americans really do call people honey.

'We had a friend; he'd joined up. They were rushing to join up, to do their bit, to end the war . . . but John . . . John was special; he was clever and good and funny and he should have lived a long, long time, and he didn't, and the rest of us, the ones left, the ones who weren't brave or clever or special, we were shocked – we couldn't cope – and we comforted one another. It didn't mean anything and then Patrick . . . He never said anything to me after it except "I'm sorry, I'm so sorry." He was so ashamed as if, as if he'd done something really terrible, sinned in some awful way. I wasn't ashamed, not till later, when I knew Holly was coming. My father was a minister and there were people in the village happy to see me go wrong, as they put it. My mother helped me; I never thought she would, but she was wonderful. She wanted me to have the baby and give it away and then go back and finish my degree and I wanted to, but I couldn't . . . I kept her. It would have been easier then; it isn't now. Tell her that when she's older.' And then she'd said the stunning words that had got through Kate's shock and had made Charlie pick up the child and hold her fiercely to his breast.

'You could put her up for adoption if you don't want her, if Patrick won't take her.'

'Does Patrick know?' The strangled voice was Kate's.

'No. I told you; he couldn't even look at me after that night and I had realized I was pregnant by the summer when I went home. Try to think of my side too, Mrs Inglis. I was terrified    no husband, a baby – it was horrible.'

She sobbed again and once more the tall, silent American comforted her. 'There, there, honey.'

'I never went back and I believe Patrick joined up about when Holly was born, just after Pearl Harbor. I couldn't tell him then. Good luck, Patrick, and by the way you have a daughter. I couldn't add that burden.'

'But you could give yer babby to complete strangers.'

'You're her grandfather,' said the girl defensively. 'And it's for Patrick to say, isn't it? He's all right, isn't he?'

And Kate had stood and watched Charlie with the child and thought of Patrick on the train speeding home; Patrick who was going to the seminary, Patrick who wrote that he had finally come to terms with himself. How could he come to terms with this?

She had stood as if carved from stone. Charlie spoke, the girl babbled, and Kate heard nothing but the shattering of her dreams around her. It was over, all over. The seminary would never take him now. It never occurred to her to try to bargain, to argue, to somehow get rid of that tousled little bundle in Charlie's arms. Dear God, why? Did I aim too high? Are people like us supposed to stay in the gutter? An education I wanted for them. Everything I never had. Is that too much to ask? And the blessing of a priest in the family? Was it for me I wanted that? Was it for God? For Mam? For Patrick?

'Go to bed afore you fall down, Kate.' They were gone. Charlie had put the child in the big chair by the fire and the firelight bronzed the red curls and showed the tears drying on the grubby little face. Patrick's child. Kate felt nothing. She looked down at the child.

'Damn him,' she said. She was frightened by her anger, her hatred. 'I never want to see him again, Charlie. Do you understand? Tell him, him and his . . . bastard.' The child opened startled eyes and looked at her grandmother and began again to sob, and it was her grandfather who bent to comfort. Kate turned and slowly, like an old, old woman, she dragged herself along the corridor and fell on her bed. She did not sleep. She did not hear Patrick's voice or the door open and close behind him.

Charlie must have undressed her for she knew she was in her nightgown and in the bed and that the doctor was there for the first time since Liam's birth. And who was this doctor? Not dear old Dr Hyslop? This wasn't even that new one. Oh, she didn't care. Let him mouth his platitudes about shock and distress. But that was when the will began to assert itself again. She didn't need a doctor. Always, always, she was the one who took care of everyone else.

'Can ye no cry, Kate, love? Ye'll feel better after a cry. Patrick's . . .'

But she wouldn't let him finish. She didn't want to hear the name, not then. Not for a long time could she bear to speak of him and she tried not to think, dulling her mind as she had always done by too much hard work.

Mrs Peden's man had returned from the war the way Charlie had returned from the first one. It would be years before the Mrs Pedens of the world could retire. The business would have to be kept going for her and for old Bessie . . . and 'face it, Kate, for yourself.' Hard work keeps painful thoughts away . . . so much salt, so many pounds of flour, the electricity bill to be paid, this new gadget called television that maybe she could afford one day for Charlie, for Charlie who had managed to cope until she had recovered and had then had another stroke, a serious one this time.

From where she stood she could just see the corner of the Great North Road. Patrick must have gone that way and one day he'd come back. He would realize, she would make him realize that she had never meant the cruel things she had said. He would forgive her when she was able to explain that it was shock and hurt and disappointment that had made her say that she had never wanted to see him again.

He must come back; he would come home and she would get over the shock of seeing the child every day. His illegitimate child. For Charlie's sake she would welcome the child and she would try, my God, how she would try not to think of what might have been.

Kate turned again to look at the hills. She would show them to Holly. She would show her the fairy ring and the

Baker's Burn and the primroses where little Patrick had played years ago. She would stand with her under the bridge while a train passed over their heads and she would wave to people on the train and she would tell Holly how her Aunt Bridie, the auntie in Canada, had wanted to own a pair of gloves.

'And Holly will never lack for gloves, Mam. I'll look after her and see she gets a good education.' Kate stopped. She was doing it again. Oh, Kate, where has your obsession with other people and their education got you? Will you never learn? Holly might not want an education. She might want the bakery. No, don't even think of plans. Think of Charlie and how you must get his children to him before it's too late.

Oh, look at the sun. It will be shining in the windows, sparkling on the glass. Patrick used to love to see the sun making paths across his books. That's where I'll write the letter, Mam; the most important one I've ever written. I'll write it on the table where he used to do his homework.

Kate walked back to the house. She was smiling. The sun was shining and surely, surely, Patrick, at last was coming home.

She was still smiling when she entered the bedroom.

He did not answer.

Charlie love, guess what I'm going to do? I'm away tae . . . Charlie?'

He was too quiet. Was he having a wee nap? Poor Charlie. His lungs, almost destroyed in the Great War, had refused to respond to the most modern of treatments and he hadn't had a good night's sleep for a few years now. He spent the long days dozing or listening to his beloved wireless. Kate leaned across him to switch it off.

'Ach, Charlie love. I should have listened to you and written afore and now it's too late.'

Kate stood looking down at her husband. He was still lying propped up against the pillows; the lines that pain had etched on his face had been smoothed away. He looked quite young and so very peaceful. The new doctor had told her it might be like this and she had actually prayed for it. Charlie had wanted to die in his own bed.

'I wouldnae like one o' the homes, Katie, and not the hospital. D'you not think they maybe help an old buddie like me on my way?'

'No, they don't, Charlie,' Kate had tried to reassure him, 'but I'll look after you at home.'

And so she had. And now it was all over. Ach, Charlie, you never had much of a life. Kate took refuge in asking help of the one person who had never failed her. *Mam, are you with my Charlie now? I was going to try to find his son for him and, as usual, I left it too late. Too late, too late. The world's saddest words, Mam. Look after my Charlie for me.*

Kate leaned over again but this time to very softly, very gently, kiss the lips that were already cold. 'I wish I'd loved you enough, Charlie.'

She stood up and straightened her shoulders thinking, thinking of all the things that would have to be done and then went to phone the 'new' doctor. Robertson, that was his name, Ian Robertson.

'He seems to have vanished completely. Well, I told her I'd try and I've tried.'

'Put an ad in the papers. Somebody'll know where he is.' George wasn't really too interested. 'Phone her and tell her.'

Margaret continued to survey herself in the glass above the fireplace. She had almost got used to owning that magnificent mirror.

'You should have come to the funeral, George. I never realized how popular he was. The whole village was there and a lot of the local farmers. Everyone but his son . . . and his son-in-law, of course.'

'Bloody hell, Margaret. I can hardly find the time to see my own bairn at this fancy prep school, never mind dropping everything to go to Auchenbeath for a funeral.' He said Auchenbeath as he might have said Outer Mongolia.

'It's not that far, especially in a Jag,' muttered Margaret. She was still looking in the mirror but she was completely unaware of the beautiful unlined face reflected in its depths. She was hearing her mother.

His last words were, 'They'll come now, Katie.' That was what her mother had told her when she had telephoned to say that her father had died. 'They'll come now.' The words would haunt Margaret all her life. Damn it, she told her serene and flawless complexion. I always meant to go down. And Elizabeth. He never ever saw Elizabeth. How could I do that to him?

'I want Patrick home, at least for the funeral, Margaret.' Her mother had sounded her old self; confident, self assured – hard. Whatever had mellowed her over the last months appeared to have evaporated. 'Has he kept in touch with you?'

'No, not a word since he was demobbed, but I'll find him for you, Mother.' In her guilt she would promise anything. Guilt and grief. Oh yes, there was grief. She had loved him and he had loved her. All her life, when she was unsure of everything else, she had known that her father loved her. And she had left him to die with just her promises. Tears started in the beautiful eyes. I meant to . . . I meant to . . . Were there more bruising words in the English language?

'How do I put something in the paper, George?'

'Get Pete Schwartz to do it. Personal column. He'll know what to say.' George got up from his desk and, putting his arms around his wife, led her to the luxurious blue sofa that set off her splendid colouring. 'I'm sorry, sweetheart. Pete'll find him for yer ma and we'll all go down. Better late than never.'

Pete Schwartz, the expensive and very clever lawyer who handled their business, did everything in his power but no Patrick Inglis ever answered his discreet advertisements in local and national press. Mr Schwartz might have had more luck if he had tried the Irish papers for Patrick had gone to Belfast to look for the priest who had been his chaplain in the army and to him he had poured out his grief and his shame.

'Different paths, Pat,' the priest had mumbled consolingly, his hand on the bowed black head at his knee.

'What do I do, Father, and there's the child, the little girl, Holly?' The two men had gone to the window and watched the tousled-haired child as she stood solemnly in the garden, thumb in mouth, not playing, not crying. She had stopped crying. Patrick thought it was because there were no tears left.

'Poor wee babbie,' said the priest. 'Well, we must try to make up for the blows life has already dealt the wee lamb, Pat. We'll need to get you a job; not easy with all the men coming back from the war but at least you have an education. You've no relatives in Ireland, I suppose?'

And Patrick had shook his head. It hadn't been stories of his grandparents that had brought him to Ireland, but this gentle man who had kept him, and so many others, sane through the insanity that surrounded them.

'We'll need to find somewhere for you, and Holly, to live. You can stay here for a few days.'

They had stayed eight years. Father O'Callaghan had found Patrick a job in a boys' preparatory school and a cottage, hardly more than a hovel, to live in. Patrick never noticed damp and cold and mildew and Holly grew up not expecting anything else.

Every Christmas Patrick wrote a card to Kate and Charlie and then sadly tore it up. They couldn't possibly want to see him. God, he felt sure, had forgiven him his sins but people forgave less readily. Was that not true?

The work in the school was pleasant, not too demanding. He was not, he felt, a gifted teacher, but he was thorough and did what the learned men who ran the school asked him to do. Holly went to the little school near their cottage and he watched her grow with amazement and delight as he had once watched trees and flowers. How much more wonderful, oh Lord, is your human creation.

And the older she grew, the more he worried. While he sat at the kitchen table in the cottage, correcting the exercises of grubby little boys, Holly roamed the beautiful Irish countryside, making friends with all and sundry and picking up an incredible and not always acceptable vocabulary. She played with the little girls in her class but often he heard her talking to imaginary playmates. Was that normal and would she not miss the absence of a woman more and more as she grew up? He had to take her back to Scotland – and oh, how much he wanted to go – to see Kate, and Charlie, to ask their forgiveness, to see if some sense could be made of his life. And as the damp winters passed he knew with a certainty that he had to go home. He had to make his peace with his mother for his daughter's sake and for his own.

Again Father O'Callaghan, older and greyer, had the answers.

'Educational journals, Pat. Or local papers. I can understand you wanting to go home with the child. It's right you should make your peace with your family. You can't work on a farm, you've not the strength for the mines, and so you must wait for a teaching place. It'll come, lad. Just wait and pray and everything will be told you.'

So easy, so easy, Patrick felt, for the priest to counsel patience. Would he have been the same? But all his life he had taken advice from those he trusted and so he waited and prayed and watched the child grow older and wilder and more dear by the minute. And he never once caught her in a spontaneous hug; he never once said, 'Holly Inglis, you are my life and whatever has been wrong, you, no matter your coming, have been so very right.' And the day came when he wished he had and he could not speak.

# 22

THERE HAD TO be a wall. Holly threw her long, skinny legs over the old dry stone dyke and with shoulders hunched, gazed at the hills while she munched her apple. This was her favourite place for sitting; she was in full view of the kitchen window should her father want her, although he never did, trusting her to get off to bed at a reasonable hour. Perhaps he didn't care enough, but Holly preferred to banish thoughts like that. It was a beautiful evening, a light breeze ruffling the golden barley like the hands of a lover in his beloved's hair. Through the trees, beyond the fields, she could just glimpse the river, in spate after recent storms, and rushing down to the Solway.

'Humbly, I accept this Academy Award.'

'Mrs Frazer, I have been invited to tea at Buckingham Palace . . . (You're peeing yourself with envy, you old bitch).'

'Prince Charles is a beautiful little boy, your Majesty. Of course he may sit on my lap.'

'What, Maestro, you would like me to sing instead of Vittoria de Los Angeles . . .? Well, if you're quite sure. I'm happy to help out . . . she has laryngitis, poor thing.'

She laughed at herself, a happy, carefree, little girl's laugh. Well, if you can't laugh at yourself. Holly was very good at laughing at herself and the foibles of those around her. It was one of those 'foibles' that had sent her to the solace of the wall. Mrs Frazer, her class teacher, disliked her. Holly was well used to sneers and sniggers. Even in Ireland she had been aware of the laughter at her expense, the giggles, the words she didn't understand, and she could never ask Dad. Dad was to be protected for he was absolutely no good at protecting himself; Holly had realized that very early in their relationship.

Actual dislike, however, Holly had never known. In Ireland she had been surrounded by affection; from the priests and brothers at the lovely old school, from the villagers, the farmworkers, everyone – but here? Here was a dislike she could not understand. Why should Mrs Frazer be so angry when she worked so hard, when with hardly any effort she came first in every test the teacher could devise? Back home, thought Holly, didn't darling Miss Day say wasn't I the cleverest girl she'd ever come across and wouldn't I be coming to take her very job off her? And why did Mrs Frazer always try to separate her from her beloved Grace, Grace with her beautiful dresses and her lovely shining curls; Grace who had been her friend from the first day she had stood in this horrible school?

'Why does that woman hate me, Grace?'

Grace had been flustered. 'She doesn't hate you, Holly. She says God says we are to love one another when she's doing the bible bit in the mornings; you know, when you have to go outside because you're a . . .'

'A Catholic, with me horns and tail. Well, the old bitch'll see my horns one of these days if she doesn't pull herself together, so she will.'

'Holly Inglis, stop pretending you're so tough. My mammy won't let me play with you if you talk nasty.'

Holly was quiet. She did not want to be banned from the cosy, comfortable council house where Grace lived with her parents and little brother and where Holly Inglis was always warmly invited to tea, although she could swear sometimes she saw Mrs Patterson frown.

But if the Pattersons were welcoming, Mrs Frazer was not. Perhaps she had no idea how to deal with an illegitimate child whose father flaunted his sin only a few miles from the very village where his mother had desperately struggled to pull herself out of the poverty into which she had been born. If only Holly would sit quietly docile like most of the other miners' children (especially the Catholics) while she educated them. But Holly, her undisciplined ginger hair sticking out round her head, much in the way Kate's black hair had done almost fifty years before, had no intention of sitting anywhere quietly. She would have her work finished almost before Mrs Frazer had written it up on the board and then she would be out asking questions, some of which Mrs Frazer could not answer, and for this would never forgive the child. Today she had used her withering sarcastic tongue, her only weapon against Holly. 'Ask, ask, ask, Miss Inglis, always asking. Well, let me ask you a question you can't answer today. Why don't you ask your father for the answer? After all, he is a teacher too like me, isn't he, Holly? I do seem to remember that there was . . . some story of the university. Did he receive an honours degree as I did . . . or did something get in the way? Answer me that, miss?'

But Holly could not answer. She had sat there while Grace had held her hand for comfort, while the others had giggled at her scarlet, unhappy face, and she had hated Mrs Frazer with a most unchristian hatred. Now she sat on her wall at the end of the garden and played her make-believe game.

One day I will be Britain's first woman prime minister and Mrs Frazer will beg to come to tea at 10 Downing Street and I'll spit in her eye.

Really, prime minister, that was most unladylike. How do you get to be prime minister? Maybe Da knows. Quickly she rejected the idea of asking him. That was one of her self-imposed rules. Don't ask Daddy anything you can find out for yourself and don't ever ask him anything that might upset him. She had asked him once about babies. Heavens, what a to-do over nothing. Old Sean Maguire up the farm had explained it all so simply but Daddy had been flustered and embarrassed.

'It'll be in a book,' was Holly's answer to her own question but she could find no book with the title *How To Get To Be Prime Minister*. Holly had long since decided to read every book the local lending library had to offer. There was not much there, in one crowded classroom, and a great many of the reference books were out of date, but she was still learning a great deal. The library was open for two hours, three times a week and the librarian had long since given up all hope of keeping Holly in the children's section. She had read them all; she loved stories of girls' schools and stories set in boys' schools; she read all the animal stories, the biographies, the poetry books. Then she started on the adult section, saying, quite untruthfully, that she was selecting books for her father. She read Agatha Christie and Zane Grey, J. B. Priestley and A. J. Cronin. Then, totally by accident, she discovered Mazo de la Roche. She had already fallen totally in love with each and every one of Georgette Heyer's Regency heroes, but it was only when the wonders of television came to the small Scottish village that she discovered the Whiteoaks.

She sat, with half the village, in Grace's mother's living room, and was enchanted by the poet, Eden; she lived all his agonies and ecstasies, and then rushed to the library to demand the Jalna series. Deep within their covers she discovered the earthier Rennie and abandoned wimpish, poetic Eden for ever.

Holly did not limit herself to the novel; she read poetry and plays, few of which she understood, and it was these she often wanted to ask Mrs Frazer about, and she started to work her way through the encyclopaedias. She invented systems, first she would read from A to Z but A could be very boring. Then she thought that subject by subject would be good, except that she found herself lost in ballet when she should have been reading birds. The best way to read, she decided, was to open the book at random . . . No, I'll maybe miss something. – No, you are more likely to find something and, anyway, by the time you are fifteen, you'll have read every book in the place. – Why do you talk to yourself? – Because there is no one else to talk to.

Except Grace, of course. She had met Grace on the first day of her time at the little primary school where Dad had enrolled her when he had got the job at the boys' school in the big town nearby.

'It's bigger than Ballinsheen, Holly,' he'd said, 'but it's a village school and we like villages better than towns, don't we?'

Holly didn't know whether she liked towns or not but she was prepared to like the village if Dad said so and she certainly liked Grace. Grace was everything that she was not. She was spotlessly clean and remained clean all day, no matter what she did. She had a frock, starched and ironed, for every day of the week, and two for a Sunday. Her long blonde hair always hung in the most beautiful, structured ringlets, and Holly thought that she looked like a fairy princess. Grace took highland dancing lessons and had a wardrobe full of kilts and costumes, a drawer full of medals, and shelves groaning under the weight of cups and shields. Standing proudly in the kitchen – the kitchen being the living room of a council house as against the back kitchen where cooking and washing was done – was a piano and on this amazing instrument Grace had a weekly lesson, and, being Grace, practised for half an hour every day without having to be told. Holly thought she was wonderful and could never quite understand why Grace had chosen her to be her friend, for if Grace looked even more beautiful and well-dressed beside her fairly unkempt friend she always came second in academics. They were good little girls and remembered all their lives the only time they had ever had the tawse.

They were in primary six and studying Scandinavia. Holly and Grace, sitting side by side by virtue of being top students, were talking not about geography but about the blueness of Howard Keel's eyes as seen on a bubble-gum card, and the magnificence of his voice as heard by Grace at the pictures in Dumfries.

'Holly Inglis, come out here and point out Denmark.'

Lost in the fathomless depths of her heart-throb's eyes, Holly would have been hard put to find Scotland.

Mrs Frazer smiled grimly. Grace would know. At last that dreadful child would be bested. But Grace, not having a taste for either Heyer or de la Roche and possessing a decided preference for real flesh and blood heroes like Howard Keel, had even less idea of the whereabouts of Denmark than her friend.

'Hold out your hand – both of you.' The rest of the class sniggered. How the mighty had fallen. Mrs Frazer whacked them both three times, making quite sure that the belt bit into Holly's wrist, but, if anything, hitting poor Grace harder because of her disappointment.

'Why didn't the old bitch say Scandinavia?' complained Holly in the playground. 'Well, for all I care, Norway, Denmark and Scandinavia can all fall into whatever blasted ocean is up there.'

The unpleasant incident was almost the end of their friendship. Grace's mother had sighed resignedly when Grace had brought the grubby little Inglis child home in primary three. Everyone in the village was talking about Patrick Inglis returning after all these years, not to

Auchenbeath, which would really have been rubbing his poor widowed mother's nose in it, but to a neighbouring village. Over the years she had become quite fond of the child, taking pleasure in Holly's delight in her home cooking, her admiration for the tidy, well-furnished little house, and hardly objecting at all to her religious denomination. 'Not her fault, the poor wain, never asked to be born. That father of hers should take more care of her, not that he ill-treats her, mind. It's just that she's allowed to run wild, and he never notices her dresses are too short until they hardly cover her bum, and as for her knickers, well, goodness knows what she sits in. And why they didn't move in with that hoity-toity mother of his . . .'

But now, for the first – and last – time Grace had got the belt, and Mrs Patterson well knew that it was Holly who had led her daughter into sin.

'This is what comes of letting you be friends with that riff-raff,' sniffed Mrs Patterson as she examined her daughter's hand. 'You're not to play with her any more, Grace. I want you to be Dux and they won't give it to you if you get tarred with the wrang brush.'

Grace looked at her parent in some surprise. Everybody knew that Holly would be Dux, the title given to the pupil with the best all-round marks, but the more important thing was to change her mother's mind about banning her friend. 'Mammy, they were my bubble-gum cards. I was showing them to Holly. Mrs Frazer doesn't like Holly because she's poor . . .'

'It disnae help her being a Papist either,' suddenly said her father from behind the *Daily Record* and, sensing an ally, Grace turned to him.

'Daddy, have you ever heard of a teacher not liking somebody because she was clever?'

'Ach, lassie, teachers are no better nor worse than anybody else but if your teacher doesn't like Holly, all the more reason you should stick by her.'

That settled it. Mr Patterson very rarely emerged from behind his paper but when he did, everyone paid attention. Now Grace could get back to the vexing question of Dux. Next morning, in the playground, she brought it up with Holly herself.

'Holly, they couldn't not let you be Dux, could they?'

'Because I didn't know where Denmark is?' laughed Holly. 'I don't know, Grace. The Dux medal goes to the person with the best marks and that's me, but grown-ups can do anything they want. I want the medal, for my dad and to spit in my grannie's eye . . .'

'Holly Inglis, that's a dreadful thing to say.'

Holly looked at her friend and thought before speaking. How could Grace, whose family was so close and loving, ever understand? She hardly understood herself. Her grandmother was always asking them to move in with her

into the historic Toll House and she was forever complaining about the length of Holly's dresses and buying
her beautiful new ones that Holly simply refused to wear.
It was because of Granny Kate's eyes; Holly knew it but
she couldn't explain it. Granny Kate's mouth said, 'Patrick,
bring Holly here; there's plenty of room and I want to look
after you both.' But her eyes said something else. Holly
knew why of course. She knew all about her father's frus-
trated plans to become a priest. She had asked him once
and he had told her everything but the telling had distressed him so much that she had decided then and there
never to ask him anything again.

So, she would argue with herself, he decided to get a
baby. What's so awful about that? Awful for a priest, certainly, but he had been a university student, a soldier. Her
grandmother had the right to be disappointed but not to be
unforgiving. She couldn't have loved him very much in the
first place if she threw him out just because he had a baby.
And what a baby! The best. *No, your Majesty. I quite agree.*
My grandmother must be very peculiar not to rave over a
grand-daughter like me. Her loss, you'll agree, dear ma'am.

Holly remembered nothing of her life before Ireland
and she never asked. Some things, she had decided, it's
better not to know. Her life was the meadows around
Ballinshean, the ruined castle where wild flowers grew
all over the walls and where she could be a princess to

her heart's content. It was Sunday afternoon tea in the drawing room at the monastery with Brother Jerome; those afternoons, when from the age of three she would sit perched on a chair sipping tea from a fragile porcelain cup because 'she has to learn, Patrick,' and listening to the beautiful, cultured voice telling her of countries and peoples and paintings and music. Next to Patrick she loved Brotheroam, as she called him, and she missed him with a pain that would not go away and that she hid because her unhappiness would hurt Patrick.

'We're going home, Holly,' Patrick had told her one Sunday after she had changed out of the best dress, the clean socks and shoes, the hair ribbon, the little white gloves that she always wore for Brotheroam who wanted her to be a lady.

'I am home, Daddy. Do you know Brotheroam says only an uneducated man needs to resort to swearing when he's angry? There are words, says he, that would knock the socks off the opposition and he's going to teach me them, starting next Sunday.'

But next Sunday had found them in Scotland, a country that had absolutely nothing going for it, thought Holly Inglis, till she met Grace. She had met her grandmother whom Patrick had telephoned all the way from Ireland. She had gone to the Toll House in her best blue frock, Brotheroam's favourite, and something about the iron gates around the bakery had frightened Holly and she had hung back and cried and generally behaved badly.

'We all need time, Patrick,' her grandmother had said and, to Holly, the mouth had smiled but the eyes had not. Every Sunday they went to the Toll House and had lunch and afternoon tea with Grannie Kate and Patrick was miserable because Holly was mutinous. And Kate? What did Kate think on these Sunday afternoons?

'I hate my grannie, Grace. She pretends to want us because she wants my daddy, and one day she'll want to know me and I'll spit in her eye, so I will.'

'Holly Kennedy, that's a terrible thing to say about your own grandmother. My mother would wash your wicked mouth out with soap. And, anyway, you'll never have enough spit in you to spit in all the eyes you want; you're too wee.'

'Want a bet, Grace Patterson?' And, hand in hand, the two little girls ran laughing round the playground.

# 23

KATE DID NOT deserve to be hated by her grand-daughter; treated with suspicion, yes – but out and out hatred – no. She was aware that the child disliked her and so she felt guilty. With her usual honesty Kate decided that she had earned Holly's animosity but, unlike Holly, she was prepared to work to make things better. She tried to find out what the child preferred to eat but her questions were met with hostility and a sullen, 'I eat anything, but I specially like anything me Da makes.'

Holly was unaware that her Sunday afternoons with Brother Jerome had taught her more than an appreciation of the world's finer and gentler qualities; she had also absorbed, like the proverbial sponge, many of the priest's upper-class sounds. That voice she used when speaking to Patrick and to her schoolmates, until they laughed at her and mimicked her. She used a heavy Irish accent with people she did not like as if she were unconsciously distancing herself from them and, at the same time, giving them what they expected. Her voice brought her grand-mother both pain and pleasure. She knew it was not the girl's real voice but, at the same time, it sounded exactly like that of the long-dead Mary Kate.

'Hello, the baker. Any chance of a cup of coffee?'

The voice startled Kate, so deep in thought had she been and, no doubt, she convinced herself, that was why her heart had started to beat so rapidly.

'Doctor.' She greeted him with genuine pleasure. 'Of course there's coffee. In fact, there's some lunch, if you have time.'

Ian Robertson, the village doctor, came in smiling, bending almost from the waist to get his considerable bulk under the low doorway without banging his head, something he had done several times in the early days of his visits to this most reluctant of patients.

'I was hoping you would say that, Mrs Inglis, for all I have in my bag is a rather tired cheese-spread sandwich.'

He smiled again and she stood for a long moment caught by his eyes before she managed to pull her gaze away. Had his presence always confused her? She had known him now, the new doctor as he was called, how many years? He had come to Auchenbeath just after the war. The vil-lage grapevine said he had been a serving soldier who had come back from active service in the jungles of Burma to find a hole where his house and his wife and two children should have been. She now knew that was true, for they had become friends over the years as they had both slowly recovered from their losses. He had treated her without, she felt, much sympathy when she had collapsed after learning of Holly's birth. He had looked after Charlie with skill and tenderness all through his final illness and, although she had never consulted him since, he had got into the habit of stopping at the Toll House on his way to and from outlying patients. First he had come for bread or pies and then, one day, he had dropped in when Kate and the bakers were having a morning break. He had been invited to join them and now came quite regularly, more and more often when Kate was alone.

'Have a cup of coffee and a scone while I heat up some soup,' Kate said briskly, 'and do please sit down. There is a lot of you, you know.'

'My wife used to say that. Ian, you'd make a better door than a window, she'd say.' He drank his coffee quietly for a moment and then stood up again and towered over Kate.

'Mrs Inglis, Kate. I've been meaning to ask you for some time. Couldn't we call each other by our Christian names? We've known each other for years.'

Kate surprised herself. 'I'd like that,' she said. 'There's no one left who calls me Kate now.'

When he had gone the bakery seemed very empty. 'Well, it is,' said Kate to herself. 'He's a very tall man.'

She found herself thinking of him as she prepared a shopping list for Sunday's lunch and, for the first time in years, it was not Patrick or winning over a resentful little girl that took most of her attention, but the effect the doctor had on her.

'I wonder if he'd like a lemon meringue pie,' she thought as she twiddled with her pencil. But, of course, it was whether or not Holly would like it that was important. Holly, Patrick's daughter, who knew perfectly well that her grandmother had turned her back on her and who now fought for her friendship because without Holly she could not get Patrick. She would ask Dr ... Ian for advice the next time he dropped in. It was so nice to have a friend to talk to. That was it; that was what she had missed most since Charlie's death, just someone to talk to. 'If he comes on Monday, I'll ask him to try the pie. After all, a man living on his own won't make pies.'

Ian Robertson did not bake and had no need to try to master the art for he was certainly offered plenty of home cooking. Every unmarried woman for miles was delighted to have a single man in the village, and there were homes where he was offered more than food, but he had become adept at avoiding potentially unpleasant or unprofessional situations. His visits to the bakery were noticed and commented upon but Kate, of course, heard little local gossip, and her employees kept quiet about any rumours that affected her. Now, totally unaware that in many homes she was already either living with or about to be married to '*the new doctor*', Kate set about winning over her reluctant grand-daughter.

'Patrick is the only person, well maybe apart from Bridie, whom I've loved from the start. I wish I loved Holly. Maybe other grandmothers just see their grandchildren and worship them immediately but I've never seen Elizabeth – I'm not grand enough for her mother – and as for Holly? If she'd let me get to know her, maybe I'd get to love her, and Patrick won't come home for me to look after him until Holly is happy here.'

That Patrick needed looking after, Kate well knew. She had been shocked by the sight of him when he had turned up that day after the almost incoherent phone call from Ireland. He had always been thin but now he was practically emaciated and his eyes shone from his death's head skull with an unnatural brightness. He had shrugged off her enquiries about his health.

'I'm fine, Mammy, a bit of a cough now and again, but I've never been fat, you know that, and I'm not a big eater, not since the war.'

They had talked for hours and hours while Holly had slept in the chair that she had slept in eight years before.

'Oh, Patrick, love, I'm sorry I was so cruel. I should have stood by you; your father would have. Such a good man, your father. If you'd just written once, I would have come over to Ireland to fetch you and Holly.'

'So many things we should have done with our lives, Mam, but I wanted to make my peace with you and Dad,' – Had he meant to say 'before it's too late,' Kate wondered – 'and to let you know Holly. She's a lovely wee lassie.'

Kate remembered her grand-daughter's shocking language at the tea table and said nothing.

'I hate bluidy peas,' the child had said and Patrick had muttered, 'Holly, Holly, stop showing off,' and the girl had kicked the table leg, Mary Kate's grandmother's table brought all the way from Ireland, and had said 'bluidy, bluidy, bluidy peas. I'll spit on them, so I will now,' she said, with her defiant eyes fixed on her grandmother.

'She's being silly since she's shy,' Patrick had tried to excuse the disgraceful behaviour, and Kate's hand had itched to smack the little backside.

'There was a brother at the school where I taught, a Lord's son, a real gentleman, and he took Holly to tea every Sunday and taught her her manners.'

Again Kate looked unconvinced but she said nothing.

'If I'd stayed at home he was going to teach me really good swear words,' had said the outrageous little girl and Patrick desperately had tried to convince his mother that the absent brother Jerome, scholar and gentleman, had been about to do no such thing.

Holly's behaviour had toned down, at least in her grandmother's presence, and the Sunday afternoons became less and less of an ordeal. Kate knew to say nothing unfavourable about Holly's clothes because if she did, Holly would be sure to turn up the next Sunday wearing a frock that long since should have been used for dusters. After lunch Patrick would insist that they wash the dishes and Kate had worried about her best china in the girl's not always too clean hands. There was no need; Holly was gentle with fine things.

'Brother Jerome had really lovely cups,' she told her grandmother who wisely decided not to rise to the bait.

'I'm sure he had, dear. Now, why don't you have a little play in the garden while Daddy and I have a little rest.'

She was aware that Holly knew perfectly well that rest was, in this case, a synonym for talk and that the talk would be about her.

'You're looking a bit better these days, Patrick, but I do wish you'd come home. Holly is getting older and older and she does exactly what she likes. Such freedom isn't good for a wee girl.'

'There's no harm in her, Mam. She's learned some swear words from the people she played with but they don't mean anything; they're unpleasant from the mouth of a wee girl but they're not words like "nigger", which I find really offensive. And she learned an awful lot from her beloved "Brotheroam", more than she knows, I think.'

Kate hesitated. There were still, after nearly eight years, things they had not discussed.

'Have you ever heard from her mother, Patrick? Does the child never ask?'

'As far as Holly is concerned, she sprang fully formed from the head of Zeus, Mam. She has no interest in her mother and none whatsoever, thanks be to God, in biology.'

'She will ask one day, Patrick, she's bound to and then what will you tell her?'

'The truth. I always tell her the exact truth. Perhaps that's why she hasn't asked me yet. She doesn't really want to know.'

He suddenly looked old and tired as he lay back in the chair. He's dying, thought Kate with a sudden and painful clarity. My son is dying and I can do nothing to prevent it. She went to his chair and bent protectively over him. 'Patrick, have you seen Dr Robertson?'

'I'm fine, Mam. The cottage in Ireland was damp so I'm left with a wee cough. You mustn't worry about me.'

'Please come home to live. You could still get to school on time from here. You could buy a wee car; I'll buy you a car. Holly would like that; we could all go to choose. If you came you could have your old room and Holly could have Margaret's. I'll ask her to help me redecorate. She could choose her own papers.' Kate stopped, aware that she was almost reduced to babbling.

'Holly's not ready.' Patrick thought for a moment before continuing. 'I'm sorry, Mammy, but the house frightened her. Maybe she remembers being left here by her mammy; perhaps she remembers being wrapped up by a complete stranger and taken away again. I don't know, but I won't push her. God in Heaven, Mam, haven't I done the lassie enough damage already? We get along fine and, oh, it's such joy to be able to walk in that door every Sunday, to smell the bakery, to see you standing there at the table. Working, working, Kate Kennedy Inglis. Aren't you always working? And here's you wanting to take on another bairn after raising your own.'

Wisely, Kate decided not to force him. She might lose him again and she couldn't bear that. No, she would be happy with her Sundays for now and see how things developed.

'Let's have some tea before you go. Is Holly still in the garden?'

'Probably sitting on the wall. I don't know what is it about walls but if there's a wall around Holly Inglis will sit on it and make up some story. She has a grand imagination. Maybe she'll be a writer.'

'She's clever enough to be anything she wants.'

Mother and son looked at one another sadly but it was Patrick who broke the silence. 'And we'll let her, won't we, Mam? We'll encourage her to be anything she wants.'

'Right now it seems to be trapeze artist,' Kate said. 'Look at her now. She's balancing on the wall talking to someone.'

'A tramp most likely,' laughed Holly's father.

Kate's heart started to do its strange little dance. It was no tramp. She knew that bulk and from the window she watched Ian Robertson lift up his arms and help her grand-daughter down from the wall. He turned and saw her watching from the window.

'Hello, the baker,' he called. 'Any chance of a cup of tea?'

'Go and bring Dr Robertson in, Patrick,' she said and bustled off to the kitchen where she could recover her composure. *What is wrong with you, Kate Inglis? A man comes for a cup of tea; it means nothing. You're a convenient stop on the road, no more.*

Without turning, she could tell he was in the room. *It's because he blocks out the light, nothing more.*

'Hello, Ian,' she said, still with her back to him. She wasn't yet ready to look in his eyes. 'You've been up at one of the farms?'

'No, Kate, no excuses today. I was out for a walk and just happened to see Holly the Magnificent crossing the Atlantic on a wire, and I rescued her just as she was about to be eaten by a shark. Kate Inglis, that was a most unlady-like snort.'

'I did not . . . snort, I mean.'

'Yes you did.'

She looked up and saw the laughter in his eyes. He was teasing her. No one had ever teased her. 'Don't be silly,' she said. 'Will you ask Holly to help me?'

'Why? Aren't I big enough to carry a tray or is it somebody dainty you need?'

'No, a porter will do.' I'm teasing him back. Am I flirting? Is this what flirting is? She pointed to the tray with a hand that shook a little but her voice, she was glad to hear, was normal. 'Will you take the dishes into the front room? I'm glad you're here. I'm a bit worried about my son. Perhaps you could have a look at him.'

Ian stayed after Patrick and Holly had caught their bus back home. Kate looked at Ian stretched out so naturally in Charlie's old chair and she wanted to touch him. Her hand ached to reach out; to feel the tweed of his jacket. *Dear God*, she thought. *What is happening to me? Never, ever, have I felt like this. It must be my age. Isn't there something strange happens to women my age? Mam, Mam, help me.*

Ian looked up and smiled slowly. 'You remind me of a chum who was in medical school with me. He could hardly wait to dissect things. Do you want to dissect me, Kate Inglis? Feel free.'

Kate blushed furiously. 'I was only wondering,' she lied easily, 'about whether I could ask you about Patrick. You must have come to some conclusions about his health. Is it wrong for me to ask?'

'I'd be happy if he would come in to the surgery, Kate, but I can't force him.'

'But one day he'll collapse . . .'

'And if that happens, and I'm not saying it's at all likely, we'll deal with him. He's not big built like me, Kate. I would imagine he's always been thin?'

She nodded in agreement.

'And then, perhaps he's still a bit well, monkish?' Again she nodded.

'Maybe Mother just wants to do her duty as she sees it, to fatten her boy?'

'Oh, Ian, you're so calming. It's so good to have a friend to talk to.'

He looked at her strangely and then he stood up, filling the room with his masculinity.

'If it's a friend you're looking for, Kate, join the Guild or for you it would be the Union of Catholic Mothers. I've decided I want more than friendship. Life is too short, don't you think? I'll trot off now. I need to visit old Mrs Flett at the Railway Cottages.'

She stood transfixed as he walked to the door. She could do nothing; she could say nothing, she could not move to stop him going. At the door he stopped and stood for a moment looking out onto the Great North Road and then he turned.

'You're some woman, Kate Inglis,' he said. 'I'll be back.' Before she could move he had reached her in one stride. How did he not break her back as he wrapped her in a bearlike hug? Kate Kennedy Inglis found herself being thoroughly and professionally kissed . . . 'for some scones,' he finished with a laugh.

The door closed and he was gone but his aura stayed in the room and Kate sank into a chair and, for the first time in a long while, thought of herself and her feelings and not of Patrick or that wretched child.

## 24

HOLLY WON THE Dux medal and received it in a dress, just a little short, which had come in one of the occasional parcels from Glasgow with which her Aunt Margaret salved her conscience. Patrick did not attend; he taught until four o'clock and it never occurred to him to ask for time off. Kate was there and Holly was secretly pleased to see her fashionably dressed grandmother among the crowd of miners and their wives who made up the bulk of the audience. Dr Robertson sat on the stage with the rest of the village hierarchy and Holly deliberately ignored his special smile of friendship. She didn't know why she did it and was rather sorry after. The doctor was, after all, according to the girls 'a bit dishy' even though he was so old.

Granny Kate and Dr Robertson took her and her books to tea at the town hotel after the prizegiving and again Holly was burdened by regret that she had chosen not to wear the beautiful pale-green frock her grandmother had bought her.

'You're a really stupid brat, Holly Inglis,' she told herself furiously as the doctor drove them to the hotel. She was aware that her grandmother was totally ignoring the fact that she was not wearing her gift, the prettiest dress Holly had ever seen. And because she was angry she became more morose than ever and had a thoroughly unhappy tea-party, spoiled even further by her intelligent awareness that the grown-ups were cheerfully pretending not to notice her sulks. She concentrated on licking the cream out of a chocolate éclair prior to eating the yummy chocolatey bits and, to her dismay, dropped a big dollop in her lap.

'Oh fuck,' she said in a voice that reached the ears of everyone in the dining room, and Holly stared in horror and rising embarrassment at her furious grandmother.

'It could have been been my new dress, Granny Kate,' she mumbled as she was hurried back to the car but her apology, if such it was, fell on deaf ears.

Dr Robertson drew them back to Patrick's little council house and, while Kate paced the tiny front room downstairs, Holly found refuge with her books.

She heard her father come in and then the three voices talking, talking, talking. No doubt they were discussing one Holly Inglis, Dux and Academy Award-winning actress who swore in public and disgraced her family. She had wanted to be able to rush to meet him, to show him her prizes. Now? Would he be furious? Would he hit her? He never even raised his voice, but this time?

'Well, Holly, show me your prizes,' was all he said when he finally climbed the stairs to her room.

Holly looked at him. He was pale and tired. He didn't really like teaching horrible little boys; they ran rings round him. 'Oh, Daddy, I'll never swear again,' she said by way of apology.

'At least wait until you learn some of Brotheroam's good words.'

He wasn't angry. He was just tired and he must be disappointed. She would make it up to him. 'Look, Daddy, my prizes. I got lots. Old Frazer had to let me be Dux, horns and tail and all. I bet you were Dux too, weren't you?'

'No, I was never the cleverest in my class. Your Auntie Margaret was the clever one. I was a plodder, a mugwump, the Yanks call it; someone educated beyond his potential.'

'I bet Mrs Frazer doesn't know what a mugwump is.'

'A singularly useless piece of information.'

'It's not useless, Daddy. No knowledge is ever useless.' She hated the times when he was sad. Desperately she sought for something to get him out of his mood, his 'I am a failure and worth nothing' mood. 'Look at this prize for geography, *A Tale of Two Cities*.'

He took the book. 'Geography prize – and you don't even know where Denmark is.' But he was laughing. Who'd told him about her getting the belt for not knowing that Scandinavia was more or less the same as Denmark, Sweden and

Norway? He stopped laughing and examined the leather-covered little volume. His face had changed, the laughter which made him look young vanished. 'This must have made Granny very happy; she always wanted to read it. Well, maybe she has now.'

'Me and Grace saw it at the pictures,' said the best English student in the class happily and ungrammatically. 'If I ever get married and leave you, Dad, it will be because my husband looks like Dirk Bogarde, gorrr-juss. Howard Keel is great for singing but, oh, Dirk Bogarde.' She did not know, and would have been horrified to learn, that her grandmother liked Dirk Bogarde too.

'Get yourself off to bed. You're a bad girl.'

'I'm a disgrace, I know. Are we seeing Granny on Sunday? I'll wear her dress and give her this book. I've read it at the library,' finished Holly honestly.

He turned away, looking exhausted, and Holly's loving heart mourned for the grief she had so stupidly caused him. 'Let me make you some tea, Daddy, and then I'll go straight to bed.'

'I'm fine.' He tried to be firm, strict, a proper disciplinarian. 'Things are going to change, Holly Inglis. I want no more swearing or spitting. I don't know why that nice Patterson girl plays with you and I certainly hope you've never disgraced me in that house.'

The long speech left him looking even more drawn.

'Don't fret, Dad. I'm a credit to you at the Pattersons. They tell everybody you're a wonder bringing me up alone. I stand with eyes downcast, looking vulnerable; butter wouldn't melt in my mouth and all the old ladies sigh. "He's suffered enough for one mistake," they say, "and has he no made up for it?" '

'Bed. Clean your teeth, brush your hair and' – dreadful punishment – 'no reading.'

When he had gone Holly obediently prepared for bed and then sat with her toes curled up on the cold linoleum and thought of the day which should have been so happy for everyone and which she alone had spoiled with her stupidity and then she lay down on the bed and cried. 'Oh, please God let it be tomorrow and I'll wear the dress and I'll be nice to Granny and I'll eat the cakes without licking the cream and I'll never, ever swear.'

But God was far too busy with the starving poor in China and Africa to put the clocks back for so insignificant a being as Holly Inglis.

'I'll put the milk bottles out,' Patrick had said, 'and the rubbish; your jobs, Holly.'

She smiled at him. So often he did her household tasks. She felt no guilt, not until later.

Holly went to bed and put out the light and, despite the problems that assailed her young mind, she was soon asleep. She found him next morning, face down in the mud that they had planned to turn into a vegetable garden. He was not dead. The doctor came, not Dr Robertson, and soon the ambulance to take him on the long journey to the nearest hospital. 'A waste of good petrol,' Holly heard one of the neighbours say. It was not meant unkindly, just stating a fact – Patrick was as good as dead – as he saw it. He was wrong. Patrick must have inherited more of Kate's tenacity than he realized for he hung on. He fought a battle against the pneumonia that developed – and won – and then he began to fight the heart weakness that they had found and that he had suspected for several years.

Holly had been left standing in the rain watching the ambulance disappear down the street.

'I'll send the district nurse down,' the doctor had said. 'She'll work something out.'

'Work something out'. Holly knew what that meant. They would put her in a home. Holly tried to imagine herself at Buckingham Palace and her friend the Queen letting her help out with Prince Charles. She could not recall the Queen's face. '*Your Majesty,*' she called silently. '*Where are you? Help me.*' This awful nightmare was the reality; her fantasies had deserted her. The picture of Dad with the mud all over his face kept intruding on her imagination.

'Holly.' It was Grace calling her, dear Grace with her mum there too, for the first time ever in the kitchen.

'Come on, Holly, you're coming home with us till we get your granny.'

This wasn't fantasy; this was real. Holly ran forward and Grace's arms went round her and they hugged, both laughing and crying.

'Come on, lassie.' Grace's mother pried them apart. What if Holly were lousy.' 'Put some of your clothes in this wee suitcase. I want to get back to my soup and then I'll phone your granny.'

Granny. No, oh dear God, no. Granny hated her, had always hated her. Wasn't it her fault that Daddy wasn't a priest? If she'd been a good girl and worn the green frock and behaved like a lady, if she'd taken out the bin like a properly brought up young girl, Daddy wouldn't have been upset and tired and his heart wouldn't have failed or whatever the doctor said it had done when he didn't realize – stupid ass, she'd spit on him – that a very intel-ligent twelve-year-old was listening.

The Pattersons' council house was calm and quiet. Holly had been many times for meals over the years, more meals no doubt than Mrs Patterson had wanted to share with her daughter's strange wee friend. Holly calmed in spite of her grief and fear. She was actually 'staying the night' in Grace's gorgeous bedroom with matching bed, dressing table and wardrobe, and pink silk eiderdown together with pink ruffled pillow that was just for show. Brotheroam had shown Holly fine china and exquisite furniture; she had seen nice pieces in her granny's living room – but this – this was a bedroom, this was fine living.

'Holly, hen,' said Mrs Patterson using the tenderest form of endearment she knew. 'I'll have to tell yer grannie.'

Holly looked at her, at her honest working-class face. Dear God in Heaven, how could she get her to understand?

'My grannie doesn't like me, Mrs Patterson.' She curled up inside with embarrassment. Brotheroam had said that God loved her for herself, swear words and all, and He wasn't interested in the slightest in her antecedents but lovely sweet dear Brotheroam had left the world of men behind and therefore didn't really understand. 'My mammy and daddy weren't married and it's been a real cross for my grannie to bear.'

Mrs Patterson, staunch member of the kirk, wife of not only elder but treasurer, had no tolerance for the young who anticipated marriage, but far less tolerance had she for those who ostracized the fruits of such unions.

'Holly, lass, you're a wean any grannie would be proud to own and you're more than welcome to bide here, but we'll need to tell yer grannie and ye'll probably be sent to stay with her till yer daddy's fine.'

The almost-incoherent story spilled out. The Pattersons heard about the dress Holly had refused to wear, about swearing in the restaurant, and Granny being furious and Daddy saying things had to change.

'And I'm supposed to take out the bin but I never do because I'm always reading or sitting on my wall and he did it because I'm so lazy and that's why he got ill.'

'Lassie, lassie,' soothed Mrs Patterson. 'Yer daddy's not been a well man for a long while. It's nowt to do with you.'

'Put her to her bed, Betty. She'll never listen to ye the state she's in and get Grace out to play. Away ye go, Gracie. Holly's needing a wee nap. You'll see her at tea-time.'

'I'll phone Mrs Inglis when I come back,' mouthed Mrs Patterson but Holly had heard.

'No, please!' she screamed. 'She hates me for getting born and when she hears that it's all my fault . . .'

'It's not your fault, Holly,' said Mr Patterson. 'Now, away to your bed like a good lassie and we'll attend to it. Come on now, you're upsetting Grace.'

That was enought to calm Holly and she contented herself with pleading quietly with Mrs Patterson while she undressed. She lay for hours in the snug bed but finally cried herself to sleep.

'She's asleep,' Mrs Patterson told her husband. 'I'll away up to the phone box and tell her grannie she can bide here the now.' She looked at her husband speculatively. 'I suppose I cannae suggest keeping the bairn while her father's poorly.'

'Suggest what ye like, hen, but her place is with her grannie.'

When the telephone rang, Kate was standing in the huge bakery, just standing looking out of the window. Her face showed clearly that the view she was seeing was not pleasant. She listened to Mrs Patterson's story attentively, thinking, Dear God in Heaven. I hadn't even remembered Holly.

'I'm on the way to the hospital now, Mrs Patterson,' she explained when the woman had stopped talking. 'The garage is sending up a car. I would be grateful if you would keep Holly today and I'll be in touch tomorrow.'

She put the receiver back and stood again, looking out of the window, her reliable iron control ready to crumple like tissue paper. Only her will, the will that had kept her working from morning until late into the night for years, kept her from screaming, screaming, screaming, against this latest hurt. Where was that damned car? If it didn't arrive she would walk the thirty miles to the hospital to get to him. Oh, Patrick, my dearest boy, this was for you, everything for you. Life was supposed to be easy for you; no hunger, no fatigue, a lovely home and education; you were supposed to have an education. Holly, Holly. It's all my fault, you poor wee lassie. I should have accepted you, but all I thought of was myself. I was ashamed of your illegitimacy, embarrassed by the sniggers of my custom-ers because my so-protected son, the boy who had been brought up to become a man of God, had fallen into what I saw as sin. As it had done day and night over the years, the full force of Kate's regret assailed her. I should have offered, all those years ago, to take Holly. It's no wonder the lassie wants nothing to do with me or my peace offerings.

At last the door bell rang. Kate picked up her coat and bag and went to open it. It was not the garage man but Ian and, quite naturally, she stepped into his arms, not caring if the whole world was passing by her door.

'Does everybody spend their life with regrets, Ian?' she asked when they were on their way.

'Only stupid people, Kate. The sensible ones decide they have made mistakes and go on from there. Now, try not to think about anything until you hear from his doctors.'

'But your own patients? What are you doing ... driving me?'

'There you go, in a panic over nothing. We have several patients in the infirmary and I'll see them today while Jim looks after the surgery.' He changed the subject. 'How long can Holly stay with her friends?'

'I don't know but I want her with me. I want to assure Patrick that she's all right and that I'm taking care of her.'

'Leave her where she is for a few days . . . at least until you see what's happening. Thank goodness school is over for the summer.'

Kate stayed quiet for the rest of the long drive. She could have been so happy sitting there in the car seeing his amazingly beautiful hands on the wheel, being faintly aware of his smell, part shaving cream part clean, healthy male. Theirs had been a strange relationship since the night he had kissed her at the door. The next time he had come to the bakery he had behaved as if nothing had happened. Kate was unaware that what she was going through with Ian was what he well knew most healthy young women experienced in their teens; he loves me, he loves me not, I want him, no I don't, I don't care if he never comes back, dear God what will I do if he never comes back? Kate was subtly being led to working out her relationship with the first man who had ever really interested her. There was also the question of working out a solution to the problem of her antagonistic grand-daughter and as if that wasn't enough. . . . Her fingers tightened on her handbag and Ian's strong left hand reached over and held them comfortingly.

'Everything will be fine, Kate. I promise.'

# 25

He would not get well. He knew it. The doctors made encouraging sounds and talked about will to live and advances in medicine and Kate thanked them and murmured all the right things. She knew, however, that Patrick's never-robust constitution had been worn down by too many damp winters in dilapidated cottages, and whatever regime he had put himself through during the war when he had seen his life as an atonement for sin.

*Oh, Mam,* she confessed, *Can I ever forgive myself if it was trying to make up to me that's brought him to this? I could have taken them in; I should have. Charlie would have, but – and desperately she tried to excuse herself – they were gone out of my life before I had a chance to think, to recover.*

She sat beside Patrick's bed and watched his face, almost as young and unlined in illness as it had been in childhood. 'I'll take care of your little girl, Patrick,' she would whisper to the sleeping form. 'You get well soon. Fight,

Patrick, the doctors say you're to fight, and then Mammy will take you home. It'll be just you and me and wee Holly. I'll teach her to bake bread ... if she wants to bake. I'll never force her to do anything.'

'Kate.' It was Ian. 'You ought to have a rest.' He had been back to Auchenbeath and she had been unaware of his absence. 'I've seen the Pattersons and they'll keep Holly for a few days. She's fine, a bit weepy, Mrs Patterson says, but keeping her chin up. Now, please come and lie down for a while; the nurses will alert you if there's any change.'

She looked up at him. Dear God, why was life always so complicated? 'I can't sleep. There were so many years of not seeing him, Ian. I have to stay here, to be here in case he needs me.'

'Then you must eat.'

He went off and came back with some sandwiches and coffee in strange plastic cups. It tasted like nothing Kate had ever experienced before. 'So this is progress,' she said and tried to smile.

'It's hot and wet. Drink it up; doctor's orders.'

Doctors really said 'Doctor's orders'. She looked at the fact critically and stored it away.

'Kate, there won't be any change for some time. Please rest.'

'I must stay with my son.' She hardly noticed when he left or heard what he said. Later, much later, she would have time to think about Ian and Holly and the bakery.

Now there was Patrick. She lifted his hand, the hand that should have been used for consecrating the host and blessing the sick. *Oh, Mam, how much was my fault? Did he ever want to be a priest? Did he ever really want to go to the university? When did I sit down with him and ask what he wanted to do with his life? I don't remember. I remember the purple berry trees in the garden and his wee face as he sat up in the cart with Charlie. Dear sweet Jesus, isn't 'if only' the most painful phrase in the English language. Let me never have to use it with Holly. I'm not too old to change.* She cried then, hot tears that ran down her face and across his white limp hand.

Was there a tightening of the hand in hers? The eyelids fluttered.

'Patrick.'

'Mam. Don't cry. I am so at peace . . . Holly.'

The eyelids fluttered and closed again.

Holly decided that the only way to handle the situation she was in was to invent a story. She couldn't really see her friend the queen in Mrs Patterson's wee front room, which was very strange because she usually had no bother at all seeing her in the shabby front room at home. She would be an American heiress, in hiding with some poor but honest folk.

'This is so good of you all,' she whispered in a throaty voice which somewhat startled her host, but Grace and her mother had lived through Holly fantasies before and went on happily eating. This particular day-dream sustained her until Sunday, four whole days in hiding from the gang of ruthless kidnappers.

She hurried off to Mass while Mrs Patterson muttered under her breath about how ridiculous, not to mention unhealthy, it was to send a wee lassie out without breakfast. The small congregation stared or did not stare – depending on their state of prayer – at 'that poor wee lassie whose father's had the stroke.'

Holly felt the eyes and was no longer an heiress in hiding. Scrubbed and pink from the exertion of hurrying up the road, her red hair, thanks to Mrs Patterson's relentless brushing, curling smoothly around her little head and shining like spun gold as the sun's rays hit it through the stained glass window, she was the sacrificial virgin knelt in prayer. She knew what the light was doing to her hair but she pretended not to notice while making quite sure that she found a seat directly in the sunlight. She bowed her head, Joan of Arc waiting for death, so humble, so beautiful, so young, and then she remembered Patrick lying in the mud and the tears were real as she prayed desperately for his recovery.

The Pattersons, all buttoned up in their Sunday best, were on their way to the kirk when she got back to the house.

'I cannae bide, lassie, or we'll be late, but a decent breakfast will do you good,' said Mrs Patterson.

Food, and Daddy in the hospital; she couldn't. She ate eggs, bacon, sausages, fried bread and potato scones, all washed down with hot sweet tea and felt better.

It's well worth fasting, she decided, her tummy distended. Protestants can't possibly enjoy their food as much as we do.

Sunday with the Pattersons was one meal after another. While eating her breakfast, Holly could smell the scotch broth simmering at the back of the stove and the roast pork spitting away in the oven. What could she do to show her appreciation? At least she could have everything ready for their return. What a pleasure it was to wash the dishes and to set the table. Mrs Patterson, who believed in Sunday as a day of rest, had the potatoes and vegetables peeled and waiting in basins of cold water. Holly rinsed them and had them ready to cook when she heard Grace at the door.

'C'mon, Holly, Mammy says we're to have a wee walk while she puts on the tatties and cabbage. Daddy's coming. It's great he's not working the day. I don't know when we last had him home on a Sunday.'

They walked through the village and down to the river, joining the parade of other good citizens out in their Sunday finery. Patrick would have been sending stones to fly across the water, jump, jump, jump, like frogs; ten bounces, he could achieve with the right throw. Mr Patterson looked shocked at the very idea.

'Ye cannot ask me to ping a stone on the Sabbath, Holly.'

'Dad would do it; he's the champion skimmer of all time.'

The river lay broad, flat, enticing. Here and there a few stones ruffled the surface, pushing the water up further for the sun to play with. And Holly knew, for suddenly he was there with her. She could feel him, even experience the dear smell of him.

'Ach, Daddy,' she whispered. She picked up a stone, a nice smooth flat stone and stood carefully balancing herself. Absolutely the angle of the pitch was important.

'. . . seven, eight, nine, ten, eleven.' Was it only the wind in the trees that chuckled?

'We'd best be getting back, Mr Patterson, before you're drummed out of the kirk for harbouring the infidel.'

'Ach, it's all right, Holly,' said Grace loyally. 'Nobody expects you to behave better.'

Holly smiled, a very grown-up smile. Yesterday, she thought to herself as she tried to deal with the dreadful tight pain across her chest, yesterday I would have said, 'I'll spit on them all, so I will.'

Grace felt the difference in her friend. She took Holly's hand as they walked home behind Mr Patterson, unfamiliar in his Sunday suit.

'Is something the matter, Holly? Mammy'll cheer you up. She's got a rhubarb crumble, your favourite, ready just to pop in the oven. Daddy, if the tallie comes, can we have ice cream with our crumble?'

'Aye, what's a crumble without some kinda cream? Listen for his bell from the front room while we're waiting for our soup.'

The house smelled wonderful, better than school dinners, better fare than the smells at the Toll House. She would stay with the Pattersons for ever. She could be the maid. She would go to school behind Grace, carrying her books, and she would never, ever beat her in an exam again.

The policeman came in the middle of the roast pork which Holly had been unable to eat. She had forced down a few spoons of soup that had threatened to come spilling back up again and the effort to keep it down had helped her cope with the incredible pain. Now she played with crackling as Grace's voice said, 'There's Jimmy Black's dad at the door. There's not been an accident at the pit, surely?'

Her father, a fireman at the local pit, looked at her while the noise of the doorbell rang around the room, and, suddenly frightened, at Holly who kept her eyes down as she pushed peas around the plate. They absolutely must not wander off that fine gold line or the prince would never ever ever find the princess.

'I'll go,' he whispered.

'It's maybe the pit, Holly,' said Mrs Patterson.

'This is the best dinner I have ever eaten, Mrs Patterson,' said Holly, who never ate pork again.

They sat, forks down, trying to talk, waiting for the door to close again behind the policeman.

Grace's father entered the room. 'Holly, lass,' he stopped and looked at his wife who almost sprang to Holly's side. 'I'm really sorry.'

Mrs Patterson pressed the silent Holly to her generous bosom.

'Don't cry.' It was Holly who spoke as Grace started to howl. 'I knew at the river and he's very happy now. He wasn't a very happy man, my daddy.'

She eased herself from Mrs Patterson's arms and stood up. 'Could I just go out for a wee while, by myself? I'll be fine, but I have just got to get out.'

Kate found her, hours later, sitting on the wall at the bottom of Patrick's wee garden. There had to be a wall.

'He said Holly,' whispered Kate and her old, old granddaughter looked at her.

'I know,' said Holly.

'I want you to come home with me, Holly. I promised your daddy.'

Holly climbed off the wall. 'I'll never swear again, Granny Kate.'

# 26

SHE WOULD TAKE the girl; she would send her to a good Catholic boarding school, the one where she would have sent Margaret. New clothes and a haircut; music lessons; dancing lessons; elocution; . . . and in the holidays . . . she could live here and Patrick would come home too and it would be as it should have been. She would make Patrick well; this time it would be all right; she would make it all right.

These had been the thoughts going through Kate's head in the hospital and, of course, as with so many of her plans throughout the years, it had gone wrong. Patrick had died as she had really always known he would and she was left not with *the girl*, but Holly. Her grand-daughter.

Holly had been delighted to stay with Grace; to live out one of her daydreams, the dreams that stopped reality from rearing its sometimes ugly head. Every now and again, the seriousness of the situation would dawn upon her; the thought that if . . . if the awful happened, she might be forced to live with her formidable grandmother in the

Toll House – a house that somehow she could not like – that made her stomach churn with a fear that she had desperately tried to hide. At eleven though, it never occurred to her that Kate was as afraid of rejection as she was herself.

Holly's warm heart reached out to embrace all three Pattersons and she would never love lightly. What she loved, she would love for ever. 'I'd rather be here with you, Mrs Patterson,' she said sincerely, and then added very politely, 'Thank you for having me.'

It was not Granny Kate or Dr Robertson who finally came to take Holly to live with her grandmother. With Grace beside her she had stared transfixed from Grace's bedroom window as a bottle-green Jaguar car purred to a halt outside the Pattersons' council house. Out of it stepped the most beautiful creature Holly or Grace had ever seen. Painted hussy was how Mrs Patterson later described her.

The girls came downstairs to find the vision sitting rather disdainfully on the very edge of Mrs Patterson's spotless settee, sipping tea from the Sunday china. She rose and stretched out her beautifully manicured hands to Holly.

'Hello, Holly. I'm your Auntie Margaret.'

For one horrible moment Holly thought she was about to be hugged and all her good intentions would have gone right down the drain, but Margaret contented herself with holding Holly's fingers tightly in a hand wearing enough diamond rings to buy Patrick's council house several times over.

'Your grandmother asked me to fetch you home, dear. So say goodbye to your nice friends. I'm sure you'll see everyone very soon.'

Mrs Patterson seemed unable to speak. 'Aye, soon enough,' said her husband, 'we'll be at Patrick's funeral.'

Margaret reached for her alligator handbag, 'My mother and I don't want you to be out of pocket.'

Mrs Patterson found her voice; she was very dignified. 'That won't be necessary,' she said. 'The lassie hardly eats a thing. Quite one of our wee family, and always will be, Holly hen.'

And then Holly smiled. There would always be Grace and her mum and her dad. 'Thank you,' she said and allowed Mrs Patterson to kiss her. Mr Patterson shook her hand warmly and Grace, dear Grace, burst into tears and ran upstairs to the pretty pink bedroom.

Dry-eyed, Holly climbed into the fancy car. She hated the sight of Margaret's hands on the leather-covered steering wheel. *Where were you and your diamonds and your fancy car all these years, la-di-da aunty?* she asked in her mind but Margaret saw only a very quiet little girl, obviously in mourning.

Dr Robertson was at the Toll House with Granny Kate and a loud, jovial man who said he was her Uncle George, her Aunt Margaret's husband. Holly disliked him on sight. How different he was from Patrick. Kate did not touch her and for this Holly was grateful.

'I've put you in your father's room, Holly,' said Granny Kate and Holly looked at her in astonishment.

At Kate's thoughtfulness she smiled, her first real smile for her grandmother. 'Can I go there now, please?'

A few minutes later Holly was sitting on the bed where Patrick had slept through his boyhood and early manhood. She wrapped the room round her bruised soul like a healing blanket.

'We'll do it up the way you want later, Holly,' Granny Kate had said but nothing would ever ever be changed, Holly decided.

The room and its decoration was to lead to their first big row nearly four years later.

Holly had been pleased to be sent away to school. It meant fewer hours trying to make conversation with Kate. She came home on the bus from Dumfries every Friday night and went back on Sunday mornings and so she was able easily to keep up her friendship with Grace who was soon as familiar with the Toll House as she was herself. Despite her grief at the loss of her father and her uneasy relationship with Granny Kate, her teen years were a very happy time for Holly. She loved the convent, the beautiful old building with its polished wood and its carved ceilings; its tranquil gardens adrift with daffodils in the spring and a glory of auburn colours in the autumn. On her third morning an elderly nun called Sister Veronica had asked her to ensure that the embroidered cloth on her sewing machine table was always turned so that the perfect embroidery showed; Holly checked that cloth every time she passed the machine for six years even although the old lady died when Holly was in her third year.

Scholastically she did very well. She made friends but no one ever became so close as Grace. Every weekend Holly went home and was polite to her grandmother and polite to Dr Robertson who always seemed to be underfoot.

'Do you think they're living together?' Grace asked once when they had, to their great surprise, found Kate and the doctor kissing in the kitchen. They had crept along to Holly's room to sit stunned on the bed.

'Don't be silly, Grace. Granny Kate lives here and he has his own house.'

'Oh, I don't mean living together, I mean *living* together.'

'You mean . . .' At the horrifying innuendo Holly sat straight up. 'Don't be daft. My grannie's a Catholic. They don't do things like that . . . and, anyway, she's too old.'

Grace saw more films than Holly. 'They didn't look too old to me.'

'Well, I hope they're past it. The whole idea is disgusting.'

'Not with Dirk Bogarde, Holly Inglis.'

Holly laughed but spent a lot of that weekend watching her grandmother very carefully and Kate was well aware of the teenager's scrutiny.

'Holly,' she said one morning at breakfast, 'Dr Robertson would like to take you to Edinburgh, to the theatre. Won't that be nice?'

Edinburgh. The lovely city she had planned to redis-cover with Patrick. Holly stared down at her fried egg.

'Holly?'

'Why me?'

Kate looked at her almost desperately. 'She's deliberately keeping her distance from both of us, Kate,' Ian had said during the latest of their constant discussions about Holly, 'perhaps if I take her somewhere on her own, we could get to know one another better and then possibly you might come to some sensible agreement about our future.'

'Oh, Ian . . .' Kate had said despairingly.

He took her in his arms and gently and softly kissed away her doubts. Held like a child against his chest, Kate felt that she could face anything, Patrick's death, Margaret, even Holly's prickles. She had long ago been forced to admit that she loved Ian, that she wanted to spend the rest of her life with him. He wanted her to be his wife 'Now,' he said, 'not next term . . . not maybe next summer . . . now, while I've still got my own teeth.'

'I would even love you without teeth, Ian Robertson.' She felt like a young girl. This was first love with all the benefits of maturity. Her heart sang when she thought about him; she moved around the bakery, working as hard as she had always worked, but a smile constantly hovered on the edge of her lips, and every now and again she had to stop to savour the feeling, to hold it close and give herself up to it. A blessing from God; it was real. it was passionate, and only the feelings of her grand-daughter prevented Kate from fully abandoning herself to it.

But now she had a plan; she would show Holly how valuable she was to her grandmother and how precious she would always be, even when Ian moved permanently into the bakery. She should have done it, she decided, when Holly was safely away at school, but she waited for the Saturday when Holly went off, seemingly quite happily, to Glasgow with Ian. Kate should have known; it should have been obvious when Holly had suggested Glasgow instead of Edinburgh.

'I would like to go to Edinburgh one day, but I want to go alone. I hope you don't mind.'

Ian's car had hardly disappeared up the Great North Road before the decorators arrived from the south. By seven o'clock in the evening both they and Kate were exhausted, but it was the fulfilled exhaustion that goes with a day's work well done. Holly's room, Patrick's room, was transformed. Gone were the shabby boyish curtains and bedcovers. Gone was the rather sombre wallpaper. The carpets, the furniture itself, all gone and replaced with a fashionable, feminine suite in beautiful light colours.

Holly's old friend, the queen, might well have chosen such a room for her little princess.

Holly was furious. She had returned from Glasgow, happy and stimulated. It had been a good day; two intelligent people with much the same interests and appetites. Holly had greeted her grandmother almost affectionately, but at least naturally, and, pleading exhaustion, had gone straight off to bed.

'I do think it worked, Kate,' said Ian, 'and here we are so subtly being left alone together. How did the room turn out?'

He never did hear Kate's opinion of the decorators' skill. The door opened and a white-faced Holly stood there in the doorway, almost rigid with anger.

'How could you?' She hardly breathed the words, so strong were her emotions. 'You had no right. It was his, just the way he was and I wanted it like that. I'll never, ever forgive you, not as long as I live.'

At Holly's dramatic entry Kate had slowly and tiredly got to her feet. The child's angry face had drained away what little strength was left in her body.

'But, Holly, I wanted it nice for you; I wanted it to be special.'

'That's your problem, isn't it, Granny Kate? You never ask anyone. You, Almighty God, you decide what's right for everyone. Well, I hate your sissy little girl room, I hate it and I'll never sleep in it.'

Kate held out her hands beseechingly but Holly hadn't finished with her. 'And I hate you too. You've taken my father away from me and I hate you.'

She turned and ran from the room leaving Kate standing staring after her.

'Sit down, Kate.' Ian pressed her gently back into the chair. 'I'll go and see where she's gone and then I'll come back. Now, don't move . . . and don't worry. The world's greatest actress has just given the performance of her life but that's all it was, Kate, a performance.'

Kate didn't even hear him. All she could see was Holly's drawn white face with those green eyes staring at her with hatred. 'Oh, God, oh God,' she rocked herself desperately, the way Deirdre had rocked her dead babies all those years ago. 'I know how you feel, Deirdre. Now I know. Now I could really feel for you and give you help and comfort. The child was right. I never ask. Dear God in Heaven, when will I learn my lesson? She thinks I've taken her father away. I threw out some old blankets, that's all they were, old blankets, needing to be replaced even when my poor Patrick slept in them.'

Ian. Dear, kind Ian. For the first time when dealing with a catastrophe Kate felt that she was not alone. There was Ian. Ian, who loved her and who surely knew how to handle little girls. They'd had a good day. He'd make it all right.

Ian was certainly trying. He found Holly in the newly decorated room, feverishly throwing clothes into a suitcase.

Sarah Bernhardt rides again, he thought, but his voice was all professional solicitude. 'Where are you going at this time of night, Holly?'

'The convent.' The voice was muffled.

'Well apart from the logistics of how to get from here to there at this time of night, there is the small matter of the terror a ring at the doorbell in the "wee small hours" would inspire in helpless nuns.'

'I'll go to Grace.'

'Fifteen miles, lugging a suitcase. Yes. You should get there by breakfast.'

She had stopped packing and was standing staring into the depths of the suitcase.

'Did you never make a mistake, Holly Inglis?'

'Everybody does.'

'Were you forgiven for them?'

Holly wanted to shout, 'Well apart from the mistake of being born,' but she held the words in. If they came out they would be real and she would have to face them. 'Of course I was forgiven for my mistakes,' she said. 'My father was the kindest, most understanding man in the whole world.'

'Do you mean everybody including Holly Inglis is allowed to make mistakes, but Granny Kate has to be excluded?'

The girl said nothing.

'She made a mistake with your room, Holly. Mind you, in the years that you've lived with her, have you ever sat down and said, Granny I feel so close to my father in my room. No, I see that grannies are supposed to be mind-readers. We'll accept that. Granny Kate made another mistake, a bigger one, years ago, and she's never forgiven herself for that. Your father forgave her; he understood. But you didn't know her and you decided to hate her because she was upset when you were born. You're not a child, Holly. You must be able to see what a shock the unexpected arrival of an illegitimate grandchild must have been.'

'I wouldn't have been shocked. I would have taken the baby and loved her.'

He looked down at her from his great height. Part of him wanted to wring her little neck – but for her, he and Kate would have been married years before – and another part wanted to take her in his arms and make everything better for her. He was too wise to touch her.

'Holly, please, for the sake of the sleeping nuns and the poor unsuspecting Pattersons, give your grandmother another chance.'

She started to cry then and he let her sob. 'I can't stay in this room. There's nothing left, nothing.'

'Of course there is. It's still the same room and we'll see what Granny Kate did with the bedclothes; you could have those back if she hasn't put them in the bin.'

They compromised on Patrick's shabby old chair which Ian rescued from the heap awaiting pick-up by the refuse men. For the rest of Kate's long life the chair sat beside the sea-green bed, reminding her of her up-and-down relationship with Holly.

'What am I going to do with her?' Kate asked Ian despairingly as they finally closed the bedroom door on Holly who had curled up in the chair and was sound asleep.

'I'm more interested in what I hoped you were going to do with me,' said Ian, 'but I won't bother you any more tonight, Kate. I've had about as much Greek tragedy as I can take for now.'

Kate kissed him goodnight and stood watching his car until its winking lights disappeared down the Main Street. It would have been so pleasant to have had him stay; to lie curled up beside him through what was left of the night and to wake with him beside her in the bed. Charlie had never slept in that bed. She had changed the entire room after his death.

*You'd be the last to grudge me some happiness, Charlie. I wish it had been like this with you. Even those last few months hadn't prepared me for love like this. You did, at least, get some physical satisfaction, Charlie. You had that much at least, didn't you?*

She went back into the house and, before going to her own room, went to peep in at Holly. She was still asleep, still curled up in the disgraceful chair. *We're going to do some talking tomorrow, young lady.*

Talking to Holly was never easy. While Kate had been making resolutions about getting to know Holly, the girl had been deciding that her grandmother would be kept, in a dignified and perhaps rather tragic fashion, at arm's length.

'I'm sorry that I changed your room without consulting you, Holly,' said Kate as she watched Holly demolish a huge cooked breakfast. Where did the food go? The girl was as skinny as . . . well, as Patrick used to be.

'I shouldn't have expected you to understand, Granny Kate. I mean, we don't really know one another, do we?'

Was she being impertinent? 'That's my fault,' said Kate who was determined to grovel abjectly if need be in order to win Holly over. 'But we can change all that. For instance, you tell me you like St Catherine's. You're certainly doing very well. Have you thought of your future?'

'Once I wanted to be the world's greatest ballerina, but I've never had a ballet lesson. I thought I might be an actress . . . does that shock you?'

'No,' said Kate somewhat wryly. 'If that's what you want, Holly, I'm sure we can find out how one goes about it.'

'Well, I think I could become a Hollywood starlet – I've got the right background, rejected by my mother, brought up in a cottage by my father – but I'd have to be beautiful to be discovered and I'm not even pretty.'

Is she serious? thought Kate. Do I try to convince her that she's beautiful? She looks fine to me – when her hair is brushed.

'Hollywood actresses don't really act, do they, Holly?'

'No, Granny Kate, but they die a lot and I'm good at dying. It's real plays I'm interested in, like the one I saw with Doctor Robertson. I read plays at school but to be the character – on the stage – to say the words so that people really believe you're real. Just hearing them was incredible.' This was the real Holly. Kate warmed to her.

'I loved words too, Holly.' Could she tell of her longing to finish Dickens and Scott and that Fitzgerald fellow Patrick had liked? Holly gave her no chance.

'That was a nice breakfast. Thank you.' Her face had lost its animation and she had withdrawn again. For a moment Kate had thought Holly might share more of her dreams but she had obviously rejected the idea. Pray God she did not reject the dreams and put them for ever behind her.

'If it's all right with you, I'd quite like to go to Edinburgh University and study Liberal Arts.'

'Whatever you want.' Kate watched her as she cleared the dishes away and began to fill the sink with hot water. Was it too early to talk about Ian? I haven't even told him that I've come to a decision.

'I'm going for a drive with Doctor Robertson this afternoon. Will you be all right?'

'Grace is coming.'

'How nice. Ask her to stay to tea. I've got a lovely steak pie.'

'Depends on her bus.'

'She knows she's welcome any time. Perhaps her parents . . .'

The look almost of loathing on the girl's face shocked Kate. *She hasn't forgiven me. She's never going to forgive me or . . . love me. I must not let her know that I care.*

'I'm sorry, Holly, about the room and everything.' She was begging.

'It's only a place to sleep, Granny Kate.'

Kate fled.

# 27

THAT WAS ONE of the joys of being with Ian. He never talked unless he had something to say. For over an hour they drove along the valley of the Nith and Kate lay back in her seat and let the peace and beauty of the countryside apply balm to her wounded spirit.

After a while she sat up straighter and smiled at him.

'Was it so awful?' he said.

'H'm. I tried to remember everything you said about her being the great tragedienne. Sometimes I thought we were on the way to talking to one another, really talking; she told me she wanted to be an actress – West End, not Hollywood.'

'Thank God for that.'

'Ian. I almost told her we were going to be married.' She held her breath. What would he say?

'And are we? It's some time since I asked, or are you becoming so modern that you are asking me?'

'Oh, Ian, please don't be flippant. I couldn't bear it. I stayed awake all night worrying about Holly and realizing that . . . I can cope if you're there . . .'

'Like an elastoplast. Sorry, I know I'm being flippant. It's because I can hardly believe what I'm hearing. Kate, I have booked a fearfully expensive and alcoholic lunch at a charming wayside inn. After filling you full of good food and champagne I had decided to attempt to lower my rather geriatric body to its knees beside you for one last romantic attempt. Now I can enjoy the food without looking forward to the athletics. Kate Inglis, will you marry me?'

'Yes . . . please.'

'Damn it, why are there no lay-bys on this atrocious road? I want to kiss you so badly. Actually, I want to kiss you rather well . . . and several other things at which I am woefully out of practice and which, in a lay-by, would get "Prominent Dumfriesshire Doctor arrested for indecency." Kate, I could sing. I could shout. Singing's better. Do you know any songs?'

'Keep right on to the end of the road.' She could match him for silliness; he made her young and silly.

'Is that a song or an instruction?'

Kate laughed like a young girl. 'Both.'

'I'm five years old and Christmas and my birthday have come on the same day. Did you like your birthday when you were little, Kate? And Christmas? Did Father Christmas bring lots of presents?'

Kate looked at him as he sat half bent over the wheel, his beautiful hands almost clenched on the steering wheel, and tried to memorize him. 'He's only just found me,' she said and knew that no matter what the future held, this silly conversation in the car would always be among the happiest moments of her life.

At the hotel Ian produced a ring; two rows of diamonds encircling a beautiful ruby. Kate had never seen anything so beautiful and she had never owned anything so valuable. Her hand trembled as he slipped it on.

'I don't mind if you keep your first wedding ring on.'

Kate looked at the thin little circlet of gold and sighed. At last it was time to say goodbye to that part of her life.

'No. I think I'll keep it for Holly.'

They stayed at the inn well into the early evening, making plans. They would marry as soon as the banns could be read. Ian would sell his house and move into The Toll House for the time being.

'I really don't want my wife working for a living; I want her looking after me. I'm going to teach you to play golf, Kate, and to sail, and to . . . just to learn to relax would be nice. Where will we go for a honeymoon?'

'Holly's tea.' Kate started up in alarm.

'I don't know that one; a Caribbean island, is it?'

'We must get back, dear. I promised to make a meal for Holly and her friend Grace.'

'Aren't they old enough to get their own meals?'

'I promised.'

Holly and Grace had already eaten. The bakery was, in fact, empty.

'Holly must be at the bus stop. There's a bus to Dumfries at seven-thirty.'

'Then I shall scuttle away and leave you to make the announcement, or would you rather I stayed for moral support?'

'It would be better if I see her alone.'

'You haven't done anything wrong. Will she want to be a bridesmaid? I'm joking. Come here and let me kiss you as an honestly engaged woman should be kissed and then I'll go.'

Kate gave herself up to him, but, fearing Holly's return, pulled away quickly. 'I'll see you tomorrow?'

'Probably not, my dear one. I'm on call and I now have important letters to write.' They heard the front door slam. 'Is that to warn you that she's coming?'

'Probably not.'

Holly, dishevelled and with her red hair sticking up round her head like the crown of the Statue of Liberty, came into the room bringing a cold blast with her. 'Sorry, Gran, the wind's up. Hello, doctor. Had a nice drive?'

'Yes, indeed, but your grandmother will tell you about it. Goodnight, ladies.'

'We ate the pie, Granny Kate, with a salad,' said Holly when Kate returned. 'I hope you're not hungry.'

'No, I had a huge lunch but I think I'll make some tea. I have something I want to talk to you about.'

Holly was already at the door leading to the bedrooms. 'I've got some studying to do for tomorrow and if it's about you and Doctor Robertson, your engagement ring is blinding me from there.'

Dear God, don't let her be awkward and prickly, thought Kate. 'Please, Holly, couldn't we talk about it? I wanted to tell you first.'

Holly turned away. 'I have to study.' Her face was stiff. 'Congratulations on your engagement,' she said politely but then added, 'It's a little embarrassing – you're both so old  but I'm away at school most of the time and really it's none of my business.'

'We're planning a quiet wedding, perhaps mid-term.' Kate could hear the desperation in her voice. I'm begging again.

'That'll be nice,' said Holly, and went out closing the door behind her.

Kate made her tea and sat down at the table as she had done for years and years in time of trouble. But this time she had Ian and his love to sustain her. *Dratted child*, she said to herself. I'm not going to worry about your prickles, Holly Inglis. You're not going to spoil my wedding. She refused to think about her first wedding almost forty years before. *I'm going to retire and be a full-time wife. I'll sell this place and invest the money for little Miss Prickles. If she refuses to love me, that's too bad. I'll always be there for her if she ever wants me and if I've failed to earn her love then I'll just have to accept that. Oh, Patrick, my dear son, I am trying with your little girl, but it's been too late, I fear. If you can help or you, Mam . . .?*

It was supposed to be a very quiet wedding. Ian's partner and his wife, Kate's lawyer who turned out to be Ian's lawyer too, some elderly cousins on Ian's side . . . and Margaret and Holly, neither of whom came. Margaret was out of practice at seeing her mother and Holly had gone on a school trip to London.

Kate refused to acknowledge that her grand-daughter's desertion troubled her and paid for her outing quite happily.

They went to the Caribbean for their honeymoon. 'Had Holly been around, Mrs Robertson,' teased Ian on the plane to San Juan, 'we would have had a weekend in Blackpool.'

They spent a week eating wonderful food, exploring islands, getting sunburned, and walking along moonlit beaches to their private cabana. Sometimes it seemed to Kate that she was a different woman.

How could she give herself up to pleasure like this, abandon herself nightly to loving and being loved?

'Don't knock it, Mrs Robertson,' teased Ian. 'Back in Auchenbeath I'll be too tired to do anything, well almost anything but kiss you goodnight.'

And Kate arched up to him and, holding him tightly, cried, 'I love you, I love you.'

They flew home, their cases full of gifts for Holly, Ian's partners and the bakers.

'I can't believe you've never been on holiday before, Kate,' said Ian. 'We'll holiday every year.' He slipped a flat black box from a jeweller on the freeport of St Thomas on to her lap. 'Happy Anniversary.'

They had been married ten days and the box contained a pearl necklace.

'You were so busy choosing her first ear-rings for Miss Holly that I was able to buy this without your even noticing. You are an amazing woman. It never occurred to you to get anything for yourself in that Aladdin's cave of a shop.'

'Oh, Ian,' said Kate as she felt the smooth kiss of the pearls against her blouse, 'you have already given me so much.'

How was it possible to be so happy? Only Holly could spoil it.

But she didn't. Holly had made a pact with herself the night Kate changed her bedroom. She would live with her grandmother who, she decided, tolerated her only for her father's sake. The fact that Kate tried endlessly to show her that she was wanted for herself meant nothing. Holly was living a real-life role to the full and she'd got so used to it that it became real.

Life after the wedding settled down. Holly went to school on Monday morning and returned on Friday evening. Sometimes she stayed for the weekend with Grace or other girls from St Catherine's. Kate encouraged her to avail herself of all the travel opportunities provided by the school.

'Glad to get rid of me,' thought Holly but confessed that she loved foreign travel. She went to Paris, to Rome, skiing in the Swiss Alps and, when she told her grandmother about her trips, she sparkled with animation and happiness. Then she would remember her script and the curtain would come down.

Holly and Ian got used to it and referred to her as Sarah Bernhardt when she was away.

'One day she'll realize you're the most important person in her life, Kate,' consoled Ian. 'Just be patient and wait to pick up the pieces when the great actress falls off her stage.'

# 28

HOLLY WAS ACCEPTED at the university of Edinburgh and at the age of eighteen she was in the beautiful capital, delirious with excitement. Every moment was filled with promise; she covered the old town on foot, every day finding something new. New to her, of course, but old to history. She found herself wondering if Patrick had seen this or read that or felt as she did the first time she watched the sun rise from Arthur's Seat. She felt she would never tire of the Edinburgh skyline or the beauty of the Georgian New Town or the wealth of the museums and galleries.

Luckily, by the time the term really started, she had a working knowledge of the city and was able to settle down to lectures and classes. She liked the residence which was merely a grown-up version of boarding-school and was friendly with almost everyone. Boarding-school had taught her to protect herself from snobs; there were even more of them at the university.

'What they see is what they get,' Holly had decided. She was herself and would be the same to everyone, liking people for what they were, not for what they had. She threw herself wholeheartedly into undergraduate life and revelled in the joy of joining everything. At Christmas she found, to her horror, that she had done very badly in her examinations.

'How could I fail? I never had to work hard before and I've always done well?'

She crawled back to Auchenbeath where she spent most of the holidays in her room trying to work out the puzzle.

You're being taxed, Holly Inglis, for the first time in your life, she told herself with her habitual brutal honesty, a trait she shared (but this she would never acknowledge) with her grandmother, and you can't hack it.

Christmas with Ian's part of the family was like being a little girl again with Patrick. Ian pretended to believe in Father Christmas and he insisted that everyone around him believe too. They hung stockings by the fireplace and Santa visited while Holly and Kate were at Midnight Mass.

'And you saw nothing, Ian Robertson?' asked Holly.

'Cross my heart, Holly. I saw no one strange in this house.'

They were all early risers, Kate and Ian from a lifetime of habit and Holly from anticipation; she wanted to see what Santa had left. A tangerine, an apple, a small box of raisins, a bar of apple soap, everything just as Patrick had done it, and for that Holly was grateful; she could not have borne too much largesse. There were expensive gifts from her grandmother, not too many, a heavenly sweater, a tailored skirt, and books, books, books. The whole day was a delight. At bedtime Kate handed Holly a small package and inside was her thin old wedding ring on a fine gold chain. Holly stared at it without saying a word.

'I thought you might like to have it, Holly. It's a direct link with your grandfather; he held you asleep once in his arms.'

Holly looked at her grandmother, her heart too full for speech. Something more than the ring had passed between them; a warmth that Holly had never experienced with Kate before.

All too soon it was time to return to Edinburgh with New Year's resolutions to work hard. Her mind, however, was soon full of more important things. Holly fell in love.

His name was Ruaridh and she bumped into him – literally – at the library. The wind, one of those winds for which Edinburgh was renowned, had plucked the huge doors from her hands as if they were matchsticks and she and her books went flying down the steps to collide with a man who was being blown up them.

He picked himself up and then picked her up and together they rounded up the books.

'I'm so sorry,' said Holly looking up, up, up into the bluest of blue eyes.

'Not at all,' he said politely and his voice warmed Holly down to the tips of her toes. He was still holding her and for a lifetime they looked at one another and he smiled and Holly was lost. 'Must go,' he said as if he really regretted leaving, 'can't have them throwing me out.' He ran up the steps and disappeared, without a backwards glance, into the library.

She was halfway up the steps after him before she came to her senses and, blushing furiously, hurried round the corner for her bus. No one would throw you out, she said to herself as the bus chugged up the Bridges, you're too big. There was more too. It was an aristocratic voice, a public school voice. People with plummy voices didn't get thrown out of anywhere if they were late. The proletariat waited politely until they were ready to leave.

Can't abide that kind of nonsense, Holly assured herself. I'd spit in his eye, and at that reversal to childhood she giggled wildly and had to leave the bus two stops before her own for fear of being thrown off. And they'd throw *you* off, *nae bother*, she told herself.

She was back at the library two days later only to change a book and she only stayed in the entrance hall reading until closing time because it was quieter than her residence. In fact, she decided that it would be much better academically for her to do all her studying at the library. She was despondently leaving the library three weeks later when he left with her. How had he got in without her seeing him? He must have been there before she got there. Who cared. He was here walking beside her as if they were old friends.

'A night for nefarious deeds,' he smiled down at her as they struggled against the wind. 'May we drop you somewhere?' He had stopped beside an expensive dark-green car. 'My brother,' he explained, nodding towards the distinguished-looking man in the driving seat.

'No, no thank you . . .'

'Ruaridh,' he said, 'Ruaridh Granville.'

'I'm Holly Inglis.'

'Holly. How quaint. Goodnight then.'

He lowered himself into the car and it sped away with scarcely a sound. He didn't look back. Holly watched until the car was out of sight before she hurried to her bus stop.

Fool. Just because Dad said never to go anywhere with people you don't know. I know Ruaridh. She stopped. I know Ruaridh, she said again quite loudly this time so that anyone passing could have heard and a bubble of pleasure welled up inside her. 'A night for nefarious deeds'. Did people really talk like that? Ruaridh did. Thirty minutes later when she was finally sitting on a bus heading up the Bridges she was wishing again that she had accepted a lift. But I could never have spoken to his brother. And then she remembered that she had been unable to say anything to Ruaridh either, except her name finally and that didn't count.

She tried to stay away from the library but students need books or so she told herself. She tried to banish Ruaridh from her mind but if she caught a glimpse of a very tall man she rushed forward, hoping against hope that it was he but it never was. His voice came unbidden into her mind at odd moments and his blue eyes came between her and almost every word she read.

This will not do, she scolded herself. Anyone might think you ... you what? God, Holly, you can't lo ... like him. You've only met him twice. And then she plummeted into an incredible abyss of despair for she realized that she *did like* him and she could see no way in which someone like Ruaridh could ever like her back. She thought of the few things she knew about him; public school accent, expensive cars, understated but very well-cut clothes. He'll spit in your eye, Holly.

The next two weeks were a mixture of pain and pleasure and Holly tried to attend to her lectures. She would never see him again; she would bury herself in her books and carve a wonderful career for herself. She felt better. God, what a relief. Obviously she was not in love because she felt nothing over the thought of never seeing him again. The next moment she felt as if she wanted to die. Oh don't be stupid, you've seen him twice and all you ever said to him was your name and you're escalating it into the love affair of the century. The king and Mrs Simpson. That cheered her up. Old Wallis caught him.

She stopped looking for him at the library and so she met him at The Chocolate House on Princes Street late one Friday night. She was just about to dig into an enormous pile of ice cream and chocolate sauce that she had been saving up for for weeks when he appeared in front of her.

'You can't possibly eat all that.'

She was so surprised that she dropped the spoon but for once her wits did not desert her. 'Then why don't you help me?' And at her audacity she turned as red as a beetroot.

'Done, hold that spoon till I dig up another chair.'

He was back in no time. Where had he found the chair? The Chocolate House was always crowded but even worse at the weekends. Somehow she knew that Ruaridh Granville would always be able to find himself a chair.

A waitress came over immediately. And he would always be able to summon up waitresses, probably even waiters.

'Would you be kind enough to bring me a . . . spoon?' He looked at the waitress who knew she should be cross but who couldn't resist his charm. 'My friend has a small appetite . . . but later we'll have some hot chocolate.'

Holly could hardly believe it was happening. Could this possibly be termed a *date*? He had been at the Usher Hall for the Scottish National Orchestra. They had this dynamic new conductor, Alexander Gibson. Surely she had seen him?

Holly had never been in a concert hall in her life but she knew where she would be every Friday evening from now on. 'Not yet,' she stalled.

'What about your friends?' she asked later as they waited for their drinks.

He looked around vaguely. 'They're here somewhere. Did you think me rude, Holly? It's every man for himself in The Chocolate House, you know. They will have . . . yes, there's Anne over there, and . . .' He slewed around in his chair and waved wildly. 'Gairn!' he yelled, 'Yes, everyone has found a seat. It's a grand group of chums, you must meet them.'

The hot chocolate was finished. There was no excuse for staying. She wanted to stay for ever just watching the play of light on his beautiful face, listening to the music of his voice. She stood up. 'I really must go.' She wished later that she had allowed herself to be talked into staying longer.

'Gairn's car is on George Street. We'll all take you home later . . .' He was already calling his friends over to take over her table.

The introductions were so fast that she assimilated very little. Anne was out of the same drawer as Ruaridh but, like him, warm and friendly. Gairn was like his name, rough and strong, a woolly bear. She wished she could stay but she was outside and they were already deeply involved in one another.

She hurried across Princes Street to her bus stop and then the miracle happened. He was running after her, yelling, 'Where do you live?' as the bus pulled away and she was yelling back and inside her stomach butterflies were exploding and she felt she would never, ever again feel so happy as she waved to him as he stood, oblivious of traffic, in the middle of the street.

Had there ever been a more beautiful spring? Not in Holly's memory. Almost every Saturday Gairn's solid old Citroën drew up outside her residence and she squeezed in beside Ruaridh and Anne and sometimes even one or two others and off they went to the nearby Pentland Hills to walk.

Here, near Edinburgh, Holly experienced the same joys in walking that her grandmother had enjoyed almost fifty years before; she revelled in the health of her strong young body which allowed her to keep pace with Ruaridh's long strides and to throw herself down – not in the least out of breath – on the moors beside him while they waited for Anne.

'It's exhilarating,' she said.

'Have the decency to pech a little!' teased Gairn when he and Anne finally caught up with them. Gairn was indestructible and could easily have beaten even Ruaridh to the summit, but it was always Gairn who waited for any stragglers and Anne was always a straggler.

'I fail to see what pleasure you get out of these walks, Ruaridh,' Anne complained petulantly. 'You walk too fast to see anything.'

Ruaridh merely smiled at her and went on chewing grass and Holly saw the smile and decided that it was the most beautiful smile she had ever seen.

Then Ruaridh took his flute out of his knapsack and he played while Anne and Holly and any other girl who was with them prepared their picnic. Sometimes, as she lay on the warm grass listening to the mellow tones of the flute, the happiness welled up inside her and she felt that she could not possibly be any more content. This was *life*; this was living.

'He should become a professional,' she murmured to Gairn who lay beside her.

'A Granville, my dear!' drawled Gairn in a poor imitation of Ruaridh's polished tones. 'Big brother wouldn't even let him be in the British Youth Orchestra.'

'Big brother?' He of the expensive, dark-green car.

'Ask Ruaridh if you want to know anything but his brother brought him up and he holds the purse strings and Ruaridh does exactly what he's told.'

A cloud went over the sun and they were reminded that it was still quite early in the year and time for them to go.

Ruaridh never mentioned his brother; they had never been alone together after that one time in The Chocolate House. Holly's friends from the hostel teased her about her gorgeous boyfriend but that was hardly the case. He was male and he was a friend. Ergo he was a boyfriend but not in the way the girls meant. They were all friends; Anne and Gairn and Ruaridh and now Holly and others who were not so involved in the triumverate.

Yes, that's what it is, Holly thought despondently, a triumverate, and I'm a fourth, allowed so far into the sacred, inner circle but no farther.

Gairn was like her, not like them, Anne and Ruaridh, and he was admitted and so would she be and why not? She started going to the Friday night concerts at the Usher Hall, cheapest seats, but everybody was poor and sat in the gods, and some nights Anne was engaged elsewhere and Holly sat with the prince of the fairytales on one side and the practical, dependable farmer's son on the other and fell in love with Sibelius.

It was the done thing, of course. Alexander Gibson, newly arrived from the Royal Ballet, loved Sibelius and so everyone in that magic circle breathed and ate Sibelius too. Holly would be glad later. Because of Ruaridh, she, who had never heard classical music, who had never, ever been near a concert hall, began a life-long affair with great music. Slavishly she listened to Ruaridh and she was lucky for he had had excellent training and had superb taste. 'Brahms will be played in Heaven,' he said and Holly was only too ready to agree with him.

Her spring term results were hardly better than her winter ones. Again, Kate made no comment, but Holly sat in her room and studied and, in the summer term, she worked. They all did. Books replaced the flute, and study sessions replaced the Friday-night concerts. They sat in the Chaplaincy Centre at the university and Holly, Gairn and Anne studied while Ruaridh changed the records on the old machine. Mozart's flute and harp concerto became Holly's favourite piece of classical music.

What are you doing during the hols? That was the most-asked question. Holly wanted to work. It never occurred to her to ask Kate for a job at the bakery which had not yet been sold.

The choices boiled down to hotel work or looking after children. Holly knew less than nothing about children. Could she possibly convince prospective employers that she would adore their horrible brats? To try to do so seemed the lesser of two evils. She bought *The Lady* and read the wanted ads. Some sounded quite good.

'Look at this one,' she told her friends as they lounged at lunchtime in the Students' Union, listening to records and drinking coffee. '"Delightful country cottage in exchange for occasional care of three delightful children. Professional parents in town weekdays. You would be in complete charge. Other help kept." '

'Three children; they may all be toddlers,' said Anne.

'Or worse, they could be teenagers,' suggested Ruaridh.

'But I'd have my own "delightful country cottage" . . .' began Holly.

'A hovel . . . that leaks . . . woodworm, rising damp and little you would be in sole charge of the brats while Mama and Papa swan around London all week?' This from Gairn.

'There would be other help.'

'You must be joking. What do you think, Ruaridh? You're the only one of us with experience of nannies and all that.'

'Don't apply. I was a holy terror and there was only one of me. When Charles went away I gave the help a terrible time.'

'But I really feel I need to work. Work is good for the soul.'

'Come and spend the summer with me,' smiled Ruaridh, 'if you don't mind an all-male household . . .' He sat up, suddenly alert. 'You could marry Charles. I've been trying to marry him off for years.'

The words, uttered in jest, shot through Holly like a physical pain. Marry Charles. Suddenly, painfully, sweetly, she knew whom she wanted to marry. She managed to recover. 'Well, thank you I'm sure, but I want to work. I want to gain all kinds of experience. There was a nanny wanted with an army family in Germany; I would love to go abroad.'

'Then go to France and pick grapes,' said Gairn. 'I was going to work on a farm there but my dad thinks it will be better if I work with him; sensible and cheaper, not so much fun. I'll bring you all the information, Holly. It's an international students' organization that arranges jobs in vineyards, farms, on digs . . . you name it, they can organize it.'

'What about your grandparents, Holly,' asked Anne. 'Won't they miss you?'

'They're practically newlyweds; I'm a bit in the way. I shall go to La Belle France and make glorious wine.'

And so Holly went to France and looked for traces of French heroes she had met in books in a vineyard in the south of France. D. K. Broster had introduced her to doomed but heroic lace-clad aristos and she looked for them in vain in the faces of the French farmers.

And in Auchenbeath her grandmother relaxed in her love for Ian Robertson but watched the post for occasional cards from her grand-daughter.

'She didn't want to come home, Ian,' she sighed, 'not even for a little while.'

'Neither did I when I was at medical school, Kate,' lied Ian. 'Young people want to travel, to meet others, to find what they call life. They go home when they need a hot bath; when they run out of money.'

'Holly won't . . . run out of money, I mean. She's very careful. Two more years and she'll graduate and I'll lose her completely. I've failed again. First with my children and now with my grand-daughter.'

'Holly needs you, Kate. I think she even loves you. She may not know it yet. Deep down she is aware that you are there and one day she'll need you and come running home.'

Kate allowed herself to be soothed. Was he right? Would Holly ever need her?

'I think I'll sell the bakery. If Holly comes home at Christmas we could look forward to buying a new house together.'

'Or building one. I like the idea of building something brand new out of the ashes of the past. It could be our retirement project, Mrs Robertson.'

Kate looked at him in surprise. Retire? She had never really considered age but, of course, the time had come to hand over to younger people.

'How silly I've been, Ian. Why I have hung on to this place . . .? Habit, I suppose.'

'I'll talk to my partners tomorrow; lots of new people around looking for practices.'

'And I'll put this place on the market.'

The decision was made. She would not change her mind. The years that were left; and surely they could not be many, would be devoted to Ian . . . and Holly, if she'll let me.

# 29

*I'M A DIFFERENT person returning to university,* Holly told herself on the ferry to Dover. *Holly Inglis has worked in a foreign country, has learned a foreign language, well, more or less, has 'done' Paris, and has even flirted with other men.* She had been surprised at how easy that had been. The camps had been full of eager young men from other countries, Holly had even joined a mixed party of students who had gone together to Paris. There she had wondered at the magnificent buildings, filled her heart and mind with the paintings in the Louvre, drunk wonderful, cheap wine at pavement cafes and listened with tolerance, and some amusement, to at least three protestations of undying love.

How could one possibly fall in love with someone in less than a month? Had the new, sophisticated Holly Inglis forgotten how long it had taken her to fall in love with Ruaridh? She had fallen in love with him that first day in the library and stayed in love with someone she had no reason to feel she would ever see again. That was different, she told herself.

She laughed to herself, a warm low chuckle that made two elderly gentlemen walking the deck look at her and smile at her rosy cheeks and bright eyes and wish they were forty years younger. As if she could read their thoughts, Holly smiled at them, a smile that said that she was young and healthy and in love with life.

They helped her off the ferry with her suitcases and her parcels with gifts for everyone. She had a blue silk scarf, the most expensive of the presents she had bought, for her grandmother and a bottle of wine for Ian. For Grace there was the most expensive bra she could find; a delicious confection of lace and fake pearls which, she had decided, she could give her only when they were alone. For Grace's father she had French cheese and for Mrs Patterson a scarf with the Eiffel Tower emblazoned on it.

It was a lovely home-coming. They loved their gifts. Dear Grace laughed about the bra.

'I'll never be able to wear it, Holly. Can you imagine hanging anything so decadent out on the line?'

'Yes I can, but it'd be pinched and we'd have great fun trying to work out which pillar of the kirk was wearing it.'

'Or which wee holy Roman.'

'Mrs Wilson.'

They collapsed with laughter at the thought of such a formidable bosom inside that scrap of lace and were called to order by Grace's mother. 'Will you two ever grow up?'

'I hope not,' said Grace's father.

Holly had not giggled and laughed over her presents to her grandparent. They had met her at the station, Ian wisely standing back to allow Kate to greet her granddaughter alone.

'You look different, Holly,' she said truthfully. There was a glow about the girl.

'I'm a traveller, Granny Kate. Travel changes people.'

So does love, thought Kate, and she asked Holly if she had met anyone nice in France. Holly rattled off the names and nationalities of a dozen people who were *nice*, but it was obvious that she was not in love with any one of them.

The glow became almost a light when Holly spoke with pleasure of returning to the university.

'It'll be so different this year. I'm not afraid of the big city or of the lecturers. I sent cards to all my friends; I can hardly wait to see them.'

Kate watched her face. Oh, Holly, my dear, she thought. You're so transparent. It's a him you're thinking of, not them, and I hope and pray he feels the same way about you.

'Will we see you at mid-term, Holly? It would be fun to look for a new house together.' She saw the shadow of doubt on Holly's face and babbled, 'Or we could come to Edinburgh and do some touring from there. Let us know what you would like.'

'I'm not sure, Gran. Things come up . . .' She stopped.

'We're here, Holly,' said Kate. 'We'll always be here. Bring your friends . . . whatever.' She could say no more. She could only hope that Holly understood.

Holly could hardly wait until it was time to return to Edinburgh. She went as far as Thornill on the bus with Grace, who was going on to Dumfries to start work at the Royal Infirmary.

'I'll come up to Edinburgh my first weekend off,' Grace promised, 'and see how wonderful Scotia's capital is – or maybe it's the men in Edinburgh who make it such a fab place.'

Holly smiled. 'Come up to see the sights in all their glory, Grace,' was all she said. She was still smiling when the Edinburgh bus arrived but never, it seemed, had the bus crawled so slowly up through the hills. She was going back to Edinburgh. Happiness swelled inside her so that she felt it must burst out of her and be obvious to everyone on the bus. She had done it; she had passed her exams . . . the butterflies in her stomach made her giggle. Oh, God, how could she explain her behaviour? Please God, don't let anyone look at me because I'm so happy and excited that I feel that I could fly to Edinburgh all by myself. She giggled again and got a disparaging look from the matron across the aisle but Holly was unaware of the overt disapproval because . . . Oh, Holly, at least admit it to yourself, it's Ruaridh. Ruaridh, Ruaridh, this year would be different. Surely their friendship would develop this year; they would be an acknowledged pair, not just part of the group; Anne, Gairn, Ruaridh, and Holly. It would be Holly and Ruaridh, Ruaridh and Holly.

The bus rolled along in time to the names and at last they were pulling in to St Andrew's Square. She felt like the heroine going on to the stage for the final act. It was going to be wonderful. Life was wonderful and every day it was going to get better and better.

There was a card in Anne's handwriting, waiting; 'S.N.O. concert, Friday. Then Chocolate House. Luv Us.' Holly refused to yield to the tiny feeling of disappointment that the card was not from Ruaridh and that there was no talk of meeting for five whole days. It was the beginning of term, of course. Everyone was much too busy. Well she would be busy too.

And she managed . . . almost. She found herself visiting the central library, not to borrow a book or to do research although she pretended to do both, hoping to bump into Ruaridh.

Oh, how gutless I am. If he doesn't want to see me until Friday I shouldn't chase him.

But she couldn't stop. She had no self-respect. She hated herself; she castigated herself; no man was worth this; yet every day she just happened to find herself near the library.

Thursday night. It was raining, and, as usual, Holly had forgotten to put a hat or scarf in her bag. The rain dripped down her neck, her hair was plastered to the sides of her head and drips of water hung from her ears – not her best feature – and her nose. She had almost forgotten Ruaridh; she needed to get inside that beautiful building where it was warm and dry.

She rushed up the steps and bumped into a man who was just coming out.

'Holly. How wonderful.' He sounded delighted to see her. Surely he couldn't pretend such evident pleasure. 'Must you use the library?' he asked. 'I was going to the catacombs for a coffee. Come with me. I'm dying to hear all about your holiday.'

He took it for granted that she would comply and she couldn't have denied him even if she had wanted to. Clinging tightly to his arm, she skipped along beside him in the rain and suddenly it was true, all that nonsense in the songs about the sun shining even when it was pouring or snowing and being unaware of cold or rain; it was all so gloriously, wonderfully true. He looked down into her shining eyes and, for the first time, he saw that she was beautiful.

The catacombs was fairly quiet and they were able to find a table where they could sit and talk. How many cups of coffee did they drink? Holly couldn't remember. They talked about the holiday, the 'vac', Ruaridh called it. He didn't elaborate on his experiences.

'The usual . . . family and all that . . . we do the same things year after year, quite predictable. I would never have dreamed of going off picking grapes.'

443

'It seemed more exciting and a better use of time than working in a hotel. Perhaps you should have had a job?'

He flushed slightly. 'I've never done a job of work in my life . . . quite useless, I'm afraid.'

'No point in working if you don't have to . . . keeps someone out of a job who needs it. Gairn worked for his father, I remember, and Anne . . .?'

'The Mediterranean part of the time. Holly, you look different.'

'It's my mascara; it must be all over my face.'

He took out a clean, folded linen handkerchief. Holly noticed that there was a tiny yet flamboyant R embroidered by hand on one corner. He gently wiped the mascara and rain from her face.

'Funny little Holly,' he said gently. 'No, it's not the warpaint. Have you done something absolutely dreadful . . . like grow up?'

'It's time we grew up, isn't it, Ruaridh?'

'God, no. Wouldn't it be nice to stay like this for ever and ever? Me sitting here, wanting to kiss you and you holding up your face so trustingly to be kissed.'

Holly leaned closer across the table. She could see herself mirrored in his eyes. Her whole body was crying out, please, please, but for what? At last, at last, his lips touched hers, so softly and gently. She had closed her eyes. Had she been brushed by a butterfly's wing or was she herself the moth struggling against the power of the candle flame? She did not know; she did not care.

'Oh, Ruaridh, I love you so.'

He drew back. 'Holly, Holly, I could take such dreadful advantage of you. Come on, before I forget I was born a gentleman. I'll take you to your bus stop.'

Her heart sank. She had not wanted the evening to end. She wanted to feel his lips on hers again, to hear his beautiful voice saying her name. She was going to cry. How stupid, how dreadfully stupid. One little kiss and she had told him that she loved him. Where had all her sophistication gone?

'No,' she stammered. 'I'll manage.'

But he was beside her, helping her on with her coat. It was still raining. At the bus stop he sheltered her against him. Please let me stand here for ever, she thought. The bus came.

'Goodnight, funny little Holly. I'm awfully fond of you too.'

She was on the bus, her hand pressed to her lips to hold the kiss he had left there. Had he kissed her again? He had, he had. Dear God, she would die of happiness. I'm awfully fond of you too. He loved her. He loved her. Ruaridh loved her; hadn't he said so? She was still holding his handkerchief and she pressed it against her face.

'Are ye planning to pay yer fare, lassie?'

The conductress brought her back to earth with a bump. Holly handed her a half crown.

'Keep the change,' she said grandly.

# 30

'I can't believe it.' Kate put the letter down on the table and frowned at it as if the bad news it contained was the fault of the paper and not the writer.

Ian waited for a moment and then, since evidently she was too upset to say more, asked gently, 'What's she up to now, sweetheart?' He had brought the letters in from the mat in the hall and had seen the all-too-infrequent handwriting.

'She's not coming for Christmas. How could she? She knows how much Christmas means to you.' She was still sitting, looking down at the offending sheet of paper.

'But I don't mean anything to Holly, dear, and why should I? My feelings don't come into this. Christmas for me will be wonderful since you're part of it. Knowing you're unhappy will take some of the fun away. Are you going to tell me why?'

Kate handed over the paper. 'She's in love; I knew that in the summer.'

Ian hunted around for a few minutes.

'They're on the fireplace, beside your newspaper.' Kate smiled. Ian was a neat and tidy and well-organized person but he could never remember where he had left his glasses. She could see them now, staring balefully at their owner from the sports section of the local paper.

'When I forget why I waited so patiently to marry you, Kate Robertson, I only have to have you find my specs.' He retrieved them and read the letter.

'Be happy for her, Kate. Her own happiness spills out of this.'

'I know you won't be disappointed for, after all, you have Ian,' Holly had written.

Disappointed, Kate had not seen Holly since her granddaughter had returned to the university at the beginning of October. I always want everything, Kate thought sadly. Ian should be enough for any woman, but . . . Holly. Holly, her heart cried the name silently and she could feel that awful pain in the very centre of her being that no patented medicine could reach. Failure, failure. She looked at her husband who was rereading the letter. With everyone but him, she thought, and a small flicker of flame began to melt the ice that had gripped her heart.

'We should be happy for her, dear,' said Ian again. 'We'll think of her sitting at the Watchnight service in St Giles with this Adonis of hers and we'll be glad.'

'It's really the very first time he has asked me out with just him,' Holly had written. 'We go everywhere together, Anne and dear old Gairn, who is a bit like Ian, Ruaridh, and me. Every Friday we go to the Scottish National Orchestra Concert in the Usher Hall. Anne and Ruaridh are very wealthy but we all climb up to the gods because Gairn has to watch his expenses. I love classical music, the flute especially. Ruaridh plays the flute.'

'Says it all, doesn't it, Kate dear. Ruaridh plays the flute.'

'I'm afraid of wealthy boys who play the flute.'

'It's because you've never met one before. Courting a young lady by lying on the grass playing the flute sounds a bit medieval to me. Used to take all my women to Murrayfield to watch rugby.'

Kate, who had never watched a rugby match in her life, laughed. 'Just as well I wasn't a bright young thing.'

'For you I would have borrowed a flute, my dear, or even a lyre if that would have pleased you.'

She went into his open arms. 'Oh, my darling. Whatever did I do to deserve you,' she whispered.

Later she read Holly's letter again. For this boy Holly was prepared to stay in a boarding house in Edinburgh while all her other friends were at home enjoying the break. What did she plan to do on Christmas Day or the days before this wonderfully romantic Christmas concert on Christmas Eve? She was surely trusting that she would see the boy, that she would be part of his Christmas. It was not obvious to Holly's grandmother, however, that this would be so. 'Ruaridh has asked me to go to the Christmas carol concert at St Giles on Christmas Eve. Anne has gone to Switzerland with her mother who is in the process of getting another divorce and Gairn has gone to his sheep farm in the Highlands, so it will be just Ruaridh and me. I've bought a green Christmas coat and my very first hat – green too. I think I look a bit like Robin Hood but the girl in the shop said it was just the thing.'

'And after Christmas, Ian, is she hoping that he'll be so devastated by the hat . . .? Oh, what, I don't know what modern young girls think. While she's staying alone in some awful boarding house this young man is having a lovely family holiday.'

'Perhaps he doesn't have a family?'

'No, she mentioned him last year. He's the rich one who lives in a great mansion of a place with his older brother and I'm sure there are servants. He'll be waited on hand and foot while my little Holly is hanging around in a boarding house waiting for him to shout. What happens after the concert, Ian? He'll take her to her digs, I suppose.' A dreadful thought entered Kate's remarkably naïve mind. 'Oh, Ian, you don't think . . .'

'No, I don't. What I do think is that he has made a fairly innocent suggestion, since Holly has so obviously fallen in love, not just with him but with music, that she come with him to this rather nice concert on Christmas Eve.

It probably hasn't occurred to him that her home isn't in Edinburgh and when he realizes that she is staying in a boarding house, naturally his family will ask her to Christmas dinner and if there are parties and dances . . . as there will be for golden boys like our Ruaridh, then she'll be asked along. She'll probably phone you asking at long last for some extra money for party frocks. She'll be the belle of the Edinburgh ball, our little Holly.'

Kate relaxed. How sensible Ian was. 'You're right, of course, and perhaps I should just send a cheque for some pretty things as an extra Christmas present. Perhaps she'll bring her friend here after Christmas. I could suggest that, and then she could have her gifts here. I was going to post everything but it will never get to Edinburgh on time with the Christmas rush. I'll try to think of her having a lovely time with nice people, Ian dear, and we'll have a lovely quiet Christmas on our own.'

The bakery, which would not pass to its new owners until the spring, was especially busy at Christmas time and Kate had little time to dwell on her grand-daughter's affairs. For the first time she realized what an enormous burden the bakery and its employees had been all these years. What differences there would have been in her life if she had. She would have had time and money to invest in her relationships with her children. Would Liam have gone off to Glasgow to his death? Would Margaret have run off to marry George? The marriage had lasted. They seemed to be happy. They certainly appeared to have money. Even the little paper in Auchenbeath mentioned George and his entrepreneurial skills once in a while – local boy makes good. And Patrick? Kate thrust the thoughts away. I could do nothing else. If I made the wrong choices with my life God will punish me. I tried. God knows I tried.

A beloved voice thrust the thoughts away. 'Kate. Is there coffee?'

Ian always entered the bakery the same way, as if he didn't really belong. The local doctor on the way back from a patient. Kate lifted her face to her husband and smiled, her heartache eased. Oh, Margaret. I hope you have realized that your gold spickets don't matter. It's this that matters.

'There's always a cup of coffee for you, doctor,' she teased in return, 'and a bap if you have the time.'

This time Ian had not been seeing a patient. True to his word he had retired and spent his days, while he waited for his wife to rid herself of her burdens, in scouring the locality for suitable land for their retirement home.

'I've found it, Kate, three acres high on the side of a hill overlooking the Nith and about halfway between Auchenbeath and Dumfries. It's about a half mile from the main road so we'll never be isolated and Holly will be within shouting distance of her precious Grace. The farmer is willing to sell; he's readjusting boundaries.'

'It sounds wonderful.'

'Water, plumbing, power, everything is handy. Won't it be fun?'

Kate looked at him. People their age were looking for a retirement home that would cosset their ageing bodies, not starting from the side of a hill to build one.

'It will be wonderful fun,' she said honestly, for with Ian everything was fun. With him she was twenty again, with all the energy she had had but none of the burdens. 'Shall we put up a tent on the site while the builders are in?'

'No doubt you are tough enough to stand it, Mrs Robertson, but my old bones require cosseting. I've enquired at the Fern Inn . . .'

He stopped and she looked at him, joy written on her face. At the Fern Inn they had celebrated their engagement and had returned frequently since their marriage.

'Oh, Ian.'

'I didn't deliberately set out to find a spot so close, or perhaps subconsciously I did but they'll have us as soon as we like.'

No time to think of Holly while her mind was full of the new challenge of building a house. No time to worry while she prepared for Christmas. Once and for all Kate had abandoned regrets. She had loved her children; she had grown to love her grand-daughter. She was here if anyone needed her; Holly, Margaret and her family, Bridie happily looking after Colm in Canada, Deirdre and her host of grandchildren.

Ian brought a tree, the largest that had ever fitted into the bakery and they decorated it and piled their gifts under it. The bakery was open until late on Christmas Eve and Kate closed the door on the last baker to leave with almost unbearable happiness. It was over. That part of her life was over and her new life would really start when they moved at the beginning of the year.

'Are you going to Midnight Mass, Kate?' There was concern in Ian's voice.

'No. I'll go to Mass tomorrow. Tonight I'm almost too tired even to eat. Let's sit by the fire and watch the lights on the tree for a while.'

Ian piled the fire with logs and they sat in the light cast from the fire and the twinkling fairy lights and listened to Christmas music.

'I'm going to fall asleep right here, Ian,' murmured Kate, her head on his shoulder, his arm around her – loving, protecting.

'Me too, very romantic but we would wake up in the wee small hours stiff as boards with the fire out. You turn off the tree and I'll attend to the fire.'

'Oh, no, who can that be?' asked Kate as there was the undoubted sound of a car in the yard. 'Someone lost, I suppose, and using us as a turning point.'

The door opened and Holly stood there. Kate could see the sturdy figure of the local taxi driver behind. No young man, no suitcase. They looked at one another.

'I haven't the fare,' said Holly in a voice breaking from fatigue or unhappiness.

Ian reached for his wallet. 'I'll handle it,' he said. 'Into the warm, Holly.' They could hear his voice out in the large courtyard. 'Awfully good of you to bring her.'

'It's Christmas,' said the taxi driver. 'And yer credit's good, doctor.'

Inside the warm house Holly still stood. 'I changed my mind,' she said in an attempt at normality and with the door still wide open.

'Come in, dear,' said Kate, 'and close the door.' Wisely she did not mention luggage.

Holly turned and slowly and solemnly closed the door behind her. She turned back to her grandmother who still stood, exhaustion forgotten, as if rooted to the floor.

The two women looked at one another, across the room, across the years.

'Oh, Granny, he didn't want me after all,' said Holly and quite naturally threw herself into her grandmother's open arms.

Kate led her to the sofa and sat with her arms around her grand-daughter while the girl cried until she was exhausted. Ian came in and went off to the kitchen where Kate could hear him bustling about. She smiled; for a doctor he had amazing belief in the restorative power of a cup of tea.

She soothed Holly as she had sometimes soothed the girl's father, "There, there, lambie, it's all right; everything is all right.'

Ian's records were still playing on the gramophone. 'Hark, the Herald Angels Sing'.

And then the story tumbled out. 'I must have fallen in love with him the first time I saw him, Gran. He was so beautiful and his voice . . . I can't describe his voice, like Brotheroam. I suppose I thought he was like Jerome in other ways too. He would never, ever, hurt . . .' The tears came again and the paroxysms of painful grief.

Wisely, Kate waited. The heavenly choir in the background was, at last, quiet.

'We were at The Chocolate House, Granny Kate, having supper, Anne and Gairn and Ruaridh and me. We'd been to the concert . . . it was super . . . he conducted Finlandia, Gibson, that is. We hummed it all the way to Princes Street and then Anne mentioned the Christmas concert in the cathedral.'

'We're not going,' she said. 'My mama is following her money into exile in Switzerland.'

'I've got a job on the post,' said Gairn. He's nice, Gran, Gairn. I thought he was a gypsy; his hair is so untidy all the time and he's tweedy and . . . fun, I suppose.'

She was quiet, the sobs subsiding, but she stayed within her grandmother's arms and Kate held her there.

Let him who dared try to remove her child from the safety of her arms.

'Why don't you come, Holly?' Just as simple as that. And I thought, stupid, vain me . . . How could a boy like Ruaridh like me, Gran? I thought . . .'

'It's all right, my dear,' soothed Kate, rocking them back and forth. 'Everything is all right.'

'I thought it was a date. How stupid of me. I can't believe how stupid. What a fool I've made of myself.'

Anger is better, thought Kate. Let it out, Holly.

'He said nothing about the days between the end of term and Christmas. I got a job on the post like Gairn and I waited and waited for Christmas Eve. I bought a coat and a hat . . . and gloves, Gran . . .' The words stabbed Kate's heart. 'Brotheroam said that ladies always wore gloves.'

She was crying again. My God, where did a young girl's tears come from?

'Oh, it hurts, Granny. I can't bear the pain.'

'I'll get Ian . . .' began Kate and was surprised to hear a strangled laugh and to feel her arms being gripped tightly.

'It's not that kind of pain, Gran.'

Kate waited. With Holly in the circle of her aching arms she would wait for ever.

'There was a Christmas card . . . today . . . Christmas Eve . . . God, how could he . . . Christmas Eve . . . and a silly little card . . . Dear Holly . . . my brother says I must be with my family. Enjoy the concert, Ruaridh. Just like that. No apology, no . . . I'll see you next term . . . nothing except enjoy the concert. I couldn't believe it. I waited; it had to be some mistake, I said. I dressed. I put on my new coat and that stupid little hat and I waited . . . He didn't come.' The voice was very low, the words so quiet Kate strained to hear them. 'I wanted to die.'

Kate held her even more tightly. I'll take your pain, Holly, her heart was crying. God, let me share her pain.

'I walked and walked and then I was at the bus station and I smelled bread. There was no one there but I smelled bread. Granny Kate. That was all I could think of, Granny Kate. I put the coat and the hat in the paper bin in the lavatory and I came . . . home.'

Had Ian been waiting for the voices to quieten? He came in with a tray. 'I'll take myself off to bed and leave you ladies. Father Christmas won't come while we're up.'

He bent to kiss Kate and laid his hand affectionately on Holly's shoulder. 'It's great to have some real Holly for Christmas.'

'He's nice, Gran,' said Holly.

Ian had made tea and toast and, more aware than his wife of the amazing restorative power of a young healthy body, had reheated the stew Kate had been too tired to eat. Kate sat beside the girl and watched her eat and listened, listened, listened, as all the stories of all the years came out. Sometimes Holly laughed; more often, she cried. There must be a well, thought Kate. I don't ever remember crying like that. Once, after Mam died. Mam, do you see us? My Holly has come to me to help her, to love her. I'll never let her down.

Finally Holly stood up and stretched. 'You must be exhausted, Granny Kate. I'll wash these and then go to bed.'

Kate knew better than to leave her alone to let the memories of the pain come back as they surely would. Tonight, this Blessed Christmas morn, Holly should have a barrier between her heart and Ruaridh's unthinking cruelty. 'Let's leave them, dear. Perhaps Grampa Ian's Santa will wash them but if he doesn't . . . who cares?'

They walked along to Holly's room and Kate went with her and, for the first time, helped her grand-daughter undress. 'Try to sleep, my dear,' she said as she tucked her into bed.

'I'll try, Granny Kate, but when the pain comes I'll think of you and that will help.'

'Shall I stay?'

'No. I'll be fine. I've got to face it alone sometime. You know I've never really liked The Toll House but somehow tonight it feels . . . I don't know how to explain it, but as if . . . there were other people here.'

'There are. They're called love, Holly.'

Kate kissed her grand-daughter gently and went back along the corridor to her own bedroom. 'They're all called love.'

# Welcome to the world of *Eileen Ramsay*!

Keep reading for more from Eileen Ramsay, including a recipe that features in this novel and a sneak peek at Eileen's next book, *The Crofter's Daughter* . . .

We'd also like to introduce you to MEMORY LANE, our special community for the very best of saga writing from authors you know and love and new ones we simply can't wait for you to meet. Read on and join our club!

www.MemoryLane.club

Dear Readers,

I wanted to be Georgette Heyer when I grew up – but failed Higher Latin because I was reading her books instead of Caesar's *The Gallic Wars*. I had written a Scottish-set Regency as part of my Master's degree at university in California and was thrilled when an agent, to whom I was introduced shortly after returning to Scotland, sold the book to an American publisher. The publisher did not ask for another and the agent said, 'Write a saga, write about what you know.'

I thought about what I knew, and made a list: teaching, music, dance, motherhood, travel and love. I would write about love or loving, and that was where I stuck until one day a picture of the village in Dumfriesshire where I grew up came into my mind. A coal-mining area, there were still acres of fine farmlands and woods where thousands of primroses rioted every spring, and there were streams running into the mighty River Nith that were deep enough for us to swim in and shallow enough so that parents did not worry.

There was a school at one end of the village. On my first day, aged five, I met my first friend and, although our career paths were very different, she is still my friend today. A little house next to the school had been the site of a toll gate and in the middle of the main street a shop had replaced a public lavatory that had been bombed during the war – or perhaps it was the other way around. We did not live there during the war.

At the other end of the village stood the Roman Catholic Church and just a little farther out was the home of the much-loved, local doctor. Was there anything this doctor could not do?

He was at the pit if there was an accident, at the primary school if there was a playground accident and – since most babies born in the area were born at home – he knew every household and every baby very well.

Local tales of difficult births or tragic accidents resurfaced and the blank pages of my notebook began to fill with ideas. I remembered being in a first-aid class taught by the doctor and I remembered my friend's aunt who gave me lunch every Friday because I wouldn't eat the school meal – which was perfectly fine, by the way. I remembered Friday afternoons when we wrote compositions, which I loved, and the days when the teacher read to us, a few pages of a classic novel that I then checked out of the local library. And I remembered the evening when my soldier father returned from the war and I remembered being terrified when this tall strong stranger threw me up into the air.

I had all the ingredients I needed for my story. I saw my heroine and her fight for an education, and I saw the boys who went to war – the man or men my heroine and her daughters would love or with whom they would imagine themselves in love. And somehow the toll gate became a bakery and my heroine became a baker who could, if she so chose, become a very wealthy woman.

I hope you'll understand her and love her as much as I do.

Best wishes,

Eileen

# Kate Inglis steak pie

## You will need:

900g/2lb stewing steak, cut into cubes
1 tbsp plain flour, seasoned with salt and pepper
1 tbsp butter
2 onions, sliced
2 carrots, chopped
2 sprigs fresh thyme
570ml/1 pint stout (or hot beef stock)
salt and pepper, to taste
225g/8oz shortcrust (or puff) pastry
plain flour, for dusting
1 egg, beaten

## How to make the pie:

1. Pre-heat the oven to 190°C/gas mark 5.
2. Toss the stewing steak in the seasoned flour. Set aside.
3. Melt the butter and sauté the onions until soft. Add the carrots and thyme for 5 minutes, then the stewing steak and any remaining seasoned flour. Stir thoroughly, then quickly add stout (or beef stock). Bring to a simmer.
4. Put mixture in an ovenproof dish and place in oven for 2½ hours until sauce is reduced and the meat tender. Place in pie dish.
5. Meanwhile, dust a clean work surface with flour and roll out pastry to the thickness of a pound coin. Place on top of pie dish and pinch to seal edges, then trim. Make small slit in the middle of the pie. Brush pie lid with egg. Cook for 45 minutes or until golden-brown. Delicious served with greens or peas.

MEMORY LANE

# Kate Inglis loaf

**You will need:**

500g strong white flour
1 tsp salt
1 tsp sugar
I sachet of fast-action yeast
3 tbsp melted butter
300ml lukewarm water

**What to do:**

1. Combine flour, salt, sugar and yeast. Make a well and add melted butter and water. If the dough feels stiff, add a little more water (1–2 tbsp). Combine well, then knead. Once smooth to the touch, place in a lightly buttered bowl, cover, and leave in a warm place for one hour until doubled in size.
2. Pre-heat the oven to 220°C/gas mark 7.
3. Line a baking tray with greaseproof paper.
4. Knock back the dough and shape into a round. Score and place on a lined baking tray. Prove for another hour until doubled in size.
5. Place in oven for 25–30 minutes until hollow when tapped on the base. Serve with fresh salted butter.

·MEMORY LANE·

**Enjoy this sneak peek at Eileen's new novel**
*The Crofter's Daughter*

# CHAPTER ONE

In the spring of 1900 Mairi McGloughlin discovered that she loved the land. She was just nine years old: in fact she had just passed – not celebrated – her ninth birthday. With her best friend, Violet Anderson, she was walking home from the village school. They skipped and walked down Pansy Lane and then Mairi saw the first of the year's snowdrops, virginal white, the lovely heads standing straight and tall on delicate stems, their dark green leaves cradling them protectively.

'Look, Violet,' she said, her voice full of awe, 'snowdrops.'

Violet skipped on the spot, not losing the beat. 'Seventy-eight, seventy-nine – they're just flowers, Mairi – eighty-four, eighty-five.'

Mairi knelt down in the damp soil beside the flowers and she spoke for herself. 'No, they're not, Violet, they're more, they're harbingers of spring.'

She was top of the class and had seen that posh word in one of the Dominie's reserved books.

'Harbingers of spring,' she said again, liking the sound of the phrase. 'Look at them, Violet. They've come up out of the ground and they're pure white; the muck hasnae stuck to them.'

'Ach, you're daft, so you are, Mairi McGloughlin. Of course dirt doesnae stick to them.'

'Well, why not, since you're so smart, Violet Anderson? Why doesn't muck stick to them?'

For a moment Violet was perplexed. She had not expected to be questioned on something unquestionable, on an irrefutable fact. 'It just disnae because ... because God made them.'

'Aye, and he made Billy Soutar too and all the mud in Angus is stuck to him.'

At the thought of Billy Soutar, the little girls dissolved into laughter and ran giggling down the path, all thoughts of flowers and muck and their place in the great scheme of things gone from their minds.

They parted at the end of the lane. Mairi had to continue another mile to the farmhouse but Violet's father's cottage sat four-square to the road almost beside the path. Her mother was in the garden throwing potato peelings to the hens that bustled frenetically around her feet as if terrified that there would not be enough for all.

'There's scones just out the oven, lassies,' she called as she went on feeding the hens, 'and a nice jug of fresh milk in the larder, for Violet.'

Mairi sighed. Pheemie Anderson was a fine baker. 'I cannae today, Mrs Anderson. I've a pot of soup tae put on for the week.' The pot of soup would have been ready if her brother, Ian, had not let the fire go out. Ian's head was usually busy with anything but what he was supposed to be doing and yesterday he had got so involved watching a blackbird building a nest that he had forgotten not only to keep the range stoked but also to bring in the cows. Mairi had gone for the cows but too late to save her brother from their father's righteous anger. This morning Ian had been too sore to go to school and Mairi had lied and told the Dominie that he had a cold. Mr Morrison had said nothing but at hometime he had given Mairi a lovely bound Shakespeare.

'If Ian is still unwell tomorrow, tell him to read *Richard II* and I want him to go on with his history book and the composition he was going to write for me.'

Glowing, Mairi had put the precious book carefully in her bag. She and Ian and the teacher's horrible son, Robin, were the only children who were allowed to read the reserved books. Ian and Robin had fought for the position of top of the class for seven years since the day they had entered the little school together. Sometimes Robin was top, sometimes Ian. Robin always beat Ian in the arithmetic examinations and Ian beat Robin at compositions. Aggregate scores were what counted for top place and Mairi was hoping that Ian would be Dux. Then maybe, just maybe, Father would allow him to stay on at the school beyond the date when most farm boys left.

'He'll need to count well enough to buy in seed, not be diddled, and to pay his men what they're worth. He doesnae need to speak poems.' That was Father, who would never understand his son, mainly because he would not try.

Mairi carried on up the road until she reached the farmhouse. The dogs, Ben and Dog, rushed out to meet her and she hugged them both, careless of the fact that they were working dogs and not, according to Father, to be petted like lap dogs. Dogs were the most satisfactory of all animals. They loved totally and without question; everything these strange human creatures did was perfect and Mairi, with her cuddles and scratching of just the right spot under the ears, was the most perfect of all. They even tolerated Ian's forgetfulness and waited patiently when he forgot to feed them. Their master did not have the same forgiving nature.

'Oh, you beautiful babies,' crooned Mairi. 'Have you missed me then?'

Their tails wagging vigorously, to show her how much she had been missed, they followed her into the house.

'You'd best lie down in the kitchen while I see where Ian is.'

If they could have, they would have told her that Ian was ploughing with his father. Mr McGloughlin had promised his wife that the children would attend school but here was Ian, perfectly well and doing nothing. He did not have to sit down to help with the plough.

When Mairi realized that the house was empty, she cut herself a slice from a loaf of bread that she had baked herself. She spread it liberally with their own butter and sat down at the scrubbed kitchen table to eat it. Then she changed from her school frock into a working day dress and began to prepare vegetables for the soup: carrots, turnips, leeks and a cabbage all grown either in the garden or on the farm. She washed some of their own barley and left it sitting in a bowl of water while the stock simmered on the range. The stock she had made from the bone of the mutton joint that had been their Sunday and Monday dinner. The soup started, she peeled potatoes and then went out into the garden to gather some of the last of the Brussel sprouts. How good it would be when the spring vegetables began to appear; Brussel sprouts were, unfortunately, such a serviceable vegetable. Mairi could not think of one good thing to say about them and, in fact, sometimes wondered why farmers bothered to grow them. She was only nine years old, not a great age, but, in all that time of living and experiencing, she had never met anyone who admitted to liking them.

'When I'm choosing the garden vegetables,' Mairi informed a particularly tough plant, 'there will be no sprouts.' She sat back on her heels beside the plants. There would be flowers. That's what there would be and something called asparagus that she'd seen in one of the Dominie's books, and strawberries, of course, which grew beautifully in Angus soil under Angus skies, and potatoes, even though Father grew them on the farm. The Dominie had a book about growing vegetables and it said that potatoes cleaned the ground and left it nice and ready for the next crop. Yes, asparagus. Mairi had never eaten, never even seen asparagus, but the gentry liked it and so it must be good. The Laird had a glass house called a succession house and he grew peaches in it. *Peaches.* Mairi had seen them when the Laird had given a picnic for his tenants. Oh, earth, soil, good clean dirt was a marvellous thing; it grew potatoes and peaches both. Even the word peach was good. *Peach.* When she was a farmer she would have a succession house and she would have a peach tree in it. The Laird would help her. He was a nice old man. He did not chuck her under the chin and expect her to like it as so many elderly and not so elderly men did. He had spoken to her, one gardener to another. Yes, she would not be afraid to ask the Laird. No doubt he had asparagus. She would go to see it at the next picnic.

Mairi jumped up. She had better get the sprouts and the tatties on. If Ian had done nothing to annoy Father they would have a nice time sitting around the table together, even though the soup would not be at its best until tomorrow. But if she made a nice Shepherd's pie and that and the sprouts were ready to be served just as Father walked in from the fields, maybe he would speak to Ian with the soft voice he always used for Mairi and that her brother very rarely heard addressed to himself. She stopped at the back door, her eye caught by a glimpse of white against the garden wall – more snowdrops.

'When I'm the farmer,' began Mairi, and then she stopped, for she would never be the farmer. She was a girl. She would grow up and keep house for her father until Ian married and then, unless she herself married, she would share the chores with her sister-in-law, for it was Ian who would be the farmer, Ian, who was only completely happy when he was reading a story or scribbling away in his secret notebook.

'It's daft,' said nine-year-old Mairi McGloughlin, 'but it's the way it is and there's nothing I can do about it.' She thought for a moment and smiled a slow sweet smile that was older than time. 'I'll marry Jack Black and bully him.'

Her future decided, Miss McGloughlin hurried into the kitchen and finished preparing the evening meal. Then there were a few precious minutes to do her home-work. She was clever like Ian and the horrible Robin and so the sums took her no time at all. The parsing and analysis of the three sentences took her a little longer because she was happier just reading and understanding lovely words than cluttering up her mind with parts of speech and suchlike nonsense. Ian now, and that spoiled brat who lived in the Schoolhouse, could happily parse and analyze all the day long. She was about to say that such a failing showed just how horrid was Robin Morrison when she realized that the same label would have to attach itself to her beloved Ian. She vented her spleen on Robin by viciously slicing two sprouts into slivers and tossing them into the soup pot. Father would have been sure to ask her what on earth she was trying to do to his laboriously grown vegetables. Sprouts were cooked whole. Everybody knew that.

Colin McGloughlin and his son, Ian, were welcomed home by the smell of good food, beautifully cooked. Ian had managed to keep his mind on his work all afternoon long and so his father was as pleased with him as he ever got. A good hammering had done the boy the world of good, which proved that Ian did not need 'patient understanding' as the Dominie was always saying, but discipline. There was a time for books and a time for remembering to mend the fire and, of the two, the fire was the more important. Without a fire, wee Mairi could not cook and he had never yet seen Ian ready to eat his books instead of a succulent Shepherd's pie. For a moment Colin toyed with the idea of approaching the School Board to allow Mairi to stay at home. There was necessity; he was a widower with two children. Ach no, he had promised Ellen and besides, the lassie was only nine. She could finish the primary school and then she could stay at home where she belonged and take care of the house. She would not do hard farm work, not his wee lassie. Too much work had killed her mother, a shop girl from the town who should never have married a farmer. But Mairi should be spared the hard work that was the lot of every daughter of the farm and if she did marry, and she had to he supposed, she should marry onto a farm that was owner occupied where there was a bit of extra money for a kitchen maid as well as a dairy maid. But not yet, not for a long time yet.

The little family ate their meal and washed it down with mugs of hot sweet tea. Then Colin went to the fire and sat down, the dogs at his feet. He would sit for an hour or two and then, once he had seen the children to bed, he would take himself off to his lonely room.

Ian too left the table and after assuring himself that his father was safely ensconced in the inglenook, he took the book that Mairi had brought him from the Dominie and carried it with pride and care to a seat on the other side of the roaring fire. He was soon deeply involved in the fourteenth century and totally removed from the world around him. Mairi accepted that she would clear the table and wash the dishes; that she would put the oats to soak for the morning's porridge and that she would fill the stone pigs that warmed the beds. That was woman's work. She could barely keep her eyes open by the time her jobs were finished.

'I'm away tae my bed,' she announced to her father and to her brother but neither heard her. She was not hurt. She did not expect a loving and protracted goodnight ritual. She smiled fondly at her menfolk as if they were her children and took herself off up the oak staircase to her little room under the eaves. She liked her room with its view over the fields towards the Firth of Tay. It was dark and she was tired and cold, but once she was stripped to her vest and knickers she pulled the handmade patchwork quilt from her bed, wrapped it around her shoulders, and sat on the window seat looking out at the night. There were one or two fishing boats on the water. In the moonlight, against the dark sky, they looked like etchings. Mairi waited and waited and there, at last, was the train. It ran like a wheeled jewel box between the fields and the sea. It was going to Dundee, to Edinburgh, to York, maybe even to London itself.

'I'll be on you one day, Train,' she told it. 'Maybe all the way to London, but at least as far as Dundee. You wait and see.'

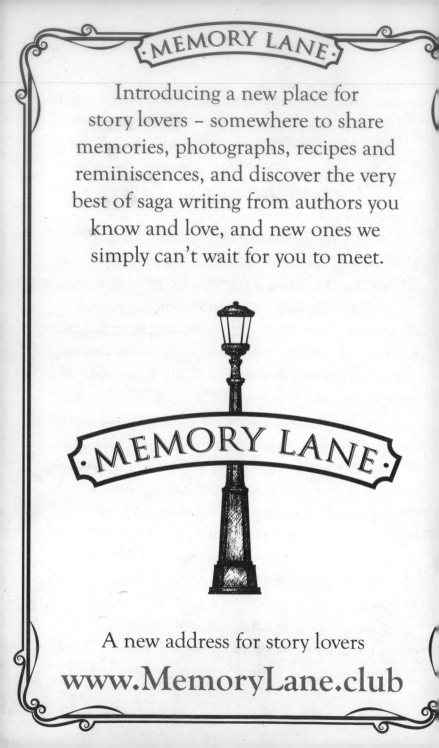